CHILD POSSESSED

'You know, I wish you'd go back to Germany now. You ain't doing this little... girl much good.'

'What little girl?' the voice became strident again.

'The little girl whose body you are in. Look what you did to her arm. It's bleeding.'

Mary looked at her arm and saw the blood. 'Oh. Did I do that?'

'Yes. With that knife.'

Mary looked at the knife. Her eyes grew wide and she opened her grip on the handle. It fell to the floor. 'I'm sorry,' the voice said. 'I didn't mean to hurt nobody.'

'Course you didn't; will you go now?'

'Yes.' Mary looked at her parents. 'I'm sorry for what I did to your little girl. I didn't mean to do her no harm.'

Mary's body stiffened and swayed. Josiah took two strides forward and caught her before she fell.

Also by David St Clair
MINE TO KILL
and published by Corgi Books

David St Clair

Child Possessed

CORGI BOOKS

CHILD POSSESSED

A CORGI BOOK 0 552 11132 5

First publication in Great Britain

PRINTING HISTORY
Published in the United States of America as WATSEKA
Corgi edition published 1979
Corgi edition reprinted 1980 (twice)
Corgi edition reprinted 1981
Corgi edition reprinted 1982
Corgi edition reprinted 1983 (twice)
Corgi edition reprinted 1984
Corgi edition reprinted 1986
Corgi edition reprinted 1987

Copyright © David St Clair 1977

This book is set in 10/10½pt Pilgrim

Corgi Books are published by Transworld Publishers Ltd.,
61–63 Uxbridge Road, Ealing, London W5 5SA,
in Australia by Transworld Publishers (Aust.) Pty. Ltd.,
15–23 Helles Avenue, Moorebank, NSW 2170, and in New
Zealand by Transworld Publishers (N.Z.) Ltd., Cnr. Moselle
and Waipareira Avenues, Henderson, Auckland.

Printed and bound in Great Britain by
Hazell Watson & Viney Limited,
Member of the BPCC Group,
Aylesbury, Bucks

This book is dedicated to
Alberto Aguas
Powerful healer
Devoted friend

Acknowledgments

No author ever really writes a book 'alone' and in this case there were a number of people who helped me.

In Watseka itself I must thank, first and foremost, Mrs Jacqueline Bicket of the Watseka Public Library. Thanks also to her assistant Mrs Rosann Miller. Special thanks also to Mrs Dorothy Long, whose knowledge of local history saved me hours of frustrating research. And thanks to the members of the Iroquois County Historical Society Museum, especially Verla Herron McCullough, Mary J. O'Neill Miller, Jannette Garfield, Eleanor Sites and Frank W. Smith, thanks to Mr and Mrs Glen Strickler for their friendship and facts on early Watseka; to Mr and Mrs Ivan Looker for allowing me to roam through their home – the old Roff residence – and to ask a thousand questions; to Mrs Golda Sobkoviak for permitting me into the old Vennum residence, and special thanks to Artie Bratcher of the Watseka Police Department for opening doors and filing cabinets all over the county.

Special thanks to J. Ronald Bogart, genealogist for the Central Illinois Conference of the United Methodist Church, Bloomington, Illinois, for biographical data on Reverend Dille and Reverend Baker.

And thanks to Mrs Evelina Smith at Kent State University, Trumbull County Branch, in Warren, Ohio, for supplying me with priceless old books about spiritualism of that era; to Dana M. Bailey of Warren, Ohio, for his backlog of spiritual anecdotes and friendship; to my parents Mr and Mrs Lee St Clair of Warren, Ohio, for letting me write part of the manuscript undisturbed in an upstairs bedroom; to Joanna and Bill Woolfolk of Los Angeles, California, and Darien, Connecticut, for giving me the sanctuary of their home for further writing and revision.

Thanks definitely to James Brown for agenting the idea and to Jody Ward for daring to commit herself and Playboy Press to doing it.

And last, thanks to *them* and all *they* have done. *They* gave me the idea, helped me research it and helped me write it. I am deeply appreciative.

PART ONE

The doctor reached his hand into the glass jar and caught one of the rusty black leeches by the head. It squirmed and lashed as it was lifted away from the sticky mass of its friends on the bottom of the jar.

He had sent the girl's parents out of the room. It was always messy when a bleeding took place. The girl's mother was pregnant again and the doctor didn't want the unborn child affected by the sight of the leeches. Children in the womb had a way of being frightened by things, everybody knew that. The girl's father looked as if he was about to faint when he saw the jar. Strange how a wealthy lawyer and real estate investor could go weak as a babe at the sight of these slimy creatures. The African maid refused to come into the room. Good. That was one more person he didn't have to contend with.

The mouth of the first leech pulsated, sucking in the warm perfumed air of the bedroom. The windows had been closed for several days. The doctor hadn't wanted germs from outside attacking the girl. The doctor didn't like night air, either. He'd seen too many cases worsen when someone left a window open after dark.

It was to be hoped that Mary's case would not worsen. If it did she would have to be committed to the asylum. That much he knew. The whole town agreed. It wasn't safe to have a girl like Mary in the streets. Heaven only knew when she would have one of her fits and do somebody harm.

Usually the harm she did was to herself but you never knew how she would act. That was the problem with Mary's illness. Sometimes she could be so normal you'd never think there was a thing wrong with the child and other times there would be such screaming and raving that it seemed as if the Devil himself had gotten a hold on her. But the doctor didn't believe in the Devil. Not medically, at any rate. As a good Methodist he believed in a heaven and a hell but he didn't think the Devil had ever come up to the surface of the earth. Not since the temptation in the desert. Now, the Devil had his hands full with the villains who had brought on the war. Brother against brother and state against state. It was a horrible thing to have happening to the country. It had started three years ago, in 1861, and was still going on. People dying every day. African people wearing chains. Entire cities in the South being burned and their citizens killed off. Thank God Mr Lincoln was President. He had kept Illinois out of the war. The fighting was going on in other places. Not in Illinois. Not in Watseka. If the rebels wanted something to invade, they would attack Chicago, 90 miles north of Watseka.

The first leech clamped down on Mary's temple. The doctor had pushed back her auburn hair so it could get a firm hold. It lashed its tail for a few seconds, almost as if it was still swimming, until the warm blood began to fill its body. Then it calmed down and stuck to the business at hand, the business of sucking out the bad blood. Then another leech came out of the jar and the doctor placed it on her other temple. A third he placed on the left side of her neck. Right on the jugular vein. There was a slight slurping noise as the creature began to drink. The doctor fumbled with the buttons at the neck of her high-collared nightdress. He tried not to think of the warm breasts that brushed his hand as he did this. Professional ethics did not permit him to uncover those breasts. If Mary had been conscious at the time and had unbuttoned her dress herself and then covered her nakedness with a towel, he might have applied the leeches on those breasts, but the base of the neck would have to do. Two leeches. One on each side of her neck, just above the collarbone.

Dr Fowler stood up and admired his work. The leeches

hung and drank and filled with blood exactly as they were supposed to. He was the only doctor in Watseka who applied leeches. The other two doctors in town, Bennett and Pittwood, didn't want to be bothered with them. The leeches came all the way from Louisiana, right up the Mississippi and over to Watseka by railroad. In spite of the war traffic on the river, medical supplies were still given express service. Bennett and Pittwood didn't hold with leeches because they didn't believe in them. Didn't believe that bleeding was at all important. Dr Fowler snorted to himself. They didn't believe in leeches, yet they hadn't been able to help Mary either. Mr Roff had called them in separately, and when they couldn't do anything, they came in together but even then the child didn't get better. Matter of fact, she got worse. When Mr Roff called on Dr Fowler and suggested he bring his leeches, the doctor felt he had won a moral victory in town. Lots of people in Watseka didn't like leeches but Asa B. Roff had finally requested them. If he could cure Mary with his little pets, then everyone in town would want him when they needed a healing. Business was bound to improve. Then, maybe, he could get that new buggy he'd seen over at Hoober's Wagon & Carriage Shop. It was the first one made in the area that hadn't been immediately shipped off to the Union army. That new buggy would call attention as he drove down Walnut Street.

The doctor walked across the room to look out the front window. He had to pull back the red satin drape and the white lace curtain that covered the large arched window from ceiling to floor. While the drapery smelled musty from lack of fresh air, the windowpanes were free of dust. The black woman did a good job of keeping the large house clean. How she managed to do the cooking, take care of five children and two adults and still keep that huge home clean was a miracle. People said Africans were lazy but this woman Loozie certainly wasn't. She was different from most Africans, people had to admit. Of course, they didn't have too much to compare her with. This Loozie woman was the only African in Watseka. She was a freedwoman working on a salary for Mr Roff. There were other freed Africans in Chicago, it was said, and some runaways too. People in Watseka thought they knew just about everything there was to know about everything, the doctor mused. Smalltown people with smalltown minds. They hadn't traveled as he had. Being born in England the way he was and then coming to Virginia with his family and everything. He had traveled. The only reason he had come to Watseka two years ago was because he couldn't abide the Rebel sentiments back home.

The girl on the bed moaned and changed her position. She hadn't moved a muscle in three days. Three days she had lain there, barely breathing, barely alive. The healing powers of the leeches had started working. Of course her parents were frightened sick that their darling Mary was going to die. Dr Fowler had showed them how to feel the girl's pulse and to put a mirror near her nose to see if she was still breathing. It was a most unusual case. Most unusual.

He turned back to the window. From the Roff home at the top of the hill, he could see straight down Fifth Street, all the way to Walnut Street, five blocks away. Walnut was the main street. Most of the shops were on it, as was his doctor's office. Mr Roff's first home could be seen from his second one. That home had been the first wooden house built in town. Asa Roff was a man of vision. He knew the town would thrive once he diverted the railroad through it. Watseka had only been pasture and woodlands before the railway cut across it. Most of the folks had lived by the river. The early settlers, 30 years ago, had settled on a bend in the Iroquois River and shipped skins and hides to Chicago. Wood was plentiful and when a few permanent houses went up somebody called it Middleport. A natural name for a port stop in the middle of the river. There were a hotel and three drinking establishments. The first building the county erected was a jail. That more or less told an outsider what kind of people he would be dealing with. Watseka had a better jail now and a new courthouse abuilding. The doctor could see the scaffolding of the courthouse from the Roff second-floor bedroom. Until it was completed Asa Roff's home would still be the most imposing brick building in town. Watseka was bringing in money and Roff was taking a large share of it. He did it honestly though, everyone admitted that.

'Water ... a glass of water ... '

The doctor hurried to the side of the bed. The girl had opened her eyes.

'A glass of – ' she whispered hoarsely.

'Yes. Yes, now just a minute and I'll pour you one.' His hands shook with excitement as he filled a water glass from an ironstone pitcher on the dresser. She was coming around, and *he* had done it. 'Here you are, Mary dear. I'll hold it for you.' The girl struggled to touch the glass but her hands were tied. 'No, you just let me hold the glass for you. Don't do no good to struggle like that. They had to do that, tie your hands down. You almost scratched your brother's eyes out when they put you to bed. Now just let the water trickle in. That's right. That's a good girl.'

The water that didn't hit her open mouth ran down her chin, soaking the patchwork quilt that had been drawn tightly around her. Her body, under the quilt and in that July heat, was soaking wet with her own perspiration. 'That's a good girl, just finish this last little bit in here.'

The doctor reached up and plucked off one of the leeches, carefully pulling it sideways so she didn't see it. He dropped it, much fatter now than when it had started drinking, into the large-mouth jar. The one on her other temple came off easily. The two above her collarbone were reluctant to leave and the one on her jugular vein put up a fight. Dr Fowler had to put his hand over Mary's eyes and tugged with the other hand to free the creature. There was a Y-shaped mark where it had been. He dropped them into the jar and with a handkerchief from his back pocket wiped away the bloody marks around her head. Mary pulled at the ropes that kept her hands bound to the wooden slats beneath the bed. 'Don't do no good to fuss so, child. I'll go and tell your folks you're feeling better.'

The doctor went down the wide wooden staircase and into the back parlor. It was the room the family used when they weren't having company. Mr Roff was trying to concentrate on the daily *Iroquois Times* and Mrs Roff was combing the hair of little Frank. As he leaned against her a careful observer could see that under the full skirt and petticoats she was expecting another child. In those skirts it was always difficult to tell if a woman was in the family way. The oldest child, Minerva, was working a needlepoint cushion seat. She was 20 years old, which made her three years older than Mary. The cushion seat was for her hope chest. She was engaged to a boy named Henry Alter and they would have been married by now, but he had joined the Union army a few months ago and so the marriage had been postponed. Minerva felt like a war wife and read each battle report as it was printed in the *Times*. Minerva – all her friends called her 'Nervie' – wasn't as pretty as Mary but she had many accomplishments. She played the piano and sang in the church choir. She could knit and tat and do crochet work and she could even clerk in a store. Henry would have quite a wife when he came back from the war. *If* he came back.

The two remaining Roff boys, Joseph and Fenton, were outside playing. Joseph was nine and Fenton a year younger. Asa Roff had kept his wife producing babies like a prize brood mare. She had given birth to nine children and another was on the way. Two boys had died before Nervie was born, another boy died the year after Mary was born and another son had lived about a year and died when Ann was carrying Frank. Five alive out of nine was just about the average for prairie life, Dr Fowler reckoned. On the East Coast there were ways of saving sickly babies, but out here you never could be sure that a child would live until he was in his teens, and even then if measles or diphtheria hit him, he would be a goner.

Everyone stopped their activity and looked up as the doctor came into the room. 'Asa ... Mrs Roff ...' he gave a slight bow in her direction. 'Your Mary has regained consciousness. If you want to come up and see her now.'

Both parents rose quickly and hurried up the backstairs. Nervie followed after them and little Frank made up the tail end of the procession behind the African woman and the doctor. Mrs Roff was the first one into the room.

'Mary,' she said as she sat on the bed and brushed the girl's hair with her hand. 'Are you feeling better?'

'Yes, Ma. Much better, thank you.' She still had no strength in her voice.

'You want something to eat, child?' Loozie's voice came

from the circle of faces around the bed. 'I've got some broth simmering down there.'

'No thanks.'

'You sure? I can have it up here in a jiffy.'

Mary shook her head. 'Pa, what did they do to my hands?'

'We had to tie them to the bed slats. You would have hurt yourself if we didn't.'

'But – '

'You were kind of out of your head, daughter. We didn't want you to hurt yourself.'

Water started to gather in the corner of her eyes. 'Did I ... did I do something crazy again, Pa?'

'You just had another of those spells,' her mother answered.

'Oh, no.' The tears welled. 'Did I hurt somebody? Again?' Her voice broke. 'Ma ... oh Ma, I don't remember. It was just like the last time, wasn't it?'

The mother's hand went out to smooth her hair. 'Now don't you fuss. It's all over and you're my little girl again. The important thing is that you're well.'

'That's right, Mary. Ma's right. The important thing is that you're well again.' Nervie was standing close to the bed and dried Mary's tears with a handkerchief.

'Pa, what did I do?' Her eyes were pleading. 'I didn't hurt one of the boys, did I?'

He shook his head. 'You just rest now. We'll talk about it later. Anyway, it's over and you've come back to normal.'

Mary's eyes went to each face in turn. 'Loozie, did I hurt you? Did I do something to you?' The black woman shook her head.

'It was Tessie!' Frank blurted out in his baby voice. 'You hurt my Tessie.'

'The cat? Ma, did I hurt the cat? Did I?'

'She was an old tabby anyway,' Mrs Roff answered soothingly. 'It doesn't matter none.'

'What happened to Tessie?' Mary's voice got louder. 'What did I do to Tessie? I love that cat!'

'You chopped off her head!' shouted Frank. 'That's what you did and when Ma tried to take Tessie away from you you pushed Ma on the ground and then you,' the boy gasped for more breath to continue, 'then you licked the blood that was coming out of Tessie!' He was furious with his sister. 'That's what you did. You hurt Tessie! And Pa had to put Tessie in a box and we had a funeral!' He began to cry. 'You killed Tessie! You killed my cat!'

Nervie grabbed the boy and let him continue to cry in her full skirt. Tears streamed down Mary's face. 'I can't believe it... Ma,' she struggled to reach out but her hands were held down. 'Ma, you know how much I loved Tessie.' She looked at her father. 'Pa, didn't I love Tessie? Didn't I?'

'Course you did. You just weren't yourself. But it's all right. It's all right. We'll get another tabby cat. Mrs Parker's cat is about to have kittens. I'm sure she'll give us one of them.'

Mary began to sob, deep body-wrenching noises. Mrs Roff looked worriedly at Dr Fowler. 'She'll be all right,' he said. 'It's the shock of the deed. She'll feel better once she's had a little nourishment.'

'Mary,' Loozie said above the noise of the sobbing, 'honey, do you want something to eat now? You ain't had a bite of anything for three days. Shall I fetch some of that broth?'

Mary shook her head and looked at her mother. 'Ma, untie my hands.'

Mrs Roff looked at the doctor. He shook his head.

'Not just yet,' Mrs Roff said. 'The doctor thinks it better if you don't exert yourself too much.'

'Ma,' Mary spoke a little louder. 'Untie my hands. Please?'

This time her father answered. 'Mary, the doctor thinks it would be better if we waited awhile. After all, he *is* the doctor.'

The sobbing stopped. Abruptly. Mary's eyes were suddenly clear and dry. She glared at Dr Fowler. 'I asked you,' she said calmly, 'to untie my hands.'

The doctor stepped toward the bed. 'Not just yet, Mary dear,' he said.

Mary took a deep breath. The sound of the air entering and filling her lungs could be heard all over the room. Her eyes grew cold and then glittered even though there was no direct light in the room. 'Didn't you hear me?' she said in a low voice. A deep voice. 'Didn't you hear me?' Her voice deepened as it got louder. 'I said untie my hands!'

'Mary!' her mother exclaimed. 'That's no way to talk to Dr Fowler.'

'That man is a fool!' the deep voice inside her throat growled. 'A fool and an idiot!'

'Now just a moment –' Mr Roff started.

'And you are a fool and an idiot for calling him!'

Mrs Roff looked pleadingly from her daughter to her husband. 'She doesn't know what she's saying,' she apologized. 'She didn't mean to be –'

Mary's face became twisted. Her eyes glowed. She contorted her body, pulling at the ropes that held her down. The bed creaked with the sudden movement. 'I said,' she shouted in that deep voice, 'to untie Mary's hands!'

Her body rose up halfway in the bed, her eyes shut tight in the effort to free herself. The veins in her neck and forehead were pulsing double their normal size. 'Get these goddamned things off me!'

There was a creaking sound, then the sound of splintering wood. Mary sat up in bed, triumph written across her face. Her hands were free. From each wrist dangled the length of thick rope. From each rope hung a piece of wood that had been broken from the shattered bed slats underneath.

'Now,' she said slowly and in her normal voice, looking at the startled faces around her, 'now, I'll have some of that broth.'

To all outside appearances Mary Roff was a normal girl, even a pretty girl. At seventeen she was well-rounded under her buttoned-down blouses and jackets and even though nobody ever saw them, she had nicely shaped legs. She had the Roff rounded jaw, wide blue eyes, and an almost classic nose. Her hair, auburn like her mother's, had hung to her waist. Now, after she had gone a little crazy and chopped it off last year, it was parted in the middle and pulled smoothly back behind her ears. It was the latest style. Mrs Lincoln wore her hair that way and what the President's wife did most of the other women copied. The monthly ladies' magazines always showed the newest styles from Washington.

The cutting of her hair and the killing of old Tessie weren't unusual incidents in the Roff family. Things like that had been going on for years, ever since the first fit took hold of the girl when she was only six months old. The Roffs were living in Warren County, Indiana, then. Asa was in the boot and shoe business. He'd take his catalogue and a case full of sample miniature shoes and get orders from the various farmhouses.

Then, Asa hadn't yet figured out what he really wanted to do. In those days you either went into your father's line of work or else you got an education and set yourself up in something. He didn't have time to remember his father, for when Asa was three his father was kicked in the head by a horse and died almost instantly. His uncle took charge of him after that because it was all his mother could do to raise the two older boys. The uncle lived in Rochester, New York, and Asa was expected to help with the chores around the house and work as an apprentice to a local shoemaker. The small amount he received in wages was handed directly to his uncle once a month. As the years went by, Asa began to hate the smell of shoe leather, hate Rochester and hate his uncle. There had never been time for school and never any money left over for books or learning. The shoemaker's wife knew how to read and sometimes she would teach Asa new words; so in spite of his uncle he learned to read and write.

His uncle had signed a contract that Asa would work for the shoemaker until his nineteenth birthday. Asa being his legal ward, there was nothing the boy could do to get out of it. There was another boy in town who had been indentured the way Asa had been and once he ran away. They found him a few days later (he couldn't get very far without a horse) and when they brought him back his employer, a blacksmith, had him publicly whipped. The sight of the blood streaming down his friend's back, streaming from flesh that was loose and open, altered any ideas Asa had about not living up to the contract. It also altered the personality of his friend, for after the beating he talked almost not at all and walked with a dull stare in his eyes. One morning they found him hanging from the rafters in the blacksmith shop. They found the body of the smith too, kneeling on the floor with his head on the anvil. Or at least what was left of his head after the boy had pounded it with the sledgehammer. Everyone talked about it for days. Asa thought about it and decided not to run away. It wasn't so bad, he reckoned, not as bad as the Africans he heard about in the Southern states. They wore chains and were indentured for life; at least he would be free when he was nineteen.

He celebrated his nineteenth birthday, in 1837, by walking into a tavern and getting drunk. He had managed to save three dollars over the years and 75 cents of it was spent in the bar. He bought drinks for everyone and then everyone bought him a drink. Early the next morning he staggered home and awoke his uncle. The old man sat bolt upright in his bed, his nightcap askew over one eye.

'Uncle Jeffrey,' Asa said, 'here is my contract with old Mr Simpson and his blamed shoe business.' He tore the sheet of paper into small pieces and threw them on the bed. 'And you,' he added, pointing a finger, 'you can go to hell and be damned!'

He walked out of the room, out of the house and out of Rochester. Much later that morning he collapsed and slept under a tree in a farmer's field, his fortune of $2.25 wrapped in a leather pouch and tied to his leg.

In the morning he headed east, intent on reaching Albany and finding a decent job. When he got to Syracuse, two weeks later, a man who owned a leather tannery needed an assistant. The pay was eight cents a day. Asa agreed to take the job if he could sleep in the tannery. For a month he ate fresh fruit from the trees on the owner's property and bought an occasional boiled egg or link of smoked sausage. At the end of the month he told the tanner he had to move on and started walking toward Albany. He had an additional $1.38 in his bankroll.

In Albany he found a job and lived with four young workers in a small house near the factory, but people were talking about the West. President Van Buren had just been inaugurated and there was a lot of commotion about opening the West. New opportunities for young men who weren't afraid to rough it. Well, he had never been afraid of anything in his life. Anyway, there had been riots in Albany that year, and many businesses had closed because of the Great Commercial Panic. The newspapers always put it in capital letters. Jobs were scarce and many men were laid off where he worked. Asa hadn't been one of them, but he could see it coming. Why stay and suffer in the East when he could go West? So he went to Buffalo and signed on a boat that was taking barrels of flour to the town of Detroit.

It was too cold for him in Michigan. The wind off the lake and the lean-to cabin he rented were not his idea of living. When the winter snows melted he started walking south and got as far as Fort Wayne, Indiana. The food was plentiful but working for someone else was not his goal. In his spare time he made a canoe and, in August, paddled down the Wabash River to the hamlet of Independence. It looked like a good spot to stop for a while.

That's when he met Ann Fenton, a pretty girl of fourteen whose family had come from Virginia to farm. The Fentons insisted Ann wait until her sixteenth birthday before she married Asa and he agreed. They would have stuck to it except Ann became pregnant, and a hasty marriage was performed two months before that birthday. When the baby was born, they named him William and Asa started selling ready-made shoes from a Chicago catalogue. A year later George was born but he died. Ann's parents were greatly concerned when she became pregnant again, and Mary was born when 'Nervie' was just past two years old.

'Asa! Asa!' Ann's voice called to him as he drove the horse and buggy toward their small wood-frame house. 'Oh, Lord, Asa, come quick. Something's happened to the baby!'

He rushed past his wife and into the only bedroom, the room right off the kitchen. Nervie was standing in her bed. She looked through the wooden bars of the headboard at her tiny baby sister in the smaller bed. It wasn't so much a bed as it was a triangular shelf that Asa had nailed into a corner and tacked on a guard board so the child couldn't fall out. Ann had put a blanket in there for a mattress and cut some muslin to size for sheets. The baby's pillow was a muslin sack stuffed with goose feathers. The small form on the ledge didn't move.

'She is breathing,' Asa assured his wife. 'She's not dead.'

'The poor tyke,' Ann said trying not to cry. 'She's been like that ever since morning. Look.' She lifted up one of

Mary's tiny arms and it fell back heavily onto the bed. 'And look,' Ann removed a needle from the hem of her apron and pushed its sharp point lightly against Mary's foot. There was no reaction. 'She's been like that since morning,' Ann repeated dully, 'stiff as a board.'

'It was just after you left and I was washing up the breakfast things when I heard her cry. Well, it wasn't her feeding time so I didn't pay no mind. Nervie was in the kitchen with me playing under the table. The crying got louder and my hands was all soapy so I just let her be. Then came this awful scream like she was strangling or something. When I ran in to see her, she was all bunched up tight like a ball. Her face was red and she was crying so hard and I put my hand on her head and it was hot! Asa, her little head was as hot as fire!' Ann reached out again to touch Mary's forehead. 'It's cool now, but it was just as hot as a coal in the grate. So I got a cloth and some cold water and when I touched her with it she began having the most terrible fit. Her eyes rolled back in her head and she screamed like a hog being butchered and her legs and arms began jerking and kicking and her face got all purple and . . . ' she paused, remembering, and the tears started again. 'And then she gave a quick jolt and her arms and legs got stiff and she didn't move at all after that.' The tears were falling faster now. 'Not a bit after that. She's been like that going on five hours.'

'What did the doctor say? You did fetch him, didn't you?'

'Mrs Simpson's boy went and brought him here. Mrs Simpson said it looked like a fit to her and Doc Davis said it was. He said it was unusual to see one in a child so young. But that's what it was.'

'Did he give her any medicine?' Asa asked.

'He said there was nothing to do for her, that whatever it was would go away. I couldn't give her no medicine even if he did leave some. She won't swallow nothing. I tried putting some water down her throat but her lips is stuck tight.' She sat down on the edge of the bed, her hands in front of her face. It was difficult for him to make out her words through the sobbing. 'I don't want to lose this baby! Oh Asa, I don't want to lose this one! They took away my Willie and my George . . . Please Asa, don't let them take little Mary away from me. Please!'

The young father, who'd been holding Mary, put the rigid body back on the little bed and walked from the room. Outside there was a chilly November wind. He closed his eyes to keep the tears from falling and took deep gulps of the cool air. He couldn't hear his wife's crying out there. He didn't want to hear it.

Mary stayed like that for several days. She didn't move, she didn't wet herself, she didn't eat. Neighbors dropped in during the day to see the child and make suggestions. Doc Davis came around and listened to her heart. He said there was nothing he could do. Ann, when Asa was out selling shoes, spent hours beside the immobile form reading from the Bible and praying. Asa said prayers too. Sometimes he shouted them aloud as he drove through open countryside. In the evenings Asa and Ann would read the Bible together and at night they put Nervie into bed with them, lavishing their pent-up affection on her. Mary lay stiffly on her bed. It was like having a dead baby in their bedroom, a dead baby that for some reason couldn't be buried just yet.

On the twelfth day she cried. The noise startled Ann and she spilled cake batter down the front of her apron. In the bedroom Mary was crying and kicking and flexing her fingers. Ann's first reaction was to pick her up and hold her very close. Then she unbuttoned her blouse and Mary's mouth found the milk-gorged nipple. 'Thank you, God,' Ann sighed. 'Thank you.'

Just before Christmas Asa decided to move to Illinois. There was a settlement called Middleport and he was told a young man with ambition could make a good living there. A road, of sorts, was being built to the big city of Chicago and there were rumors that Middleport would become a main stopover for all river traffic headed into or out of Chicago. Indiana had been fine for a while but Asa wanted to move again. Ann wasn't too happy about changing, her folks were there as were most of her friends, but Asa was determined. He even suggested that maybe it was the Wabash River air that had taken their two boys and had given Mary her fit. Everybody knew that illness came down a river, especially in warm weather when rotting things floated and the mud oozed between your toes along the banks. The Iroquois River was wider and deeper at Middleport and the town had two doctors. Asa had checked it out. Both of them had studied at school to get their diplomas, not like old Doc Davis who got his learning by himself from a book. Middleport had other advantages too. There was a sawmill, so wood for houses could be bought cheaper and without all the hauling and cartage fees that you had to pay in Independence. Middleport even had a gristmill, so corn and wheat from their fields could be ground right away and if they planted enough of it maybe they could sell their excess to merchants coming down from Chicago. At least the flour would be fresh when Ann bought it. There were all kinds of bugs and worms in the barrels of the stuff that came into Independence. There were shops too, places to buy things you needed right away without having to order from a catalogue. A man could buy a new gun or get a new saddle and a woman could buy bolts of dress material right off the counter. There was a hotel that catered to travelers but served meals to anybody who had the price. There was a school with a real teacher. And if she wanted to, Ann could even get on a train and ride to Chicago. The North–South Railroad tracks were being laid right then. So in the spring they loaded their few belongings into an open wagon and started out for Middleport. Asa drove the team of horses and Nervie sat between him and Ann. Mary, completely recovered, wriggled in her mother's arms and looked at everything with the intense curiosity of a one-year-old child.

Middleport proved disappointing. The plot of land Asa had purchased for his homesite was high and dry. And the activity wasn't what he expected it to be.

In 1852, after five years in Middleport, Asa bought a half interest in a sawmill that was being constructed in the middle of a woods everybody called Watseka. Nobody lived there and it took him a good hour by horseback to get to the mill. The land was cheap and he bought many acres. If Middleport kept growing, people would eventually farm the Watseka land he was clearing. He hadn't been able to raise the entire amount by himself, so went into partnership with a man named Josiah Matzenbaugh. He had come to Middleport from the East and seemed to have money to buy land and buildings. Everyone said he probably was Jewish. Josiah was a young man (just turned twenty) but a big man. He was tall and broad-shouldered, the kind of man who got instant respect no matter where he went and no matter how much money he had in his pocket. Josiah didn't want to run the business, Asa could do that. All he wanted was the profits from his investment. He considered Asa, seven years his senior, as an older brother, and it was while he was visiting one Sunday for supper that Mary had her next serious fit.

'Now don't go fussing around Uncle Josiah's things, Mary,' her mother called as she saw the six-year-old girl near the man's hat and coat. He had thrown them over a chair by the door as he always did when he came visiting. The new pegs on the wall of the room were filled with the Roffs' own things. The idea of built-in closets hadn't yet come to Middleport.

'I ain't doin' nothin',' Mary said.

'Just see that you don't.' Ann was busy with the potatoes while Nervie put the plates on the table. The two men were in the backyard inspecting a brood sow Asa had recently purchased. Even though they lived in town, they had chickens and pigs and a milk cow in the backyard. So did everybody else.

'Blood,' said Mary. Her mother didn't turn around. 'Ma, look at this here blood.'

Nervie was the first to scream and dash toward her younger sister. She stepped back as Mary brandished the knife just inches from her face. 'Don't you touch me, Nervie. You keep away. You hear?'

In Mary's hand a knife glistened; the tip was red with blood. The blood came from Mary's left arm, from the large cut she had made in it.

Ann rushed to the girl but was held back by the knife. 'Mary. Mary, you give me that thing right now! Oh Lord in Heaven just look what you did to your arm. Give me that thing or I'll thrash you!'

'You come any closer, woman, and it'll be your blood on the end of this here knife!' Ann stepped back against the kitchen table. She was unable to think for a few seconds so shaken was she by the drastic change in her daughter's voice.

'She sounds like an old lady, Ma,' Nervie said.

'Now Mary, you cut out this foolishness. You cut it out

right now. You hear?' Ann was shouting now.

'The only thing that'll be cut out will be your heart, if you come any closer!' It wasn't Mary's voice.

'I'm going to bring your Pa in here and he'll settle your hash, young lady,' Ann threatened, her eyes still on the blood that was dripping from her daughter's arm onto the kitchen floor.

'My Pa?' the voice laughed. 'My Pa's been dead for more years than I care to remember.' The strange laughter returned. 'My Pa!'

Ann backed toward the kitchen door. 'Mr Roff,' she screamed. 'Mr Roff, come in here! Quick.' Even under stress Ann remembered her manners. Married ladies never called their husbands by their first names when company was present.

'What is it? Supper about ready?' Asa called back.

'Will you and Josiah *please* come in here? It's Mary. Something's happened to Mary.'

Both men came running into the kitchen, not stopping to scrape the mud from their boots. They stopped almost at the same time and stared at the girl in the corner.

'That's my knife she's got,' said Josiah. 'I left it in my coat pocket.' He glanced over at Ann. 'I'm sorry. I shouldn't have left it there.'

'Now, come on, Mary,' Asa commanded. 'Give me that knife. It don't belong to you and you already hurt yourself. Give it to me.' He walked over to the girl, his hand outstretched to receive the knife.

Mary slashed the air in front of his fingers. 'You keep your distance!' the voice almost whispered. 'I got this knife and I'm gonna keep it.' She slashed again at the empty space between herself and Asa.

'Now Mary, I ain't about to tell you again. Give me that—'

'Mary?' the voice rose loud and questioning. 'Why do you people keep calling me Mary? Ain't none of you got no sense?'

' 'Cause your name's Mary!' shouted Nervie, 'and you'd better be careful about talking back to Pa.'

'Ain't nothin' worse than a brat!' the voice said. 'My name ain't Mary!'

'It is too!' Nervie shouted. 'Your name is Mary Roff and Pa is really gonna get you!'

The girl lunged toward the group, which pulled back together as if tied to the same string. 'I told you my name ain't Mary! Now stop calling me that. Don't like that name!'

Asa started toward the girl but Josiah held him back. 'Wait, Asa,' he cautioned. 'Don't do anything. Don't go near her just yet.' He was looking at the girl in a new way, as if seeing her for the first time. 'Just stay calm and let's see what'll happen.'

'What'll happen?' Asa demanded.

'Yes. Back east, in New York City, I saw something like this once. It was at a spirit meeting. A lady got taken over by a spirit and it changed her whole way of speaking.'

'A spirit? What in hell are you talking about?'

'A spirit came down from someplace and took over the lady's body and made her say all sorts of things. Do crazy things, too.' Both Ann and Asa were looking at him. 'I seen it with my own eyes. It looked just like this thing that's got Mary.'

'Oh, Josiah,' Ann was indignant. 'There ain't no spirit got Mary! There ain't no such thing as spirits!'

'That's right,' Asa agreed. 'Ain't no such things as spirits.' Then after a moment he added, 'Anyway, spirits are the work of the Devil, and Mary is a Christian child.'

'The Spiritualists are Christian too,' Josiah said, never taking his eyes from Mary. 'They believe in Jesus just like you do but they don't believe that all spirits is from the Devil.'

'Well, where can they be from then?' Ann asked.

'From the spirit world. They can even be the relatives and friends who have passed into the spirit world. You know, passed away. Died?'

Mary had stopped brandishing the knife and was listening in fascination to what Josiah was saying. 'I believe that,' she said in the strange harsh voice. 'I believe that because I've seen spirits. Back home I saw spirits more than once.'

'Now, Mary,' Ann started to say but Josiah signaled for her to be still.

'Back home?' he asked slowly. 'Where do you come from if you ain't from around here?'

'Germany.' The reply was instant and definite.

'Germany?' Josiah repeated.

'Near Koblenz. Near the border. You ever been there?'

'No,' said Josiah. 'Never been out of the United States. But my father was born in Germany. He came from Eltville near Wiesbaden.'

'Oh yes,' the voice grew softer and a smile crossed Mary's face. 'That's on the Rhine. My folks and I been through there once when we was on the way to Mannheim.'

Ann became exasperated. 'Now Mary Roff, you stop that lying. You know you've never been to Germany and neither have we!'

'It ain't none of my concern where *you* have been,' the child said. 'But my folks and I come from Germany.'

'Mr Roff,' Ann insisted. 'Do something!' All Asa could do was look at Josiah, who shook his head.

'*I* believe you were born in Germany,' he said soothingly. 'What's your name? Will you tell me?'

'Katrina Hogan.'

'How old are you?'

'Sixty-three years.'

'How did you get from Germany over to Illinois?'

'Through the air. I always come through the air.'

Neither Asa nor Ann said anything.

'You know, I wish you'd go back to Germany now. You ain't doing this little girl much good.'

'What little girl?' the voice became strident again.

'The little girl whose body you are in. Look what you did to her arm. It's bleeding.'

Mary looked at her arm and saw the blood. 'Oh. Did I do that?'

'Yes. With that knife.'

Mary looked at the knife. Her eyes grew wide and she opened her grip on the handle. It fell to the floor. 'I'm sorry,' the voice said. 'I didn't mean to hurt nobody.'

'Course you didn't; will you go now?'

'Yes.' Mary looked at her parents. 'I'm sorry for what I did to your little girl. I didn't mean to do her no harm.'

Mary's body stiffened and swayed. Josiah took two strides

forward and caught her before she fell. Ann began to cry and caress her daughter's forehead. 'She's fainted,' Josiah said. 'Better get her to bed.'

He carried her rigid body into the room she shared with Nervie and placed her on the bed. 'She's like she's carved out of stone,' he said. 'She ain't moving nothing.' He started toward the door and the horse he had left tied to the post in front of the house. 'I'll go and fetch Doc Pittwood. Maybe he can be some help.'

Asa hurried after him, catching him by his sleeve. 'Josiah, this ain't the first time Mary's been sick like this. Once back in Indiana she was like a board for twelve days after a fit.'

'Did she talk like somebody else before?'

'She weren't even six months old then. Don't tell Doc Pittwood.'

'Don't tell him what?'

'That business about the spirit. Just tell him she had a fit and to bring the right medicine.'

Josiah looked into Asa's eyes and smiled. 'I understand,' he said. 'Don't worry.' He laid a large hand on Asa's shoulder.

That had been in 1852. By 1860 the Roffs were no longer living in Middleport and they were no longer in the shoe business. And they were no longer poor. Asa and Josiah Matzenbaugh had become rich.

In 1858 the Peoria & Oquakwa Railroad wanted to expand its lines as far east as the Indiana border. Since Middleport sat almost in a straight line to the east of Peoria, it was only natural that the railway company would want to pass through the town. And it was also a junction point with the line that ran from north to south.

But almost from the beginning, the railroad officials ran into problems. Some senior citizens in Middleport didn't want all the noise and soot that another train would bring. Some said it was bad enough having the north–south line running so near the town's center, without having another railway running east–west as well.

It wasn't good for neither animals nor children, some said. A farmer, whose horse was about to give birth, became frightened by the train whistle and broke her leg, then had to shoot both mother and unborn colt. Some chickens somewhere in Ohio had all stopped laying when the train came by, it was said. Someone else heard that corn didn't grow very well wherever a train ran. All that shaking and vibrating wasn't natural for the seeds and the ears grew crooked and small-kerneled.

The town fathers argued with the officials for a month, finally agreeing only if the railway company would pay an exorbitant fee to their treasury. The officials said they would have to go back to Peoria to think about it.

The day after they departed, Asa and Josiah drove their buggy to Peoria. Aside from their clothes and several bottles of good booze, they had a tin box with maps and deeds of the land they owned about a mile south of the town's limits. It was land they had purchased to get lumber for their sawmill. The Peoria & Oquakwa could come through *their* land, if it wanted to, for much less than Middleport was asking and the two men would even construct a depot at the spot where the two lines would cross. They could call the spot South Middleport if they chose, but everyone referred to the place as Watseka, after an Indian woman who lived there with the area's first white settler. Watseka had been good to the white man, Asa said, and Watseka would be good for the P. & O.

The officials checked their maps with the maps the men brought. It was good flat land and they only had to deal with two people, not an entire town. The papers were drawn up in two days. Asa and Josiah stayed drunk for three.

In 1859 the railroad started clearing the land and laying the ties and the rails. At the place where the two lines crossed, Asa and Josiah built a depot. Then they took a sheet of paper and a straight-edge block of wood and mapped out their holdings, plotted and constructed their new town. The town of Watseka.

There was 50 feet on the right side of the tracks that the railroad owned. On the left side where the depot and the side tracks were to be, they got 100 feet. Bordering the north–south tracks Asa drew a line and called it First Street. Then another vertical double line was drawn and it became Second Street. He drew the lines up and down on the paper until he had created Sixth Street.

The horizontal streets were next. Because he and Josiah had originally purchased the land on account of its fine stand of virgin timber, it was only fair that the horizontal streets be named after different species of trees. They had made most of their money by selling walnut boards and planks. So the main street, the one immediately north of the railroad tracks, was called Walnut. It was to be the main commercial street, serving the railway junction and all the people who would later move into town. The next one north was Oak, then came Ash and Hickory. The last one was simply called North Street.

To the south of the tracks, running parallel to them, were Cherry, Locust and Mulberry. The two men looked at their handiwork and laughed. 'I feel like the Lord who created the Earth and then rested,' Josiah said.

'This must be just how He felt,' Asa commented, 'creating something out of nothing.'

'Except He didn't have anything to put in His bank account,' Josiah said, 'and we do.'

'Oh, Mr Matzenbaugh, we most certainly do!'

The two men were the owners of a town. They had arrived. Asa was forty-one, Josiah only twenty-seven.

It didn't take long for the population to shift from Middleport to Watseka. Businesses moved nearer the railroad junction and so did their owners. When residential construction started, Asa was the first to build himself a house, and as soon as he was able to put more money in the bank he built another house, Watseka's first brick home. It was modern, with arched windows, a wide front porch and two parlors (most people only had one), plus a carriage barn and a hand-carved stairway that led to a second floor with four large bedrooms. The acreage behind the house was magnificent, running almost a mile through good rich land and a grove of fine trees until it stopped at the banks of the Iroquois River.

Asa, rich from the sawmill and his land investments, dedicated himself to making his town a better place. He jumped feet first into politics and civic affairs. He was named postmaster for four years in 1854, and then became sheriff for another four.

Then, in 1857, after reading law books and sending to New York City for a home course, he took his bar exam and became a lawyer. In just a few years he had become one of the most influential and important men for miles around.

Each time Mary's fits returned Dr Pittwood was summoned. But only afterward. Neither Asa nor Ann wanted the rest of Watseka to know about the changes that came over Mary when these attacks occurred.

Once the girl claimed to be a woodsman and she spoke English with such a strange accent nobody could understand her. He had heard some people speaking French back in Rochester and they rolled their tongue and spoke through their nose just the way his daughter did. Another time she pretended, when the fits struck, that she was burning up, actually being consumed by flames. She cried and beat at her body and tore off her clothes to get rid of the terrible heat. Ann tried to hold her on the bed but Mary's strength was such that she shoved Ann across the room. Mary staggered from the house and rushed toward the pigsty. It was only when she threw herself into the wet mud and rolled in it for several minutes that the fit stopped. Ann and Nervie picked her up and carried her back into the house. Then they had to cut the clothes from her body. When she was clean and covered with a blanket Doc Pittwood was summoned. As usual there was nothing he could do, but he did have an idea.

'I don't know whether you've seen this in the paper,' he said, taking a folded copy of the *Middleport Weekly Press* from his black bag, 'but it might help if you sent Mary there.'

Asa took the paper eagerly. He read aloud the two-inch advertisement:

'Peoria Water Cure, Peoria, Illinois. This institution is pleasantly located on the Bluff. The building is commodious, and the rooms large, well ventilated and comfortably furnished. The diet will be phizzo ...' he stumbled.

'Physio-logical,' put in Doc Pittwood.

'The diet will be phizzy-o-logical and the treatment strictly hygienic. A department of the Institution is devoted to the treatment of all forms of female complaints.'

'Female complaints!' Ann blurted out. 'For heaven's sake, they put things like that in the paper? For everyone to see?'

Asa glared at her. 'Arrangements are completed for administering the Electro-Chemical Bath, so celebrated for the eradication of mineral drugs, and infectious diseases, and for various ... various ...'

Doc Pittwood adjusted his rimless spectacles on his rather plump nose: 'For various Neuralgic, Paralytic, Rheumatic, and Nervous afflictions. Terms in accordance with the Times, from five dollars to forty-two dollars per week.'

'Forty-two dollars per week!' Ann sat heavily on the horsehair sofa. 'Who could possibly pay all that?'

'That's only for the fancy deluxe apartment suite,' Doc Pittwood said. 'Mary wouldn't need that. I reckon she could go in there for about eight or ten dollars a week. That would give her a private room and her food and the doctors would be there all the time.'

'But would it help?' Asa asked. 'Do you think Mary has any of those things they talk about in the paper?'

Ann was still indignant over the words that had been read aloud to her. 'Well, she's too young to have any of those female problems, that's for sure. My Mary's only going on fifteen.'

'Has she been having her monthly discharge?' the doctor asked.

Asa reddened and Ann looked away. 'I ... I suppose she has. Nervie told me she once saw Mary burning some rags that had blood on them but, you know, Doctor, there are some things a mother just doesn't talk about with her children.'

'Of course, Mrs Roff. But the medical men at Peoria will have to know these things if they are going to treat her.'

'Treat her for what?' Asa repeated.

The doctor sighed and sat down on a red velvet chair, the dark carved wood legs creaking as it received his large body. 'I really don't know what ails your daughter,' he said. 'I'll confess, and I've said this to you time and time again, I've never seen such symptoms in a child before. It could be something in her blood. Maybe the water cure could get rid of it.'

32

Asa wanted to know, 'If we take her to Peoria, could they check her for whatever ...?'

'Oh yes,' the doctor assured him. 'It's a very modern establishment. If Mary goes there she'll be given special mineral waters to drink and she'll take baths in special medicinal waters that will get into all of her ... ah ... orifices ... if you'll excuse the expression, Mrs Roff.' She nodded and looked away. 'And they'll give her special foods and keep a close watch on her. Also they have –'

'Could we visit her?' Ann interrupted. 'I mean it won't be as if she's in a jail or something, will it?'

'Oh, no,' the doctor laughed. 'They have regular visiting days and visiting hours. You and Asa can even stay overnight right there if you choose.'

'Eight to ten dollars a week.' Asa looked at his wife and shook his head. 'That'll take quite a bite out of my savings.'

'But if it cures Mary –' Ann said.

Asa looked sharply at Dr Pittwood. 'If I spend all that money and she is not cured, then what?'

'Then, Asa, I don't think you have more than two choices.'

'Which are –'

'Mary dies one day by having a fit and choking on her tongue or else you have to put her in the loony bin.'

'You think my daughter is crazy?' Ann asked quickly.

'Those fits, if they aren't physical, must be mental. As she gets older she could become dangerous. You probably couldn't handle her at home. You'd have to put her away someplace. For her own good.'

'Mr Roff,' Ann said, looking up at her husband, 'tell Doc Pittwood to make the arrangements. Let's try this Peoria place. I can't see as we really have another choice.'

They packed a large trunk with Mary's clothes and books and some of her toys as well as her tatting and crocheting things. Ann stayed at home with her children. Nervie, at seventeen, could have taken care of Joseph and Fenton and Frank, the three boys born in Middleport. Joseph was six years old and Fenton was five. Frank was not quite two. Ann didn't really want to travel with Asa and Mary. She was pregnant again; the doctor said the baby would be born around July of that year. The problems with Mary had put

Ann's nerves 'right under her skin', and taking care of three healthy, noisy little boys was almost too much for her at times. Fortunately there was Loozie. Between Loozie and her oldest daughter Nervie, Ann was able to get a little rest and take walks in the woods to clear her head.

They could trust Loozie. Ann called her 'my African godsend'. The woman, somewhere in her early thirties, had come into Middleport when Ann was pregnant with Frank. She was a freedwoman and showed everyone her papers. Her owner, a cotton planter named Lozier from Mississippi, had sold his farm and freed his slaves, then moved northward into Ohio. Loozie went with him to help his family get settled, then continued westward hoping to get to Canada.

Loozie hugged Mary hard as she helped her up the steps onto the train. 'You take good care of yourself now, girl. You do what them doctors tell you. They ain't interested in seeing how stubborn you can be.'

'Oh Loozie, I'll be all right. I promise. You just help Ma and Nervie to take care of Pa and the boys.' Mary hugged the black woman.

Loozie dug into the pocket of her full-length coat and took out something wrapped in a bit of red cloth. She pressed it into the girl's hand. 'Now you take this and you keep it near you. Don't let nobody else touch it. You understand?'

'What is it?'

'It's something my Ma gave to me once when I was smaller than you and was feeling poorly. Somebody made it for her. A woman who lived on the farm where she was born.'

While Asa made sure all the baggage was being loaded into the car, Mary unwrapped the red cloth. Inside was a human figure, about two inches long and carved from dark wood. The figure had one of its hands over its heart and the other on its buttocks. Instead of a face a single blue bead had been inserted into the wood.

Mary made a face. 'It's ugly! What is it?'

'It wasn't made to be pretty. It's to keep away evil spirits and ghosts and things. My Ma gave it to me and now I'm loaning it to you. Loaning it, I said. I ain't giving it. When you get back from Peoria, I want it back.'

'What do I do with it?'

'Just keep it near you. It'll protect you. It sure has me.'

Mary stuffed the carving into her purse as Asa finished with the porter and came back to her. 'Loozie, you take the buggy back now and be sure and tell Mrs Roff that everything is all right and that I'll be back just as soon as Mary gets settled.'

'Yes, sir,' Loozie answered. 'You have a safe trip now and me and the missus will take care of things till you get back.' Then she hugged Mary, whispering in her ear: 'You keep that thing around you. Hold it tight when you need it. You hear?'

Mary shook her head and gave the woman a kiss. 'Goodbye, dear Loozie, and thank you.' She kept her head out of the window watching Loozie and the depot getting smaller and smaller until the woman's waving white handkerchief disappeared from sight.

Both Dr Mordecai Nevins and Dr Sarah Kenyon were at the front door of their clinic to receive Mary. After taking her to her room (Asa had relented and consented to a fifteen-dollar-a-week special accommodation) they showed him their diplomas and invited him to take coffee in their office.

'Of course, Mr Roff, there is nothing we can tell you right now,' Dr Nevins said, crossing his neatly pressed black and gray-striped trousers. 'We will have to make exhaustive tests, first.'

'I understand,' Asa nodded. 'But she is only fourteen years old. This is the first time she's ever been away from home and things are bound to be strange in the beginning.'

Dr Kenyon nodded. Asa looked at her curiously. He had never seen a woman doctor before. 'Mr Roff, you may be completely assured that we will take excellent care of your little Mary. We have had many children here who were even younger than she. Her days will be supervised and we will make sure she continues her schoolwork as well as her domestic projects like knitting and tatting. There is a Saturday afternoon tea for all clients and visitors and, of course, on Sunday, there is a Protestant church service.' She paused. 'Your faith *is* Protestant, isn't it?'

'Methodist.'

'Excellent. Now once we have decided upon the best method for restoring your daughter to health we shall put her on a special regimen that will include diet and exercise. She will also be given the beneficial treatments from Dr Nevins's special Electro-Chemical Bath machine. The doctor invented it and its remarkable curative powers have been of benefit to so many of our clients.' She smiled at Dr Nevins and he nodded majestically to Asa.

'I stand in awe, Doctor,' Asa said, 'of your profession. As a practicing member of the bar, I have always admired those who could heal the mind as well as the body.'

Dr Nevins took out a thick notebook and turned to a fresh sheet of paper. A quill pen, briskly removed from its holder, was poised in his hand ready to begin work. 'And your daughter's condition is more mental than physical?'

'I don't know, Doctor. It is something that comes and goes. She can be in the best of physical health and then suddenly become violently ill. Dr Pittwood, he's our doctor in Watseka, calls these seizures "fits". I myself,' and he coughed politely, 'don't like the word.'

'Well, then we won't use it,' said Dr Kenyon soothingly. 'When these seizures come on the child, what exactly takes place? I mean does she suddenly become rigid or is there some manifestation in other parts of her body?' The pen was waiting to write.

'I don't know exactly what you mean,' Asa hesitated.

'Does she just become immobile and go unconscious? Or is there more?'

'More?' Asa began stalling for time.

'Does she lose control of her body functions?' Dr Nevins asked.

'Uh . . . no. That seems to stay normal.' Did he dare tell them of the old German woman who grabbed the knife? The woman who spoke of Germany as if Mary had actually been there? 'If you mean do her bowels malfunction and things like that, no.'

'Does she show signs of restlessness or lack of appetite before these seizures?'

Should he tell them about the voice that claimed to be a sailor? The one that used the foul language and demanded whiskey?' 'No, her appetite has always been fine.'

It was Dr Kenyon who asked, 'How about melancholy? Sadness? How does she react to her brothers and sisters before one of these attacks?'

Should he tell them of the time Mary began to laugh in a high-pitched voice and grabbed little Frank from his crib, threatening to throw him from the upstairs window? It had taken Ann and Nervie ten minutes to talk her into giving the baby to Loozie.

'How is she with animals?'

'Fine,' Asa replied quickly, not adding that once during a fit she twisted the necks of seventeen chickens in the hen house.

'Mr Roff,' said Dr Kenyon, 'you aren't giving us very much to work with.'

'I'm sorry, but I am a lawyer and a businessman. You are the medical people. It will be up to you to decide upon the best method for her.' He rose to leave.

'Would you like to see the rest of the clinic?' Dr Nevins asked.

'No. I really must be getting back to the depot. My wife and the other children are expecting me back tomorrow.'

'Would you like to say good-bye to Mary?'

'I've already done that. No, I must be getting back. Thank you.' He shook hands with both doctors and left a check for one month's service on the desk. He walked quickly from the room and out into the warm afternoon sun. The train depot wasn't far from the clinic. The walk would do him good. It would give him time to reconcile himself to what he hadn't told the doctors. They would find out for themselves, he shuddered. They would find out for themselves.

At the beginning of the third month, Asa received a bill from the clinic and a notation that Mary seemed to be in good spirits and was eating regularly. They had examined her thoroughly and discovered nothing. A new diet had been started and she seemed to relax in the Electro-Chemical Bath. Each evening, right after supper, she was given a special herb tea. It helped her sleep.

The world seemed to go mad that spring. In April Southern cannon opened fire on Fort Sumter and killed several Northern soldiers. Many folks had seen it coming; in fact, the *Middleport Weekly Press* had been filled with rumors and stories ever since Lincoln took the oath of office. Asa had voted for Lincoln and believed in him. He also hoped that a man from Illinois would do more for the state. Lincoln was the first President from the West. Asa had actually shaken hands with Mr Lincoln when he came to Kankakee to debate with Stephen A. Douglas. Both men wanted to be state senator. Now Mr Lincoln was President and the nation was at war with itself. The only consolation was that it would be over within a few months. The South just didn't have the modern machinery for war that the North had.

Mary wrote regular letters asking when she could come home. Asa and Nervie wrote replies, telling her of family events and gossip of her friends in Watseka. Since she had gone, the tension in the house had eased considerably and Ann was able to rest more comfortably at night.

Ann had her baby, a boy, in late July. He was a frail child with pale skin and clear blue eyes. They named him Charles. In early September Ann felt strong enough to have Mary return and Asa wrote to the doctors. He wanted Mary home for her birthday, her fifteenth, October 8. The day after he posted the letter, he received one from Dr Nevins.

My Dear Mr Roff.
Sir:

It is with the greatest reluctance that I write to inform you of a relapse in the condition of your daughter, Mary. It came most unexpectedly and without the slightest provocation. I am, dear sir, at a loss to explain it and loath to detail it on paper. However, as her parent and benefactor, you must be apprised of the situation.

It was five days ago [the letter was dated September 12] and Mary was in the music room as was her usual wont after luncheon. She was seated at the piano playing her favorite hymn 'We Are Coming, Sister Mary' and singing with Miss Greene and Miss Whitfield (two elderly ladies who frequent this establishment annually for the water cure) when she began to pound upon the keys and shout in a loud voice. Both Misses

Green and Whitfield attempted to soothe her but Mary began to shout obscenities at them. Miss Greene swooned into a chair and Miss Whitfield hastened to the door to summon one of the attendants but Mary ran ahead of her and closed the door, bolting it from the inside. At this, Miss Whitfield began to scream for assistance. Mary jumped on her, knocking her to the floor and sat astride her back, and tugging on the lady's hair began to pull at it and call her all sorts of vile and wicked names. By the time I and my staff were able to enter the music room we found Miss Whitfield's clothes to be torn and in complete disarray (her skirts had been rent in two) and Mary was beating the unfortunate woman's bare buttocks with the woman's own belt. Mary was laughing and speaking in a very low voice and shouting about the necessity of thrashing a sinful nun. When we overpowered your daughter (it took four of us) she said she was a Jesuit priest and that Miss Whitfield had broken her vows and needed to be castigated. Mary was placed in a separate room with no windows, and dressed in a special restraining jacket. She insisted that she was a priest and that we would all be excommunicated (Mr Roff, sir, you *did* say that you raised her a Methodist, did you not?) and would all suffer for the rescue of the nun (Miss Whitfield).

I attempted to administer a sedative to her but to no avail. She would not swallow it, but spat it out, one time directly into my face. Then just as rapidly as this fit took her, it released her and she fell onto the floor. We placed her on her bed where she remains today, five days later, and still in her restraining jacket. I cannot arouse her even though her heartbeat, her pulse and her breathing are normal.

If I am to continue my treatment of your daughter, I beg you sir to inform me whether anything like this has ever happened before and if so *when and under what circumstances*? Mary has been a perfectly normal girl and a model patient since the first day she was admitted. This episode, I do not need to tell you, has upset not only the staff but the other patients as well.

A complete reply by return post will be appreciated and is anxiously awaited.

Your obedient servant,
Dr Mordecai Nevins, proprietor.

Asa, instead of writing, took a train the next day to Peoria. 'I'm sorry,' he told Drs Nevins and Kenyon. 'That's the entire story. I should have told you everything when I was here.'

'Why didn't you?' Dr Nevins asked.

'I was afraid that if I told you, you'd think my daughter was crazy and wouldn't have admitted her at all.'

'That *she* was crazy?' Dr Kenyon said in her low voice, 'or that *you* were crazy for giving credence to an idea such as spirit possession?'

Asa looked down at the floor. 'That I was crazy too, I suppose.'

'Do you believe in spirits? Aside from those in the Bible, of course,' Dr Nevins asked.

'I don't know,' Asa replied truthfully. 'One part of me says it's all superstition and yet the other part . . . the part that's seen what comes over Mary . . . tells me that something must be there. *Something.*' He looked from face to face trying to imagine what they must be thinking as they sat examining him. There was a long pause, broken only by the ticking of a large clock on the far wall. Asa coughed and crossed his legs, then uncrossed them and brushed a bit of mud from the cuff of his trousers. They were still looking at him. 'I don't know what to believe,' he said defensively. 'The Bible says there are more things on earth than man can dream of. I don't believe we have all the answers.'

'About spirits?' Dr Kenyon inquired in her flat now-I'm-questioning-a-patient tone.

'About *anything*,' Asa replied quickly. 'I think there are many things here on earth that man cannot explain away by his own reasoning. Like how a seed grows into a flower, for instance . . . ' He was searching, knowing they were examining him ' – and why a man can have an idea and turn that idea into a real thing like an invention or a business. Things like that.' He felt good that he had expressed himself on their level.

Dr Kenyon adjusted her long skirt so that the hem hung evenly above her buttoned shoes. 'Do you consider yourself a Christian man, Mr Roff?' She pronounced 'Christian' as if it had three syllables. Chris-ti-an.

'Yes. Of course. I was born into the Methodist faith and am a member of that faith today. So are the members of my family.'

'It was thirteen years ago,' she said, 'that some hysterical girls, they were the Fox sisters, deluded the world into thinking they had communicated with the spirit of a dead peddler – '

'Imagine,' Dr Nevins broke in, 'a *peddler*!'

'Supposedly the man had been killed and buried in the basement of their home. This was before they moved into it with their family, of course, but he had been killed and after several nights of knockings on the walls and foolishness like that they claimed to have communicated with the man's spirit.'

Asa nodded. 'Yes. I believe I've heard about it.'

'Well because of all the nonsense that followed it these girls have become some sort of heroines, especially to the ignorant and impressionable, and they have amassed a large following of foolish persons, the Spiritualists, anxious to communicate with the dead.'

'But they did find the body, didn't they?' Asa asked.

'What body, Mr Roff?'

'Why, the body of that peddler. Didn't the knockings on the wall tell them where to dig in their cellar, and when they dug in that spot the body of the peddler was uncovered?'

'Yes,' said Dr Nevins, 'and that's what started it all.'

'But if they actually found the body,' Asa continued, 'then the information the spirit . . . or the knockings if you prefer . . . gave them must have been correct.'

'Coincidence,' Dr Kenyon said between pressed lips.

'Yes. Coincidence,' Dr Nevins repeated.

'But a rather unusual coincidence,' Asa said.

Dr Kenyon said, 'It was exactly because it *was* unusual that this whole spirit nonsense started. And,' she looked at her companion for confirmation, 'and since that incident many young girls have deluded themselves into thinking they can communicate with spirits.'

Asa wished he could light up a cigar, but he was in the presence of a lady. He would have to wait. He needed it to keep his hands busy as he tried to put his words together. 'Are you telling me that you think *my* Mary has been imagining all these things? That she is, somehow or other, trying to emulate these Fox sisters?'

'It is a possibility,' said Dr Nevins.

'I don't think so,' Asa said. 'I can't see how. Mary had her first fit when she was just six months old. Six months! That was almost two years *before* those girls heard the knockings! And anyway,' he searched for the words, 'how could she have been trying to delude herself at that tender age?' He got up from the chair and walked to the window. The trees were leafless outside, leafless and cold. As cold as the attitude of the doctors in the room, he thought. 'May I have a cigar?' he bowed slightly toward the lady doctor. She nodded her assent. He pulled the silver case from his waistcoat pocket and snapped it open. He removed a thin black stick of tobacco and a wooden match. He bit off one end of the cigar, twirled it around in his mouth for a second, then struck the match against the sole of his shoe. The warm aroma filled his lungs and cleared his head. The entire process had given him time to think and now he turned around to face them. 'The first time Mary's personality really changed,' he said carefully, 'was when she said she was a German woman and took the knife and cut her arm. Mary was six years old at the time. Six! How could she have heard about the Fox sisters at the age of six?'

'Maybe she heard you and your wife discussing the matter,' Dr Nevins said. 'Children can be most impressionable.'

'No,' Asa was on firmer ground now. 'A friend of mine was in the house when it happened. It was his knife Mary used. He told us about the Fox sisters for the first time only *after* Mary had that attack.'

'Again coincidence,' said Dr Kenyon. 'It is exactly these coincidences that have built this spirit nonsense into what it is today. That's what we have been trying to tell you.'

Asa ignored her. 'In my profession as a lawyer, we look for coincidences to help our study of the cases we get, but in

42

your profession I would think you would look deeper than coincidence. *Anything* can be turned into a coincidence. Have you questioned Mary as to her knowledge of these Fox sisters?'

'We have not had the opportunity, Mr Roff,' Dr Kenyon said, 'after all we didn't suspect any of this until Mary attacked the two ladies the other day. And being as she is still unconscious and cannot hear us —'

'Or *won't* hear us,' Dr Nevins put in.

' — we have no way of knowing just how much she is aware of this so-called spirit madness.'

Asa turned back to the window. He didn't like the bars but he supposed they were a necessary precaution. He took a long pull on the cigar. 'I've come to a decision,' he said. They were both watching him. 'Mary is in no condition to be taken home. I don't know if being here will help her or not.' He put up his hand to stop Dr Kenyon before she could interrupt. 'She cannot come home because she is an unsettling influence on my wife and the other children. I will keep her here a few months longer, hoping she can be cured. I am willing to pay for better and more direct treatments, if necessary. She is to continue her studies and I am to get a full report once a month. And,' he waved his cigar for emphasis, 'I want you to thoroughly investigate this theory you have about her imagining she is possessed by spirits. If you should be correct, she must be broken of this habit. If you are *not* correct, you had better find out what her *real* ailment is.' He walked toward the door, putting on his heavy greatcoat. 'And,' he added, 'for all the time and money I will have put in here, I want to be presented with proof. Not coincidences!'

They moved Mary into a bedroom suite after that. She awoke in a new room and in a new bed, the restraining jacket removed. A nurse, a middle-aged lady whom Mary liked, sat in the corner of the room rocking and doing her needlepoint.

'Mrs Jacobs . . . ' Mary called and the woman hurried to her bedside. 'Mrs Jacobs . . . I'm so thirsty.'

'Of course you are, my darling,' the woman soothed, 'I'll get some water right away.' She was gone several minutes, when she returned she had Drs Nevins and Kenyon with her.

All three fluttered around the girl for a few minutes, asking how she felt, if she were in pain, taking her pulse and listening to her heartbeat. Mrs Jacobs combed her hair after she had sponged off her face, 'Does that feel better, Mary dear?'

'Yes thank you.'

'You have been a sick little girl,' Dr Nevins said. 'We were quite worried about you.'

'And so was your father,' added Dr Kenyon.

'Pa? Is Pa here?' Mary tried to sit up, but Mrs Jacobs pushed her gently back onto the pillow.

'He was here yesterday,' replied Dr Nevins, 'but you were too sick to see him.'

'He's gone? Back to Watseka?' She started to cry.

Mrs Jacobs hushed her in a sing-song voice.

'But I wanted to see my Pa! Was Ma with him or Nervie or the boys?'

'No, he came alone. He came as soon as we called him. As soon as it happened and you were resting.' Dr Kenyon brushed back a hair on the girl's forehead.

Mary stared at her. 'As soon as *what* happened?' she said.

'That scene in the music room,' came the reply.

'The music room?' Her eyes were wider now. 'Did I do something in the music room?'

Doctor Nevins glanced at Dr Kenyon and then at Mrs Jacobs. 'You *do* remember being in the music room? With the Misses Greene and Whitfield?'

'Yes,' Mary said slowly. 'That was yesterday.'

'That was *ten days* ago,' said Dr Kenyon. 'You've been in a coma ever since.'

The girl put her hands up over her face. It was easier to cry in front of these people if her face was hidden. 'Oh no. It's started again.'

'Apparently *it* has,' Dr Nevins said sarcastically. 'Whatever *it* is. We have one opinion and your father has another. What we would like,' and he tapped the pencil against the pad impatient to begin writing, 'is to know what *you* think it is.'

'What *I* think it is? How can I tell, Doctor? I never seem to remember nothing when it's over. Nothing.'

'Have you ever *tried* to remember, child?' This time Mrs Jacobs asked the question.

'I have. I really have, but it's like it didn't happen to me. Like it was happening to somebody else.'

'Somebody else?' Dr Kenyon's voice rose as she glanced at her colleague. 'How could it happen to somebody else when it happens to *you*. To Mary Roff. To you!'

'I don't know,' she flinched as Mrs Jacobs wiped her cheeks with a handkerchief. 'It seems that one minute I'm me, then something happens and people say it's somebody else and then when I wake up I'm me again.' Dr Nevins was writing it down. Mary saw they didn't believe her. 'I'm sick, ain't I? I'm sick and I ain't never going to get well.' There was no answer. 'That's what you told Pa, isn't it? That I'm real sick and I have to stay here forever.' The tears came faster now.

'You are sick, yes, Mary, you are,' said Dr Kenyon, 'but you are here because we want you to get well. We want you to get well just as much as you do. As much as your father does.'

'But if you don't know what ails me—'

'We have a theory,' Dr Kenyon continued. 'And,' she coughed politely into her hand, 'your father has another.'

'What does Pa think? Pa has seen me when these things happen. What does he think?'

'He thinks,' Dr Kenyon said slowly, 'that you are possessed by spirits.'

'Pa thinks I get taken over by a ghost? He said *that*?' Mary shook her head, still not quite believing what she was hearing. 'A ghost? Why, we don't believe in ghosts. Ma told me there ain't such things. I asked her once,' she said hurriedly, trying to convince them that she was telling the truth, 'and she said there were no such things as ghosts. That when a person dies he stays dead a long time.'

'And your father? What does he tell you?'

'I . . . I can't remember my Pa ever talking to me about ghosts.' She shook her head, watching everything she said being written down. 'He talks about his business a lot and what's happening in town and sometimes he tells us things that happened to him when he was a boy and growing up and all, but we never talk about ghosts.'

'Well then,' said Dr Kenyon, 'who is it that tells you about ghosts and makes you *imitate* them?' When she said that, Dr Nevins glared at her quickly. He wasn't quite ready to get to that point of the questioning.

'Imitate?' repeated Mary.

'You know, pretend. Play that you are somebody who has passed on and has come back to haunt somebody else.' Mrs Jacobs suggested.

Mary shook her head. 'Nobody.'

'Then you get these ideas all by yourself?' Dr Nevins was writing.

'I don't get *any i*deas.' Mary said trying hard not to set the tears in motion again. These people never believed anything she said. She had been through their questioning before. Sometimes they put words in her mouth. Her Pa had told her to tell the truth but not to let people get the wrong idea. 'You have the wrong idea,' she said boldly. 'I don't pretend. I don't know what happens. One minute everything is fine and the next thing I know I've done something horrible and it's several days afterward. I don't tell lies. My Ma doesn't want me to tell lies.'

'Then that means you are telling us the truth. As you see it.'

'Yes,' she sighed. 'I am.'

Dr Nevins closed his notebook. 'We shall see,' he said. 'We shall see for ourselves.'

They watched Mary closely after that but weeks went by and nothing out of the ordinary happened. She took her Electro-Chemical Baths and ate the special diet and studied her schoolbooks during the day and wrote letters or played the piano in the music room after supper.

Several times over the next few months her parents came to visit her. Asa was all for taking her home and saving the expense but Ann was still weak and nervous. The birth of the last son – their tenth child in twenty years – had weakened her more than anyone had suspected. Asa would hear her crying softly beside him during the night and each time he asked her what was wrong she said it was only her nerves. The four small boys, even with Nervie and Loozie to help her, were more than she could handle. She loved Mary – she loved all her children – but the strain of having her home, of never knowing when she would have another of her fits was too much for Ann. She kept asking Asa to let

Mary stay in Peoria 'just a little while longer.'

Mary did come home for Christmas in 1861 and again for Christmas in 1862. She seemed to be calmer and had put on a little weight. The younger boys didn't remember her at first and this bothered the girl; yet when Asa took her for a ride through the town, people waved at her and called her name. They asked her how she was feeling and wished her a Merry Christmas and made her feel part of the community again. Some of her classmates even envied her for being in the big city of Peoria. A couple of times some friends even came to visit her, taking her to lunch with their parents and asking her all sorts of questions about the clinic and about Peoria and she asked them about her own family and about happenings in Watseka. She was always so excited when her friends appeared that she didn't notice how their parents looked at her, watched her. For it was common knowledge – back in Watseka – that Mary was in Peoria because she might be going crazy. Might be, mind you. It wasn't definite, but rumor had it some strange things crossed the girl's mind every now and then. It was every pious citizen's fervent prayer that Mary would recover and be able to return to Watseka soon.

By May of 1863 nothing unusual had happened to Mary. There were no fits, no screaming, no sudden changes of personality. The doctors were unable to find anything wrong with her, unable to investigate her so-called spirit seizures because nothing had occurred since October of 1861.

However, both Drs Nevins and Kenyon were pleased with their work. They wrote Asa he could come for his daughter and take her home for good. They told Asa they were positive their Electro-Chemical Baths and their diets had cured Mary. They told each other that what really had cured her was their constant vigilance and watchfulness so that the child soon learned who was in command and didn't dare try any of her foolishness on them. They assured Asa that Mary would never have another occurrence of whatever it was that bothered her.

And, indeed, it did seem as if Mary was another person now. She was calm and considerate and helped her mother with the boys and Loozie with the housework. She became interested in things that girls of her age were interested in. She made herself a blue velvet dress and tatted a wide white collar for it. She joined the church choir.

One day shortly after she returned, Loozie confronted her.

'You still got that little carving I gave you before you went to that clinic?'

Mary nodded. 'It's upstairs in the old dresser. Come on, I'll show you.' The two went up the wide wooden stairway and into the front bedroom that Mary and Nervie shared. The two beds in the large room were made of dark wood with high backs detailed with roses twining around Grecian columns. There was a red velvet chair with carved mahogany legs. It almost matched the new parlor set downstairs with its carved back and crushed red velvet seats. There were a few scatter rugs on the floor. There were pictures of little children on the wall, dressed in heavy silks and satins, being guided by angels or playing with dogs or picking flowers. There were also embroidered mottoes in several different colors and types of stitching, asking God to protect the house.

Mary knelt down and pried at the base of her dresser. The carved strip came off in her hand, nails sliding easily out of their worn holes. There was a small space where the strip had been set into the side of the dresser. She picked up the carving, unwrapped the piece of red cloth, and showed it to Loozie. 'See. I still have it. They never found it even when I was in Peoria.'

'Well, you see that you keep it and that you don't tell nobody else. Not Nervie and not any of your brothers either. Someday you'll be needing that and it can't have lots of other folks' finger marks all over it.' The black woman caressed the small figure. 'My mamma gave me that and it sure brought me good luck. Got me my freedom.' She handed it back. 'Now put it in there and put back that strip of wood. Don't let your Pa know you're tearing apart his furniture.'

The year of 1863 passed uneventfully in the Roff household. On Christmas the Roffs invited several friends for dinner.

Mary baked a cake for the Christmas dinner. It was a

special recipe she had copied from the newspaper in Peoria, calling for raisins and orange peel, walnuts and filberts. She spent an entire day rounding up the necessary ingredients and fussing in the kitchen. On Christmas Day it was all Asa could do to cut it with a butcher knife. The family laughed (especially the boys, who never lost a chance to tease any girl) and Mary burst into tears and ran to her room. After a few minutes, while the family sat around the table concerned that maybe this would bring on one of her 'fits', she came laughing back into the dining-room. 'I felt so angry with that cake,' she said taking her place, 'but when I started to remember how funny Pa looked trying to cut it with that big knife, I had to laugh.' Everyone else at the table laughed and the tension was broken.

Everything seemed to be going well. Then came the month of June and along with the heat and the sudden thunderstorms came Mary's next attack. She grabbed Tessie, the family cat, and chopped off its head, licking the blood and shoving Ann to the ground when she tried to stop her. When Mary finally passed out, screaming in some language nobody understood, they managed to get her into bed and Dr Fowler was called. That's when they bound her with ropes and she used the foul language.

For the rest of the month Mary ate sparingly and would sit for hours on the big front porch, rocking and reading and thinking. She could not remember killing the cat. But she must have done it. Her own mother said she did it. Her own mother said she cut Tessie's head off and then licked the blood that came spurting out of the severed body. They only talked about it that one time, that time she had come to her senses and found herself tied down in her own bed. They never mentioned it again and she was so ashamed of what she had done that she didn't talk about it either. She wondered who else in Watseka knew about it, wondered who Dr Fowler had told. Asa had made him promise that, as a professional, he wouldn't tell anyone what had happened. The man kept his promise, yet did tell several of his clients that he had successfully been bleeding Mary Roff and suggested they try the same treatment. When they asked him what ailed Mary this time, he would just shake his head and smile. They smiled along with him. They were not surprised that the clinic wasn't able to cure her of her craziness.

Mary stopped going to choir practice with Nervie, and on Sundays when the preacher gave his sermon she couldn't look at him. He always talked about sinning and being sorry before God for what you did. She knew she had sinned. She was sorry. She told God that a thousand times and asked for forgiveness. Not just for killing Tessie but forgiveness for all the trouble she was causing her Pa and Ma and forgiveness for all the money she had cost her Pa in that clinic. She asked to be forgiven for the thoughts she sometimes had of doing away with herself. She knew suicide was a sin. It said so somewhere in the Bible, but after she had killed Tessie she began to think about killing herself. She pictured herself jumping into the river and watched her body sink, then rise and float downstream past old Middleport. She pictured drinking a glass of poison and clutching her stomach and falling on the floor while everyone in the family cried. Maybe she would jump in front of the train.

Every night she got down on her knees and asked God to forgive her for these thoughts. She asked Jesus to bless her and protect her. Sometimes she would remain for an hour or more beside the bed, begging, pleading, crying for guidance. Nobody in the house knew of these prayers. After she had killed Tessie and had been put to bed, Nervie was moved into a bedroom by herself and the boys doubled up in their rooms. The lock was taken off her door and the hole was plugged with a wad of cotton. Asa thought it would be better if she couldn't lock herself in her room. He put new locks on the other bedroom doors and told the children to use them when they went to sleep at night. They didn't ask why – they still had the memory of Mary attacking Tessie with that butcher knife.

Dr Fowler came twice a week with his jar of leeches and Mary began to look forward to these visits. Unlike the rest of her family, she found the creatures attractive and would reach into the jar and apply them by herself. She liked the tugging pressure they made as they hung from her veins. She liked to feel them growing from cool to warm as they gorged themselves on her blood. When they were full she would caress them and hold them in her hand. She wanted Dr Fowler to let her keep them at home but he refused, and cautioned Asa that his daughter had 'an unusual fascination' with blood.

On Saturday morning, July 16, dark clouds hung over the farm when she awoke. They were low and motionless, filled with rain almost to bursting, yet holding back. Holding off from lowering the heat, holding off from washing away the tension. It was all she could do to get out of bed. The pressure in her head was the worst she had ever experienced. It seemed to start in the center of her forehead and move out in waves that lapped against her temples. Her father had gone either to his office or the post office and her mother was shopping with Nervie and Loozie. The three of them could carry the parcels home without any trouble. Ann needed their help; her unborn baby was giving her occasional dull spasms of pain. They left before Mary was out of bed, hoping to get their shopping done and get back to the house before the rain began.

Her four brothers had finished their breakfast when Mary came into the kitchen. Loozie had left a pot of oatmeal on the stove with enough in it for Mary's serving. Joe and Fen had gone to spend the morning with a friend. Frank and Charles were outside, shooting at each other and hiding, and galloping and dying and charging as they played Union and Rebel. Because Charlie was the youngest, he was always the Rebel soldier no matter how much he protested.

Mary sat down at the kitchen table and stared at the small white flowers on the oilcloth. The boys' dirty dishes, their spilled sugar and their toast crumbs were scattered across the design. She added some sugar, then some cream from the icebox to her oatmeal, stirred it listlessly, not hungry but feeling she should eat something. Dr Fowler had told her to eat, even when her stomach told her differently.

The room was dim, with the sunlight hidden behind the enormous watery clouds. Maybe if she lit the lantern some of the gloom around her and inside her could be chased away. The kerosine lamp hung from the ceiling, on a long chain, directly over the table. She tugged on the counterbalance chain and the lamp came down to her level. Now she needed a match. Loozie kept a box of them on the stove shelf. As she reached for the matches something sparkled and caught her eye. It was a butcher knife. A brand-new butcher knife that had replaced the one she used to kill Tessie. Loozie had been given strict orders to lock up all the knives. In her haste to get to the market she must have forgotten to lock up this one.

Mary smiled and picked up the knife. It felt good in her hand. She turned the knife over and over, running her finger slowly down the cutting edge, being careful not to cut herself, yet enjoying the sensation.

She examined the knife, pleased with its newness, pleased that she had discovered it, pleased that she was all alone in the house.

Her body trembled and she thought she was going to fall. Reaching out, she steadied herself against the back of a kitchen chair. She looked down at the chair, its rush woven seat taut in perfectly aligned valleys and ridges. She stared at its pattern, at its man-made perfection, at its smugness at being whole and united. Its completeness annoyed her. The flawless woven pattern made fun of her. It was in order. She was confused. It was serving a purpose. She was worthless. It had a reason. She had none. She had none and the chair had to go. It couldn't sit there and make a fool of her. With one loud cry and a sharp thrust, she drove the knife into the seat. She laughed and plunged the knife again and again into the seat until it was no more than a mass of loose ends hanging limply from the wooden rim. Then she went from chair to chair slashing, tearing and laughing as their mocking perfection was destroyed.

She stepped back to admire her work. The cluttered table still stood there, solid and observing and whole. The knife tore into the oilcloth, shredding it and separating the flowers in the design. The knife hit the dirty porridge bowls, breaking some, knocking others onto the floor. The cream pitcher sloshed its contents across the ravaged surface of the table.

Then she ran out the door, slamming it with satisfaction at a job well done. Frank and Charlie, loudly killing one another on the front lawn, didn't hear her laughter as she ran down the back steps and out into the field behind the house. As she ran she waved the knife at the low hanging clouds, trying to slash them as she had slashed the chair seats.

As she ran she swiped at the tops of tomatoes, slashed at beans tied to poles and delighted in the sweet sticky smell on the knife blade when she cut through a young stalk of corn.

The woods began at the edge of the clearing. She slowed down to a fast walk now, brushing against the rough trunks of the trees and lifting her feet so as not to trip over the exposed roots. Birds, resting uneasily in the branches because of the impending storm, rose in startled flight as she passed under them.

She fell and rolled down an incline into the midst of a large clump of elderberry bushes. Still laughing she crawled into the bushes, going deeper and deeper until their tall stems and thick green leaves hid her from the world. She held the knife in front of her. She could barely see it in the semidarkness but she could feel it. She could feel its edge and remember its avenging point. It could do in one second what her adored leeches took several minutes to do. It would release her pent-up blood. It would take away the lump of pain in her head.

It was a simple and quick action. Raise the knife, position its point in the center of the left arm right where those red and blue veins were, and then push. Push in and then pull. Pull down and feel the pressure followed by the pleasure of the skin parting and the muscles being severed. Feel the warm air inside her arm, warm almost down to her wrist. Feel the blood run out hot and thick across her skin. Feel the blood falling onto her closed eyelids as she lifted her arm above her face. Taste the warm blood as it trickled down her cheeks and into her open mouth. Drink the blood directly from her veins as she sucked and licked the wound. The lump of pain on her head was gone. The delight in the warm fresh blood had chased away every other sensation. The pressure was leaving. Drowsiness was setting in. She could hear the first large drops of rain falling on the elderberry leaves, trying to enter her secret place and soak the ground that was slowly being soaked with blood.

The search started as soon as the women returned and discovered the havoc in the kitchen. The three searched every room and closet of the house, calling Mary's name. Ann sent Loozie to fetch Asa, and she stopped everyone she met on the five-block stretch to ask if they had seen Mary. Loozie held her skirts high as she ran and she prayed as she cried and blamed herself for not locking up that knife. There was no doubt about the knife. The damage in the kitchen. The missing girl. The missing knife. It was all her fault, she told herself, she had let harm come to that girl because of her own stupidity. If anything happened to the child she would die.

She found Asa in the post office and told him what had happened. She kept apologizing as Asa shouted to his staff of three to close the front door and round up others for the search.

The first few large drops turned into a million smaller ones as the clouds broke wide open over the town. The warm dust of Walnut Street turned quickly into mud. The postal workers ran from store to store along the street telling the proprietors and their customers what had happened and what was expected of them. In many shops, clerks were dismissed, doors were closed and buggies were harnessed to search for the missing girl. The sawmill stopped cutting, the feed store stopped sacking, the farmers in the open market stopped selling. The important thing was to find Mary.

Five hours after she had crawled into the elderberry bushes, Mary was found. Her dress was soaked in blood. Her hair and face were coated with it, some congealed, some still wet and sticky where it had mixed with the rain. Her heart was beating faintly and blood still oozed from the gaping wound in her arm. One of the men who found her took out a handkerchief and tied it tightly above the slash. Another picked her up in his arms and carried her out of the woods toward home.

In an instant she was wide awake. Her eyes looked into the face of her rescuer and she wrenched her body from his grasp and fell onto the ground. She landed on her knees and like a dog on all fours she screamed at him: 'Don't you touch me! Don't you touch me! I'll kill you if you do!' Her voice, high pitched and cracking, stung the five men in the group.

'You all will be killed,' she snarled at them. 'I'll kill you all!' Her hands dug into the plowed earth and she started pelting them with dirt and rocks. 'I'll kill you all! Don't you dare touch me!'

The biggest of the group, a muscular farmer named Simpson, lunged at her, almost falling on her as he grabbed her around the waist. Mary struck out at him, hitting him squarely on the side of his face, knocking him down. 'I told you not to touch me, you bastard!' she screamed.

The others looked at each other and began to close in on her. It was an instinctive move on their part, as if they had surrounded a wild animal and were going to capture it with their bare hands.

'Keep back!' the high voice screamed. 'Keep back or I'll kill you!' Mary's eyes went from face to face; she was on her feet now, turning slowly toward each man as he advanced on her. 'I'll cut your goddamned hearts out if you touch me, you bastards!' she shouted. 'You'll see. I'm warning you!'

The men were murmuring, 'Now Mary. Now Mary,' as Simpson reached out from his position on the ground and grabbed her ankles.

Mary doubled over, like a marionette whose string has been cut, and began to bite his hands. He yelled and pulled away, swearing at her.

'I warned you,' she called. 'I warned you.'

The others backed off slowly, still circling her. 'Come on back to the house now, Mary,' one of them said in a low voice. 'Come on. Just relax now and let's go home.'

'Shit on you!' she spat. 'Don't touch me!'

'Mary ... let's go, Mary. Your Pa is up at the house ...' he coaxed.

'I said shit on you!' she screamed and jumped about four feet across the row of tomato plants, landing on the man and bringing him down with her. Her hands clawed his face, drawing blood. 'I told you to leave me alone!'

The others fell on her, pushing her to one side to free their fallen friend. Two men grabbed her arms and held them behind her back. She cursed and struggled and kicked but two more managed to grab each of her legs. They held her upright, off the ground, and started to carry her toward the house, keeping clear of her teeth as if they were carrying a dangerous animal. They sloshed through the rain, soaked to their skins. Mary's full-length dress, stained with blood and mud and water, dragged along the ground.

The entire family ran into the fields to meet the five men. When Ann saw Mary's condition she stopped short and gasped. Asa tried to put his hand on Mary to let her know he was there.

They carried her past the spot where Ann was standing. 'Oh my God, Mary,' she moaned, reaching out one ineffectual hand toward her daughter.

Mary glared at her. 'Fuck you, old woman! Fuck you!'

Ann crumpled into Nervie's arms but Asa, dumbfounded by what he was seeing and not being able to believe what he had just heard, grabbed his daughter by her matted hair and slapped her across the face.

The men stopped, looking first at him, then back at Mary. The girl, with blood running from the corners of her mouth, looked at Asa and said quietly, 'Oh Pa,' and fell unconscious.

Dr Fowler came quickly with his leeches. Asa called Dr Secrest. Dr Pittwood came on his own accord. The news raced through Watseka faster than a summer storm.

'Did you hear that the Roff girl tried to kill herself?'

'They said she took a knife and cut her arm.'

'She completely ruined the kitchen, I heard.'

'Well, I heard the sofa and chairs in the parlor was covered with blood!'

'I can't repeat the things she said to her mother!'

'I don't know how dear Ann can put up with that child.'

'It took five grown men to hold her down, and she a little body of not even a hundred pounds.'

'She lost almost all her blood and still had the strength of ten men! I can't understand it.'

'If you ask me that girl is dangerous.'

'Well, if she can grab a knife anytime she pleases, a soul isn't safe walking down the street!'

'I'm not going to let my children go over there anymore!'

'She must be plumb crazy, that girl!'

'Did you see the bruise on the side of Ed Simpson's face? Why, that girl has the strength of a maniac.'

'Asa is such a fine man. What a shame this is happening to him.'

'It sounds to me like the Devil possessed her.'

'Why did they bring her back from Peoria?'

'Crazy people running loose in the streets! I don't care who the Roffs are, that girl of theirs ought to be locked up.'

'My Cindy read in the paper about a case just like Mary's.

56

The girl died a horrible death, and when she did snakes crawled out of her eyes.'

'That girl ought to be locked up.'

'Isn't there something we can do? A petition or something?'

'That girl ought to be locked up.'

Mary was unconscious for five days. Again she barely breathed, couldn't eat and nobody could force a drop of water down her throat. Ann spent a great deal of time sitting beside her bed, crying and praying and asking a benevolent Jesus Christ to save her little girl. Asa didn't go to the post office or his law office those five days. He had partners and assistants who would handle things. He didn't want to leave the house, didn't want to see anyone outside his immediate family. His hand still stung where he had slapped his daughter. Ann said it was his imagination, but he could feel it. Feel the tender flesh flatten and stretch in pain as he hit her. There was a large bruise on Mary's face where his hand had landed. There was a large bandage in the crook of her arm where Doc Pittwood had put in stitches and some healing salve. Mary didn't feel the needle as he sewed the gaping wound. Everyone, the doctors included, were astonished at the strength she had shown even though she had lost all that blood. Five hours of bleeding and yet five men could barely control her. Asa supposed he would have to send her back to Peoria. Or worse. Maybe he would have to put her in the insane asylum in Springfield. If she continued like this he couldn't keep her at home. The next time she might hurt one of the children or maybe Loozie or even Ann. God, what would he do if anything happened to Ann? How could he manage without her?

Mary recovered after five days and, as usual, didn't remember anything that had happened to her. Ann didn't want to tell her but Asa thought she should know what she had done. He told her about the mess in the kitchen, finding her in the bushes with an arm wound, and her fight with the five men. He also told her he had struck her. He didn't tell her why. He couldn't bring himself to repeat the words she had used, had spat, at her mother. He never used those words even with the men down at the railroad, so he certainly couldn't say them to his eighteen-year-old daughter.

Dr Fowler came with his leeches every day until mid-August, draining the girl's blood and weakening her. Dr Secrest and Pittwood both told Asa there was nothing they could do for Mary. They didn't have any pills or potions that would keep her from repeating what she had done. They hinted that perhaps no doctor of the body could help her. They suggested Mary stay in bed and that an eye be kept on her at all times. They were opposed to Fowler's leeches but if they calmed the girl down perhaps they were of some use.

Then Ann lost her baby. She awoke one morning with terrible pains in her swollen stomach. Loozie and Minerva ran for the doctors while Asa held her hand. When Dr Pittwood arrived the sheets and mattress were already soaked with blood. Asa was told to leave the room. Loozie was told to stay and help. Three hours later, while Ann screamed and Asa drank whiskey in the parlor, Loozie came out of the bedroom carrying something wrapped in a bloody blanket. While Asa sat on the edge of the bed, watching his wife's white and immobile face, the African woman buried the little body in the blanket deep in the woods. She never told anyone where it had been buried and nobody asked. If they had been curious they would have discovered a patch of loose earth, covered with leaves and handfuls of grass and broken twigs and blobs of melted candle wax.

No one in the family doubted that if Mary had not had that terrible fit, the baby would have been born normally and at the right time.

The Reverend Dille, John Barr Dille, became minister of the Watseka Methodist Church about that time. He liked the town, and the people of the town seemed to like him. He had met the Roffs once or twice before Mary had her fit but now that she was well enough to receive visitors he decided to pay a call. After all Mary and her family were members of his church, and Mr Roff was one of the richest and most important men in town. For the sake of his church, he had to pay his respects. And for another reason as well. He had been doing some reading, material his brother sent him from New York, about Spiritualism. Some of the things he read seemed to fit some of the things he heard about the Roff girl's case. Losing control. Speaking in a strange voice. Great strength. Not recalling anything afterward.

Reverend Dille waited in the parlor while Ann and Loozie combed Mary's hair and helped her into a dress – with long sleeves to hide her bandages – so she would be presentable.

The Reverend was impressed with the Roff home. Aside from its being the largest home in Watseka and one of the few solid brick homes anywhere in the area, it was well furnished and clean. Most houses that held four small boys were jumbles of clothes, muddy footprints and dog hair but there was none of that here. He supposed it was because the African woman was such an industrious Christian. She was a fine example of what could be done when The Word was revealed to the heathen. Perhaps he would use her as an example in his appeal for missionary funds. He heard footsteps descending the stairs and turned to wait for Mary and her mother as they came through the wide doors into the back parlor.

He was surprised at how thin Mary was and how the circles under her eyes added to her age. She was wearing her hair loosely around her shoulders, not parted in the middle and pulled back the way he recalled seeing it. She wore a filmy white lace cap, held in place by several pins. Her dress was deep blue, while around the collar, the floor-length hem and the long sleeve cuffs there was a thin line of white piping. She smiled, timidly. Aside from the family and the doctors, he was her first visitor. She extended her hand and he held it for a second, feeling the small bones under the pale white skin. 'I'm so happy to see you are able to be up and around again, Miss Roff,' he said. 'My wife extends you her wishes for a rapid recovery, as do I.'

Mary thanked him and Ann offered him a seat on the red velvet sofa. Mary sat in the matching parlor chair next to the sofa while Ann took a wooden rocker several discreet feet away.

The Reverend chatted about the weather and how fortunate they were that August was cooler than July had been and how the covered-dish dinner last week had been a success despite the fact that Mrs Roff had been indisposed and unable to attend. (Ann's miscarriage was never referred to, not even by her minister.) He mentioned a stained-glass window he had seen in Springfield that he wished the church could afford to install and the fact that everyone in the choir missed Mary and sincerely hoped she'd soon be well enough to rejoin them. Mary smiled and said she also looked forward to it. He expressed his concern for her health and how shocked he and Mrs Dille had been when they received word of the accident. Mary glanced quickly at her mother at the word 'accident', but the Reverend Dille pretended not to notice. Finally he reached the subject he had come to discuss in the first place.

'Mary, as your pastor I have an obligation to try and help you as much as I can and as much as the Lord wishes you to be helped. What you experienced out there with the knife and afterward with your rescuers, others have experienced before you.' He paused to let his words sink in.

'Others?' Ann asked. 'What others? Here in Watseka?' He could hear the relief in her voice.

'No, not in Watseka, but in other places around the country. Indeed, in other places around the world. It seems that whatever it was that took ahold of Mary has taken ahold of others.' Ann pulled back, watching him suspiciously. 'These others went through the same type of physical and mental anguish and in almost every case they, like Mary, could not recall what had taken place.' He looked at Mary and then at her mother. 'Do you understand what I am saying?'

'I think so,' Mary said softly.

'I am saying that there seems to be an increasing amount of evidence that something outside ourselves can come in and take ourselves over. To possess us, if you will.'

Since this was the first conversation she had ever had with this new minister Ann advanced cautiously. 'My husband and I have heard something of this, Reverend Dille, from Mr Roff's business partner Mr Matzenbaugh.'

The minister nodded his head. 'Josiah Matzenbaugh, yes. I have met him on occasion, but we have never discussed this subject.' He smiled and adjusted the points on his waistcoat. 'This is not a subject that most ministers *do* discuss.'

'Frankly, Reverend Dille,' said Ann, 'I am surprised that you, a member of the clergy, would be interested in these... these... spirits. If that is what they really are.'

'On the contrary, Mrs Roff, as a member of the clergy I should be most interested in spirits and everything they are capable of doing. After all I preach – and I'm sure you believe in the Holy Trinity – the Father and the Son and the Holy... *Ghost?*'

Ann raised her hand to her mouth and Mary opened her eyes wide. 'I never thought of it that way,' she said. 'The Holy Ghost...'

The Reverend smiled, happy that he was reaching them. 'Indeed, the Bible is full of references to ghosts, spirits, possessions, all sorts of things that we don't believe today.'

'But we believe in the words of the Bible, Reverend Dille,' said Ann. 'Our family often reads the Bible together.'

'I'm not saying you don't believe in the words of the Good Book, Mrs Roff, please don't misunderstand me. What I *am* saying is that there is biblical reference for what might have happened to Mary. I say *might*, of course, because I don't fully understand what the entire circumstances were.'

'I thought everyone in town knew,' Mary said bitterly.

'Everyone in town knows the external appearances of your incident,' he said, smiling at her, 'but few can even guess at the internal reasons for what happened.'

Ann was still not sure of her footing with this man. 'Then it is your contention, Reverend Dille, that Mary was possessed by... by the Devil?'

He turned quickly to her and shook the index finger of his right hand. 'Oh no,' he said still shaking the finger, 'I never said I thought it was the Devil. On the contrary my dear Mrs Roff, I don't believe it has anything to do with the Devil. Just the opposite. No, not the Devil.'

'Then you think it was an angel?' Mary asked, her voice rising. 'Do you think an *angel* would have done the things I did or said the things I said?'

His finger wagged in her direction now. 'Not an angel. A *spirit*. The spirit of someone who has gone before us and yet hasn't gone far enough.'

'But,' Ann put in, 'we all go to either heaven or hell when

we die. How could a spirit not have gone far enough, as you call it?'

'Granted that we all go to either heaven or hell. It seems, however, that some spirits don't go directly to heaven or hell. It seems that some stay here on earth after they die.'

Ann looked at him coldly. 'I don't recall seeing that in the Bible.'

'Oh yes, it's in the Bible. I looked it up.' He hurried on before they could ask him to quote chapter and verse. 'It appears that some spirits don't know they are dead and stay here on earth. I have heard tell of the ghosts of our brave boys killed at Gettysburg being seen by visitors to the site. It is said that they are looking for their units and can't understand what has happened to them.' He shook his head. 'Most sad. Indeed.'

Mary shook her head. 'Indeed.'

'But why does God in all His mercy permit this, Reverend Dille?' Ann asked.

He shrugged his shoulders. 'Who knows why the Almighty does what he does and who are we to question His judgements?' Mary and Ann lowered their eyes. God was not to be questioned, of course. 'There are many things on earth that man cannot explain.'

'Possibly man should not know about them,' Ann added.

'Possibly. But when man *does* know about them he must examine them and try to discover how they influence his life and thought.'

'How long, Reverend Dille,' Ann began, 'and I'll admit that here in Watseka we are sometimes unaware of progress being made in other places, but how long has the Methodist Church believed in this Spiritualism?'

'Mrs Roff, while the Methodist *Church* does not believe in Spiritualism, that does not mean that I, as an individual, do not believe in spirits. There is a difference between spirits and Spiritualism. One is a religion. The other is our immortal soul. And I believe in our immortal soul. Indeed I do.'

Mary had been listening and evaluating. 'Reverend Dille, why would a spirit want to do those things to me? Why *me*?'

'I cannot answer that, my dear. I don't know just as I

don't know why a spirit stays on the earth when it could just as well be in heaven.'

'Maybe the ones who are here don't want to go to hell,' she suggested.

'Possibly, but quite often in some seances held in the East and in England spirits of people who were quite honest and quite honorable have reappeared and spoken to entire groups of people. And,' he added, hoping to convince them, 'been *recognized* by their friends and loved ones!'

'Recognized?' Ann said rather loudly. 'You mean people saw their faces and recognized them from their *faces?*'

He sat back comfortably on the sofa now. 'Exactly. Saw their faces, heard their voices and received answers to questions that no one but the deceased spirit could have known. Really, it has all been most remarkable.'

'Have you ever seen a ghost?' asked Mary eagerly.

'No. Not personally, nor have I attended any of the seance meetings. I've not had the opportunity as yet. I have read a great deal on the matter and have given it much thought. I try,' he said brushing at a bit of lint on his trouser leg, 'to be well read and as scientific as I can be. As a minister I must know what is happening everywhere.'

The two women nodded in agreement. Mary had another question. 'If this is a spirit that enters my body then how do I get rid of him? Is there anything I can do to make him go away?'

He shook his head. 'I don't think so,' he said. 'It seems that they come and go as they please. It is true that at a seance they are called into the room but no amount of pleading will make them go away before they choose to go. Or to stay either, for that matter.'

'Why then,' asked Ann warming up to the man and the subject, 'does this spirit affect Mary's *physical* body? Like making her unconscious for days at a time or giving her such strength that five men are unable to contain her?'

He shook his head again. 'I don't know. I wish I did, but I am a healer of the soul and not a healer of the body. Those are questions that only a medical doctor can answer.'

'Are these ghosts . . .' Mary began, 'these spirits that take control of me, are they always around me or do they come and go?'

'Come and go from where?' her mother asked.

'I don't know. Just come and go from wherever they live.'

'They don't *live* anywhere, Mary,' said her mother. 'They're dead.'

'I know that. That's not what I was asking. I was asking if they are always here. You know, in the air and invisible.'

'I suppose they are,' said the Reverend. 'If they don't go anywhere then they must stay right here. There may even be some of them in the room with us right now.' At this Ann and Mary looked quickly around them. 'I don't mean to startle you,' he said, 'but dozens of them may be listening and watching right now.'

'Watching?' Mary's voice rose. 'Do you mean that even when I go to the – ' she stopped short. It was not polite to mention the word 'bathroom' in public, especially to the minister ' – when I am getting dressed?' He nodded. 'Oh, how embarrassing!'

'I don't think we can do anything that would embarrass them,' he laughed.

'Not to them. To me!' At this Ann began to laugh with the minister and Mary, seeing the humor of it, laughed with them. Ann was glad. It had been the first time her daughter had laughed since the accident.

'There is another interesting phenomenon that often accompanies these spirit possessions,' the Reverend said. 'Often the person who experiences these things takes on abilities that are not common. Like knowing things in advance or being able to read things through a sealed envelope.'

'Through a sealed envelope?' Mary doubted that.

'Yes. It is said that these people acquire special abilities that cannot be explained by natural causes, like knowing when someone is about to die or seeing things as they happen a great distance away.'

'With a telescope?' Ann said.

'No, with their minds. Some people are actually able to tell what is happening at a distance where their eyes cannot see.'

'That would be fun!' Mary laughed. 'That way I could see what the boys were doing and catch them at it!'

'Very practical,' laughed Ann.

'Do you want to try it?' Reverend Dille asked Mary.

'Me? Now?' He nodded.

'Why not?'

'Well, I don't think I could . . .'

'You never know until you try.'

'But I'm sure I . . . it all sounds so silly!' She laughed, then became serious. 'Do you really think I could do it? See what was happening somewhere else? Like in another room?'

'Would you like to try?'

She looked at her mother and Ann nodded her head. 'Yes,' said Mary. 'I'll try it with you. How does it work?'

'You go into another room and I'll do something in this room. Then when I call you back you tell me what you think I was doing.' Reverend Dille was already off the sofa and pacing the floor. He was about to begin his scientific investigation at last. 'Go upstairs or wherever you choose and I'll do something here in the parlor. You try to *see* me – it's important that you try to actually see me. Don't *think* of anything at all. Just pay attention, close your eyes and *listen* to whatever images come into your mind.'

'Like a photograph?'

'Yes. Exactly. Pretend that your mind is taking a photographic image of me. Then when I call you, come back into the room and tell me what developed on the camera plate.'

Mary got up and walked quickly from the room. 'I'll go into the kitchen,' she said. The excitement had added a lilt to her walk and Ann smiled at the minister in thanks.

Reverend Dille closed the double parlor doors. He put his finger up against his lips as a sign that Ann was to make no noise. He looked around the room for a moment and then walked toward a round lace-topped table near the casement windows. There was a porcelain figurine of George Washington astride a horse on the table. The general held his hat in his hand and one of the horse's hooves was raised. Part of the general's uniform had been painted but most of the figurine was left in natural white. He smiled at Ann, as she watched him with both amusement and curiosity, as he took the figurine and carried it across the room and placed it on the fireplace mantel. Then he picked it up again, walked with it extended in his hands back to the table and set it down. He picked it up again, walked across to the fireplace, then returned it to the table. He did this several times, staring at the figurine all the while. Then he opened the sliding doors, shouted to Mary that she could come back and hurried to his seat on the sofa.

She entered the room, a frown on her face. 'What's the matter?' asked Ann.

'It didn't work.'

'What didn't work?' the Reverend wanted to know.

'The experiment. The photograph I got was so silly.'

'Silly?' he asked. 'In what way?'

'It couldn't have been right. I didn't have an impression of anything in this room.'

'Did you see me?' he asked hoping for a positive answer.

'No. I didn't see anybody. I didn't even see this room.' She was obviously disappointed.

Ann asked, 'What did you see, dear?'

'Reverend Dille asked me to see him doing something and all I could imagine was a white horse running back and forth across a field! Every time I tried to push that horse out of my mind, it would come back again! We don't own a white horse.'

The Reverend jumped up off the sofa. 'Mary, do you know what you've done? You made the experiment work! You did it!'

For several weeks after that the Reverend and Mary conducted experiments: he dreaming up foolproof tests and she passing them easily. Once he had her stay at home while he walked to a certain brick wall in town and chalked a large white number on it. Mary was told to see and report the number. She picked up '88' correctly. At other times he would hand her a book, usually one from his own library that the girl could not have examined in advance, and ask her to tell what the first word was on a certain page. She almost always came up with the correct word. He gave her sealed envelopes and she told him what was in them. He once found a dead bird and, after wrapping it in several layers of cloth, put it into a large pasteboard box and covered it with heavy paper and sealing wax. When Mary held the box she burst into tears, asking him why he had not buried the 'dead thing' inside it.

While the Reverend Dille didn't want Mary to become

possessed again, he was hoping that if it *did* happen he would be there to see it. He felt he had gained Mary's confidence and that she would listen to him so that he could rid her of whatever it was that held her. He had been reading voraciously on this subject ever since that first experiment in the parlor. His brother sent him books from the East and he subscribed to such magazines as *The Spiritual Telegraph* from New York, *The Banner of Light* from Boston and the *Spiritual Messenger* from Springfield, Massachusetts. While the bulk of these publications dealt with the Spiritualist religious movement, there were many articles and letters from readers throughout the country reporting on strange occurrences, the results of seances, and matters that seemed to defy explanation. He kept these magazines and newspapers locked in a trunk in his bedroom, away from his congregation and his family. There were people in Watseka who thought he was doing the Devil's work, even though he told those who asked that he was conducting scientific experiments that could only bolster the Methodist faith if proven.

One of the minister's most vocal opponents was Lavinia Durst. Lavinia lived in a large wooden home on Hickory Street, about three blocks from the Roff home. Lavinia's husband, Harold, had been in the shipping business. He dispatched and received items coming into and out of Watseka. One day when he could no longer stand Lavinia's scratchy voice and vicious tongue, he left town, never to return. Lavinia didn't care. The house was in her name and her children (two boys and one girl) had married and moved away. She received monthly checks from an estate in the East so she didn't have to earn a living. Instead, she spent her time minding other people's business. She was good at it because she was so self-righteous. No one had ever heard her say that she had been wrong about anything. No one had ever heard her say 'I'm sorry' or 'excuse me'.

Now Lavinia had a new matter to handle in her own meticulous way: Mary Roff.

It seems that the Roff girl had gotten worse after that last attack instead of better, in spite of what that old fool Doc Fowler said. Everyone could see that the girl was not her old self at all. She was thinner and had dark circles under her eyes. If you ever saw her eyes, that is. It was shameless the way she would meet a body on the street and not look at them directly. Wouldn't hardly say 'good morning' or 'good evening'.

The girl was strange. Of course, that was not news. She had been strange for a long time, even before Asa spent all that money on that clinic in Peoria. It didn't do her a bit of good. Just a lot of nonsense and a way to legally steal from Asa's pocket. He had a lot of it in his pocket, that's for sure. More than most people in these parts had. More than Lavinia had, more than she would ever hope to have. Now, probably because Asa was so rich and so important in town, he thought that he owned the place. Well, he didn't. Lavinia paid her taxes and went to church regularly and was respected just the way he was. She would not do what he was doing if she had a daughter in Mary's condition. She would have had her committed. She would have sent her to the asylum in Springfield. That was the place for crazy people, not on the public streets menacing innocent citizens.

And now what were these mysterious goings-on with the Methodist minister? Lavinia hadn't liked him from the first. He wouldn't have been tolerated more than one Sunday if he had been preaching at her Baptist Church! People came to church to hear about Jesus and to be saved before their souls were cast into hell. They didn't come to listen to nonsense about spiritual guidance and tolerance and some kind of scientific poking around. If Reverend Dille wanted to be a scientist then let him become one, but let him vacate the pulpit to someone who was more interested in God than in sealed envelopes.

Sarah Thayer agreed with Lavinia. She was a Methodist and was shocked by the Reverend Dille's comportment. He was making his church and himself a laughingstock in town. It was reported in the paper last week that an experiment had been held at the Roff home and Mary had told the mayor and the newspaper editor what was in envelopes they had in their pockets! It was disgraceful that these upstanding citizens should openly attend such experiments. They were experiments with the Devil, that's what they were. A body wasn't safe. That child could just as soon look in *anyone's* house and snoop into *anyone's* business if she wanted to and nobody would be the wiser. And you never knew when she was going to grab a knife and come at you. She could switch from girl to devil faster than a horse could trot. She was dangerous, that's for sure. Why, it took five strong men to grab hold of her and bring her back home that time. Something had to be done. Sarah agreed wholeheartedly with Lavinia. If Asa and Ann didn't do it themselves, then others more responsible would have to see that it was done.

Mayor Conrad Secrest was intrigued by Mary's supposed abilities. He had read a little about this sort of thing and he had always suspected that maybe there was something else out there. When his mother-in-law had died he was in Chicago studying medicine, and as he turned the corner he saw the woman's reflection in a haberdasher's window glass. It had made him stop short and look again. It was definitely his mother-in-law and she was looking back at him. Then she smiled and vanished. It was a good thing there was a saloon nearby, for he needed strong whiskey to settle his nerves. When he returned to Watseka the next day his wife told him the news. Her mother had passed away just a few minutes before he had seen her image on the window glass. His wife cautioned him not to mention it to anyone and he never had, but now Mary and some of the things she could do seemed to have a relation to that image. Exactly what, he couldn't be sure. But there was something there and it was happening in his town. As mayor he deemed it his duty to investigate *anything* suspicious that took place in Watseka.

A meeting of several selected guests had been scheduled at the Roff home that night. Asa had personally invited them at the request of Mary and the minister. Asa wasn't too happy with these public experiments and he was the first to admit he couldn't explain what Mary was doing, but she seemed to enjoy them. She appeared to be getting stronger. Both he and Ann noted the color returning to her cheeks and the sparkle in her eyes growing brighter. She ate better too, and was beginning to put back some of the weight she lost after the accident. Asa still referred to it as the 'accident'. He knew his Mary too well. She had not done those things deliberately. It must have been an accident. His daughter had had several 'accidents' and he prayed that she would not have another. It had been a full six months since the last 'accident'.

Reverend Dille thought that the experiments were acting as a release for the tensions that build up inside the child. He believed Mary might have more energy than most girls her age and this energy had to be released. If it wasn't released she exploded. Her last 'accident' had been such an explosion. Mary was like a steam kettle. If the spout was sealed off, the kettle would burst. That's why Asa had agreed to these sessions. He had heard the rumors in town. He knew what Lavinia Durst and Sarah Thayer were saying, but he didn't care. Those two busybodies were harmless and if these sessions, supervised by the minister, were helping Mary, then he would hold as many as necessary.

The guests arrived about 6 p.m. that cold evening in January of 1865. Loozie had prepared dinner: pumpkin soup, baked ham with mashed potatoes and candied yams and stringbeans baked in a mushroom and cheese sauce. There were apple pie and peach pie for dessert and freshly ground coffee.

The dinner was a success. Mary didn't eat a great deal but her appetite was returning slowly. Nervie was the only other Roff child at the table; the boys ate in the kitchen with Loozie. The Reverend Dille ate well and Mr Hogle was there (he owned the biggest dry goods store in town, selling everything from undersleeves to bed sheeting). Mr A. G. Smith was there (he was the editor of the *Iroquois County Republican*), Mr Lile Marsh also (he owned the hardware store in town) and the mayor and his wife were there. Mrs Secrest was the only one of the wives who attended. The others had been invited but for one reason or another declined. Ann knew that Mrs Marsh had the flu and that Mrs Smith had visitors from Ohio. The Reverend Dille's wife never accompanied him when he went to the Roffs. She didn't believe in anything he was doing and warned him about tampering with things he knew nothing about. At times he wished it was not a mortal sin for a man of God to divorce his wife. Mrs Hogle claimed she had sciatica and could hardly walk. The real reason she stayed home was that she had no intention of being part of the Devil's handiwork.

The guests left the comfortable dining-room and walked into the back parlor. The Reverend Dille had asked that the furniture be arranged against the wall and a circle of straight-backed chairs be placed in the center of the room. He was going to try something different that night. Something that would go beyond sealed envelopes and words on the pages of a book. He had discussed it with Mary and after he had assured her that nothing would happen, she had agreed. He would be at her side at all times. She had nothing to worry about and it was an important step in their experimentation.

The Reverend Dille showed the guests where to sit. 'We must place the women and the men as evenly as possible for the best results,' he said. 'Mary will sit here. If this were a clockface, then this chair would be at twelve o'clock. Mr Smith, you will please sit at Mary's left and I'll sit at her right. Nervie, you sit beside me, and the mayor will sit next to you. Mrs Roff will please take the seat next to the mayor and Mr Roff, sir, the seat directly opposite Mary. The six o'clock seat, if you prefer. Mr Hogle please sit at five o'clock and Mrs Secrest at four o'clock and Mr Marsh, please, directly across from the mayor at three o'clock.'

Loozie was standing in the doorway to the dining-room, a small oil lamp in her hand gave off the only illumination. She had done as the minister asked: closed all the windows and pulled the drapes and blown out all the lights but one. 'Will you place that light on the table behind us?' the minister asked. 'Thank you. Now you may leave the room.'

Loozie hesitated. She wanted to stay. Mary had told her it would be all right if the minister said so. 'Could I just watch from over here?' she asked.

The Reverend Dille shook his head. 'There must not be any disturbances outside the circle. I'm afraid I'll have to refuse you.'

'But Mary said – ' Then she remembered her position in the household. 'Yes, sir.' She went out and closed the door behind her.

'I was hoping Loozie could stay,' Mary said timidly.

'That would be out of the question, dear,' Asa replied.

'If we were only family,' Ann added, 'but, my dear, we have guests.'

Mary lowered her eyes. 'I understand . . . but it would have been nice to have Loozie here.'

'Maybe next time,' the minister said. 'She can sit in on it next time.' He smiled at Mary and then at everyone in the circle. He voiced his thoughts: 'I am searching for religious *truths*,' he said, 'trying through Miss Roff to understand the nature of the spirit. Attempting to make contact with a departed soul in order for that soul to describe where he is and what heaven looks like. I believe that once we understand what happens to our souls when they leave our bodies we will have a better understanding of not only where we will go after death but a better understanding of why we are here in life.'

'Aren't these matters better left alone?' asked Mr Marsh.

'That's the problem, sir. They have been left alone for far too long and they have created fear and confusion among the living. Even among the most faithful of the church there is fear of dying. I have ministered to many devout Christians on their deathbeds who have been terrified to leave this mortal shell and enter into the world of spirit. I believe, sir, that it is time for progressive men to examine what is on the other side of this vale of tears and to traverse it and permit light and understanding to come to us.'

There was a general murmuring of agreement, and nodding of heads. 'My own sister,' said Mrs Secrest, 'went to church every Sunday and read the Bible each evening. Yet when she died, God rest her soul, she cried and clung to life. That pitiful scene has been stamped on my mind forever.'

The minister was delighted. 'Exactly what I am trying to dispel. That fear of the unknown. That fear of God rather than the unquestioning love of God that we should all have.'

'Maybe there are some things that God does not wish us to know,' put in Mr Hogle. 'Then where are your investigations?'

'If God does not wish us to know certain things, then we shall not know them! It's quite simple. Should He not wish my experiments to succeed, He would make them fail. I bow to the will of God.' Again, general agreement. 'But He has *not* made my experiments fail. Just the opposite. Almost every experiment with Miss Roff has been completed with great satisfaction!' He looked at each face in the dimly lit circle. 'Does that not indicate to you what God wills in this case?' Murmurings of 'yes' and 'of course'.

The Reverend reached under his chair and pulled out an odd-shaped wooden box. 'I have here a metronome. An ordinary metronome that we who play the piano are quite familiar with. I am going to release the spring and set the arm into motion. As it counts time Miss Roff will begin to relax.' He released the metal arm and it swung and created an audible 'tick'. Then it swung in the opposite direction and 'tick' again. Back it went. 'Tick.' Forward. 'Tick.' Back. 'Tick.' 'Tick.' 'Tick.' 'Tick.'

Ann coughed and the mayor's wife looked at her husband across the circle and he smiled at her. 'Before we begin, there are several rules that must be observed,' said the Reverend Dille. 'First is silence. Until I give you permission there must be no talking of any kind. Do you all agree?' They all did. 'Secondly, when the time comes that you are permitted to ask questions, please make the questions simple and direct. The more complicated the question, the more difficult it will be to get a correct answer.'

'What kind of questions?' the newspaper editor wanted to know.

'You shall see when the time comes, sir. Now I want you all to get comfortable in your chairs and put your feet flat on the floor.' There was a rustling of satins and taffeta as the ladies arranged themselves. Mr Hogle had been sitting with his legs crossed and his shoe made a sound as it hit the chair leg and settled firmly on the floor. 'Now I want you to hold hands. Take the hands of the person next to you. Mr Marsh, you'll have to uncross your arms, sir, and take Mr Smith's hand and Mrs Secrest's hand. Yes. Fine.' He inspected his circle. They had done as he had asked. At his feet the metronome went tick... tick... tick...

'Would you all close your eyes and bow your heads in prayer?' Again they did as they were asked. 'Our Heavenly Father, be with us at this time and grant us the right to know You better and to better understand Your mysterious workings. I especially ask You to protect us this evening and not to permit anything contrary to Your divine judgement to enter into this circle. We ask that Mary Roff be protected and blessed at all times. That she be guided into Your divine paths by Your divine hand. Amen.'

'Amen,' the others repeated.

Tick. Tick. Tick.

'You may open your eyes now.' They did. 'Now, Mary, I want you to close your eyes and listen to the ticking of the metronome.'

Tick. Tick. Tick.

'As you listen I want you to imagine that you're descending a long staircase with each tick of the metronome. Do you understand?' She nodded her head. There was silence. Tick. Tick. Tick. 'Do you see the staircase?'

'No, not yet.'

'We shall wait. Tell me when you see it.'

Tick. Tick. Tick.

All eyes were on Mary's face, which was partially concealed by shadows. Ann squeezed her husband's hand and he returned the pressure. 'Do you see the staircase, Mary?'

'I think I do,' she said softly.

'Don't force it. It will come naturally.'

Tick. Tick. Tick.

'I see the staircase clearly now. It's made of dark wood and has a red carpet running down the center of the steps.' She paused. 'It's a long way down there.'

'Can you see the bottom step?'

'No.'

'Are you afraid to go down those stairs?'

'No.'

'Mary, as I count down the steps, and there are twenty-one of them in front of you, I want you to listen to the metronome and see yourself descending the stairs. See your body actually going down each step as I count down. Do you understand?'

'Yes.'

'Are you ready?' She nodded and he looked at the others in the circle. All eyes were on Mary's darkened face. Tick. Tick. Tick. 'All right, Mary. Let's start down the steps. You are on the top step, the twenty-first step. Now see yourself going down to twenty. Now down to nineteen. Eighteen.

Seventeen. Sixteen, Fifteen.' Tick. Tick. Tick. 'Fourteen. Thirteen, twelve, eleven, ten.'

She sighed.

'Are you all right?'

'Yes.'

'Down to nine. Eight. Seven. Six. Five.' Tick. Tick. Tick. 'Four. Three. Two. One. You are now at the bottom of the stairs. Am I correct?'

'Yes,' the voice was faint.

'Do you see a large chair, Mary?' She shut her eyelids tighter and tilted her head to one side as if looking around. She nodded. 'Fine.' Tick. Tick. Tick. 'Now, Mary, I want you to sit in that chair and wait. You will wait until someone comes out of the door in front of you and speaks to you. Do you understand?'

'Yes.'

'Are you in the chair?'

'Yes.'

'Fine. Now wait until the door in front of you opens and a person comes through that door and walks over to you. Do you understand?'

'Yes.' This time very faintly.

Tick. Tick. Tick. Tick. Asa wanted to loosen his collar. It seemed to be too tight but his hands were being held by Ann on his left and Mike Hogle on his right.

Ann had nearly stopped breathing as she strained to see her daughter's face across the dimly lit circle. She glanced at Nervie, on the other side of the Reverend Dille, but Nervie didn't notice. She was staring intently into her younger sister's face. Staring and praying that everything would go the way it was supposed to.

'Where are you now, Mary?' the minister asked softly.

'Still in the... the chair.'

'Has the door opened?' She shook her head. 'Can you see the door?' she nodded. 'Then let's just wait a little longer. Someone will come through the door.' At least he hoped someone would come through the door. This method had been used successfully in New York and Boston and had been reported in *The Spiritual Telegraph*. God help them all if anything were to go wrong.

'Yes . . . ' Mary spoke. 'Yes. The door is opening. I see someone.'

'Who?' He reached down, breaking the circle for an instant, and stopped the ticking metronome.

'A lady. It's a lady and she's wearing a long black dressing gown.'

'Does she frighten you?'

'No. She's a nice lady. She's smiling at me.' Ann squeezed Asa's hand in relief.

'Will you describe her more fully?'

'She is about . . . oh, sixty years old, I would say, and she wears a lace cap on her head. She is holding out one hand and pointing to it with the other.'

'Why?'

'I don't know.'

'Is she trying to call attention to something she is wearing on that hand?' the minister asked.

Mary pushed her face forward a little as if trying to get closer to the hand. 'Oh, the poor thing!' she said softly. 'She doesn't have a little finger! There are only three fingers and a thumb on that hand!'

'My God!' said Mr Marsh.

The Reverend Dille glared at him. 'Shhhh!'

'But I think I know that woman,' Mr Marsh insisted. 'My first wife was missing the little finger on her left hand!'

'Is this woman Mr Marsh's first wife, Mary? Ask her.'

Mary sat silent for a few seconds. 'She says her name is Lizabetha. She says you spell it with an "L" instead of an "E" and you put an "a" on the end of it.'

'Oh my God!' Mr Marsh began to perspire. 'That was the way my first wife spelled her name. She thought it was more elegant than plain Elizabeth.'

'Yes,' said Mary, a little faster now, 'and she says you had two marriage licenses at home because she made you go back and get another one with her name spelled correctly on it.'

'That's true!' Mr Marsh said excitedly. 'The clerk spelled it the normal way and neither of us noticed it until we got home. She made me go back and get another one with the correct spelling. She said she didn't consider herself married until her name was correct on the license.' His eyes filled with water but he was smiling. 'We used to laugh about that, afterward. Yes, that must be Lizabetha.'

'Do you have anything you want to ask her?' the minister was looking at him.

'A thousand things, I suppose,' he stammered, 'but I can't think of one of them right now. I really wasn't . . . ' he glanced at the others '. . . wasn't prepared for anything like this.'

'Nor were any of the rest of us,' said Mrs Secrest.

'Yes,' Mr Marsh spoke up. 'I do have a question for her. May I ask it?' The Reverend Dille nodded. 'Lizabetha,' he said slowly, 'were you in much pain at the last? Did the medicines and the poultices take away some of the pain?' His eyes were intent on Mary's face. 'I tried my best, you know.'

'She says,' Mary spoke slowly, 'that there was no pain toward the end. The pain was in the fact that you seemed to want her to die.'

'I never!' Mr Marsh almost shouted. 'I loved my wife!'

'She says,' Mary continued, 'that you felt you had spent enough time with a woman who was always ill and whose doctor bills never ceased. And she says you had already met the present Mrs Marsh before she died and were planning to wed her as soon as the proper time had elapsed after the funeral.'

'Reverend Dille,' Asa's voice was heard, 'I don't think it quite proper that my daughter . . .'

'That is not your daughter, sir. That information is coming from the first Mrs Marsh.'

'But still my daughter is saying those things and I find it improper conduct toward a guest in my home.'

Mr Marsh looked at Asa. 'Please,' he said, 'Mary is only repeating what Lizabetha is telling her. We asked her to do just that, if you recall. And it is true,' he sighed, 'quite true that I wished for her passing. The surgeons who removed her little finger thought they had removed all the disease with it. But it continued inside her body for several years afterward. It's all perfectly true. Including the part about my wanting to marry Lillian while she was still alive.' The others sat in stunned silence. 'I'm a grown man and I take full responsibility for my actions and deeds. Don't berate your daughter for telling the truth.'

'She is going now,' Mary said. 'She said she understands and forgives you. She says that where she is, all things are understood and most things are forgiven. She was a lovely lady, Mr Marsh.'

'Yes, Mary, she was.' He broke the circle of clasped hands long enough to take out his pocket handkerchief and blow his nose. 'She was lovely and pleasurable to be with. The disease destroyed her.' He put the handkerchief into his pocket and joined hands with the editor and the mayor's wife.

'Now what do you see, Mary?' the minister's voice was gentle.

'There is someone else trying to come through the door. A young man with a small baby in his arms. How strange! I wonder why a man would hold a baby.'

'Why don't you ask him?'

She nodded and was silent for almost a minute. 'He says that this baby is his little brother. He says that he went into the spirit world just after this baby was born and that it followed soon after and he has been taking care of it. He says his name is Ray and the baby's name is Ronald.'

Mr Smith, the editor of the town newspaper, said in a calm even voice. 'I don't know how you got that bit of information. There is no one in town who knows that.'

'Knows what?' the minister asked.

'That I had a brother named Ray who was struck by lightning when he was sixteen years old. Three weeks after his death my baby brother Ronald died of diphtheria. It was a sad time for my family, two funerals in one month. Who told you about this, Mr Dille?'

'Told me? Sir, nobody has told me anything.'

'But there's no way Mary could have guessed that about my family. That happened years ago in Pennsylvania. She couldn't have guessed it.'

'She is not guessing, Mr Smith,' the minister said. 'She is being *told* the information.'

'Mr Smith,' Mary said. 'Your brother Ray wants to prove he is really here. Will you permit him?'

'Proof? Yes. Let him – or you – *prove* it to me.'

'He is pointing at a flat wooden box. It has been painted bright red but the outside lid has the letters "A" and "R" on it in white. He opens the box and there are two pipes. Smoking pipes. Now he closes the box and places it where it is hidden by straw and earth. It is cold there but he says the cold will not harm the pipes.'

The editor was silent for several seconds. 'That is incredible,' he said choosing his words carefully, 'my brother and I had such a box and it was painted red. The letters stood for my name, Adam, and "R" for his, Ray. We stole those pipes from a tobacconist one time when we were visiting Philadelphia. They were expensive pipes and nobody in the family ever knew about them except Ray and myself. We would sneak off to the woods near our farm and smoke where no one would see us. Especially my father. We kept the box hidden in a woodchuck hole that we covered over with weeds and dirt.' His voice broke. 'Ray, I'm sorry I doubted you. You were my favorite brother. I really missed you when you died.' He fought to hold back the tears.

'He's telling me to tell you not to grieve for him, that he is happy where he is and is learning every day and he enjoys taking care of little Ronald. He says he sees little Boney ... Bonnie ... I can't make out the word,' she complained.

Now the tears welled up and over the rims of the editor's eyes. 'That's little Boniface, our mutt dog we named after a Pope Boniface I read about in a book. Even though we were not Catholics my mother was shocked that I would use a holy name for a dog. We were not allowed to call him Boniface. It was always Bonnie. I ... I'm sorry ... I can't seem to control my voice.' He let the tears run down his cheeks.

'Mr Smith,' the minister said, 'there is no reason to hide or be ashamed of true emotions for others.'

'I cried at Ray's funeral. We had been so close.'

'But now he is happy,' said Mary softly. 'Now there is no need for tears. He tells me to tell you to cry for the living and to be more considerate of the feelings of the living, for they need compassion more than the dead do.'

'Does he mean the way I will sometimes report a news item? The way I write about someone in the paper?'

'He says you know what he means,' Mary replied. 'He says you always knew what he meant even when you were boys together. There was never any misunderstanding between you, and there should not be any now.' She turned her face, eyes still closed, toward him. 'Do you understand?'

'Yes. I understand what you have said,' he added quickly, 'but I don't understand where the information came from.'

'We are not asking for understanding, Mr Smith,' the Reverend Dille said. 'Until we have the answers, all we ask is an open mind.'

'Then that, sir, you have. I promise you.'

'Thank you.'

'Thank *you*!'

'He is going away now,' Mary said. 'He's going out the door. Now he's gone.' She was silent for a few seconds. 'There is a movement at the door again. This time it's a lady, a very old lady who walks with a cane.'

'With a cane?' the minister repeated, looking quickly at the faces in the circle for some sort of recognition.

'Yes. She has a cane. She had two canes. One of wood and the other was silver overlay. She never liked the silver one but would carry it sometimes when she went calling on friends if the family insisted.'

The mayor looked at his wife. Her eyes were large. She was about to say something but he shook his head.

'Does anyone recognize this lady?' the minister asked. Again the mayor and his wife exchanged glances.

'She tells me that Tad is there with her and so are Samuel and Delbert. She can't find David. She has looked for him but she can't find him. There are some places she is not permitted to go. Perhaps David is there.'

'Doesn't anyone here acknowledge this woman?' The Reverend Dille looked at each face. 'If not, we shall have to send her back.' Silence from everyone.

'She's showing me a bean crock. A large brown bean pot. She says it doesn't matter anymore.'

Again the minister searched the faces in the circle. 'She seems to think she belongs here. Can't anyone identify her? Mr Roff? Mrs Secrest?' Both Asa and the mayor's wife shook their heads.

Mary's eyes were tightly closed, her mouth pursed. 'I'm trying to understand what she is saying. It begins with the letter "P" . . . a strange word or difficult name . . . I can't seem...' Then her entire body shook. The sensation rippled through the hands of the others in the circle. Ann gasped as Mary's head dropped forward as if in deep sleep. The Reverend Dille held his breath. Then she raised her head and turned toward the mayor's wife.

'The word is Punxsutawney!' she said in a completely different voice. 'It's no wonder this poor child didn't understand it. But you understand it, Martha. Your parents were born there and you know who I am.'

Mrs Secrest's eyes were wide. She looked at her husband.

'Martha, you know who I am!'

'Yes, Grandma. I know.' The mayor's wife's voice was almost inaudible.

'I don't know why you didn't speak up when I came in! You know how I hate scenes and this little girl is in no physical condition for scenes.' The voice was that of an elderly woman, a woman who was accustomed to commanding and getting her own way. 'I was trying to tell you that your uncles are here with me. I can't find David. I can't find him anywhere. Do you know where your father is?'

'Father is not dead, Grandmother,' Mrs Secrest said. 'He is still alive. That's why you can't find him.'

'Still alive?' the old voice rose questioningly. 'But good heavens, child, he must be very old by now.'

'He will be ninety-two his next birthday.'

'Is he with you?'

'No.'

'Well, where is he?'

Mrs Secrest looked at her husband again; this time he gave her no signals. 'He is in the insane asylum in Harrisburg, Grandmother. He has been there for many years.' She was glad it was so dark in the room because her face was burning with shame. Her father's insanity had been a well-guarded family secret. Now her friends and everyone who had voted for Conrad would know that the mayor's wife had a father who was in an asylum.

'He is being well taken care of,' the mayor said to Mary. 'He gets the best. We see to that.'

Mary's face turned quickly toward him. 'Now he gets the best,' the old woman's voice said. 'But when you had anything to do with it, *you* got the best. And you took it!'

Asa sat in shocked silence. That this should be going on in his home and to one of the most respected men in Watseka was unthinkable. Yet he didn't dare interrupt. He didn't dare do anything to startle Mary.

'I don't know what you mean, Grandmother,' said Mrs Secrest. 'If you really are my grandmother,' she added.

'Oh, I'm your grandmother! There are times when I wish I weren't. What I am talking about is the money in the bean pot. The money you and your husband stole from me when you ran off and got married.'

Asa struggled to keep silent.

'We didn't steal the money,' the mayor said angrily. 'You promised it to us and then you said we couldn't have it.'

'I had the wedding all planned, Gran'mother. We had to have the money.'

'Yes, you got married and none too soon either!' the old lady laughed under her breath.

'Really, Reverend Dille,' said Asa aloud. 'I must protest that this is going too far. I want you to end this immediately.'

Mary looked at her father, her eyes closed and her lips pressed tightly together. 'You listen, young man,' the voice said to him, 'I have a few things to say to this granddaughter of mine and I don't cotton to interruptions.'

'Mary!' Ann exclaimed loudly.

'My name is not Mary! Never did like that name. Too common,' replied the old woman's voice. 'Every Tom, Dick and Harry called their children Mary.' Her tone softened a little. 'Martha, I did not come all this distance to argue with you. I came to tell you that I really don't care about the money anymore. Over here I've learned that there are more important things to think about. I came because I was concerned about David. I couldn't find him. Now I know why.'

'Grandmother,' said Mrs Secrest, 'I'm sorry about the money. I really am.' She began to cry. She and her husband had avoided her grandmother after the wedding and moved away as soon as they could. She never saw the woman again and had only been back to Punxsutawney once to sign the papers that committed her father to the asylum. The money they got from his farm helped them get settled in Watseka.

'Martha –' her husband tried to calm her.

'Let her be, Mr Secrest,' the minister said. 'She'll be all right.'

Mary's voice was softer now but still cracked with age. 'Well, I'm going now. I'm sorry I upset you, Martha. You too, Conrad. But I wanted to find out about David.' Mrs Secrest tried to speak but tears lodged in her throat. 'And Martha, I love you. I always did love you more than the rest. You know that, don't you, child?' Mrs Secrest nodded. 'That's why it hurt so when you did what you did. But I forgive you. And now you can forgive yourself. Does that make you feel any better? That you can forgive yourself?'

Mrs Secrest managed to say 'Yes' through the tears.

'Good.' Mary looked around the room. 'Well, I'm going now. No need wearing out this poor child. She's remarkably easy to come through, but there should be more of a guard. More protection.'

'What do you mean by *protection*?' the minister asked.

'Just protection,' came the reply. 'I can't put it into any other word. Protection. I don't mean to tell you your business, sir,' she said, 'but if I were you, I wouldn't let her do this anymore until there is adequate protection.'

'Thank you,' said the minister. 'I'll remember that.'

'And so will I,' spoke up Asa.

'Well, good-bye Martha. And Conrad. I shall pray for you. I love you both.' Mary's head flopped down, her chin pressing against her neck, her shoulders hunched over, her hands limp in the grip of Mr Smith and the Reverend Dille. Everyone took a deep breath. The others were looking at the floor or down at their laps, not wanting to look at either the mayor or his wife. Nervie kept her eyes on Mary's face. Because Nervie was the only one looking at Mary's face she was the first one to scream.

Mary sat with her face tilted toward the ceiling. Her mouth was open and her tongue licked her lips. The veins in her neck stood out, even in the darkness, and seemed to be pulsating more than normal. Mary jerked her hands, suddenly, and freed them from the circle. She ran her hands through her hair and scratched her scalp as if it were itching.

Asa unclasped his hands and started toward her. The Reverend Dille motioned him back to his seat. Ann couldn't look. Her hands covered her face. She knew what was coming. She had seen it happen before.

'Well!' said Mary looking around the group and scratching her head. 'Isn't this lovely! Look at all you people come to see me! Ain't this a real honor, though?' She opened her legs and stretched her skirt as tight as it would go, feet firmly on the floor. Then she bent over and rested her elbows on her knees, her head cupped in her hands. 'What did you come for this time?' Her voice was harsh, almost guttural, and there was an accent with it, an accent that was difficult to place.

The circle of hands broken, the others had instinctively pushed back their chairs.

'Well, what is it this time? Another dead cow? A barn on fire?'

'Mary, I think it's time we went to bed,' said Ann.

'Did one of your dogs produce a litter of kittens?' the voice inside Mary laughed. 'Well, what is it this time?' No one said a word. 'Well, speak up! I ain't got all day. To what do I owe this honor?'

'Mary, I think your mother is right. It is past your bedtime –'

'Past my bedtime?' said the voice. 'You want to put me in a nice soft bed? Hah! That's certainly different. Does the bed have a snake in it? Or maybe a scorpion?'

The Reverend Dille was frightened, yet fascinated. He didn't want what was happening to happen, yet now that it had he was pleased. He tried to take command of the situation. 'What is your name?' he asked and touched Mary on the shoulder.

She pulled back and knocked the hand away. 'What kind of a question is that? "What is your name?"' she mimicked. 'You know damned well what my name is!' She looked around the room at the broken circle of chairs. The mayor had managed to get over to his wife's side and Asa stood with his arm around Ann. 'Funny,' said the voice. 'You know who I am and yet you ask me my name. I don't know who you are and haven't asked your names.'

Nervie tried to help. 'My name is Minerva and –'

'I don't care what any of your names are! I just want you to tell me what you want this time and then get out! Get out of my house and off my property!' She stood up and took a few steps. The others backed away.

'Why should we want anything?' asked the Reverend, trying to keep his investigation going.

'What else would you be doing here?' she snarled at him. 'Everytime something happens in the village you come running here accusing me of doing it! Well, what happened this time? What am I supposed to have done now?'

'Nothing,' he said.

'Nothing? Then get out!' She walked toward him and he backed slightly away. He didn't dare show anyone that he was losing control.

'We are your friends,' he said weakly.

'Oh yes, *friends*. I've lots of friends in this village, I have! Come here all the time for coffee and cakes and candies!'

'Who are you?' he asked again. 'Maybe we have come to the wrong house.'

'I'm Katrina Hogan and you know it. And you haven't come to the wrong house. You know exactly where you are and what you are here for, and *I* want to know what is being blamed on me now! I did not make that baby sickly the last time. But you wouldn't believe it.' She glared at them all. They moved backward a few more steps. 'None of you would believe it! Now get out of my house!'

'We want to help you, Katrina,' said Nervie. 'We love you.'

'Yes, we love you,' Ann added. 'Please go away and give us back our Mary. Please.'

'Love?' Mary walked over to Ann and looked at her, her eyes still closed. 'That's a strange word coming from the likes of you folks. I've never seen any love. Not around here. All I've seen is hatred and fear. You hate me and you fear me and you blame me for things and I don't know why. You don't even let me go to church on Sunday.' She went near Mrs Secrest, who was staring at her with horror. 'They don't even let me into the church,' she said, softer now, 'can you believe that?' She reached out and touched a ribbon in Mrs Secrest's hair. 'You look like a nice lady,' the voice said, 'can you believe they won't let me in church?'

Mrs Secrest started to say something but Mary walked away. She looked at Mr Hogle and then at editor Smith. 'I don't know you,' she said tiredly. 'I don't know you and yet you come here to persecute me. Why can't you leave me alone? I'm an old woman. I have no husband, no children. I have done nothing to you. Why can't you leave me alone?' She crossed her arms and hugged her shoulders as if she was cold. 'Why don't you people leave me alone?' She began to cry. It wasn't Mary's voice but they were Mary's tears and they ran down Mary's cheeks to be absorbed in the cloth of Mary's dress.

She stood like that for almost a minute until Ann got up enough courage to put her arms around her daughter. 'Come on,' she said quietly. 'Come on, it's time to rest.'

Suddenly Mary opened her arms and the force threw Ann onto the floor. The wooden chairs of the circle crashed as she hit them.

'Don't touch me!' Mary screamed. 'Stay away from me! This is my house! Why don't you all get out of here!'

Nervie helped Ann to her feet as the mayor and his wife ran toward the parlor doors. Mr Hogle and Mr Marsh were right behind them.

'Get out!' the voice screamed as Mary looked around with blind eyes to find something to throw at the intruders. The metronome was snatched from the floor and hurled with force against the wall. It barely missed Mr Hogle's head. The table behind where she had been sitting had a cut glass vase with flowers. She threw it at the fleeing guests and it smashed against the wall just as the mayor found the handles and slid open the parlor doors.

'You leave me alone!' the voice shouted at editor Smith as he stood staring at her. She picked up one of the chairs and raised it over her head. He stepped aside just in time as it came crashing inches away from him.

'Do something, Reverend Dille!' Ann screamed. 'Do something before Mary kills someone!'

'I don't know what to do!' he confessed. 'I can't control her any longer!'

Asa was leading Ann toward the door and editor Smith was protecting Nervie with his own body as another chair came sailing through the air and smashed against the wall. All four of them made it through the door before the next chair shattered after them.

'Now you,' said Mary to the Reverend Dille. 'You get out of here too!' Eyes still closed, she glanced around and grabbed the flickering oil lantern. 'You came to burn me like a witch, didn't you?'

He shook his head. 'I wanted to help –'

'You want to see me burn?' she demanded. 'You want to see us *all* burn?' She held the lantern high over her head and pulled back her arm. 'In a few seconds this house will be in flames. Isn't that what you want? Then will you leave me alone?'

'Mary!' A voice boomed from the doorway. 'You put that lamp down.' Loozie's black face was even blacker as she shouted at the girl.

Mary's arm wavered but the lantern stayed poised for the throw.

'Put the lamp down, child. See what I have in my hand.' Loozie walked slowly toward the girl, her eyes never leaving her face. She held a small piece of carved wood in one hand. Mary's arm wavered.

'Open your eyes,' Loozie commanded. 'Open your eyes and see what I am holding.' Mary's eyelids began to flutter. 'That's right, open your eyes and look at this.'

With great effort the girl managed to raise her eyelids. Mary blinked, trying to focus. Then she saw what Loozie was holding. She stood still and stared at the carved figure. The Reverend Dille caught the oil lamp as Mary fell unconscious onto the floor.

News of the scene at the Roffs quickly spread through town. A meeting was held in Lavinia Durst's living-room. She was pleased that seven women showed up.

'I don't think I have to tell you ladies what has been going on in the Roff home.' It was a statement rather than a question and she looked at the satins and silks and feathers they were wearing rather than into their eyes. 'We all know and love the Roffs.' General agreement. 'And we certainly feel for dear, dear Ann at a time like this.' More general agreement. 'But something has got to be done regarding their daughter Mary. She cannot be permitted to roam loose in the streets of our town!' Louder agreement, faster munching on sweet cakes. 'I have called this meeting of you concerned citizens to discuss what must be done in order to preserve our safety. Someone had to take the responsibility of starting this movement and as much as I love dear, dear Ann, I have willingly assumed the burden.' There was even light applause from two ladies who had already put their cups back on the table. 'Asa Roff is a respected man and an important man in town. However, he has no right to inflict his family's illness on others.'

'My Adam said he didn't think it was anybody's business what happened to Mary as long as Asa assumed legal responsibility.' Harriet Newman couldn't decide anything without her husband.

'That's hardly the point, Harriet!' Lavinia replied sharply. 'What kind of legal responsibility could Asa assume if Mary plunged a knife into *your* heart?' Harriet clutched her bosom.

'Ann told me that since the time it happened she personally locks up all the knives in the kitchen. Even the African woman has to get her key if she needs a knife.'

'There are other knives in Watseka,' spoke up Sarah Thayer, as Lavinia nodded her head in agreement. 'Marsh's hardware store is full of them!'

'Certainly Lile Marsh would have more sense than to give that girl a knife,' said Alice Thompson. 'Lile is a responsible merchant.'

'How could he stop her if she was determined?' Lavinia wanted to know. 'He is only one man, and not in the best of health either. Look what she did when *five* men' – she held up the fingers of one hand – 'when *five* men tried to hold her down! You think Lile Marsh is stronger than *five* men? And she don't need a knife to hurt someone. She could hit them with a brick or with a hammer or anything.'

'And by the railroad tracks,' someone said. 'There're all kinds of spikes and sharp stones.'

'She could get ahold of a rifle,' offered someone else, 'and shoot up the town.'

'She don't need anything in her hands,' Lavinia reminded them. 'Just recall the bruise on the side of Willie Simpson's face. She did that with her bare hands.' She paused for effect. 'With her *bare* hands.'

'And another thing,' Sarah had been awaiting her cue, 'as if the murderous intent is not enough, what about this Devil business? What are we going to do about that?'

'Devil business?' Millie Hawkins asked.

'You know,' Sarah lowered her voice, 'those things that have been happening with her when the Devil comes and takes her over.'

'I hadn't heard about any Devil – ' Millie started to say.

'Nobody actually called it the *Devil*,' put in Lavinia, 'but that girl has to be powered by something evil to do the things they say she does. Reading things that are sealed in envelopes! Knowing what's happening in one room when she is in another! And fooling around with ghosts!' She paused and stared at her friends.

'Right,' added Sarah. 'Jesus says in the Bible to let the dead lie and to let the dead bury their dead. That's a direct commandment from God.'

'Well, I heard that the Reverend Dille was doing some kind of scientific work with her when that happened. Certainly you can't accuse my minister of helping the Devil?' Mrs Thompson was a pillar in the Methodist Church and Lavinia was a Baptist, therefore automatically suspect when it came to badmouthing her church. 'The Reverend Dille is a man of God.'

Lavinia backed off a little. 'I'm not saying your preacher is working with the Devil, Alice. I'm saying that while his intentions have been pure and Christian, the Devil has somehow managed to intrude upon his experiments.'

'He would throw out the Devil if it appeared,' Alice said angrily. 'He is a *minister* and trained to do just that!'

'Christ couldn't throw out the Devil,' said Pauline Wilkins. 'It says right in the Bible that the Devil bothered Our Lord for several days when He was in the desert.'

Alice glared at her but said nothing. Another Baptist!

'Why hasn't the mayor done anything about this?' Millie Hawkins wanted to know.

'The mayor?' snorted Lavinia. 'The mayor and Martha were there the very night the Devil came through! Sitting in a circle and holding hands with Mary as she did her diabolical work! Don't look for the mayor to do anything where the Roffs are concerned.'

'Well, what can *we* do?' Millie rephrased her question.

'We can get up a petition and have decent people sign it and force Asa Roff to put his daughter where she can't harm innocent folks, that's what we can do. If we got enough signatures Asa wouldn't dare do nothing else but go along with us. He may be one of the richest men in town and have powerful friends but Watseka is still a democracy. Our boys in blue are still fighting so that we may have our democracy!' That patriotic chord vibrated in all of them.

'Who is going to draw up this petition?' Millie asked.

Lavinia reached for a sheet of paper. 'I have already done that,' she said with a flourish, 'and you ladies may be the first to sign.' She passed the page and slid the pen and ink to Alice Thompson sitting on her right. Alice read the statement demanding Mary be committed and then looked at Lavinia. Then she looked at the others, who were all looking at her. She bowed her head, picked up the pen and signed her name.

'More tea, anyone?' Lavinia asked sweetly.

The petition circulated slowly but surely during the months of February and March, 1865. Lavinia didn't let it out of her sight and personally carried it to friends' homes and places of business. More women than men signed it. The women were afraid for their lives and their children's lives but the men were afraid that if Asa saw their signatures on the document he'd hurt them financially. Asa was a powerful man in town. He had the law on his side, and as a lawyer knew how to twist things around. Shop owners didn't want his wrath brought down on them. Many people didn't want to sign it because they just didn't like Lavinia. She was a gossip and a troublemaker. If it came to a showdown between Lavinia and Asa, few doubted that Asa would win. It wasn't good politics or good business to side against him. So they declined and Lavinia went away, the paper tucked in her purse, to corner someone else.

Relations with the Reverend Dille had come to an abrupt halt after that night. Asa told him firmly – and not too politely – that he didn't want him conducting any more of his 'scientific experiments' on his daughter. He told him a minister's place was in church talking to God and not in parlors talking to spirits. He asked the Reverend not to call on Mary again or on any other member of his family.

Nothing appeared in the newspaper about that evening. Asa and the mayor asked editor Smith not to write it up. It wasn't really *news*, they told him, and would only create more gossip than the town needed. Editor Smith hadn't really planned to print the story, knowing that when people started asking questions those in the room would only suffer more than they already had. He was concerned over Mary's health and angry at the Reverend Dille's interference. And Asa was a steady advertiser. So instead of the truth about the evening being written for all to read, half-truths were whispered for all to hear.

Ann first noticed the cooling of the women toward her when Dr and Mrs Fenner gave a reception for his sister who was visiting Watseka from Indianapolis and she and Asa weren't invited. The Fenners (he was a dentist) had been to the Roff home many times. They rarely gave parties, but when they did, the Roffs had always been on the guest list. Three days later Ann had tea with Mrs Marsh and the mayor's wife. Both of them had been to the Fenners but neither wanted to tell her what was being said about Mary and the plans if the Roffs didn't do something about her.

Because she had stopped going to church after Asa ordered the Reverend Dille not to return to their home, Ann missed the gossip at the sewing circle, held on Thursday afternoons, and the covered dish supper, held the first Sunday of each month. With Ann not present, the ladies could say what they pleased and they were not pleased with the fact that 'Mad Mary' lived on the hill and could see into their homes and bedrooms whenever she had a mind to. They had had time to think about it and more of them were coming around to Lavinia's point of view: Mary was a danger to society.

April 9 was Palm Sunday and almost everyone had been to church except the Roffs. Toward evening the bells began ringing again, and the telegraph key at the newspaper clattered out the news: General Grant had sat down with General Lee that afternoon and the war was over.

Small boys ran through the streets shouting the tidings at

the top of their lungs. Several farmers raced their horses down Walnut Street. Tommy Osterman, who had run away to be a bugler boy for the Union at twelve and had returned without his left leg at the age of thirteen, hobbled on his crutch and blew his bugle.

There was a hint of frost in the air as Ann bundled up the children so they could run out and join their friends. She and Asa wrapped warmly and walked through the streets with Minerva and Mary, stopping to congratulate and shake hands with everyone. Even Loozie came along that night. She had tied her head in a bright red cloth she'd been saving for the occasion and wore the golden earrings the Roffs had given her for Christmas the year before. She was happy because it meant that soon her man would be coming for her. She wished she could see some black faces so she'd have somebody to hug and somebody to understand what it meant to people with her skin color, but she was the only African in town. So she hugged Mary and kept a sharp eye on her. There would be lots of time for hugging and laughing when her man came for her.

Mary didn't know when she had heard such noise or felt such excitement. The war had never been real to her. It had never even come close to Watseka. The fighting had been miles away and involved other people. She was happy for Nervie. It meant that Henry would be coming back for sure, that the danger of his being killed had passed and Nervie would get married after all.

The crowds were heading for the corner of Walnut and Fourth Street, where civic celebrations usually took place. Some men had already begun nailing the speaking platform into place. While the Watseka marching band waited for the stragglers to arrive so they could line up, one-legged little Tommy Osterman hopped around and blew his bugle and everyone applauded.

Kerosine lanterns appeared in shop windows and four of them were placed on the platform so everyone could see the speakers. A large barn lantern was suspended over the platform by cross wires and made a large hole in the darkness.

The mayor arrived and was roundly applauded. The fire

chief and police chief joined him. Ministers from the various churches clambered onto the platform, too. People stood because nobody had thought to bring chairs. The mayor spotted Asa in the crowd and urged him onto the platform. Several people called his name and applauded him. He was a good man and everyone, even the poorest farmer, knew him from the post office.

The mayor waved his hands for silence, and just as he was about to speak the marching band struck up 'Yankee Doodle'. Everyone laughed and tried to sing at the same time. When it was over and he started to speak, they broke into 'The Bold Soldier Boy'. Everyone laughed again and many joined in the singing.

Loozie felt a chill through her heavy clothing and turned to see what had caused it. Not more than ten feet away stood Lavinia Durst. She wasn't singing. She was looking at Mary, staring at her with contempt.

Mary started to say something to Loozie about the dress the mayor's wife was wearing, but when she looked at her she followed the African woman's gaze. She saw Lavinia. She got the same chill. 'That's the woman, isn't it, Loozie?' she said in a low voice. The African nodded. Loozie had come up behind Lavinia one afternoon at the butcher shop and overheard her make a remark about Mary. She had called her 'Mad Mary Roff' but the lady she was talking to saw Loozie and signaled for Lavinia to be quiet. Lavinia had a sheet of paper in her hand that was almost completely filled with signatures. Loozie didn't know what was written on the paper because she didn't know how to read, but the way Lavinia snatched the paper back and walked quickly out of the shop, she knew it wasn't good. On her way back to the house she stopped at the little vegetable stall and asked Blind Annie what was going on. Blind Annie knew everything that was going on and said even she had been asked to sign the petition against Mary. For three days she debated about telling the Roffs and when she did both Asa and Ann said they knew all about it and it wasn't important. They hadn't asked her not to tell Mary, so she told her. She felt the child had a right to know what was going on so she could defend herself if anything came of it. Mary had cried for a few minutes and then dried her tears. She wasn't surprised that people in town were afraid of her when these fits took over.

After the mayor spoke, the police chief spoke, followed by the newspaper editor and finally Asa. The crowd had grown restless and many of the children had gone off to play hide-and-seek in the darkened shop doorways. Fenton and Frank had vanished and while Ann knew they had to be nearby she became concerned and asked Loozie to see what they were up to. Loozie, glad for a chance to move her legs after standing all that time, gave Mary a hug and went looking for the boys. Mary stood behind her mother and her sister, listening to what her father was saying.

Asa spoke of the nation being united again and what that would mean as far as getting mail to the South and hearing from loved ones who had been cut off by Confederate politics. Ann turned and asked Mary if she was warm enough. Mary said she was.

After Asa spoke, three young men who had fought in the war and who had been shipped back to Watseka minus parts of their bodies got up on the platform to tell the crowd of the horrors of war. They were cheered and you could have heard a pin drop when they related their experiences on the battlefield.

'That Davis boy is very handsome, even without his arm,' said Nervie over her shoulder to Mary. 'He'd make you a good husband.' Nervie laughed and waited for Mary to comment on her joke. Benny Davis had been an ugly boy when he enlisted and losing his arm had only made him more so. Instead of a reply, there was silence. Nervie turned to her sister but Mary wasn't there.

'Ma!' Nervie grabbed her mother's arm. 'Mary's gone!'

Ann turned quickly and gave a small cry. 'Where'd she go?' she asked Nervie. 'She was standing right here! Why didn't you keep an eye on her?'

'She was here just a minute ago,' Nervie said. 'She couldn't have gotten far.' Nervie stood on tiptoes and tried to stare over the heads and hats around her. 'I don't see her,' she said.

'See if she's on the curbstone. Maybe she got tired and went to sit down.'

'Did she go with Loozie?' Nervie asked, even though she knew Loozie had gone alone.

Ann shook her head. 'Go find her. Please.' As Nervie started away from her Ann reached out and touched her sleeve. 'Don't cause a scene, Nervie.'

Minerva knew what she meant.

When the three veterans finished, the Baptist minister offered up a prayer that peace would last and be just for both sides. The band struck up 'Glory, Glory Hallelujah', and while many cheered, others just stood with tears in their eyes. Then the crowd began to break up, friends talking with friends, others shaking hands, farmers heading for their buggies and children being herded off toward home and bed.

When Asa rejoined Ann she told him Mary was missing. She said it in a soft voice and with a smile on her face. Since Mary's seance people looked at the Roffs in a new light and she knew people were watching her now. She didn't want to let these strangers know any more than she absolutely had to. 'Nervie's gone to look for her. Loozie and the boys are over on the other corner.'

'How did you let her get out of your sight?' he asked, smiling. They had rehearsed their public appearances as if they were visiting royalty. He waved to a friend who had tipped his hat in his direction. 'It was your responsibility to watch her,' he said under his breath. 'Now God only knows where she has gone.'

Loozie, standing on the corner shepherding the four boys, was grim. 'I'm sorry, Mrs Ann,' she said. 'But you did tell me to fetch the boys. I thought Mary would be all right with you for a few minutes.'

'Hush,' Ann was still smiling. 'It's not your fault. Nervie and I should never have turned our backs on her. You take the boys on home and watch carefully as you go. Perhaps Mary went that way.'

Loozie herded the four boys up Fourth Street. The Roff home stood at the end of it. By peering through the just budding tree branches Loozie could see the lantern light in the upper bedroom window. She never went out at night without leaving that light on. It was a beacon drawing the family home and an amulet keeping enemies away.

Ann and Nervie started walking down Walnut Street toward the place where the railroad tracks crossed the old road that led into Middleport. Asa went across Walnut and down into the railroad yard. Mary liked the large depot and sometimes would chat with the stationmaster. Perhaps she had gone there to rest on the long wooden benches inside the large, warm waiting-room.

Lavinia Durst walked three blocks with Sarah Thayer, chatting about the end of the war and what it would mean to certain people in town. She would have discussed seeing 'Mad Mary' at the gathering but Sarah didn't have time for more gossip. She turned to the right and Lavinia went left. The double-globed parlor lantern in the window was still glowing. She always left it on when she went out.

Lavinia pushed open the front door and went inside. She hadn't locked it when she left. Few people in Watseka locked their doors. She hung her long cloth coat in the closet built under the staircase and walked into the front parlor. There had been so much excitement tonight that she wasn't quite ready for bed. Maybe she would read some more of *Moods*, that new novel by Louisa May Alcott, and have a cup of tea.

Walking into the dark kitchen she groped for the match safe attached just inside the doorway and struck one to light the wall lamp. She raised the wick a little and the flame grew brighter, illuminating the room.

And illuminating the figure of Mary Roff sitting at her kitchen table.

Lavinia put her hands to her mouth but couldn't scream. She heard the noise inside her but couldn't force it from her throat.

'I was wondering how long it would take you to get back here, old woman.' Mary uttered the words but it wasn't Mary's voice.

Lavinia stood stock still.

'I thought I'd drop in for a cup of tea,' said the voice inside Mary. 'You have been wanting to meet me so I thought I'd save you the trouble.'

Lavinia's strength started to return. 'You get out of my house, Mary Roff,' she commanded. 'Get out before I have to call your father.'

Mary looked over her shoulder. 'I don't see nobody here named Mary,' she said. 'Don't try your tricks, old woman. I've been on to you for a long time.'

'Now, Mary Roff, you git! Do you hear me? You git out of here!'

'I'll git when I'm good and ready. I've come for a chat. You know why I'm here.' The voice was feminine and harsh and cracked with age. 'You have been causing lots of trouble, old lady, and I aim to find out why.'

Lavinia backed against the wall, wishing she were nearer the kitchen sink where she kept her knives. 'You aren't going to hurt me none, are you?' she asked.

'I should!' said the voice. 'I should churn you into a grease spot! You'd do the same to me if you had a chance. You've already gone too far fooling around with that poor girl.'

Lavinia was stalling for time to think. 'What girl?'

'That poor Roff child. The one you have been meanmouthing all over town. You think I don't know about it? I've heard you telling folks she should be put away. If anybody should be put away it's you!' Mary got up and walked toward Lavinia, who was shaking under her long skirts. 'You leave that girl alone! Do you hear me? She belongs to *me*! Not to you! Do harm to your own kin, but not to mine.'

'I don't know what you're talking about,' said Lavinia, her courage coming and going in waves. 'I think you're crazy and I want you to clear out of here.'

'Crazy? That's what you'd all like to believe. Everytime something happens they come running to Katrina Hogan, accusing me of being crazy or being a witch or even worse. Now you leave me alone and you leave my girl alone.'

'I think you are crazy,' said Lavinia. 'You're as crazy as a bedbug, Mary Roff, and I'm going to see that you get locked up good and proper. Locked up and the key thrown into the Iroquois River!'

Mary lunged at her but Lavinia had anticipated it and ducked. She twisted and managed to get to the sink. Mary came after her as Lavinia kicked a kitchen chair. It fell and Mary fell on top of it.

'You bitch!' she howled and as she started to rise Lavinia kicked her in the side. Mary groaned and fell back onto the floor. Lavinia kicked her again, but this time Mary grabbed the hem of her skirt and started pulling the woman down. Lavinia began screaming and resisting the force of Mary's grip. There was a ripping sound and the lower half of

Lavinia's skirt was torn off. The older woman stepped over Mary's body and ran for the front door. Suddenly propriety entered her mind. She couldn't go outside with her skirt missing!

Mary got up and came charging after her. Lavinia was up the stairs and into the first bedroom by the time Mary figured out where she had gone. The girl thundered up after her. Lavinia, known for not being anyone's fool, opened a door on the other side of the bedroom. A door that pulled inward and opened out onto a small summer porch with a high railing. She hid behind the door, and the moonlight caught Mary's attention as she came into the room. She dashed across the room and out onto the upper porch. The second she stood there, startled to find herself outside and alone, was all the time Lavinia needed to slam the door shut and to slide in the heavy wooden crossbar. The bar had been installed to keep the winter winds from rattling the door. It was thick solid, so that no matter how hard Mary pounded it wouldn't give in.

Lavinia changed her dress, combed her hair and went first to the sheriff. Then she went to Asa Roff. Then she went to Sarah Thayer's to sob out her story and ask for overnight protection.

The sheriff found Mary unconscious on the floor of the porch and he supervised while Asa, with two deputies, put Mary into a buggy and carried her home. Because Asa was who he was, the sheriff left Mary in his charge but warned him that the next time something like this occurred he would have to lock the girl up. He also warned Asa that the people of Watseka were not going to stand for much more of Mary's shenanigans. If Asa knew what was good for him he would see that the girl was committed to the asylum in Springfield as soon as possible.

Ann took to her bed right after they brought Mary home. She complained of dizzy spells and swelling in her hands and feet. Loozie and Minerva were in charge of the boys and ran the household, trying not to think of what had happened.

The Saturday following the attack on Lavinia a meeting was scheduled to discuss Mary's future with Asa. It wasn't just Lavinia and some of her cronies but the mayor, the sheriff and some important citizens of Watseka. The meeting had to be canceled, out of respect to Mr Lincoln. Some mad actor had shot the President the night before and he had died. Mr Lincoln's death was more important and more traumatic than Mary's commitment. Shops and businesses closed in mourning and Asa promised the sheriff he would keep a close watch on his daughter. He put a lock on the outside of her bedroom door and insisted on going into the room each time someone else did. Loozie brought the chamber pot when Mary asked for it and Asa turned his back as she used it. He sat across the room while she ate her meals. He didn't dare let her out of his sight. He didn't dare risk another scene like the one with Lavinia Durst.

Toward the end of May, after the month of official mourning had passed for President Lincoln, the group met in the Roff home. Asa listened to what each one had to say, neither agreeing nor disagreeing. Ann didn't attend the meeting. She said she didn't want to hear them talk about her daughter. Mary didn't know about the visitors. Thanks to Dr Pittwood she had been on sedation for almost the entire month. Asa himself personally put a few drops of the brackish liquid into a glass and stood there while Mary drank it twice a day. It didn't quite put her to sleep (too much would have put her to sleep forever, the doctor cautioned) and she could move about a bit and pick at her food, but she was far from being aware of everything that was going on.

The meeting didn't last as long as Asa had feared it would. It was actually rather cut-and-dried. (Lavinia Durst was not in attendance, for her nerves were still 'shattered' by the incident; yet her presence was everywhere in the room.) The sheriff had a court order demanding Mary Roff be committed to the Hospital for the Insane in Springfield. The commitment was to be carried out as soon as Asa could complete the 'necessary arrangements'.

'And if I refuse?' he asked them.

'Then I'll have no choice but to take the girl into custody and take her to Springfield myself,' said the sheriff.

'I thought you were my friend,' Asa replied.

'I am,' he said, 'but I'm also sheriff in this town and the protection of the people is what I get paid for.'

'If I take my daughter to a private hospital,' Asa asked, 'rather than the state hospital, would that be all right? I was thinking of that place in Peoria where she went one time. They have the water cure and an Electro-Chemical Bath.' He had seen how patients were treated in Springfield.

'What guarantee do we have that you won't bring Mary back to create her confusion all over again?' Sam Thayer asked. His wife Sarah sat close by, saying nothing, but planning on reporting to dear Lavinia every word that was said. 'That place didn't help her the first time, as I understand it.'

'I'll give you my word that she won't come back to Watseka until she is completely cured.' Asa tried to keep his voice level.

'As sheriff, I'd want some kind of guarantee from that Peoria place when she is cured. If the doctors there say she is ready and if the doctors here in Watseka say she is ready,' bargained the sheriff. 'That's the only way I'll agree to it.'

'You can consult all the doctors you wish,' Asa answered, feeling he was winning the battle now, 'and until all of them say she is cured, she will stay out of town.' He looked around the room. 'Agreed?'

They glanced at each other and one by one began to nod their heads.

'Fine.' Asa stood up. 'And now if you will all excuse me, I must inform my wife of this decision and get ready for my trip to Peoria.'

Sarah told Lavinia that it felt as if Asa had thrown them out of the house. That Asa's face was white with anger until he had finally gotten his own way. Of course, they both agreed, that awful girl would never come back to Watseka. There wasn't a doctor in town who would be foolish enough to allow her to roam the streets again. Having her spend the time in Peoria was just about as good as having her locked up in Springfield. Both cities were far enough away from Watseka to please everyone concerned.

Even though it had been a little over two years since Asa had seen the Drs Nevins and Kenyon, it seemed that they were wearing the same clothes and smiling the same smiles.

'If I understand you correctly, sir,' said Dr Nevins, 'your daughter has had more than one of her seizures since she was with us.' Asa nodded. He'd already told them of the suicide attempt in the woods and the attack on Lavinia Durst. He hadn't told them about the seance. Somehow he couldn't.

'Has she been eating?' asked Dr Kenyon.

'Now that she is under sedation, not a great deal,' Asa replied. 'She ate rather well before, however.'

'Have you been bleeding her?'

'No. There have been no leeches for a while.'

'And, as happened here,' Dr Nevins asked, 'I suppose there are no advance warnings to these seizures? No way to foretell their coming and to prepare for them?'

'I thought I'd already explained that point, Doctor.' Asa realized he had never liked this man. 'If there was a way to tell when these attacks were going to occur, then we would have taken the necessary precautions to see that they *didn't* occur.'

'Exactly,' the doctor said and looked at his partner. He rose and extended his hand. 'Mr Roff, Dr Kenyon and I must consult about this matter. There are things that must be evaluated before we agree to having your daughter as a patient again. We will write you of our decision.'

'Write me? I've come all the way from Watseka and I must have a decision now!' Asa was on his feet. What kind of a game were they playing with him? 'This matter is most urgent,' he said. 'I have to make the arrangements *now*.'

'And if we refuse to accept your daughter?' Dr Kenyon asked in a calm voice.

'Then I shall have to commit her to the asylum in Springfield,' said Asa. 'A decision must be made. Either here or Springfield.'

'Then it will have to be Springfield.' Dr Nevins was still smiling as he walked closer to the door, hoping Asa understood that the interview was over.

'But why?' Asa demanded.

'We are about to receive several adult males from the army,' Dr Nevins said. 'Soldiers who have sustained severe battle shock. This will hardly be the place for your young daughter.'

'But I am willing to pay!'

'The government pays better, sir, and for a longer period of time.'

'But ...' Asa had not expected this refusal. 'What can I

do?'

'Springfield,' said Dr Kenyon. 'It's not *that* bad.'

'It's terrible! I've been in there. I've seen how they treat their patients. They are all mad over there. My daughter is sick, not crazy!' Asa was shouting now.

'That's what you say, Mr Roff. Loved ones are always "sick". No one has a loved one who is "crazy".'

'Well . . .' Asa fought to put words and not emotions in his mouth. 'Well, where else can I go? If you can't take her, is there another place like yours? I don't want her in a crazy house.'

'There is no other place like ours,' said Dr Kenyon. 'We are unique in medical practice in this state.'

'Another state?' he searched eagerly.

They shook their heads.

'You must help my daughter!' Asa grasped Dr Nevins by the lapels of his jacket. 'Don't refuse her! She's only a child. Please!'

Dr Nevins removed Asa's hands and smoothed his jacket. 'From your actions, sir, it would appear that this madness runs in the family,' he said coldly.

'I'm sorry,' Asa muttered. 'I lost control for a moment.'

'Mr Roff, your daughter is mad. She is not sick. This was evident to us when she was here two years ago and everything you have told us indicates we were correct. Now she has grown progressively worse. This is not a madhouse. We operate a clinic for those who can be saved.'

'My daughter can be saved!' Asa shouted in his face.

'No, she can't,' the doctor replied. 'Only the madhouse. Only in Springfield.'

'I'll pay you double. Triple!'

'We do not want her here for a hundred times the regular fee. No, Mr Roff, take your daughter to Springfield. Now if you will excuse us, we have other duties that need our attention.' Both doctors walked quickly from the room, leaving Asa standing alone and unable to stop the terrible pressure that was building up behind his eyes.

Rather than stay at a hotel in Peoria he took the night train to Springfield, sitting up in the coach unable to sleep or eat. He wished he had a bottle with him; at least the whiskey would help him relax.

He didn't spend more than ten minutes in the director's office of the insane asylum. The Watseka court order had already been received and was on file. The director asked him to have Mary there no later than July 5. They would try and give her special consideration. Did he wish to see the institution? Well then, did he wish to see the ward where Mary would be kept? He understood. Then good-bye until the fifth.

Ann cried a great deal after Asa told her the results of his trip. Nervie and Loozie both went about their chores with red, swollen eyes. Ann and Asa decided not to tell the boys.

Asa called upon the sheriff and then on the mayor to tell them that Mary would be going to Springfield on the fifth. There was a train that left Watseka at 7.45 a.m. and arrived in the state capital by nightfall. Until that date Asa would make certain that Mary was guarded at all times and would not be permitted to leave the house. She would not have another chance to bother the good citizens of Watseka. Asa also would appreciate it if word got around that he didn't want any visitors until after Mary went away. Ann was not in a fit nervous condition to receive callers and he, quite frankly, wasn't interested in seeing anyone. There was a sigh of relief all over town. 'Mad Mary' was going away. 'Mad Mary' was going to be locked up and everyone could relax once more.

Asa decided not to tell Mary what was about to happen to her. He also took her off the sedative potion. He wanted her to return to her old self for these last two weeks. In a few days she was back at the family table, helping Ann with the housework and Loozie with the cooking. She started to make a set of napkins, large butterflies in the center and tiny roses in each corner. Each time Ann saw her working on them she would leave the room in tears. She knew Mary wouldn't be allowed to finish them, since no needles were permitted where she was going. The atmosphere in the house was heavy. Nervie cried and Loozie prayed. Asa abandoned his work and spent as much time as he could with Mary. At night he'd lie awake thinking about the dreaded moment when he would leave Mary at the asylum.

On July Fourth the family celebrated more loudly and

more noisily than any of them remembered. Asa bought firecrackers, pinwheels and sparklers. That night, just after supper, Asa informed Mary that they were going to take a trip. They would leave early in the morning and take the train to Springfield. He wanted her to spend the rest of the evening packing the clothes she wanted to take along for a few days or a couple of weeks, whichever he decided after they got there.

Mary looked at him. 'What are we going to do in Springfield?'

'Take a vacation,' he said. 'You always wanted to see the state capitol building and I have some business there. I thought you'd like to come with me.' How he hated himself for lying to her.

'Are you coming, Ma?' Ann shook her head. 'Nervie?'

'No, Mary. It'll just be you and me. You ain't ever had a vacation with just your Pa,' he smiled, wanting to reach out and hold her but not daring to display any emotion that would give himself away.

'It'll be good with you, Pa,' she said. 'And maybe on the way back we can go through Decatur and see Cousin Mary Lou. Do you think we could?'

'We might,' he said and walked quickly toward the front door. 'I think I'll get some air before bedtime,' he called back to her. 'Pack your bags now.' He hoped she didn't see his tears.

He was waiting for the sun when it shone through his window the next morning. Another sleepless night. Ann was asleep. She had taken to drinking a few drops of Mary's potion before going to bed.

He glanced at the clock on the wall. Not quite 5.30. Not quite time to get dressed and started on what would be the saddest journey of his life.

Suddenly he heard a piercing scream from Mary's room. It rent the warm damp air with its shrillness. Asa jumped out of bed and ran across the hall. Nervie had heard it too and was right behind him. He opened the door and looked in his daughter's bed.

Mary was lying with one arm hanging over the side of the bed. Her eyes were open.

She was dead.

PART TWO

Lurancy Vennum was not considered a 'pretty' girl. Her mother hoped that when she got older, with her large bones and long legs, she would be viewed as a 'handsome' woman. She was only thirteen now, with long arms, big hands and feet and features that didn't quite complement each other. Her nose was a little too wide at the end, her eyes a little too large and her mouth a little too big. She did have nice hair, though, of that her mother was glad. It was jet black and naturally wavy. Lurancy's hair was the only characteristic that seemed to come from the Smith side, her mother's side, of the family. The large features and the gawkiness came from the Vennums. They were large-boned, loud-mouthed farmers.

The Vennums were a mixture of German and Dutch, and many people in Watseka thought they were Pennsylvania Dutch just because Tom was born in Pennsylvania. Thomas Vennum, Lurancy's father, was born in Washington County, Pennsylvania, in that lower left corner of the state that borders West Virginia. Lurinda came from St Joseph County, Indiana, near South Bend. It had grown in those forty years since she'd been born. Her Pa was granted some land in the territory of Iowa and moved the whole family when she was not quite in her teens. The Vennums, unable to make a go of it in Pennsylvania, had also moved to Iowa. She met Thomas and they liked each other and they had married.

Thomas never had a cent but what he was able to dig up out of the soil and they moved around too much after their first son Henry was born. Henry was just a babe when they tried to make a go at farming in Milford Township in Illinois. Bertram, their second child, was born there but he was always sickly. Then Lurancy was born in 1864, one year before the war ended. That same year Tom decided to go back to Iowa and live with his in-laws for a while. After their second daughter, Laura, was born Tom got into a fight with his father-in-law over some empty feed bags and pulled his family up again all the way across the state of Illinois to some land a few miles outside of Watseka. Baby Laura died almost as soon as Lurinda got the furniture, such as it was, moved into the house. Then Tom moved again, to a better job (he thought) on a better farm on the other side of Watseka. That's where they lived when Bertie died.

Lurinda had had enough of farm life and insisted Tom move into town. They rented a small house on the outskirts of the city. Tom took a job as farmhand and Lurinda enrolled Henry and Lurancy in the Watseka school. They went three times a week during the winter but neither child did very well. Tom blamed it on the teachers, and Lurinda blamed it on their Vennum blood. Lurinda could read and write some. She joined the Methodist Church and tried to go every Sunday. She made a few friends but Tom was so belligerent that it was difficult for her to invite anyone for tea or whatever the other ladies did when they went visiting. Then too, she was ashamed of her home. It needed painting on the outside and fixing up on the inside. It needed nice furniture and not the battered old stuff she and Tom had hauled all around two states. She didn't expect to own nice parlor things like Lavinia Durst had or what she imagined was in the Roff mansion at the end of Fourth Street, but she did pine for a nice rug and for a fine china oil lamp to set in the window.

She had never seen the inside of the Roff house, of course. She wasn't the kind of person Ann Roff associated with. She had *seen* Mrs Roff several times on the street but didn't do any more than just glance at her out of the corner of her eyes. That woman was always so elegant. But then why not? Her husband had all that money and all that land and was the most important lawyer and judge in town. He had once been the postmaster, someone had told her, but gave that up when he started to travel. The Roffs and the Matzenbaughs were close, she knew. The Matzenbaughs had a fine home in town but were almost never there. They had land in Texas and Mr Roff went to see them on several occasions to help with legal matters. She knew all this from reading the *Watseka Republican* and talking with some of the other women in town. Lavinia Durst claimed she knew all about the Roffs and Lavinia would stop her whenever they met on Walnut Street to tell her the latest gossip. Lurinda wondered why Lavinia bothered with her at all, especially when she almost never had anything interesting to tell Lavinia in return. Finally she decided that Lavinia just liked to gossip and it didn't matter who she talked to. Once when she and Lavinia were standing in front of Hoober's store, Ann Roff came by with her daughter, Mrs Alter. She saw both women stiffen and turn their heads as they passed Lavinia. Lavinia had become flustered and couldn't get her tongue together for a second or two. When Lurinda said she thought Mrs Roff wore beautiful clothes, Lavinia said she didn't have anything to do with those people because they were 'impossible stuck-ups'. Another time when the church was getting ready for a money drive to help an orphanage near Chicago, Lurinda had suggested to the committee chairman that the Roffs should be asked to contribute. The lady replied that the Roffs didn't want anything to do with the Methodist Church. They had been members once, but that was several years ago. Something had happened and they had asked that their names be removed from the church roster. They didn't go to any church now but instead traveled to bigger cities and sat with people who were involved in Spiritualism. Lurinda had been shocked. Spiritualism! She had heard about people who sat in dark rooms and called on the dead but she had never actually known anybody who did it. To find that the wealthiest family in Watseka believed in such nonsense was almost too much to believe. She told Tom about it and he said he had heard it too and that he always did think that old man Roff had a screw loose somewhere. Someone said the Roffs had a daughter that went loony and killed herself. Not that he had ever talked to old man Roff of course. Asa Roff and farmhands hardly ever had a chance to meet. He'd seen him on the street, and once Asa had tipped his hat good morning to him, but he'd never really spoken to him.

In 1875 Lurinda's father died and the Iowa farm was divided five ways between her brothers and sisters. After paying the taxes and his funeral costs they each ended up with almost $600 apiece. Tom wanted her to buy a farm but she refused. She had had enough farming in the early days of their marriage. She liked living in town and wanted her two children to stay in school. When the money came, she paid $400 cash for the house they were renting. She used another $100 to paint it and to buy some decent furniture and some clothes for herself and the children. The last $100 she gave to Tom and he rented several acres of good farmland and started caring for his own crops instead of the crops of others. That had been two years ago and he actually made enough money from summer cabbages and winter wheat to show a profit both years. He was pleased with himself and she was pleased that no matter what happened she and her children would always have a place to live.

It wasn't a very elaborate house, not at all as fine and large as the Roff or the Matzenbaugh home. But it was better than renting and better than living on a farm. It was just inside the town limits on Sixth Street between Mulberry Street and Mechanics Avenue. Sixth was the last street, and vacant farmlands and plowed fields faced their front porch. The house was two stories and made of wood. Each room had two windows, not arched or anything fancy like that, but large enough to let the sunlight in. You came up the path from the street and onto the porch and then through a door that led straight into a large square room where Lurinda had a sofa and a dining-room table and some chairs. The coal-burning heating stove was against the far wall. It was the only source of warmth in the house except for the kitchen stove. Lurinda would have liked a fireplace. Maybe Tom would build one someday. Straight behind that room was the kitchen. It wasn't very big but there was room for a stove and a dry sink and some cupboards and a cutting board. Off that room was an even bigger room, 18 feet square, that was used for company. Right now all it was used for was storing old trunks and tied-up newspapers and old clothes that she intended to tear up someday and use to make hooked rugs. That room had four windows, two on the front and two on the side. She put fancy curtains at each window and then pulled the blinds behind them. That way people would think the room was furnished with fine things instead of being used for storage.

Right off the kitchen there was a small room where she kept potatoes, flour, onions, things like that, because there was not enough space in the kitchen. She had several crocks of pickles and sauerkraut working there. It also had fancy curtains and shades on its windows.

They used the upstairs for what it was intended: to sleep in. There were four bedrooms. She and Tom had the front bedroom directly over the closed room on the ground floor. Henry had the room at the rear and Lurancy had a small room in the corner that had two windows but a sloping ceiling. Lurinda had arranged the girl's bed so that it took most of the space under the slope. She often warned the child not to sit up suddenly in bed or else she'd bump her head. If Lurancy grew any taller she didn't know what she'd do. There was a square bedroom but it was piled with farm tools and junk Tom refused to throw away.

Rancy – as everyone called her – was a sickly child at times, so she needed a bedroom with the afternoon sun and the cool breezes that blew from the river.

Her poor health began in 1873 when she had the measles. She kept moaning and Lurinda kept running up the stairs with cold compresses for her head and camphor-soaked flannel for her chest. Doc Pittwood said she had a severe case, and if she had been an adult she might have died. She lay unconscious for two days before her fever broke. She'd mumbled and talked out aloud but it wasn't anything anyone could understand. 'Fever ravings,' Tom had called them and Lurinda had agreed.

After that she caught colds more often than other girls did and would complain of weakness in the stomach and in the legs. She started having her monthly cramps and bloody discharge when she was twelve and it frightened her as much as it did Lurinda. She had to tell Rancy about birth and babies and what the blood meant for a woman. Rancy became fascinated with the bloody rags she collected each month and showed them proudly to her mother.

On the night of July 4, 1877, Rancy came to sleep with her mother, complaining that there were people in her bedroom. When Lurinda took a lantern and showed the girl there was no one there, she still refused to believe it.

'Ma, there was somebody in there and they kept calling my name. "Rancy! Rancy!" I'm afraid.'

'Nonsense. There ain't nobody in here.'

'But I heard them. It sounded like a whole lot of people.'

'Young lady, I know you been eatin' something you shouldn't,' Lurinda scolded.

'Can I stay with you? Just tonight?'

'Well, your Pa won't be coming home, not after an afternoon of drinking with his friends at Ebert's barn. Come on.' She pulled down the coverlet and Rancy got into bed. After Lurinda blew out the light, Rancy said, 'Ma, I really did hear somebody call my name.'

'It was probably just God watching over you,' her mother replied. 'Now good night and get some sleep.'

On the next night, July 5, after everyone was settled down for the night and the lamps were out, Rancy started to yell. She ran into her parents' bedroom. 'Ma. They've come back.'

'Who?' Lurinda tried to make out the figure standing beside her.

'Those voices,' the girl said. 'The same ones as last night. They keep calling "Rancy, Rancy." Ma,' she started to cry, 'I'm afraid. Come and see.'

'Oh, Rancy! There ain't nobody there! It's just your imagination.'

'Come and see,' the girl pleaded. 'See if you can hear them too!'

Tom's voice rose from the darkness beside her. 'Go and see what the gawd-damned trouble is! No use waking up the whole house!'

Lurinda got out of bed and lit the candle on the table. She led the way down the short corridor to the girl's bedroom. Rancy followed close behind her. 'You see?' she said holding the candle high so it lit up most of the small room, 'there ain't a soul in here! I knew there wasn't anybody here!

Now you get back in that bed and let us all get some sleep!'

'Ma, I don't want to sleep in here alone!'

'Well, you're not sleeping in here with me and your Ma!' Tom shouted.

'Ma, stay in here with me.' The girl was trembling. 'Please.'

A shudder ran down Lurinda's spine. Maybe Rancy was coming down with something. Maybe she hadn't been giving the child the attention she needed. Rancy was her only daughter and she remembered how her own mother never seemed to have enough love to spread around. 'Tom? I'm going to sleep in here with Rancy.' They both laughed as they heard his snoring. Rancy, wrapped in her mother's arms, slept soundly that night.

Five nights had gone by and the voices hadn't returned.

On the afternoon of the sixth day something happened.

Lurancy had been working on the rags that were stored in the front parlor. She'd torn them into strips, braided several into five- or six-foot lengths and carefully sewn them together to form a circle.

Lurinda came in from the backyard carrying fresh curtains for the parlor. 'Rancy,' she said in passing, 'you had better commence getting supper. Your Pa and Henry will be home before you know it.'

Rancy put down her sewing and closed her eyes. 'Ma, I feel bad. Real bad,' she said in a low voice.

'You'll feel worse if your Pa gets home and supper ain't ready.'

'Ma, I feel bad.'

'Where?'

'Right here.' She put her hand over her left breast and started to get up from her chair. She rose about halfway, then screamed. Her eyes closed and she began breathing loudly through her nose. She fell on the floor, her head barely missing the edge of the sofa. She pulled her legs up to her chest and then violently pushed them back. She began foaming at the mouth, opened her eyes, showed only the whites to her mother and then screamed.

Lurinda dropped her curtains and rushed to her side. 'Rancy! What's happening?'

The girl flipped over onto her back, stretching her legs as

far as they would go and pointing her toes at the ceiling. Then she raised her arms straight into the air for a few seconds before they fell heavily to the floor beside her. After that she didn't move a muscle.

Doc Pittwood was away and Lurinda didn't want to call Doc Fowler. His solution to everything was leeches and she couldn't stand the sight of the horrid things. So she and Tom hovered over Rancy as she applied cold compresses and prayed.

Tom had carried Rancy up to her bedroom and remarked that she felt like a cord of wood, she was so stiff and unmoving. She was rigid for five hours, returning to her senses around eleven that night. When her mother asked her how she felt, she said 'Very strange.' Then she fell asleep. Lurinda sat up all night watching her.

The next morning Rancy said she felt fine and took her breakfast with the family. Lurinda kept watching her out of the corner of her eye, waiting for what, she wasn't sure. But she watched.

Suddenly Rancy slipped silently off her chair and fell on the floor.

Lurinda screamed and knelt beside her. 'Oh my God, Rancy! Not again! Please, dear Lord, not again!'

Rancy's arms and legs were twitching. Foam started to appear at the edges of her mouth and her eyes were closed.

'Oh my God!' Lurinda ran into the kitchen, returning with a wet cloth and a piece of ice she had taken from the ice chest.

Rancy's body quivered and then stretched to its fullest. Her arms and legs became rigid and heavy. Lurinda tried to put Rancy's hands on her stomach but she couldn't make them bend at the wrist or elbow.

'Ma...'

'Rancy! Rancy child! Can you hear me?'

'Ma...' her voice was only a whisper.

'Ma's here, Rancy. Ma is here.'

'Ma... how strange I feel.'

'Does it hurt? Tell me where it hurts.'

'It don't hurt.' She tried to shake her head but couldn't. 'I ain't hurting none. It's just strange...'

Lurinda pressed harder on the icy cloth. 'You just save

your energy, now. Don't try to talk till this goes away.'

'But don't you want to hear?'

'Hear? Hear what?'

'Where I am,' Rancy replied softly. 'What I'm seeing.' There was a note of wonder in her voice.

Lurinda smoothed her daughter's hair from her forehead. 'I know where you are. Here with me. Now you just relax and this will go away. Just like it did yesterday.' How she wished Tom or Henry were here.

'No, Ma,' Rancy said. 'I know I am with you but I'm also in another place. I'm seeing other things.'

'Now, darling. I asked you not to use your energy.'

'But Ma, it's so beautiful.' She smiled. It seemed her mouth was the only part of her body she could control. 'Grandpa is here, Ma. He's looking at me.'

'Grandpa Smith?' Lurinda asked.

'Yes and he is smiling and walking toward me.'

'Now, Lurancy, you know better than that. Your Grandpa Smith is dead and buried.'

'He ain't dead, Ma. He's here and he's smiling at me.' The smile on her face grew broader. 'He says to tell you hello.'

'Oh my God!' Lurinda pulled away from her daughter. The sickness had touched her brain.

'And he says he didn't care that you and the others sold the farm. He says the people who bought it have made it even better. He says he's glad you bought this house. It was a smart move.'

'Now, you stop that Lurancy!' Lurinda got up and walked halfway across the room. 'You stop that fooling around with your Ma! You know I don't like these things!'

'But Grandpa Smith is here, Ma. And he says there is nothing to be scared of. And Ma, look! There is little Laura and she's with Bertie! Ain't it nice to see Laura and Bertie again?'

'That is devil talk!' Lurinda screamed. 'Devil talk! Your sister and brother are dead!' She ran toward the upstairs door. 'I won't listen to this kind of talk. It ain't fair, Rancy.'

Lurinda broke into tears and dashed up the stairs, closing her bedroom door after her.

Lurancy stayed on the floor for another twenty minutes,

smiling and talking silently with her long-dead relatives.

When Lurinda heard Rancy moving around downstairs she came out of the bedroom and went into the kitchen. She splashed some cold water on her face and ran a comb through her long wavy hair. She didn't say anything to Rancy. Didn't even look at her. After another hour had gone by and Rancy had returned to her rug braiding, Lurinda walked through the room on her way out the front door to the market. 'You feeling all right, child?' she asked over her shoulder.

Lurancy didn't look up. When she had come to she'd been lying on the floor. She didn't remember falling and she didn't know how long she had been lying there but she knew that whatever had happened had upset her mother. It was best not to talk about it. 'Yes, Ma,' she said. 'I'm fine. You going to the store?' Lurinda nodded and hurried from the house.

She debated about telling Tom all the way to Culver's Grocery and back again. Tom would be furious with Rancy for playing a trick like that on her and probably would punish the child. Lurinda prided herself on being a strong woman but she couldn't abide anything to do with dead people. It was something that she was terrified of as long as she could remember. Lurancy knew that. Why did she suddenly start playing those games? Years ago, when she was just a girl back in Iowa Territory, old man Hinckle had died and kids said they saw his ghost walking around his barnyard. She was afraid of that place after that and wouldn't go near it, not even on a dare. When her mother died they laid her out in the parlor and friends came to pay their respects. Someone had asked Lurinda for a drink of water because they were feeling faint and she had taken the glass pitcher to the well. On her way back she saw her mother. Her mother was standing in the kitchen doorway looking at her. Lurinda screamed and dropped the pitcher. It broke into a dozen pieces and Aunt Nell insisted she go to bed and stay there. The doctor had said it was nerves and when she told him about her mother he said it was her imagination. The shock of the death had been too much for her. He gave her some pills and she slept. When she awoke the coffin was out of the house and in the ground.

Lurancy knew that. Why did she do what she did? She

wouldn't speak to Tom about it *this* time, but if Lurancy ever pulled anything like that again she would get a licking. That was all there was to it.

Ten days went by before it happened again. Lurinda and Rancy were in the garden in the back of the house picking snap beans for supper when the girl suddenly stood up, put her hands over her eyes and fell over into a row of onions that had been left growing for seed. Lurinda screamed and grabbed Rancy's hand to pull her to her feet, but she couldn't budge her.

'Rancy!' she yelled. 'You get off them onions! Your Pa will be furious!' But the girl just lay there, not moving a muscle. 'Rancy! Did you hear what I said?' Lurinda knelt down beside her. 'Are you having another of your fits or are you play-acting again?'

'Ma...'

'Oh dear Lord,' Lurinda said under her breath, 'don't start that again.'

'Ma... he's back.' She had a faint smile. 'Grandpa's back.'

'I won't stand for this, Lurancy Vennum!' she screamed. 'I won't stand for this!' She got to her feet, knocking over the basket of snap beans as she tried to get away from the girl. 'You cut that out! You hear? You cut that out right this very minute!' She took a few steps, blindly, almost falling over the tomato stakes. 'I'm going to tell your Pa on you, Lurancy. I'm going to tell your Pa!' She lifted her long skirts and ran out of the garden and in through the kitchen door.

Lurancy smiled. 'She don't want to talk to you, Grandpa,' she said, 'but I do. Don't pay her no mind. She's just nervous.' A ladybug lit on her hair, making a sudden red dot on a black background. 'Did you bring little Laura and Bertie this time?' The smile was complete now. 'Oh, there they are! How good you are to bring them again, Grandpa.'

Tom was in a bad mood when he came home. He had stopped at Ebert's barn for a glass of whiskey and heard that prices were lowering on field corn, and the crop wouldn't even be ready until the first frost. A man works all spring and summer and then some people in the city wearing ties and frock coats take it all away from him.

Lurinda met him in the front room. 'Tom, I want you to

speak to Rancy. She is becoming impossible.'

'What's the matter now?' He was in no mood for squabbles at the house. 'She ain't doing her chores?'

'No, it ain't that. It's something else.' Lurinda took a deep breath. 'She's been scaring me.'

He had started toward the back door and the outhouse and he stopped. 'What do you mean, scaring you?'

'She pretends she is seeing my Pa and Laura and Bertie!' Lurinda was almost in tears again, remembering it. 'She falls on the ground and acts silly and then scares me.'

'What do you want me to do about it?' he asked. 'You're her Ma. Do you want me to beat her?'

Lurinda shook her head; no, she didn't want that. 'You don't have to whip her, just give her a talking to. Maybe she'll listen to you.' She wiped her hands on her apron, even though they weren't wet. 'Spilled the snap beans. Broke off the tops of the onion plants.'

Tom stopped. The conversation was getting around to his world now, to the garden he had hoed and planted. 'She did what?'

She had to tell him about the onions; he'd see them, sooner or later. 'In her tomfoolery she fell down when we was in the garden and broke off the tops of those onions you're letting go to seed.'

'Goddamn it! Ain't I got enough to do at the farm? Do I have to do your job here as well?' Lurinda rubbed her hands on her apron. 'That kid is supposed to be your responsibility. Not mine!'

'I try to keep my eyes on her,' Lurinda defended herself, 'but I couldn't stop her from falling. She wasn't close enough for me to catch.'

'Where is she now?' Lurinda pointed upstairs. 'Rancy!' Tom shouted up the staircase. 'Rancy, you get down here this minute.' He glared at Lurinda and stormed out into the backyard to inspect the damage to his onions. He saw them, about a dozen tall hollow stems had been cracked off, crushed into the dirt. He swore and stormed back into the house, slamming the screen door.

Lurancy was waiting for him, standing in the center of the room, her hands behind her back and her eyes downcast. She didn't speak to her father. He didn't give her a chance.

'What in the hell are you doing breaking up my garden?' he shouted.

'Nothing, Pa,' she replied timidly.

'Nothing? You call breaking my plants nothing?'

'I'm sorry, Pa.' Her voice was still low.

'Sorry? A helluva lot of good being sorry does! Sorry ain't going to put those plants back together again!'

'I know.'

'Oh you know? Well why did you do it ... if you know so damned much?'

Before Rancy had a chance to reply, Lurinda put in: 'And about scaring me, Tom. Ask her why she did that?'

Tom glared at her. His onions were more important. 'Why are you scaring your Ma?'

Rancy looked at her mother and then back at her father. 'I didn't mean to scare her.'

'You did too! You pretended that you was having a fit and then you scared me with tales of seeing Grandpa Smith and Bertie and little Laura.' Lurinda rubbed her hands on her apron. 'You did all that deliberately and you know it.'

Rancy opened her eyes wider and looked at her mother. 'I said I saw Grandpa Smith?' She looked at her father. 'And Bertie and little Laura?' She tilted her head to one side as if that would help her remember. 'Did I say that, Ma?'

'You certainly did. Both times!'

'That I saw Grandpa Smith? And Bertie and Laura?' She closed her eyes and shook her head. 'I don't remember saying that, Ma. Are you sure?'

In a sudden movement Tom swung his open palm outward and hit Lurancy full in the side of her face. She staggered and fell, her eyes open in surprise. 'Don't you sass your Ma!' he shouted.

Her cheek stung and her jaw felt loose. 'But I didn't sass her.' Then the tears came. 'I am trying to tell you ... both of you ... I don't remember saying anything about Grandpa or Bertie or Laura. Honest I don't.'

Her mother stood over her, their long skirts brushing. She didn't like to see her Rancy punished, but when it was necessary it was for the child's own good. 'You pretended to be having a fit and then you told me you saw them!'

'I don't remember ...'

'And you don't remember breaking off the onions or anything?' Tom was still shouting.

'I don't Pa. I really don't,' she sobbed.

He reached down and dragged her to her feet. 'You don't remember or are you calling your Ma a liar?' He shook her, ready to slap her against the wall if necessary. 'Are you going to tell me the truth about this?' He shook her.

'I don't remember anything about Grandpa Smith,' she said through her tears. 'Ma, I really don't.'

Tom freed one hand and drew it back. She slumped, trying to avoid the blow that was coming. His wife reached out and caught his arm.

'Don't, Tom,' she said quietly. 'I think she's telling the truth. Rancy ain't one to lie to us.' She shuddered and stretched out her arms. Rancy fell into them crying. As she smoothed the girl's hair she looked at her husband with a worried frown. 'She's telling the truth, Tom. She really don't remember.'

He lowered his raised arm and put his hands into his pockets. His daughter was sobbing. His wife was looking at him in a way he had never seen before.

'Oh God, Tom,' she said in a whisper. 'Something's happened to our little girl. She don't remember. Tom? What's happening to our Rancy?'

Two weeks passed before Lurancy had another fainting spell. When she started to talk, Lurinda left the room and didn't go near her daughter until she came out under her own power. She could hear Rancy talking with someone. Asking questions and seemingly replying to questions being asked her, but Lurinda didn't try to hear the words. She busied herself so as not to hear what was happening.

She told Tom about it that night and he suggested they call Doc Pittwood. Lurinda said no, she didn't want it spread around town that Rancy was sick. Maybe sick in the head. 'Doc Pittwood will tell his wife and that's the same thing as putting it on the front page of the *Watseka Republican*.'

The week before school opened in September Rancy had another attack. It happened on a Sunday morning when Lurinda was in church and Tom was still in bed. Only her brother Henry was there and he was fascinated.

'What's Grandpa doing now?' he asked Rancy, who was

stretched out on the back lawn where she had fallen as she was collecting apples for a pie.

'He's got a long black hat on,' she said calmly, 'and he's laughing.'

'I know that hat!' Henry said. 'That's the one he and Uncle Sidney bought when they marched in the election parade for President Lincoln. Is it a stovepipe?'

'Yes. With a long feather in the band.'

'That's the one,' he laughed, 'he took a feather right out of a turkey's behind and stuck it in the hatband.'

'He wants to know if you believe him,' she asked suddenly.

'Believe him?' Henry asked. 'In what way?'

'That he is dead yet can still talk to me?'

'I guess I can. I heard a lot about this stuff from the Glazers over in Milford. They believe in spirits. They ain't dumb people, neither.' Henry was kind of sweet on Millicent Glazer, so anything her family did was fine. 'Millie don't like it too much. She says it scares her.' He paused, looking at his thirteen-year-old sister. 'But it don't scare you none, does it?'

'It don't scare me because there ain't nothing to be scared of.'

'Grandpa is dead. That sure scares Ma,' he said.

'That's because she can't see him. If she could see how fine he looks, she wouldn't be scared.'

'Yeah. She's probably thinking that he's a skeleton or a sheet or something.' Henry laughed.

'Did you ever hear of Blue Bell tooth powder?' she asked suddenly. 'That's all I see now, a box of tooth powder with the name Blue Bell on it.' Her eyes were closed and her legs were as stiff and immobile as her arms, but she felt relaxed. This time with Henry near she was relaxed. He seemed to understand and that made it easier somehow.

He shook his head. The name Blue Bell meant nothing to him.

'And Lois?' Rancy asked. 'She is big and fat and her fingernails are so red! I never seen anybody with fingernails that red. I wonder what she's done to them?'

'Don't know no Lois except Lois Deeming and her fingernails is natural as far as I can recollect.' Henry thought for another moment. 'Yeah, they are normal as yours and mine.'

Rancy was still seeing the fat lady. 'She says she is a cousin of Polly's.'

'Polly?'

'Polly.'

Again he shook his head. 'Only Polly I know is Mrs Glazer. Her name is Polly, but I never call her that.'

'The fat lady is nodding her head. It *is* Mrs Glazer she's talking about. She says to tell her everything is in order where she is and not to worry.'

'In order and not to worry,' Henry repeated it and laughed. 'Okay, I'll tell her.'

Rancy grew silent after that, then the stiffness left her body. She sat up on one elbow, the fallen leaves sticking to her dress and hair. She didn't remember where she had been but her first words were quick and pleading. 'Oh Henry, don't tell Pa and Ma! Please.'

That afternoon, after dinner, Henry rode over to see Millie. He came home just before midnight. Rancy was in her bedroom, working on some embroidery. Henry glanced at his parents' bedroom door to make sure it was closed, then he went into his sister's room, closing the door after him.

'I asked Mrs Glazer,' he said. 'She did have a cousin named Lois and the woman was big and fat. She lived in Baltimore and once she painted her fingernails bright red with some house paint. She did it after she read of some ladies in France painting their hands. It shocked the whole family.' He laughed. 'Mrs Glazer says she was scandalized but wished she could have painted her nails too.' He took a deep breath. 'And about the everything being in order, her cousin Lois couldn't stand a messy house. She was always picking up after people, washing plates before dinner was over and things like that. Mrs Glazer said when she was dying, Cousin Lois's husband let the house go to wrack and ruin and it looked like a pigsty when the family came to take away the body.' He smiled at Rancy. 'Mrs Glazer says you must have a powerful spirit working with you to show things so true. She says maybe, if Ma will let you, you would do this over to their place sometime.'

Rancy shook her head. 'I don't know if I want to or not.

Ma would never let me.' She sighed. Now that she was beginning to understand what was happening to her, she wasn't sure if she liked it or not. Henry got up to leave. 'What about Blue Bell tooth powder?' she asked. 'Did that make any sense?'

He sat back down on the edge of her bed. 'I almost forgot the best part,' he laughed quietly. 'Mrs Glazer said that her cousin Lois liked to smoke cigarette tobacco . . .'

'A woman smoking cigarettes!' Rancy was shocked.

'Yep,' he laughed, 'and she kept her tobacco in an empty box of Blue Bell tooth powder. Took it with her everyplace she traveled and nobody ever was the wiser.' Henry laughed out loud. 'Mrs Glazer said her cousin was a real hot pistol.'

'She must have been. She didn't *look* like that kind of a woman. I hope she don't come back no more.'

The new school building opened in September – a week late – but it opened, and Rancy was there every day. She still didn't like reading and writing any better than when she was in the old school but her seventh grade teacher asked them to do original compositions and Rancy liked that. It gave her a feeling of importance to be able to write 'I' and 'me' and 'my'.

'I want you to take your pens and ink out now, class,' Miss Blades said, 'and Charlene will hand out the paper. Today we will write about the animal kingdom. I want you to tell me your favorite animal and why, a true story, not made up. Maybe you like horses, maybe you have a pet dog or a pet cat or maybe you have a wild animal that you especially admire.'

The lined paper was passed from desk to desk. Rancy took a sheet and sat for a moment trying to think what to write about. They didn't have a dog or a cat; her Ma didn't want hair all over her furniture. The iceman had an old horse that would eat sugar out of her hand, but he wasn't very exciting. One time Henry had found a crow with a broken wing and had nursed it back to health but it flew away. Or the time the skunk met Aunt Nell face to face in the outhouse back on the farm in Iowa. That would be a good one. Her Pa always told it and everyone would laugh, except she didn't know if she would be permitted to use a word like 'outhouse' in a composition.

Some of the children had started writing while others gnawed on the ends of their pens and looked off into space searching for an idea. The girl across from her would be writing about her dumb old cat, Rancy was certain of that. The girl thought everything her cat did was special and she talked more about that cat than she did about her own brothers and sisters. Rancy peeked across the aisle. There it was, in large script at the top of the sheet: 'My Cat.'

Rancy went back to her own paper. She put her name and the date, September 21, 1877, and Miss Blades's name in the upper right-hand corner. She had decided on her theme. 'The Crow.' She wrote it at the top of the page in large letters, admired it, for a second, then bent over the paper and started to write.

Miss Blades was the first to notice it. Lurancy Vennum was writing with her eyes closed. She wrote rapidly, filling the lines and dipping her pen into the inkwell in short stabbing motions. Miss Blades walked slowly toward her, peering down at her work, reading the first sentences. 'Lurancy,' she said, 'this is to be a factual composition. Not from your imagination.'

Lurancy kept on writing, came to the end of the page and flipped the sheet over.

'Lurancy!' Miss Blades spoke louder. 'You are not doing what I told you to do!' She reached out and touched the girl on the shoulder. Rancy sat bolt upright; the pen fell onto the floor. She turned and stared into her teacher's face. Her eyes were still closed. Then she shuddered and let out one high-pitched scream as she slumped forward onto her desk, her eyes open now but still unseeing.

Miss Blades stepped back and the others in the room stopped writing and stared at Lurancy. Nobody said anything. The only sound was Lurancy's heavy breathing.

Miss Blades put her hand on the girl's shoulder. 'Lurancy,' she said softly, 'are you all right?' No answer. 'Lurancy, do you hear me?' Still no answer. 'Lurancy?'

'I think she's fainted,' said the girl who owned the cat.

'What the hell do you know?' the voice boomed out of Lurancy's throat. 'Stupid brat!'

Stunned, the girl sat for a second, realized she had been insulted in front of everyone and burst into tears.

'Now you stop that this instant!' Miss Blades said quickly, 'or I'll send you to the principal.'

'Go yourself!' the voice was old and ragged.

'Lurancy Vennum!' Miss Blades had never had a student speak this way to her. 'You go directly to the principal's office!'

'And you march directly into the fires of hell!' the voice inside Lurancy cracked as it laughed.

The children gasped as Miss Blades grabbed the girl by the hair. 'You sit up!' she shouted.

Lurancy rose up out of the seat. She turned and swung her fist at the teacher. Miss Blades screamed and ran toward the door. Lurancy ran after her, yelling something about having her hair pulled as the children screamed or sat in stunned astonishment.

'Now, Lurancy,' Miss Blades pleaded from the doorway, 'you behave yourself!' She must try and show the class she wasn't going to be bullied. 'You settle down and behave yourself. You hear?'

'No gawd-damned bitch pulls my hair!' the voice said under its breath. Lurancy's fingers, clawlike now, grabbed for the soft mountains of hair the teacher had piled on her head. As she grabbed and tore at the hair, Miss Blades screamed. Lurancy forced her almost to her knees, shouting at her and using words many of the children had only heard their fathers use when their fathers thought they were out of earshot.

The teacher fell to the floor and Lurancy was on top of her, pulling her hair and laughing. Some of the boys tried to drag the girl off the teacher. Some of the girls ran down the hall screaming and crying for help.

The janitor and the algebra teacher managed to hold Lurancy so that Miss Blades could get out from underneath. The science teacher led her back to her desk where she sat and sobbed. The two men hustled Lurancy down the hall, still kicking and screaming and shouting obscenities. The principal led the way, opened a storage room next to his office and helped them push her inside. Then they closed the door and locked it. Lurancy pounded against it, swearing and demanded to be freed.

Lurinda was washing clothes when they came for her,

three boys running and shouting for her to come quickly to the school because something had happened to Rancy. She didn't bother to change her clothes or even comb her hair but hurried back along the dusty paths with them. They didn't know what had happened and Mr Haley, the principal, had told them not to talk about it. Mrs Vennum would see when she got there.

Miss Blades was sitting in a chair by the principal's desk. She had composed herself by that time, had washed her face and redone her hair. The only sign of trouble was a long scratch on the right side of her face and her red, swollen eyes.

Lurinda sat in another chair, facing Mr Haley's desk. He refused to tell her what had happened until she was seated.

'Mrs Vennum,' he said slowly, 'your daughter is very ill.' Lurinda rose in the chair, but he motioned her back down. 'She is resting now in the infirmary room, but she gave us quite a turn.'

'I want to see her,' Lurinda got up again.

'She is resting now, Mrs Vennum. Please don't be disturbed. We have had quite enough disturbance here for one day.' He looked at Miss Blades, who was staring at a sheet of paper in her hands. He was a big man and he spoke softly. Lurinda was afraid of big men who didn't raise their voices.

'What do you mean my daughter is very ill?' she asked, knowing that Rancy must have had one of her spells. This one in public. Oh God. Please dear God! 'How is she ill?'

'She attacked Miss Blades in the classroom today.' He gave a deferential bow toward the silent woman in the other chair.

'Attacked?' Lurinda didn't think she heard correctly.

'Yes, *attacked*!' Miss Blades said suddenly. 'She pulled my hair and knocked me down and gave me this.' She pointed to the long red scratch. 'Your daughter is very ill.'

Lurinda was at a loss for words. 'But . . . I don't understand . . .'

'Neither do we, Mrs Vennum,' Mr Haley said. 'We are hoping you can clear the matter up for us.'

'She was fine when she left for school this morning.' That was all Lurinda could say about Rancy's health. 'She ate a good breakfast and was fine.'

'She was fine most of the morning,' put in Miss Blades. 'It came on her sudden like.'

'Came on her?' Lurinda asked, afraid to hear where the conversation would lead.

'Like she was possessed!' Miss Blades said.

'I'm sorry,' Lurinda said. '... I am truly sorry.'

Mr Haley turned his attention from the scratch to Lurinda. 'Has this ever happened before?'

'This?' Lurinda repeated. 'This what?'

'Attacking innocent people,' he said. 'Turning on them for no reason.'

Lurinda shook her head. Truthfully, she had never known Rancy to attack anyone. 'No. Never.'

'Do you speak German?' Miss Blades's question surprised her.

'German? No.' She shook her head. 'We don't know any German.'

'Isn't Vennum a German name?' Mr Haley asked.

'I really don't know. But we never spoke German.' She looked at them. 'Why?'

'This.' Miss Blades held out a paper.

Lurinda reached for it but the teacher pulled it back.

'This is a composition your daughter wrote in class today just before she ... she attacked me.'

'And it's got German in it?' Lurinda asked.

'It has,' said Mr Haley.

'But Rancy don't speak no German.'

'She wrote this paper!' Miss Blades waved it at her. 'There's German in it!'

Again, both of them stared at Lurinda. She felt uncomfortable but she didn't know what they were talking about or accusing her of. She shrugged her shoulders. 'What does the paper say?' she asked timidly.

'Miss Blades asked the children to write a composition...'

'A composition about animals,' Miss Blades took over. 'And everyone in the class knew it was to be about animals. It was to be a true narrative.' She looked squarely into Lurinda's face, trying to judge her silence. 'Your daughter wrote this paper' – she held it as if it were dipped in sewer water – 'and when I stopped her she attacked me.'

Lurinda looked at both of them and shrugged again. 'What . . . what does it say?' she asked.

'May I read it to Mrs Vennum?' Miss Blades asked. Mr Haley nodded. 'Well, she started out by putting her name and the date in the upper right-hand corner.'

'Isn't that where it was supposed to go?' asked Lurinda.

'Yes, it is. That's not the point.' She glared at Lurinda. 'The point is that she wrote "The Crow" and then . . .'

'The Crow?' said Lurinda. 'What crow?'

'I don't know *what* crow,' Miss Blades said sharply, 'the point is, it's not about a crow at all!'

'Oh,' was all Lurinda said. It would be better if she remained silent and let the teacher read the paper.

'The Crow,' Miss Blades turned on her precise reading voice. 'One day my brother Henry found a crow in the woods that had a broken wing. He brought it home and cared for it.'

'Oh, *that* crow,' Lurinda said.

'He put a piece of wood on the wing and tied it there. The bird tried to fly but the stick sick and tired of you people and your interference in my life. When will you leave me alone?' Miss Blades shoved the paper across at Lurinda. 'That's where the writing changes,' she said. 'Right after "stick" comes "sick" and "sick" looks completely different from your daughter's normal handwriting.'

Lurinda tried to examine the paper, but Miss Blades pulled it back. 'You won't let me live my own life and you come and meddle in it all the time. Then some words in German, and you'll know it when I do it to you. I have taken all your accusations that I, and some more words in German, the church can burn down for all, more German words, and the German word "priest" can German, German, German, which is what he deserves. Your cattle and children shall suffer mightily if your meddling does not cease. I will start to do some of the things you have falsely accused me of . . .' She looked at Lurinda. 'That's where she was when I touched her and she attacked me.'

'Has anything like this ever happened before?' Mr Haley asked. 'Anything at all similar?'

Lurinda wondered how much she should tell. The fallings

and the ghosts? Should these people know about these incidents?

'Have you had your daughter see a doctor?' Miss Blades asked.

'No,' Lurinda shook her head. 'Mr Vennum and I don't much like doctoring. He says sickness should stay in the family and not be gossiped all over town.'

'Gossiped?' Mr Haley was curious. 'Why should a sickness be gossiped. A doctor is a scientific man. There is no shame in being ill. The shame is not doing anything about an illness and permitting it to worsen. I have great faith in doctors, oh my yes. I wouldn't hesitate for an instant to call upon their services should the need arise.'

Miss Blades was looking at Lurinda, trying to read what was under that plain farm-woman face. 'Has your daughter been in need of a doctor, Mrs Vennum, and haven't you called upon one?'

Lurinda looked down at her hands. They were red from the harsh laundry soap and were nestled in the dirty apron that rested on her worn housedress. The two people looking at her were neatly dressed and well educated. They were respected members of the community. Especially Mr Haley. They weren't people she should lie to. These people should be told the truth. Maybe they could help 'Maybe you could help,' she heard herself saying out loud.

'Help?' Mr Haley's voice rose a little. 'We should be glad to help in any way we can.'

'Well,' Lurinda began, 'Mr Vennum and I have been worried about Rancy lately. She hasn't been herself. She has been acting poorly and doing things to scare me.'

'Scare you?' Miss Blades asked in a surprised tone.

'Yes. She falls down and pretends she sees ghosts and things and she *knows* that scares me. She does it on purpose, too. Mr Vennum has punished her once for it and I know he'll punish her again when he hears about what she's done here today. He'll really hit her hard!' She began to cry, her shoulders shaking. When she looked down at her hands, she couldn't see them through the tears. 'My Rancy is a good girl. She never did any of this before.' She looked at Miss Blades. 'I lost two babies and I don't want anything to happen to Rancy! She's my only daughter!' The tears came faster and Miss Blades rose quickly and put her arm around the woman.

When Lurinda had finished telling them in detail about Rancy's fits, her falling on the floor, her rigid limbs, her seeing dead people and talking with her dead grandfather, she asked if she could take Rancy home. There was no objection. Rancy was lying on the padded table in the infirmary room, staring at the ceiling. When she saw her mother come in she swung her legs over the side and sat up. Lurinda hugged her and Lurancy began to cry. Mr Haley and Miss Blades excused themselves from the room.

Lurinda asked, softly, 'Why did you do that to Miss Blades?'

'Ma,' she said through her tears, 'I didn't mean to do it. I don't *remember* doing it! Believe me, Ma. I don't remember doing anything at all!'

Lurinda patted her and hugged her closer. 'I believe you, child. I believe you.'

Lurancy wanted to wait until the halls were clear before they left the school. She couldn't face any of the other students. She knew it must be all over school by now. The number-one topic of conversation. As they hurried down the corridor toward the front door, Mr Haley appeared from his office.

'Mrs Vennum,' he said calmly, 'I think it would be better if Lurancy stayed at home until she feels better.'

Lurinda nodded. 'I will keep her home for the rest of the week.'

'No. Keep her there until we give you permission to enroll her again. And that,' he coughed politely, 'might not be for a long time.'

'But I'm all right now,' Lurancy spoke up. 'I don't want to miss school.'

'You keep her home until you hear from us, Mrs Vennum,' he said ignoring Lurancy completely. 'And I think you had better have her see a doctor. And you should see your minister.'

'My minister? You mean Reverend Baker?' Lurinda was puzzled. 'Why?'

'Your minister is a man of God. You may need God's solace before you are through. Good afternoon, Mrs Vennum. Good-bye, Lurancy.' He went back into his office and shut the door.

'Would you have just a little more tea, dear?' Lavinia poured from her silver pot with great authority. 'It will take some of the November chill from the air.'

Mrs Baker nodded and accepted another cookie at the same time. It was her first visit to Mrs Durst's home and it had turned into a society gathering (to be written up in the next issue of the *Iroquois County Times*) where Watseka and most of its distinguished citizens were discussed and praised. Praised if they were present, of course. Lavinia was not one to speak well of someone who was absent. This afternoon most of the prominent families were represented so there weren't too many people she could gossip about.

Mrs Baker had heard about Lavinia long before she had actually met her. When Mr Baker assumed his pastoral duties in Watseka the year before, Lavinia Durst was a Baptist. The Bakers were Methodists and Lavinia had been gossiping about the Reverend Russell (Mr Baker's unhappy predecessor) so much that the stories had penetrated as far as the church's central offices in Bloomington. It had to do with a fund-raising drive, the proceeds of which, gossip said, went into Mr Russell's pocket rather than the church coffers. Naturally an investigation had been made and the gossip was proved to be wrong. But the Reverend Russell wanted out after a year in Watseka and Mr Baker had been given the church. It was quite a promotion for Benjamin and they both knew it. He'd only been a Methodist minister for two years in the small town of Lexington, Illinois, before he was asked to assume the much larger congregation in Watseka. In a way Martha Baker felt a debt of gratitude to Lavinia Durst.

After the Bakers had been in town for nearly a year, Lavinia had a fight with the Baptist minister. She gossiped behind his back and he denounced her one Sunday from the pulpit. He didn't actually mention Lavinia by name, but everyone knew who he was referring to. Lavinia flounced out of the Baptist Church and soon decided to become a Methodist. She worked hard for the church.

The Reverend Baker used Lavinia and her friends to find out what was happening in town.

'I am impressed with Reverend Baker's acumen and knowledge,' said Lavinia to Martha Baker. 'Such a young man and such a great understanding of the world around him.'

'Thirty-six,' Martha replied.

'Oh, he doesn't look it,' put in one of the other women. 'I could have sworn he was much younger.'

Martha beamed. 'I suppose God is looking after my husband,' she said. 'Except for his war wounds he is in excellent health.'

There was a murmur of agreement.

'And he has done so much for the church!' a lady said.

'More than a lot have done,' added Lavinia. 'His day is completely filled with church matters or family counseling and charity works.'

Mrs Baker took another sip of tea. 'Some folks don't appreciate his counseling, however.'

'You mean like those Vennums over on Sixth Street?' Lavinia wondered when the conversation would get around to that family.

'Is it true that Tom Vennum ordered your husband off his property?' another lady asked.

'With a gun in his hand!' Martha said.

'Some people just don't want to be helped,' Lavinia said in her usual self-righteous manner. 'If Tom Vennum thinks he can keep a crazy girl loose in this town, he's got another think coming! You all know what happened to me that time when the Roff girl went mad?' She looked around and they all nodded and sympathised. 'Well, I ain't about to let it happen again.'

'Well, I heard,' one lady said, 'that she can't get out. That they keep her in the front room with the doors locked.'

'She could get out the windows,' another voice suggested.

'No,' said Lavinia, 'he nailed some boards across them. Haven't you seen that house now?'

'I wouldn't go near it!' a lady said.

'Poor Lurinda,' someone put in. 'She has had such a bad time of it.'

'That husband's no help.'

132

'Drinking almost every evening over at Ebert's barn!'

'Young Henry seems like a nice fellow.'

'I heard that Lurancy has been expelled from school.'

'Well, who is to be surprised about that? After what she did to poor Miss Blades.'

'It was Miss Blades who insisted on it,' another lady said. 'I happen to know that she told Mr Haley that she refused to teach there one more day if he allowed that crazy girl back in her classroom.'

'Well, who can blame her?'

'But do they feed her? This Vennum girl, I mean.' A lady asked, 'Do they let her come to the table? That could be dangerous.'

'Mr Baker says,' the minister's wife spoke up, 'that they pass the food in to her through a special hole in the door. I suppose Tom Vennum put it in. But they don't give her any knives or forks or anything like that.'

'And what about her . . . ' the voice faltered. 'You know . . . her necessities.'

'She passes the chamber pot out to Lurinda.'

'Poor Lurinda,' Lavinia said. 'Such a sweet soul but with so much sorrow.'

A lady in a maroon shawl and matching bonnet was curious. She lived in Decatur and was visiting her sister. 'You must excuse my ignorance,' she said, 'but is it necessary to keep that child locked up like some animal? After all, she is a human being.'

'My dear Mrs Fitzsimmons,' Lavinia said, 'the girl is hardly a human being.'

'What do you mean?'

'After that dreadful attack on Miss Blades she got worse. She set fire to the parlor sofa and the only thing that saved the house was the fact that Lurinda managed to haul the flaming thing outside. Then she took a butcher knife and threatened to kill her mother . . . and would have succeeded if she hadn't tripped over the rug and knocked herself unconscious.'

'And the horse,' someone spoke up. 'Tell her about the horse.'

'Well,' Lavinia sat back in her chair, pleased that her tea party was a success. 'Mr Palachek delivers ice here in town.

Palachek,' she repeated. 'From Hungary but a very nice old man. He had an old horse that pulled his wagon. That horse never went faster than it possibly could.'

'Sometimes you wondered whether your ice would be melted by the time that old nag got to your place,' someone said.

'Well, that old horse always ate sugar from children's hands. Lurancy Vennum was no exception. One day after she had done that terrible thing at school she was walking around the courthouse and she met Mr Palachek and his horse and wagon. Well,' she looked around to make sure that everyone was following her story, 'she walked over to that horse, just as she had done a thousand times before, and that horse took one look at her, raised up on his hind legs and started whinnying. Just as if he had seen a snake in front of him. Well, old Mr Palachek couldn't control him and he took off down the street faster than he'd ever gone before. Trouble was when he hit the railroad tracks he upset the ice wagon and Mr Palachek with it. The horse ran clear to the river dragging the wagon right behind it. When they found him, he was dead. His eyes were bulged from his head and his mouth was white with froth. And as if that wasn't enough, poor Mr Palachek broke his arm in the fall.' She finished her story. Most of them had heard it several times before but they liked to hear it again. 'And that crazy Vennum girl was the cause of it all,' she added as a final touch.

'But I don't understand,' Mrs Fitzsimmons said, 'what this girl did to frighten the horse.'

'Just her physical presence was enough!' someone said.

'But the horse knew the girl,' the visitor from Decatur was persistent. 'Maybe there *was* a snake.'

'There was no snake,' said Mrs Baker. 'He smelled evil. Horses and other animals can sense evil faster than we can.'

'I know they have faculties that we do not possess,' the Decatur lady said, 'but Mrs Baker, do you really think this little girl is *evil*? Evil is a very strong word. Does your husband think she is evil?'

'My husband has been trained in the ways of the Bible and theology. In his years in the ministry he has seen and experienced many things that we *ordinary* mortals never experience. He is *trained* to see both good and evil. He *listens* to what he hears. He knows evil and in this particular case he has been told this girl is evil.'

'Told?' Mrs Fitzsimmons raised one eyebrow. 'Who told him?'

'God did.' The lady from Decatur couldn't question the answer.

'That's why we know this Vennum girl is a menace to our city,' Lavinia said. 'The Reverend Baker has studied the case and is convinced she is evil and insane and should be locked away where she can't harm innocent people.'

Mrs Fitzsimmons looked at Mrs Baker over the rim of her teacup. 'Of course I would never presume to know more than a man of God and must respect his knowledge, but locking this child up in an insane asylum for the rest of her life because she attacked a teacher and frightened a horse seems unusually harsh punishment.'

'There are other factors, madam,' Mrs Baker replied in a voice that was beginning to take on an edge, 'other factors that most of the people are unaware of.'

'Such as?' Mrs Fitzsimmons asked.

'Such as conjuring up the souls of the poor dead and departed and making them lose their restful sleep in heaven,' Mrs Baker announced.

Lavinia sat bolt upright. 'I didn't know that!'

'What do you mean, *conjuring*?' Mrs Fitzsimmons asked.

'She falls into a deep sleep and then drags some departed spirit into her body to speak and cry and beg for forgiveness.'

'You have seen this?'

'Not personally. My husband, the Reverend Mr Baker, saw it. He was there once consoling poor Lurinda Vennum when the child went into one of her fits and before he could stop her she had pulled a soul from paradise and forced it to speak through her lips.'

'Who came through the child?' Mrs Fitzsimmons wouldn't give up.

'A demon!'

A chorus: 'A demon!'

'A demon who said his name was Stebbins and that he had been a sailor and had gone overboard off the China coast. He used language most foul and poor Mrs Vennum ran from the room in tears. Then Mr Baker made the sign of the cross over the child and the horrible voice was silenced. But, and I don't know whether I should tell this or not ...'

'But you will,' said the lady from Decatur.

'But after this demon left Lurancy, she began to bend over backward and kept bending until her head was touching the heel of her shoes. Can you believe it?'

Stunned silence.

'Mr Baker told me that he could not believe his eyes. She was just like a rag doll with no backbone at all. Just bent clean over until the back of her head was resting against the back of her shoes. He said he had never seen a thing like that in his entire life. He said it lasted about five minutes and then she straightened up as nice as you please and without even a by-your-leave went over to the sofa and fell fast asleep.'

'Well, I never!'

'Who ever heard such a thing?'

'Coming from anybody else it would sound impossible.'

'The Reverend is a brave man.'

'A man of God!'

'He's right about that girl, you know.'

'Of course he is.'

'She's dangerous.'

'To herself and to us.'

'She ought to be put away. Locked up someplace and the key thrown away.'

'Lavinia is going to draw up a petition if the family doesn't do anything on their own.'

'Are you, Lavinia? A petition?'

'I'm in the process of writing it now,' Lavinia answered. 'You can all sign it when the time comes. We'll give Tom Vennum a little while longer. Then if he doesn't do his duty, we'll do it for him. You'll sign it, of course?'

'A little more coffee, Dr Stevens?' Mrs Fitzsimmons raised the china pot.

'Oh my, no. I've had sufficient, thank you.' The doctor pushed his chair back from the dinner table and carefully wiped his mouth and brushed his beard with the napkin before placing it on his plate. 'That was a delicious meal. I want to thank you both for it. Nothing beats good home cooking. Hotel food is beginning to taste the same to me, no matter where I go.'

'How long have you been away this time?' Robert Fitzsimmons asked.

'It will be six weeks Tuesday next. My wife did manage to join me in Chicago for Christmas, however. Sometimes I wonder if the day won't come when I shall return to Janesville and my dear family won't remember me.' He laughed. It was a deep and low-pitched laugh, from that voice that had charmed thousands and supposedly cured hundreds.

Dr Edward Winchester Stevens was a man of some renown, not just in Decatur, where he had dined with the Fitzsimmonses, but all across the Union. He was a Spiritualist and a healer. He gave lectures, he used his famous 'magnetic passes' to cure various diseases and he was a specialist in spirit obsession. The advertisements for his public meetings claimed that he 'carried balm not only to wounded bodies but afflicted souls as well'. His name appeared in all the Spiritualist publications and he was often quoted or mentioned in articles that appeared about the new religion in the popular press.

He was a large man, six feet two inches tall, and broad across his chest and shoulders. He wore his beard long, covering his tie and most of his shirt front, as was the fashion before the war.

Dr Stevens was not a medical doctor in the sense that Drs Pittwood and Fowler were. He had become a self-ordained minister in the Spiritualist movement back in the fifties and had graduated from the Vitapathic School in Cincinnati in 1870. It was there that he perfected his magnetic healing passes and got the piece of paper that permitted him to be called 'Doctor'.

While his voice and his height and his beard were notable, almost everyone remembered his eyes. They were large and deeply set under jutting bushy brows, bright blue eyes that seemed to penetrate you as they looked at you, that seemed to demand the truth and seemed to know when it wasn't being told.

His wife and children lived at Janesville, Wisconsin, and

three daughters were spirit mediums. One, when she went into trance, received poetry from 'the other side'. The poems had been published but under a nom de plume, at her husband's request. At fifty-five years of age, Dr Stevens thought he had accomplished a great deal. He had no way of knowing that the postdinner conversation that very evening would change his life.

They moved into the parlor, where Robert Fitzsimmons handed him a cut crystal brandy glass and then filled it halfway from a cut crystal decanter. The Fitzsimmonses lived well in Decatur. She had inherited her father's dry goods store and he had managed it so well that the business had become what would later be called a department store. Another store was being planned for Bloomington and, if all went well, a third store would open next year in Springfield. The Fitzsimmonses were admired because they were young (both in their thirties), because they lived well and because they had money. But they were not admired for their religious convictions. Both believed in spirits and both were pillars of the Spiritualist Church in Decatur. They were the ones who had sponsored Dr Stevens's lecture, to be held the next night. He would remain there for another week, seeing private clients who needed his physical and spiritual powers.

'Have you ever been to Watseka, Doctor?' Robert asked.

'Watseka?' He shook his head. 'No, I don't believe so. Where is it?'

'Here in Illinois. Not too far from us, actually. Helen's married sister lives there.'

'Wat-see-ka,' the doctor rolled the name on his tongue. 'Strange name for a town, isn't it? Is there a church there?'

'Spiritualist church?' Helen asked.

'Yes.'

She laughed. 'Good heavens, no! They've got Baptists and Methodists and Catholics but they don't want us.'

The doctor sighed. He was all too familiar with that kind of thinking.

'The reason I asked you, Doctor,' Robert sipped from his brandy glass, 'is that when Helen was there before Thanksgiving she heard a story and we wondered if you had heard about it.'

'About a little girl who is possessed,' his wife added.

'Possessed? In Wat ... what did you say the name was?'

'Wat-see-ka.'

'Yes. Watseka. No, I haven't heard about any little girl.' He shook his head. 'What sort of possession do they say it is?'

'The Methodist minister and the town gossip mill say this little girl frightens horses, that she tried to kill her mother and that she goes into trance and demons speak through her. They have her locked in one room of the house and won't let her out even to do her private necessities.'

'Good heavens,' the doctor said. 'What kind of people are her parents?'

'From what I understand they are farmers, or at least he is. She is a nervous woman and since her daughter has been having these fits, as they call them, her health has gotten worse. She's a young woman, just turned forty, and her husband can't be too much older.'

'Any other children?'

'One. A boy. He seems to be all right. Not quite twenty, I understand. They aren't poor people. By that I mean they own their own home and manage to dress modestly and eat well. They aren't rich, but they aren't suffering either. I drove by the house and it's an average house, except for the wood that's nailed over the front parlor windows.'

'Over the windows?' the doctor's voice rose. 'What for?'

'To keep that poor child from escaping. The whole town thinks she's dangerous and needs to stay locked up. I hear her father mistreats her at times, too.'

'Mistreats?'

'Whips her when she begs to be let out and when she gets her fits he refuses to let her have any food.' Helen shuddered. 'They've reduced her to little more than an animal.'

'They are most probably ignorant people,' her husband said. 'They are afraid of what's happening and they can't explain it and it shames them.'

Dr Stevens pressed the rim of his glass against his lip. 'Maybe if I went there and saw the child I could drive out whatever it is that is holding her and restore her to health.'

Helen clapped her hands. 'Oh could you, Dr Stevens? I didn't want to ask you because I know how busy you are, but if you could do something for that girl! She's been on my mind ever since I heard about her. We would make sure you were financially rewarded, wouldn't we, Robert?'

He waved his hand at her. 'Let's not get involved in money talk right now. That can always come afterward. The important thing is that I go to this Watseka place and see the child for myself. I could be there in a week's time, after I finish with my clients here. What did you say her name was?'

'Vennum,' Helen said. 'Lurancy Vennum.'

He took out a small black notebook and a silver pencil. 'Let me write that down. Vennum. And you say the family are Methodists?'

'Well, they were,' she replied, 'until the girl's father took a shotgun to the Methodist minister and ordered him off his property. None of the family goes to church anymore.'

'Took a gun to him? Why?'

'Because the preacher said the girl was crazy and evil.'

'Too bad the gun didn't go off,' her husband said.

'Richard! I'm shocked at you!' she laughed.

'So that's two things the minister listens to,' Dr Stevens said in mock seriousness, 'God and guns.'

'And you'll need both when you get to Watseka,' Helen said. 'Just wait and see.'

Dr Stevens was not impressed when he got off the train in Watseka. He had been in many small towns and after a while they all began to look alike. The depot was large and very busy and by standing on the platform he could see the main street. He could read the sign 'First National Bank', with I. O. O. F. of the Odd Fellow's lodge rooms on the second floor. The Williams House, the hotel Helen had recommended, was just beyond it. He only had one valise (and it contained more books than clothes) so it was an easy walk down Walnut Street to the hotel. The snows of Christmas had melted and a January thaw had begun. The boardwalk on the business side of the street had been swept clean for pedestrians. Some snow still remained on the opposite side of the street, along the tracks, where it had been piled to allow the horses space to pull their wagons and buggies. There was a great deal of frozen horse manure mixed with the frozen snow. He read the signs as he passed them: Dr Roberts, Dentist; McCurdy's Harness Shop; Culver's Store, with lawyers Stearns & Amos on the second floor; Held Brothers, meats; Edinger's Boots and Shoes; office of the *Iroquois County Times*; J. G. Wagner's Dry Goods; Watseka Bank and finally the Williams House. Farther down he could have read, had he wanted to: Oren's drugstore; Kice's blacksmith shop; the Opera Hall; Weaver's picture gallery: 'You need not go to Chicago to get a fine photograph'; Burlew & Smith's wagons and the Famous Clothing House.

Miss Alice Williams had him sign the guest register and told him the times that meals were served. She gave him a key and pointed to the stairs that led to the second floor. There were two bathrooms, she said, one at each end of the hall. Hot water for morning shaving must be ordered the night before but, she laughed, with that beard she supposed the doctor wouldn't be wanting any.

The room was large with a window opening on the main street and a view clear across the tracks to the southern part of town. He hung his extra suit in the wardrobe closet and put his six clean shirts on a ledge beside it.

After he had combed his hair and brushed his beard he put on his greatcoat and his warm fur cap. He walked down to the lobby and asked Miss Williams if she knew where the Vennum family lived.

'They have a place over on Sixth, all right. Their house sits in the middle of some vacant lots between Mulberry and Mechanics. You've got to go down Fifth and then over one. Sixth don't run up into Walnut. You can't miss it, they've boarded up their parlor windows.' She looked at this imposing stranger. 'What do you want with *those* people?'

'I understand they have a daughter.'

'Who is mad as a hoot owl,' the lady said.

'I've come to see if I can help her.'

'Did Tom Vennum call you?'

'Nobody called me. I came on my own.'

'You'd better keep out of it. That girl will be locked up in another week and we can all breathe easier.'

'Locked up? In another week? Locked up where?' He was becoming concerned about the little time he had left.

'They are taking her away to a crazy house in Springfield. Next week. The papers came through yesterday and Mayor

Peters signed them. I know that for a fact because the mayor was here for lunch yesterday and told me so personally.' She centered the guest register on the counter and wiped away a nonexistent bit of dust from its cover. 'Good riddance, too. Watseka is too small to have crazy people loose in the streets.'

He nodded to her. 'Between Mulberry and Mechanics on Sixth, you said? Thank you very much. A good morning to you, madam.' He pulled his coat tighter and adjusted his cap. 'It is doubtful if I will be back in time for lunch. You did say supper was between six and seven?' She nodded. He walked out into the air.

He walked back down Walnut Street, in the direction he had come from the depot. At Fourth Street he looked across at the corner building. It was one of the few structures on that side of the street, with its rear entrance facing the tracks. A window on the second floor was opened to let in fresh air. Dr Stevens saw a white-haired man look at him, then close the window and move out of sight. He read the gold lettering on the window: Asa B. Roff, Attorney at Law.

He continued down Walnut to the next block, which was Fifth Street, and turned right, crossed the tracks, crossed Cherry and Locust Streets, and when he came to Mulberry he walked one block, turning right again on Sixth. It had been easy going until he turned on Sixth. Most of the walkways had been cleared of snow but Sixth had its own brand of desolation. There were no wooden walks, just a foot trail through ice and drifted snow.

He sensed the Vennum home before he saw it. There was a tingling down his spine and he shuddered under his warm greatcoat. The house sat in silence, back from the street, protected from the outside by two tall trees that, black and leafless, did nothing more than stand like ink drawings against the snow on the ground and the paint on the walls. And there were the slats, nailed in large X's across two front windows and two side windows. As he made his way slowly through the snow up the path to the low front porch he tried to see what was behind those windows, but the blinds were drawn.

The summer screen door was still hanging, and he had to open it to use the door knocker. It was a dainty bronze female hand, and it held a bronze ball. It was the only bit of ornamentation he could see. He knocked and waited. There was a large window a few feet from the door but it was draped in heavy ecru curtains. There were no slats nailed to its frame, however.

He was about to knock again when the door opened. A woman looked at him through the narrow space between the door and the frame. 'Yes?' she said.

'Mrs Vennum?'

'Yes.'

'My name is Dr E. Winchester Stevens and I have come to visit with you.' He removed his cap, but she didn't open the door any wider.

'To visit with me?' she asked. He could see her hand trembling on the door.

'To visit with you and Mr Vennum in hopes that I can be of some assistance to your daughter.'

'Who are you, did you say?' her voice rose slightly. 'A doctor?'

'Yes, ma'am, Dr E. W. Stevens.'

She slammed the door shut and he heard her call: 'Tom, come quick! There's a doctor here and he's come to take Rancy!'

There was a muffled shout, a masculine voice, and Dr Stevens waited to see if he would get a shotgun pointed at him.

Heavy footfalls across the inner room and then the door was yanked open. Tom Vennum stood there in an undershirt and trousers. From the way his face was shining, he had been in the midst of shaving. 'You get out of here!' he shouted. 'Ain't nobody supposed to come for Rancy till next week!'

'Now just a moment –'

'I don't have no moments! And neither do you!' He glared at Dr Stevens. 'You have no right –'

'Shut up!' Dr Stevens commanded.

'What?' Tom looked stunned.

'I said,' Dr Stevens repeated, 'shut up.'

No one had ever told Tom Vennum to shut up before. He stared at the stranger in the door as Lurinda began to whimper behind him.

'Now,' Dr Stevens took a deep breath. 'I'm sorry if I used that kind of language, but you wouldn't listen to any other.' Tom was getting the color back in his face. 'Now just be silent,' the doctor cautioned, 'I am speaking to you.'

Lurinda was crying softly now, fearing for the violent scene that she knew would take place. Nobody talked to her husband like that and got away with it.

'Good,' the doctor said in his deepest speaking voice, 'now perhaps you'll listen to me and to why I am here.' He had a way of charming audiences and of dealing with his critics. The doctor had a great deal of experience in getting what he wanted. Tom Vennum was no match for him.

'My name is Dr E. Winchester Stevens. I have not come, I repeat, sir, *not come*, to take your daughter away from you. I have come to try and help her, to cure her of her affliction so that she may return to normal health.'

'Nobody ever told me to shut up before,' Tom growled but didn't make any move toward the man in the greatcoat.

'More's the pity,' replied the doctor, 'perhaps if they had you wouldn't be in the situation you are in at the present.' He was sure of himself, now. The man was willing to listen. 'Your daughter is under severe pressure from outside influences, pressure that makes her appear as if she is not sane.'

Tom looked at him. 'Pressure? What kind of pressure?'

'I am a man of God,' the doctor said. 'My calling has been, for the past twenty years, to drive entities from the bodies of innocent victims. I believe your daughter is such a victim.'

'To drive *what*?' Tom asked.

'Entities.'

'What's that?'

'Entities are spirits that have no physical form. They can enter into physical bodies, as is the probable happening in your daughter's case, and they can make that human body do things that it would not otherwise do.'

'Spirits? Are you talking about spirits?'

'I am indeed, sir. I am talking about spirit entities that take over physical beings and perform dastardly deeds upon them.' At last, he thought, I am making myself understood to this rude farmer.

Tom was looking into his eyes now, looking hard and breathing hard. 'You get out of here,' he said in a steady voice. 'You get out of here with your spirits and your ghosts!' His voice got louder. 'My Rancy don't have no ghost inside her! She ain't working with the Devil! I don't care what you and the others say, she is a sick girl and she needs medical help. *Medical* help. She don't need no talk about evil spirits and damnation!'

Dr Stevens was taken back by this sudden twist in the conversation. 'My good man, I did not use the word "evil". I merely said that there are –'

'Used the word "spirits" and "ghosts" and all that stuff, that's what you used. I don't need you. I don't even know who you are. Now get out of here!' He walked out on the porch. Dr Stevens took a couple of steps backward.

'I assure you that I came in friendship and in God's service,' he said quickly.

'And I assure you, mister whoever you are, that if you don't get off my property I'll blow your head clean off your shoulders!'

'Just let me see the girl,' the doctor asked.

'You ain't seeing nobody! You're going to get the hell out of here!' He took a few steps forward. Dr Stevens found himself walking backward onto the steps of the porch.

'If you'd let me see the child, just for a few minutes, I could help her,' he pleaded.

'If you are not out of here in two seconds I'm going after my gun. And I'll blow your ass into the next county, mister. You can be sure of that!' He stood watching until Dr Stevens had moved down the street and out of sight.

Dr Stevens was muttering to himself. He was angry with the muleheadedness of Tom Vennum and angry that he had not been as convincing as he could have been. He blamed himself for talking about 'spirits' so early after their meeting. He should have taken another tack, talked about nervous disorders and young people's growing pains instead of entities and ghosts. The poor man was already frightened enough by what had happened to his daughter and still possessive enough about her to want to protect her right till the last minute.

He was quite accustomed to having people run the other

way when he spoke of spirits. Ignorance was a monumental obstacle to his work, he thought. Ignorance of how spirits truly functioned led to fearing them and once fear set in, it was difficult to change a person's convictions. And the good spirits suffered with the bad. Good spirits brought love and joy and messages that the dead were not suffering any longer, while bad spirits played games, lied and gave erroneous information. It was unfortunate the bad spirits did what they did, but that was the way God had set things up and if he, Dr E. W. Stevens, was to do any good he had to accept God's plan and work with it accordingly.

But he could not give up now. He had come to Watseka specifically to help that poor child. He would go to the highest official in town and get legal permission to examine the girl. It had to be done quickly, for there was only a week separating her from perpetual condemnation in the insane asylum.

He reached the hotel and walked briskly inside. Miss Williams was behind the desk, writing in a large account book. 'Madam,' he addressed her, 'can you tell me where the office of the mayor is?'

'The mayor? You mean Colonel Peters? He isn't in his office today. He only goes there once a week and then only if it's necessary. He takes care of most of his business at the bookstore,' she said, nodding in a direction to her right.

'The bookstore? He works in a bookstore?'

'He *owns* a bookstore,' she replied, 'and has people working for him. He's a fine man, the colonel.' She felt as if she had to add this.

'His establishment is nearby?'

'Go out the door, turn right and go past the Opera Hall on the corner of Third and Walnut, and halfway down the block you'll see his bookstore. If he's not up front, he'll be in the back with a book and a cigar and a cup of coffee.' She laughed. 'He makes sure he reads just about every book he sells. You order a new book and sometimes when you get it, the pages has already been cut.'

He thanked her, bowed slightly and started toward the door.

'Will you be here for supper?' she called.

'I assume so, yes,' he answered, tugged his cap tighter on his head and walked back outside.

The colonel was standing, propped against a far wall, reading. Dr Stevens walked over to him. 'Are you Colonel Peters, the mayor of Watseka?' he asked.

'I am, sir. Have you read this book?' He held it out 'The True Story of the Battle of Little Big Horn,' he read aloud. 'Fascinating stuff, this. Tells what poor Custer really went through and how that scoundrel Sitting Bull took advantage of the entire situation. Things in here that have never been in print before, including General Sherman's personal opinions of the incident. I knew Sherman, you know. Served with him in the Carolinas in sixty-four. Marched with him to the sea. Burnt the bejesus out of those Rebels.'

'I am always honored to meet a veteran of our glorious Union,' Dr Stevens said. 'I myself did not actively participate because of my work with religious groups and orphanages. Brave men like yourself saved the homeland from breaking into fragments. For that you have my eternal gratitude. By the way, I am Dr Stevens.'

Colonel Peters shook the older man's hand. This stranger, at least twenty years older than he was, had a deep voice and a serene manner. Obviously the colonel's interest in the military and in great battles did not hold the same interest for the doctor. 'A pleasure and an honor to know you, sir.' The colonel shook hands with Dr Stevens again.

'Thank you, Colonel. May I take off my coat? It's quite warm in here. Thank you. May we sit down, I have a matter in which I need your assistance, it being quite delicate.'

'Delicate?' The colonel led him into the back room where there was a desk and a sofa and piles of books. 'A cup of coffee, sir? I always keep a pot going in the wintertime.'

'Thank you. Just plain, no milk or sugar. Colonel Peters, sir, I would like you to know from the very beginning that I am a minister.' He paused, looking at the younger man who was filling two large blue coffee mugs. 'A *Spiritualist* minister.'

'You did say no milk, didn't you?'

Dr Stevens relaxed a little more. 'Does the fact that I am a Spiritualist surprise you, sir? Or bother you?'

'Bother me?' the mayor replied. 'Why should it bother

me? It is your life and your calling. If it doesn't bother you, why should it bother *me*?' He handed one of the steaming mugs to the doctor. 'I was born in Germany, sir, and came to this country with my parents and brothers and sisters when I was a year old. We settled in New Orleans, in the state of Louisiana.'

'A charming city,' the doctor said.

'No. Not for us. When I was a year old the fever took my mother and my sisters and all my brothers save one. When I was ten my father died. My brother was placed in an orphanage and I was apprenticed to a tailor who treated me cruelly. I escaped wearing only the rags on my back and with a fifty-cent coin that I had been entrusted to market with in the morning.'

'You poor fellow,' was all the doctor could say.

'Then I met a man who took me in and cared for me like a son. He died after a year, leaving me not only on my own but having to care for *his* aged mother. Who is still with me, by the way, into her eighties, and shall always be with me as long as she shall live.'

'Most commendable.' The coffee was too hot to drink.

'I taught myself to read and write, then went on to become a schoolteacher in Ohio, and when the war broke out in sixty-one I enlisted in the Ohio Infantry. I saw battle in Virginia, saw the Rebel general Garnet get his just desserts, became a sergeant, became a lieutenant and was wounded so severely at Stone River, Tennessee, that my comrades deserted me for dead. I managed to rejoin my unit after three days of crawling behind them.'

'Crawling?'

'My legs were injured, sir. I couldn't walk. But I recovered and was with Sherman as he marched through Georgia, was again wounded in the legs, this time by shrapnel while I was charging a Rebel battery at Buzzard Roost Mountain and left lying on that field for two days. A few more battles and a few more wounds and I was made a captain and then a major. After the hostilities were over, I was given the honor of becoming a colonel.'

The doctor was looking at him, puzzled. 'Why are you telling me all this, sir? Granted it is interesting, but what does it have to do with my being a Spiritualist minister?'

'Everything! My life has shown me that a man can do anything he chooses to do if he has the proper guidance. I did it. I overcame being an orphan. I overcame being wounded. I overcame moving to a new town like Watseka where I knew no one, and after buying the local newspaper I was elected mayor. I've been elected mayor twice! And I'm only thirty-four years old.'

'But I still don't see...'

'The point is, I overcame all those obstacles because I knew I had someone there who was helping me.' He sat back. 'Do you understand?'

'Someone?' said the doctor. 'You mean a guide?'

'A spirit guide. I know she was with me all the way. I know she helped me over impossible barriers. I know she saved my life on the battlefield. I know she is with me whenever I need her. I don't even have to call on her. She is there, ready to help me.'

'She?'

'My mother, sir. My mother who died when I was a baby. She is not dead. Her *body* may have died but *she* is not dead.'

'I know exactly what you are saying,' Dr Stevens said. 'Exactly. I thank the spirits that they have sent me to you. They seldom fail.'

'They never fail, sir. Never,' the mayor said solemnly.

'But,' said Dr Stevens, 'I am curious. How is it that a man with your beliefs became mayor of a town like Watseka? Surely you are in the minority. A dangerous position, I don't need to remind you, for a politician.'

'Ah, sir, there are very few people in this city who know of my Spiritualist beliefs. I learned long ago not to flaunt them in public. Certain things should remain within a man's heart and not be paraded for everyone on the curbstones to witness.'

The mayor-bookshop-owner-colonel put down his cup and opened a box of cigars. He offered one to Dr Stevens, who declined, then he selected one for himself, sniffed at it, rolled it between his fingers and bit off one end. 'But we have one point of divergence, I'm afraid.'

'What's that?'

'I don't believe that Spiritualism should ever have become a religion. I believe it should have remained in the public as a manifestation for scientific inquiry and not made into a church where it became immediately antagonistic to all other church groups. I know,' and he made a slight bow of his head, 'that you are a minister in that religion and that I should not voice an opinion contrary to your church. However, it is my opinion and I usually say what I think.' He smiled. 'Sometimes it has gotten me into hot water, but at least I've been honest with myself.'

Dr Stevens was not surprised at his point of view. He had often wondered himself if the movement hadn't made a drastic mistake by becoming a religious creed. 'I admire a man who states his opinions,' he said. 'I myself think I would have preferred that our beliefs were open to all, and not inside a church with its dogma and rituals. But it was the only way that we who believed in the same thing, in the power of spirits and the survival of bodily death, could unite to become strong enough to withstand the scorn of the rest of the world. In unity there is strength.' He paused. 'But you are a member of a church, sir? Of course.'

'Oh yes, I go to the Lutheran church in the next town sometimes and I often visit other churches on Sunday morning in my capacity as mayor. The citizenry expect their mayor to be religious ... but it must be *their* religion. Even that scalliwag Hayes has taken to going to church regularly since he has moved to Washington.' He laughed, 'God moves in strange ways.'

'The fact that you are a believer in what I profess is a direct sign to me that I have come to the right man.' It was the doctor's turn to bow slightly toward the colonel.

'Why don't you tell me how I can be of help to you here in Watseka, sir?'

'I have come to your city to try and help a poor child named Vennum. Lurancy Vennum.'

'The mad girl? Yes I know about her. Tragic case, tragic.'

'I think that I can free her from the entities that possess her. At least I am willing to try.' The coffee was cooler now and he took a sip, watching his new friend over the rim of the cup.

'From the entities?' The mayor considered the word for

a second or two. 'The entities. You know, I never gave *that* supposition a thought.'

'That the poor child was controlled by outside forces?'

'Exactly. I only took her violent acts into consideration and never the fact that she might be doing them under spirit control.' He got up and went for another cup of coffee. 'I really am quite surprised at myself,' he said. 'I should have considered every possibility rather than listening to what was said by others.'

'I think if I can see the girl, just once, I can help her. At least I'll know if my idea is the correct one.' The doctor was watching the troubled face of his companion. 'I have less than a week, I understand.'

'Yes.' The colonel was pacing the room, coffee mug in one hand, cigar in another. 'Yes. I signed the papers and gave Tom Vennum one week to deliver the child to the authorities.' He turned toward the doctor. 'You know, I'm really surprised at myself for not considering her case in a special light. That bothers me.'

'But what could you have done, sir? Imagine the repercussions if you, the mayor, had suggested the child was possessed?' Dr Stevens laughed. 'You *and* she would have been carted off to the Springfield asylum.'

'Yes, I suppose you're right,' he was still pacing, 'but there *might* have been another way, if I had used my head.'

'Everything isn't lost,' the doctor assured him, 'not if you help me now.'

'What can I do? Really, what can I do?' He sat down, facing the doctor. 'Tell me how I can do it and still keep the respect of the citizens and I'll do it in a shot.'

'Get me in to see the child. That's all I ask.'

'It won't be that easy. Tom Vennum doesn't want anyone to see her. He keeps a loaded shotgun in the front parlor.'

'Have you ever seen her?' the doctor asked.

'Not since he locked her up.'

'So you have not personally investigated the claims of others?'

'No. I am ashamed to tell you, no.'

'You can approach her father telling him that you want further proof that his daughter should be committed. That as mayor you have the obligation to double-check the statements made by others before she is to be shipped out like an animal to slaughter.'

The mayor thought for a few seconds. 'Yes, I suppose I could. I could go to Tom and tell him that I needed verification, *new* verification, and then I could say that I had asked you to give one last try to save the child.' He stopped. 'You *do* have experience in this matter, haven't you? I mean we have talked, but you haven't given me any proof that you can really help this girl.'

'I admire your bluntness and appreciate your desire for proof,' said Dr Stevens, reaching into his suit pocket. 'Here is an article written about my work in this field. Please take it and study it, and you'll know who I am, where I am coming from and what I can do.'

'Ah, the *Religio-Philosophical Journal*. Very good. I am a subscriber to it myself. Four pages on you. Very good, sir.' He smiled broadly. 'I'm most impressed. It is an honor to have you in my humble shop.'

'Please keep it and read it,' said the doctor, 'and then try and get me in to see the Vennum girl. Time is of the essence.'

'Where are you staying?'

'At the Williams House. Second floor.'

'Good.' The doctor stood up. 'I'll see what I can do this very afternoon,' the colonel promised.

The doctor returned to the hotel, added some words to his wife Olive (he wrote a few lines every day and then mailed it on Saturday morning), ate a full meal in the dining-room (the baked chicken was excellent but the biscuits were a little salty) and went out for a walk before going to bed. When he returned the hotel clerk, a young man with one eye (the other had been shot out at Vicksburg), handed him a note.

'Mayor Peters was in here looking for you, sir. He left you this.'

Dr Stevens opened it, reading to himself: 'Your good forces are still on the winning side. Tom Vennum agreed more easily than I expected. I'll be by near four tomorrow afternoon. Mrs Vennum wants the morning to clean the house and prepare her daughter. From the noises I heard coming from the locked room, you had better prepare yourself.'

The doctor read from the New Testament until he fell asleep, awakening from a troubled dream only long enough to blow out the sputtering oil lamp.

At 3.45 the next afternoon Dr Stevens was waiting in the downstairs lobby. He had passed the morning and much of the early afternoon resting, reading his spiritual manuals and considering other cases he had worked on. He wanted to be primed – both mentally and physically – for the difficult task he had taken on. It wasn't just his reputation that was at stake, but the life of a young and, quite probably, innocent girl.

Colonel Peters stormed into the hotel and the doctor rose to greet him. They shook hands. 'The buggy is outside,' the colonel said. 'I have a friend with me. He may be of help.'

There was a white-haired man sitting in the buggy, bundled up in a greatcoat of dark cloth with a dark fur collar. His face was lined and thin. The doctor imagined he had been a large and handsome man in his youth. Now he looked every year of his age, which was almost sixty. The doctor was sure they had met before.

Colonel Peters did the introductions. 'Dr E. Winchester Stevens, I'd like you to meet a good friend of mine, attorney Asa B. Roff.'

'Of course,' said the doctor, 'I saw you yesterday afternoon from the street. You have the office in the building at the corner.'

Asa smiled. 'Yes. I'll admit I was watching you. It's not that often that a well-dressed visitor walks the streets of Watseka.'

'I suppose you know everyone in town,' the doctor laughed, 'and make it your business to know those who wander in for a spell.'

'I grew up in this town, almost,' he said.

'What he really means,' the colonel remarked as he got onto the front seat and took the reins of the horse, 'is that the town grew up around him. Mr Roff here is one of the founders of the city of Watseka. He owned the land and had the foresight to bring in the railroad. Without him, this place would still be a cow pasture and a playpen for woodchucks.'

'Are you a friend of the Vennum family?' the doctor asked. 'I can use all the assistance I can get.'

'No,' Asa replied. 'I'm afraid I don't know them at all. Oh, I've tipped my hat to Tom Vennum every now and then when we'd cross in the street, but I don't know the family at all. The attorneys and the farmers don't mix that easily. My children don't know the girl, either. They are all much older than she is. My youngest, Charles, is sixteen, which of course is miles away from thirteen if you recall your youth.'

'Oh, I do indeed. When I was fifteen I thought people who were twenty were old and when I was twenty I thought people who were forty were museum pieces.' He laughed. 'Now when I hear of a man my age passing on to the other side, I'll say "Poor chap, he was so young to go!"'

The three men laughed and Dr Stevens pulled his cap down around his ears. The sun was about two feet from the horizon and there was still light in the streets but a cold wind had come up, colder than yesterday, and was starting to penetrate his warm clothing.

'We three have one thing in common, Doctor,' Colonel Peters said. 'All of us believe in the power of spirits.'

'You too, sir?' he looked at Asa.

The older man nodded his head. 'I am a Spiritualist, Dr Stevens. I believe in the power of the spirits and the validity of a life hereafter. I also believe that spirits can make contact with us humans on earth. I didn't always believe so, but many things in my life have shown me this to be true.' He smiled. 'I have also read in the various spiritual publications of your work and of your successes in this field. When Matthew told me you were in town and were going to see the Vennum girl, I asked to go along. I'd like to see you in action.'

'I'm most flattered,' the doctor said. 'When I first saw you I was a little worried that I'd have to convince a doubting lawyer at the same time I was convincing a doubting father. I'm glad we understand the same things. It always makes these sessions so much easier.'

'Tom Vennum came to see me yesterday, Doctor, and I told him –' the colonel started to say.

'Came to see you? I'm flabbergasted,' Dr Stevens said.

'Well, he didn't come on a social call. I sent one of the sheriff's deputies around with a note and told him that I – as mayor – wanted to see him. I wanted him to come with his hat in his hand rather than his gun.'

'Did you explain the situation?'

'I did. I told him that I had been wrong in not investigating the claims of the citizens about his daughter and I apologized for it. That took him off his guard. He never expected the mayor to apologize to him. Anyway, I told him that as mayor I had the power to extend the time limit on delivering his daughter to the authorities and that as mayor I had the right to try any type of cure that might help one of my citizens. In this case, his daughter. I told him about you and he said you had been to see him and that he'd chased you off his property.'

'He did indeed,' remembered the doctor.

'He said he was sorry about that, so expect him to apologize when he sees you. Anyway, he has agreed to let you see the girl, but only if others are present.'

'Others?'

'He means himself and his wife. They want to keep an eye on the girl at all times.'

'I can understand that,' Dr Stevens commented. 'There is no problem. I would rather have them there, as a matter of fact. It will give the girl more confidence and more assurance if she can see her parents.'

'I also told Tom Vennum that I was bringing Asa Roff with me. That impressed him. Asa is a well-known attorney and respected for his honesty. I told him it would be to his advantage to have a member of the legal profession there to verify the proceedings. Tom is an ignorant man, but he does respect authority.'

'I'm impressed at how much you were able to accomplish,' said the doctor and he meant it.

The horse turned down Fifth Street, bounced the buggy across the railroad tracks and continued down to Mulberry. Dr Stevens had another chance to admire some of the large new homes that were being built along the route. There must be money in farming, he thought, or else money in transporting farm products. 'Tell me more about your conversion to Spiritualism,' he asked Asa.

'Well, it happened several years ago. There was an incident in my family that caused a great deal of emotional conflict and problems. No one seemed to have the answer, yet everyone had an opinion. I spent a great deal of time and money trying to solve the problem and it almost made a nervous wreck out of my wife, yet when it was all over we were no wiser than when it had begun. I searched the various religions for the solution and finally turned to Spiritualism. The answers were there, or,' he added, 'at least some of the answers were there. My wife and I haven't found them all as yet but we are searching.'

'And Spiritualism comforted you?' the doctor asked.

'It did indeed.'

'I should like to hear of the incident, sometime,' the doctor said. 'Possibly before I leave Watseka we can meet again.'

'I would like that,' Asa answered, 'and so would my wife, I'm sure.'

Colonel Peters gave a light tug on the reins and the horse turned right, into Sixth Street. It was getting colder now; they could see the horse's breath coming out in white short spurts. The doctor checked to see that the top button on his greatcoat was fastened. The temperature had either fallen or else simply being on that street made him colder. As both men stared straight ahead at the darkened Vennum house, he shut his eyes and said a silent prayer. It was a prayer asking for knowledge, success and protection. Especially protection.

Tom Vennum opened the door for them as they stepped onto the porch. The colonel was the first to enter, followed by the doctor and Asa Roff. They all saw her at the same time.

She was sitting against the far wall of the front room, next to the coal heating stove. She perched on an old kitchen chair, her feet pulled up under her and her arms clasped around her legs. Her long pale green dress hid the fact that she had refused to put on shoes or stockings. Her hair was hanging down her face, despite Lurinda's attempts to make it pretty for the visitors. She had lost a great deal of weight and if the colonel thought he would have trouble remembering her, he would never have recognized her in that condition had he met her on the street. Her eyes were like two live coals competing in intensity and fire with the coals in the stove.

The three visitors paused for a moment, unsure if they should go into the room or not. Tom Vennum was muttering something about how honored he was to have such distinguished guests in his home while he gave orders for his wife to set three chairs near – but not too near – Lurancy.

The men took off their greatcoats and Lurinda hung them on the wall pegs. Dr Stevens took the chair nearest the girl, with Asa and the colonel beside him.

'Rancy,' her father said. 'Rancy, this here is the mayor and he has brought you some guests.' The girl glared at him and then at the intruders. 'Say hello to the gentlemen, Rancy.'

She squinted at them, then turned her face away, rocking her body steadily.

'Rancy,' her father repeated. 'I want you to say hello to your visitors. Mr Stevens here is a doctor and he has come a long way to see you. He wants to help you.'

Dr Stevens extended his hand and the girl looked at it curiously. Then she spat and he yanked it out of range just in time.

'Rancy Vennum!' Her father's voice was loud and harsh.

'That's all right, sir,' said the doctor. His voice was soft and smooth. 'That's all right.' He extended his hand again. 'How do you do?' He waited. 'I said, how do you do?'

The girl looked at his hand and then at his face. She kept rocking her body. Finally she said, 'Howdy.'

'That's nice,' the doctor said. 'I'm glad you are feeling well. My name is Stevens and this is the mayor, Mr Peters, and this man is Mr Roff. We have all come to help you.'

She glared at the other two and then closed her eyes, rocking her body. She began breathing deeply, making sounds in her throat each time she exhaled. 'Go away.'

'We've come to help you,' the mayor said. 'Please let us stay.'

'She hasn't been a bit well, Doctor.' Lurinda thought she should offer information. 'Sometimes she sits like this for hours and hours, never eating her food nor even taking a little water. I try to get through to her. I mean I try to make her hear me and do my bidding, but when she gets like this there ain't a power in either heaven or hell that can get through to her.'

Dr Stevens wanted to reassure her that he had the power of heaven with him. 'Don't be too surprised, Mrs Vennum, at the powers you will see demonstrated here this afternoon. God works in strange and wondrous ways.'

'If you could do something to help poor Rancy!' The woman began to cry and pulled her shawl around her shoulders in an attempt to muffle her sounds. 'Don't seem to be nothing nobody can do. Nobody can do nothing for my baby girl.'

Tom glared at his wife. 'Now you hush that up, Lurinda. Don't do no good for you to get upset. The doctor and the mayor and Mr Roff will do as much as they can and they don't need you whimpering and acting like a female.'

'Please,' Dr Stevens said to him, 'it's a natural reaction on your wife's part. She has been going through a great deal, I'm sure.'

'We all have,' Tom replied. 'I have too. So's my son, but my wife here gets on crying spells that I swear wear me out more than those fits Rancy gets. I can take a woman screaming and yelling but I can't abide a woman's tears.'

'Tears?' Lurancy said suddenly. 'My God, how many tears!'

'What?' Dr Stevens turned back to her. 'What did you say?' She was silent. 'What did you say about tears?' Silence. 'Won't you repeat it or at least tell me what you meant by that?'

She sat there, eyes closed, everyone staring at her. After a few moments Dr Stevens said, 'We must try and keep her talking, try and make a wedge into her mind where we can reach her and understand where she is.'

'Where she is?' Tom was surprised. 'What do you mean? She's right here. With us.'

'No,' said the doctor, 'her body is here with us but her mind is someplace else.' He had seen cases like this before, not as severe but similar. 'You see, your daughter is but a shell right now. Someone else is inside her.'

'Oh my God!' cried Lurinda. 'Oh my God. My poor baby!'

'Please Mrs Vennum,' the doctor's voice came swift and commanding. 'If we are to succeed today we cannot have emotional displays!' Then more soothingly, 'I understand what you are going through, but you must be brave and brace yourself until it is over. At no time must your daughter think she has mastery over you. She must not see your tears.'

'Tears,' Lurancy said softly. 'Tears. Why must there always be tears?' She looked at the doctor, her eyes open, the hardness gone. 'Why? Why always so many tears?'

'What do you mean?' his voice was as soft as hers.

'Everywhere there are tears. Everywhere.' She closed her eyes again and resumed rocking.

There was another silence before the doctor asked, 'Everywhere? What do you mean, everywhere? Where are you?'

'I'm here.' The voice was low and there was sadness accompanying it. 'I'm here and everyone is crying. Crying and looking.' She rocked back and forth, her knees pressed tightly against her chest. 'Looking and crying.'

'What are they looking for?' he asked.

'The boats, of course.'

'The boats?' No reply. 'What boats?' Another long silence.

'The other boats, with the other men.'

'Other men? What other men?'

She sighed. 'The ones who haven't returned, of course.' She turned toward him, her eyes open now. 'Weren't you here earlier?' she asked. 'Didn't you hear the news?' She stretched out her hand and he took it, holding it lightly in his own.

'The news? No, I didn't hear the news. Tell me about it.'

'It was horrible.' Tears started down her cheeks. 'The fire reached the powder kegs just as the boats were being lowered over the side. Some men managed to get away but others were blown into the sea. My brother is still missing. That lady over there, you see her?' and she pointed toward Lurinda.

'You mean your mother?' he questioned.

'No. Not my mother! That lady isn't my mother. My mother is back at the house, sick in bed. But that woman,' and she pointed again at Lurinda, 'that woman had three sons on the ship and all three were killed. Lars Holmquist said he saw them being blown to bits.'

'Lars Holmquist?' the doctor asked. 'Who is he?'

'One of the sailors on the ship. He lives here in the village. You know where the road turns and runs around the white house on the hill? Well, he lives just a little farther around that corner. In the stone house.'

'And you?' Dr Stevens continued, 'where do you live?'

'Where do I live?' She looked at him. 'What a funny question. You know where I live!'

'No, I do not.'

'Of course you do,' she laughed.

'No, I don't. Where is it?'

She stiffened her body and yanked back her hand. 'I don't know you! I thought you were someone else!'

'Please –'

'Get away from me! I don't know you! Don't you touch me!' Her voice was loud and fearful. 'How dare you touch me when you don't know me?' She looked wildly around the room. 'Oh God, what's happened to my brother? Where are the other boats?' She closed her eyes and started to moan, then the moaning got weaker and weaker and in a minute or two she was silent, rocking back and forth in her own silence.

'That's the way she's been,' Tom volunteered the information. 'She'll go off her head and pretend she is some imaginary person, and then just as quick as she goes on it, she'll go off it.'

Asa asked the next question. 'Does she ever become someone you know? I mean like a departed relative or friend?'

Tom looked at Lurinda. 'Once she was my father,' the woman answered.

'Did she sound like your father?' he continued.

'Pa had a deep voice and she had her ordinary voice.'

'Did she tell you anything, while she was your father, that she couldn't have known?' Asa kept at it.

'Like what?'

'Like things that only your father could have known. Personal things that might have happened and that Lurancy didn't know about.' He glanced at Dr Stevens and got a nod of approval. 'Things of a personal nature.'

'Didn't she say something about Grandma Ida Jones?' Tom asked her. 'Remember you told me something about that?'

'Oh, yes,' Lurinda said. 'At the time when she said she was my father, she told me that Grandma Ida Jones had buried her husband before he was dead. Grandma Jones wasn't really my grandma, we kids just called her that!'

'Before her husband was dead?' Colonel Peters was curious now.

'Yes. Old man Jones passed away, and being as there weren't any doctors out where he and Grandma Ida were, she made a pine box and buried him in it in the woods. Then a few years later when the church was built and they laid out a graveyard she wanted Grandpa's body to be reburied near the church. Well, when they dug up his coffin they found the lid had been forced open a bit and one of his hands was between the box and the lid. Everyone supposed that he hadn't really been dead when she buried him and then he came to and discovered where he was but it was too late. No amount of scratching and pushing would get him out. He must have suffocated in there.' She shuddered. 'I never knew about that story and I certainly never told Lurancy that story but Grandma Ida did bury her husband by herself. That's a fact. I remember the old man and remember when she came over to our farm to tell us what had happened.'

'So there was no way Lurancy could have known about the incident?' the colonel asked.

'No way,' said Tom. 'I only heard about it a few years ago when we was back home visiting, but Rancy wasn't there when they told it.' He paused in his speech and looked at them. 'Hey, wait a minute. Do you gentlemen think Lurinda's father *really* came here? I mean in Rancy's body?'

'It could very well be,' said the doctor. The other two men nodded in agreement.

'But that's impossible!' Tom said. 'The dead don't come back.'

'Anything is possible, Mr Vennum,' said Dr Stevens.

'Yes,' Asa added, 'and how do *you* know the dead don't come back?'

'Well,' he said looking down at the floor, 'I always thought it was just scary stuff telling tales about ghosts and dead people at midnight at the cemetery and all that.'

'There may be more truth in those tales than we have hitherto imagined,' the doctor said. 'We know very little about death and what really happens when a man dies.'

'I always thought that when you were dead you were dead for a helluva long time.'

'Please, Tom!' Lurinda shook her head. 'No profanity.'

'Nothing wrong with "helluva".'

'Nothing wrong with helluva,' Lurancy parroted. 'Helluva. Helluva. Helluva.'

'Lurancy!' Lurinda was shocked.

'Helluva!' the girl said louder. 'Helluva and piss and fart and shit!' She laughed. This time loud and deep. It was almost a man's laugh. 'Fart. Piss. Piss and fart!' she laughed again.

'Lurancy Vennum, now you stop that!' her mother commanded.

'Oh, Old Granny, just shut up! Everytime you open your mouth people realize you are more of a fool than they thought the first time. So just keep quiet and nobody'll know the truth.' The laugh came again. 'Old Granny, she don't have many brains in that old head.'

'Who are you?' the doctor asked.

'I'm Willie Canning.' She stretched out her hand and shook the doctor's hand. 'Who are you?'

'My name is Dr E. W. Stevens.'

'Glad to know you, sir. Is it a medical doctor you are or a horse doctor?' the laugh returned.

'A little bit of both, at times.' Now the doctor laughed. 'What are you doing here, Willie?'

'I don't know,' came the answer. 'I was just lolligagging around, not doing much of nothing, and here I am. Hey, you don't happen to have a cigar, do you?'

'Lurancy!' her mother was getting more upset by the minute.

'Now, Old Granny, just you hush. She never did like it when I smoked. Said it made me look like the Devil's rear end. With all that smoke coming out of the hole.'

'I never said a thing like that in my life!' Lurinda got up

out of her chair and the doctor motioned her back into it.

'Please, "Old Granny",' he said with a wink, 'let's not get upset. We should be happy that Willie is here for a visit.'

She sat back down, crossing her arms angrily at her daughter.

'About that cigar,' the girl said.

Colonel Peters reached into the pocket of his suit coat and pulled out a silver case. As he offered it, opened, to Lurancy it was Tom Vennum's turn to get indignant.

'Please, Mr Mayor, I won't abide my daughter smoking in my house!'

'Your house?' Willie Canning snorted inside Lurancy's body. 'Hell, mister, you don't own this place! Nobody does.' She looked at him, her eyes wide open. 'And don't call me your daughter. I ain't your daughter. I'm all man and if you want me to I can prove it. I can open my trouser front and show you something your daughter don't have, but would sure like to have!' The laugh was longer now. 'Thanks,' she reached for the cigar, expertly bit off the end and inhaled deeply as the colonel held the match. 'Ah, by Jesus that tastes good! What is it? Cuban?' Colonel Peters nodded. 'Thought so. They make the best over there. When I was in Havana we used to buy them by the handfuls.'

'You were never in Havana!' Lurinda said, then clapped her hand over her mouth quickly. 'I'm sorry,' she whispered at Dr Stevens. He smiled at her and gestured it was all right.

'Tell me, Willie,' the doctor said. 'What was your father's name?'

'Pete. Peter Canning.'

'Where were you born?'

'In Cardiff. Do you know where that is?'

'Wales.'

'Right. But I haven't been there for a long time. I ran away when I was about ten and never went back.'

'Where did you go?'

'To sea.'

'As a sailor?'

'As anything at all. Anything the captain needed a hand for.'

'Were you a sailor all your life?'

'No. When I was about twenty or so, I took a land job.

There was a gentleman in Peru who needed someone to manage his fishing boats. There's good solid whitefish off the coast and he dried them and sold them to people in Europe. But it didn't work out,' she sighed.

'Why didn't it work out, Willie?' the doctor asked.

'Politics. There was a revolution. Damn, there was always a revolution down there and his ships were destroyed. I was lucky I got out with my life.'

'What do you mean?'

'Well, the shit-eating government soldiers were coming in one door just as I was going out the other. They fired at me, but I got away.' Willie took another puff on the cigar. 'Damn fine leaf, this.'

'Willie,' Dr Stevens's voice was slow and deliberate. 'Are you positive you got away?'

Lurancy took the cigar out of her mouth and looked at him. 'What kind of a dumb question is that? Of course, I got away.'

'All right,' the doctor said. 'Assuming you did, where did you go after that?'

'After that? Well, after that I went to ... to ...' She paused, took a puff on the cigar and thoughtfully blew out the smoke. 'Well, I think it was ...'

'No, Willie.' Dr Stevens was insistent. 'I don't want you to tell me where you *think* it was. I want you to tell me where you *know* it was.' There was a long pause as the girl studied the pattern the cigar smoke made in the musty parlor air. 'Did you go anywhere after that, Willie?'

'Well, yes. I went to ...'

'To where? Come on, I must know where you went! I must hear it from you yourself.' He looked at the others in the room; they were not sure what he meant by this line of questioning. Finally he said, 'Willie, I want you to remember when the soldiers came in the front door. I want you to remember what it felt like when you heard the shooting.'

'What it felt like? What what felt like?'

'Your body, Willie. What did your body feel like when you heard the shots that were fired at you?'

She closed her eyes, as if the darkness would help her recall the incident in better detail. 'Well, they came in the front door of the house. I was in the first room and I ran toward the cooking area because I had my revolver there.'

'All right. Then what?'

'Then I got the revolver...' she said slowly, seeing the scene acted out inside her closed eyelids, 'and I turned to fire it at the two soldiers who had come after me.'

'Then what?'

'I'm trying to think!' the voice said irritably. 'Then I fired one shot and then...' The voice stopped.

'And then?'

There was silence. 'Oh my God!'

'What happened?'

'Behind me. There were others at the door behind me. My back! Dear Lord, my back!' She gave a cry and reached around trying to clutch at her back. 'The pain! Sweet Jesus, the pain!' Tears welled in her eyes. She looked at Dr Stevens as if seeing him for the first time. 'I didn't... didn't go anywhere after that.' Long pause. 'Did I?'

He shook his head.

'Dear sweet Jesus,' the voice moaned. 'I didn't go anywhere. They got me. They got me and I... I...'

'You died,' the doctor said. 'You left your body and you died.'

'Yes... yes... that must be what happened.' The tears were streaming faster now. 'I died. I really died.' Lurancy looked at her hands and then touched her face. 'But if I died why do I still have—'

'A body?'

'Yes. Why do I still have a body?' The hands were touching Lurancy all over.

'You have a body, but it is not *your* body. You have taken over the body of a young girl, Willie, an innocent young girl, and you are doing it great harm. You must leave. Leave her and never come back.'

'To go where?' The throat was filled with tears.

'To go to where you were supposed to go so many years now past. To go with the others who have given up their mortal bodies.' Dr Stevens got up from his chair and stood in front of the girl. 'Willie, would you like to go there?' She nodded her head. 'Very well, I shall try and send you there.'

He placed his hands in the air, slightly over her head, and

began to move them slowly. First around her hair, then both hands down near her ears, down to her neck and clearing her shoulders with a sweeping motion. His hands never touched her body, but he shook them as if he was shaking off something that was clinging to them, caught between his fingers. Then he stepped to one side of her and started the same movement across the top of her head, down in front of her face and the back of her head. At the base of her neck, the hands swooped out again and were shaken again. That was when she gave a muffled cry, bowed her head and sat like a rag doll all hunched up on folded legs. Her breathing was normal, the tears had stopped.

'Very good, sir!' said the colonel. 'You have sent that entity to paradise.'

'Or at least away from Lurancy,' put in Asa. 'That was well done. My congratulations. I had often read of such a thing but I've never actually seen it done. Magnetic passes, you call it?'

'Yes. It is a process that I have studied and perfected over the years,' he answered.

'How did you do it?' Tom Vennum was most impressed.

'Yes,' his wife chimed in. 'I'm so relieved.'

'I don't know what I do,' he confessed. 'All I know is that it works. In cases of spirit possession, it almost always works.'

'Then that was a ghost that was in her body!' Lurinda began to whimper. 'Oh Tom, you know I don't like these things!'

'Just hush up!' he commanded. 'That Willie person is gone.' He looked at Dr Stevens. 'He *is* gone, isn't he? Gone for good?'

'I hope so,' the doctor replied. 'I hope I have sent him into spirit land where he will understand the fact that he is dead and will begin to progress into his next life.'

'You mean he didn't know those soldiers shot him?' Tom was amazed. 'If someone shot me in the back, I'd sure as hell know it.'

'Everyone doesn't know it when they are dead,' the colonel said. 'That's why you have ghosts.'

'They don't know they're dead?' Tom would have liked to argue with him, but this *was* the mayor. 'How come?'

'From what I've been able to read,' the colonel began, 'people who die suddenly, like in an accident or are murdered, don't have time to prepare themselves mentally for death. So when they do die, sudden like, they don't know what's happened to them. Folks who die after a long illness, peaceably in bed, get ready for death and they don't have any problems in knowing when they're dead.'

'How come people don't know it?' Lurinda asked. 'Can't they feel that they don't have no body? No feet or nothing?'

'They don't stop to feel their bodies,' Asa said. 'They can see their own bodies lying on the ground or the battlefield or wherever they died, but they can also see other people who are still alive. They can hear the other people and touch them but they can't make the other people hear *them*. At least,' and he turned to Dr Stevens for confirmation, 'that's what I've been led to believe.'

'Correct,' said the doctor. 'The spirit of the disembodied then tries to make contact in some other way than words. Like throwing things, making things float across a room, banging doors or, when he has enough energy stored up, being able to make a replica of his physical life form appear.'

'That makes a ghost?' asked Tom.

'That makes a ghost.'

'But,' Tom was watching his daughter now, waiting for some movement from her, 'why have these ghosts taken ahold of Rancy? What did she ever do to them? This Willie person. We never knowed that man.'

'Your daughter is in a weakened mental and physical condition,' Dr Stevens felt he was delivering a lecture now, 'and spirits who are out there, looking for a way to make themselves understood, have found her and are using her body. Their energy powers her physical form and it is their thoughts she is saying.'

'But her voice.'

'But her voice, yes. They are using her vocal cords. Just like a piano. Your hands make a piano string vibrate. It is the piano that is making the sound but you are deciding and controlling what sounds it will make. Do you understand?' He hoped he did.

'I see that,' Tom answered, 'but I still don't understand

why Willie and the others chose Rancy. I mean, she's just a girl.'

'She is a girl and a young girl has more energy to use than an adult. Also younger persons do not know how to close themselves off from these spirits. Your daughter has been ill for quite a while. She is in a weakened condition.'

'She wasn't weak when she tried to come at me with a knife,' Lurinda interrupted.

'Don't you see,' Asa put in, 'that it wasn't your daughter that tried to kill you? It was an entity inside her that was using her energy.'

'My Rancy's always been a good girl,' the woman said.

'That has nothing to do with it,' the doctor put in. 'The goodness or the badness of people has nothing to do with whether a spirit can take over their bodies or not. You can play bar-room songs on a piano or you can play church hymns on it. The *instrument* is not what plays the songs, it is the *player*. Your daughter is not evil. Do you understand?' God, how he hoped they did.

Lurancy coughed, all eyes were turned on her. She stretched her arms and uncrossed her legs, putting her bare feet on the floor. The men could see the rope burns around her ankles where Tom had tied her to keep her quiet. No one mentioned the scars.

'Are you all right, child?' Mrs Vennum went to her and touched her shoulder.

Lurancy pushed the hand away. Lurinda stepped backward and began whimpering. 'Oh, for the love of heaven will you stop that bellyaching?' Lurancy's voice was scratchy now.

'Good afternoon,' the doctor was ready to take on one more entity.

The girl looked at him, pushing back her fallen hair to get a better view. 'Who are you?'

'My name is E. W. Stevens. Who are you?'

'Stevens?' She rolled the name a little. 'I don't think I know no Stevens. Where are you from?'

'Wisconsin state.'

'Never heard of it.' She dug her fingernails into her armpit and scratched.

'It's near here,' he said. 'Up north.'

'I ain't never been up north. Had a married sister who moved up north but she don't come and see me no more.'

The doctor put a warning hand up toward the Vennums so they wouldn't start correcting Lurancy this time as well. 'Who are you?'

She looked at him, eyes open, and then squinted at him as if that would help her to see him more clearly.

'Who are you?' he repeated. 'I've told you my name, the polite thing would be for you to tell me yours.'

She pursed her lips, frowned, then shrugged her shoulders. 'Wouldn't hurt none,' she said. 'My name's Katrina Hogan.'

Asa Roff drew his breath in sharply.

'Nice to meet you, Katrina,' the doctor continued. 'How old are you?'

'Is it really?' she replied.

'Is it really what?' the doctor was puzzled.

'Nice to meet me?' she laughed. 'Very few folks around here think it's nice to meet me. Most of them go the other way so they won't have to meet me.'

'Yes, it is indeed a pleasure to meet you.' He stretched out his hand and she looked around the room for a minute and then shook it.

'I'll shake your hand because you seem like a nice man, but don't let these other people touch me. I hate it when people I don't like touch me.'

'Don't worry. They'll keep their distance.'

'Especially that old biddy over there,' she pointed at Lurinda. 'I can't stand old biddies!' Her mother began whimpering. 'Damned old women, coming around here and touching me and asking me questions and expecting me to solve their problems and then stoning me when things don't go their way.'

'Why do they do that?'

'They say I'm a witch.' The laugh was harsh and bitter. 'They come running up the mountain when they need me, but when they don't they pretend they never saw my likes in their life. Stupid old biddies.' Lurinda sobbed out loud at that. 'Yes, you! You are a stupid old biddy!'

Tom was about to get out of his chair but all three men motioned him to stay exactly where he was. It took a great deal of effort for him to sit there and hear how his daughter was talking to his wife.

'I asked you before,' said the doctor. 'How old are you?'

'Sixty-three years.'

'Where are you from?'

'Germany.'

'How long have you been here?'

'Three days.'

'How did you get here?'

'Through the air.'

'How long will you stay?'

'Three weeks.'

'Three weeks?' he said. 'Don't you think that's rather a long time to be occupying this body?'

'What business is it of yours?' Her voice was sharper.

'I've come here to help this girl.'

'Well, help her. Who's stopping you?'

'You are,' he said.

'Me? For Christ's sake, now what am I getting blamed for?' She took back her hand and pulled her legs up under her skirt as before, hugging her knees to her chest. There was a silence. The doctor hoped he had not broken the contact.

'I'm not blaming you for anything,' he said soothingly, 'I'm just telling you that while you are here, I cannot help this girl.'

'And what am I supposed to do?' she snarled. 'Fly away again?'

'Yes. That's exactly what I want you to do.'

She spat on the floor. 'Well, fuck you!' She turned her face away from him.

Dr Stevens got very red under his beard. No one had ever used those words with him before. He didn't care if it was a disincarnate spirit he was talking with, she had to be reprimanded. 'How dare you use such language to me and,' he pointed toward Lurinda, 'in the presence of a lady!'

'Her?' the voice chuckled. 'She doesn't know what "fuck" means? How did she get to be that old and not have a fuck or two?'

Lurinda thought she was going to faint off the chair. Having a sick daughter was one thing, but having a foul-mouthed daughter was quite another. 'I'm not going to sit here another minute, Tom.' She rose and hurried toward the door to the upstairs hallway. 'I just can't take this anymore! You are supposed to be a doctor, Mr Stevens; well, *do* something! Either cure her or have her taken away! That child is not normal! That child is the Devil!' She fumbled for the door, opened it and almost fell up the stairs, tripping over her long full skirts in her haste to get away from Lurancy.

There was silence in the room after she left. All eyes were on Lurancy, especially those of Asa Roff.

'Katrina Hogan,' he said calmly, 'have you ever been here before?'

'Here? Where is here?'

'In Watseka?'

'Never heard of it. Who is this man?' she asked Dr Stevens.

'Have you never seen my face before?' Asa continued.

She peered at him through half-closed lids. 'Yes,' she laughed, 'every time I look at a cow plop!' Then the laugh came much louder.

'No, I'm serious,' Asa insisted. 'Have you ever seen my face before?'

She looked at him again, studying his features in detail. She scratched at her nose and then at her armpit. 'You look,' she said slowly, 'like somebody I've seen before, but I don't know where. Yes,' she said, 'maybe I do know you. From somewhere. Why?'

Dr Stevens looked at Mr Roff. 'Yes,' he said, 'why are you asking that question?'

Asa shook his head. 'Nothing,' he replied. 'It was just an idea that I had, something out of the past that I thought I recognized.'

'Something to do with Lurancy?'

'No. With someone else. I'm sorry,' he apologized, 'I should not have intruded.'

'You are all intruding,' Lurancy's harsh voice said. 'Why don't you all go home? Go home and let me be.'

The sun had gone down and the room was badly lit, with just one small oil lamp. Nobody had noticed the darkness settling in. Dr Stevens took out his pocket watch and consulted it. 'We have been here for almost an hour and a half.

I suggest we leave the girl until tomorrow. I don't want to overtax her. These things are always better in moderate sessions. May we come back tomorrow?' he asked Tom Vennum.

Tom nodded his head. 'If you think it can help Rancy.'

'I think it can. Mrs Hogan,' he said to the girl, 'Mrs Hogan, we are going to leave now, but we would like to come back and see you tomorrow. Is that all right?' She didn't answer. 'May we call tomorrow?' he asked. 'Will you be here?'

She waved him away. 'Yes. Yes, I'll be here. Where else would I go? Bring me a sponge cake tomorrow, will you? I haven't had sponge cake in years.'

He rose and nodded to the others to do the same. 'Of course, I will. About this same time tomorrow and with a sponge cake.'

'Fine.' She uncrossed her legs and put them on the floor, then she stood up. He was surprised how tall she was for a young girl. 'I like you,' the old voice said. 'I can talk to you. Do you have to bring the others?'

'If you'd like I can come alone.'

'That's all right. These men aren't so bad. It's that old biddy that I can't stand.' She put her arm around the doctor's shoulders and walked with him to the door where Tom was holding their coats. 'You know,' she confided, 'I once had a gentleman friend who had a beard just like yours. It smelled good too. Rosewater, isn't it?'

'Yes,' he laughed.

'I love rosewater.'

'If you'd like I'll bring you a bottle tomorrow.' He started to say something about the time of their meeting when she staggered. He tried to grab her but she twisted away from him and fell heavily onto the floor. She jerked, violently, several times kicking her legs and thrashing her arms. The four men held back, unwilling to get too close. Then she gave a short cry, stiffened her spine, stretched her legs straight out and lifted her arms straight into the air. Her breathing was deep and noisy, sucking the air in and out of flared nostrils.

'Oh God, now what?' Tom looked down at his daughter, her arms thrust like iron bars into the air. 'What is it now?'

Dr Stevens motioned for them to stand back. 'She's gone

into trance,' he said. 'I've seen this before. I can handle it.'

He got down on his knees and began the same passes over her head and shoulders that he had done previously. His hands fluttered just a few inches over her face and hair, then he'd remove them with a swooping movement and shake his fingers as if there was something sticking to them. He was breathing heavily himself.

'Mr Roff, sir,' he said, 'would you stand on the other side of her and hold out your hands like so?' He put his arms out and his palms upward facing the girl. 'And, Colonel Peters, will you get down at her feet and do the same? Just keep your palms upward facing her. I need your strength as batteries.'

The men, knowing what he was talking about, did as they were told. Tom Vennum stood there, coats in his arms, staring at his daughter.

The doctor passed his hands around her head again, and again shook his fingers. She didn't seem to be stirring.

'It's not working this time,' Tom said.

'It will.' The doctor was sure of his technique. 'Sometimes it takes longer than others, that's all.' His hands swooped down in front of her face, got as far as her collarbone and then back up again, shaking off something that only the doctor could feel.

Lurancy groaned and lowered her arms a little.

'It's working,' the colonel whispered. 'She's coming around.'

The doctor's hands fluttered, glided, swooped and shook as they passed near the girl's face. She sighed and lowered her arms slowly to the floor. Asa looked at the colonel and met his smile. The doctor let his open fingers hover over her eyes, tops almost touching her lids, but never quite doing it. He closed his own eyes and concentrated on sending the energies the girl needed down his arms and out his hands into her body. His legs were starting to cramp and, in spite of the chilled air in the room, he was perspiring. Asa and Colonel Peters never took their hands down nor their eyes from the girl, unless it was to watch the doctor's face.

Lurancy's cheek muscles twitched and the corners of her mouth contracted. Her breathing was heavier now and she flexed her fingers. She groaned and flexed one leg. Her lips moved as if she was trying to form the beginning of a word.

'She's coming around now,' said the colonel.

The girl groaned again and twisted her face to one side and then the other. She moved her head in a circular motion as if trying to get all her neck muscles into play. The groans were louder now, coming from deep in her throat. Then she opened her mouth and gulped in large swallows of air. Finally her eyelids fluttered and opened. At first only the whites were visible, then the pupils came slowly into view and finally into focus.

'Pa . . . ?' she said softly. 'Pa?'

Tom was beside her, touching her hair, pulling it away from her forehead.

'Pa?' she looked at him.

'Yes, Rancy,' he said. 'I'm right here. You just hush now. Your Pa's right here.'

'No . . . ' She turned her face away from him. 'No . . . where's my Pa?' She rose up on one elbow. 'Pa?'

'Over here, honey,' Tom said. 'I'm right here beside you.'

She shook her head. 'No.' She looked at him again, shook her head again. Then she looked into the doctor's face and into Colonel Peters's face. 'No.' Her gaze went to Asa and she stopped, eyes open, studying his features.

'Oh Pa!' she cried. 'Oh Pa! Your hair's so white! It's so good to see you again, Pa!' She sat up and reached for Asa, pulling him to her, hugging him close. 'Oh Pa!' she was crying.

Tom put a hand on her shoulder. 'No, child. That's not your Pa. That's Mr Roff. I'm your Pa. Over here.' He tugged lightly at her but she wouldn't budge.

'This is my Pa!' she said through her tears. 'This is my Pa and I ain't hugged him in years!' She pulled back, stared at him and brought him back into her arms. 'Oh Pa, I missed you so!'

Tom looked at Dr Stevens and then at Colonel Peters. 'What's this all about?' he asked.

'I don't know,' said the doctor. 'Mr Roff, sir, can you explain this?'

Asa had tears running down his cheeks. 'I'm afraid to ask for an explanation,' he said. 'You ask. You ask her her name.'

'My name?' the girl laughed. 'Oh Pa, you know my name. My name is Mary. Mary Roff! I'm your daughter, Pa. I'm your daughter Mary what's come back to you! I'm back, Pa! I'm back!'

PART THREE

The light from three large double-globed oil lamps illuminated the back parlor. Ann Roff sat on the velvet sofa, a white wool shawl around her thin shoulders, a handkerchief in her hands, listening intently to Asa.

'It was Mary's voice,' he said. 'I knew it as soon as she turned to me and called me "Pa". I knew it was Mary! I just knew it.' He hadn't been able to sit down since he'd arrived home. He hadn't even taken time to remove his greatcoat. He wore it still, as he paced in front of his wife. 'It was incredible,' he said, 'one minute she was this old hag and the next minute she was our beloved Mary. Incredible!'

'How did she look?' Ann asked. 'I mean, when Mary took her over did she change physically or was she still the Vennum girl but with Mary's mind?'

'Yes. She is still the Vennum girl but it is Mary inside her. She has Mary's voice but it's still the other body.'

'Well, what did she say? What does she plan to do?'

'She?' he asked. 'Who? The Vennum girl?'

'No,' Ann said. 'Mary. What does Mary plan to do now? How long is she going to be here?'

'I don't really know,' he answered; then he stopped, looking at his wife. A perplexed frown crossed his face. 'You know,' he said softly, 'you are reacting awfully different to this story than I thought you would. You've accepted it completely. I expected tears and doubts and even denial. You amaze me.'

Ann looked up at him. 'I've always known someday we would make contact with Mary again. I've believed that with all my heart and soul. Mary was a very special child with a very special gift. Her death was not a natural death. Her life was not a natural life. There was much to our daughter that we never understood. I've prayed a great deal, Asa. I've prayed and I've studied and I've waited. Especially the latter. I've waited, Asa, and I am ready to accept my daughter back again.'

Ever since Mary Roff had screamed in the night and been found dead Ann and Asa Roff had searched. Searched for the answers to questions that had never been clearly formulated. They read the Bible, tried to talk with doctors and ministers and finally ended up reading Spiritualist booklets, the same type of literature the Reverend Dille had read and hidden in his parsonage. It hadn't been easy finding the material and, once found, hadn't been easy understanding and believing a great deal of it. It was all so strange and farfetched from anything they had ever experienced in their lives.

They began by reading about the Fox sisters and the mysterious rappings at their house in New York State and how those rappings had turned into a question-and-response system between the girls and the spirit of a murdered peddler, a man whose body had been buried in their cellar. When the peddler's body was discovered – right where the rappings said it would be and the news got around town – an entirely new movement had begun. The Fox sisters were investigated, tested, adored and ridiculed.

Out of their experiences came others trying the same things and with much the same results. Supposed contacts were made all over the nation between the living and the dead. Spirits stopped rapping after a while and began to speak directly through the living. It became a common occurrence for someone to fall into an unconscious physical condition called a trance and have a strange voice issue from their lips. Messages from the 'other side' were given. Loved ones were reunited, secret hiding places of money and wills were revealed and physical bodies were miraculously healed.

The world called it Spiritualism but the churches and the skeptics called it hogwash. It was dangerous, they said. God had never meant for spirits to be dragged back to earth. It was the working of the Devil. It was evil. It was crazy. It was charlatanism brought to its highest degree, where people willingly paid to be deluded. It was a national disgrace. It had to be stamped out. So its practitioners were forced to form themselves into a religion with by-laws and dogma and hymnals and, as a religion in a nation where the church and state are separate, they were protected by law.

Just because they were protected didn't mean they were respected. Good God-fearing Baptists and Methodists and Episcopalians had nothing to do with people who professed to talk to the dead. Spiritualist Churches (when they got built at all) were often mysteriously burned to the ground. Known Spiritualists had their windows broken, their horses poisoned and their children stoned. Some social organizations passed rules to bar Spiritualists, while others simply ignored the existence of anyone stupid enough to believe that one could make contact with the dead.

Asa's business suffered after Mary died. As he searched for the answers to her death he drew farther away from the Lavinia Dursts of Watseka and into his own self-contained world where the only ones with whom he could discuss his beliefs were his family and a few friends in other towns. He had first made the mistake of telling people of his ideas. They made sure he suffered for it. He was never again elected postmaster. He was asked to resign from the two fraternal organizations he had helped found. His law practice suffered and people called upon him as judge only because they knew he was a fair man. The fact that they were not fair to him never entered into it. He had wisely invested some of his money in gold coins and unwisely invested a great deal of it in Watseka farmland. When the crash of 1875 hit he held second mortgages on lands he was unable to pay. No one came to his rescue and he was almost wiped out. Fortunately the family home was safe, as was his office building downtown. For all practical purposes he was living on money from the past. Others prospered after that but Asa never quite made it to the top again. Any gain he made was cut down by good citizens who abhorred his spirit beliefs.

Ann also suffered for their beliefs. The groups of women

who used to come calling – or insisted she come calling on them – evaporated like fog over the lowlands. More and more she stayed at home and took care of the boys and worried with Minerva over her marriage to Henry Alter. At times she was glad that Nervie's marriage wasn't everything marriage was supposed to be, because it kept the girl closer to her. Henry was all right but he was lazy. His war experiences had taught him, he said, that it wasn't what you knew in this world but *who* that was important. He had returned to wed the daughter of one of the wealthiest and most respected citizens in Watseka, and instead of milk and honey it had turned to sticks and stones because of their strange religious leanings. Henry wasn't happy with the situation but there was little he could do. Asa had given them a house when they married and Henry had taken a job as assistant cashier in a bank. He plodded along and did his share of womanizing – in Chicago, in the rows of those places where a man could buy the services of wanton women – and Nervie always came crying back to Ann. Ann still had her daughter. And now, it seemed, she had her other daughter back as well.

'I want to see her,' Ann said. 'I want to see this Vennum girl and see if I can talk to Mary. Do you think it would be possible?'

'I don't know,' Asa answered truthfully. 'Dr Stevens himself doesn't know how long Mary will be in her body. She said something about staying there until the Vennum girl was cured.'

'Cured of what?'

'Whatever ails her. You know, those fits and things she gets.'

'You mean Mary said she would be in that body *permanently*?'

'That was my understanding. Permanently until the Vennum girl is able to handle her body by herself. At least that's what the doctor gathered from it. I don't know. I was listening but at the same time I was so overwhelmed by it all that I couldn't really comprehend anything but the fact that Mary had come back.'

Ann looked up at him; a sudden and unsettling thought had just crossed her mind. 'Asa, do you think this is all a trick? You know, maybe some sort of a joke that awful Hogan woman is playing on us? She tried to kill Mary before when she was in her body and we drove her out. Now maybe this is her way of getting back at us.' She wished the pressure under her eyes would turn into tears and release itself. 'Oh Asa, what if that is all it is?'

'Then that's what it will have to be,' he sighed. 'I just don't know, Ann, I just don't know.'

That night in bed, for the first time in months, Asa reached out and held his wife in his arms. She slept that way until almost dawn, when she sighed and moved over onto her own pillow. He was awake when she changed positions. He was awake all that night.

Dr Stevens slept soundly, in spite of the fact that he had been tremendously excited about what had happened in the Vennum home. He wrote three pages to his wife before retiring, telling her of the girl and how he had found her and what had transpired right up to the point of Mary Roff coming into the girl's body.

'I'm not sure exactly what this means,' he wrote, 'because it is too soon to tell. The entity calling herself Mary Roff said she would be there to help the Vennum girl regain her complete physical and mental health. She said it was the least she could do to repay some of the suffering she had caused her own parents those twelve years ago. She said there had been much consternation on "the other side" regarding Lurancy Vennum and that volunteers had been requested to take over her body and keep it until her mind was normal once again. Apparently some of the spirits contacted Mary Roff and told her of the problem and she came to investigate for herself. Once she saw her own father there she willingly agreed to undertake the task.' He paused to fill his pen and to remember the expression on Asa's face. 'It was really quite moving to see the united pair,' he continued, 'father with tears down his cheeks and the little girl, who had been almost dead just seconds before, now alive and laughing and crying at the same time and hugging him and telling him how happy she was to be with him again.

'Of course the girl's father, the rude farmer I wrote you about, is at sixes and sevens over the entire thing. He cannot understand how his daughter could suddenly become someone else's daughter, and while he was pleased that his daughter was out of pain and conversing normally he wasn't at all pleased over the fact that she was a brand-new personality. His wife remained upstairs while all this was transpiring. I have no idea what opinion she has formed of it all by this time. She is a weak woman, even though physically she is large and seemingly healthy. I understand that the events of the past months have taken their toll on her nerves, so her emotional outbursts are to be expected from one with little formal education and with absolutely no knowledge of spirit workings.

'I am to return to the Vennum home tomorrow afternoon for another session with the girl. I don't know what I shall find or even if the father will permit me to enter the house again. One full day of contemplating things he does not understand just may be too much for him. I sincerely hope that I shall be able to continue my work without his interference, but one never knows.

'I shall close now, my dearest, and have this ready for the post in the morning. I miss you and the children and hope to be able to return to Janesville and my happy home in just a few more days.'

He signed his name and started to fold the paper. Then he stopped, unfolded it and dipped his pen into the ink bottle one last time.

'P.S. I suppose you think I am taking this all very calmly and that I sound as if what I have experienced is just an ordinary event. It is not ordinary and I, quite frankly, am a bit frightened by what it may lead to. I have never had a case where one entity remained inside the body of a living person for a prolonged length of time. I am concerned about the mental health of the Vennum girl should this be the case and I am frightened at what this entity who calls herself Mary may be able to do in this borrowed body. Please pray for me and for little Lurancy.' He went back to the final notation and underlined the word 'frightened'.

Asa left for his office at the normal time in the morning. He and Ann had decided it best not to tell any of the children about the Vennum girl. It was too soon to be sure of anything and they could imagine the unsettling influence it could have on others. The boys had become Spiritualists along with their parents, but it wasn't as firm a conversion as Ann's and Asa's had been. It was more of the thing to do because their parents had done it. Actually, only the two younger boys had converted to the new religion. The older ones, Joseph and Fenton, had gone off to college in the East, had married and settled down there. Asa and Ann were the grandparents of three small children they had never seen. Nervie had had a baby, a girl, but it died before it was six months old. Only Frank and Charles were at home now and Frank, at eighteen, was thinking of moving to Kansas Territory, while Charlie was interested in girls and music and liked Watseka. The only other person in the old Roff home was Charlotte, the German hired woman. She had taken Loozie's place right after the war. They heard from Loozie several times from her home in Canada. She had had three babies of her own and the first child, a boy, had been called Asa. That had pleased Asa Roff a great deal.

He unlocked the door to his office and started arranging papers for his day's work. There wasn't that much to do but it took his mind off the events of the previous evening. Took it off until the door opened and Tom Vennum strode in. Asa looked up in surprise. This was the first time Tom had ever been in his office.

Asa jumped up and offered the visitor a seat, dragging a chair nearer his desk. 'Please, sit down,' he said. 'I'm glad to see you this morning.' Tom kept standing. 'That was quite an experience we had last evening, wasn't it?' Tom didn't sit. Asa resumed his own seat. 'Tell me, Mr Vennum, how is Lurancy this morning?'

'She wants to go home.'

'I beg your pardon?' Asa did not understand.

'Your home. She says she doesn't belong at our house and she wants to go home. *Your* home.' He stood there, still wearing his heavy woolen cap and his hands in the pockets of his thick jacket. 'That's what she says,' he repeated dully. 'She ain't happy at our place and she wants to come to yours.'

Asa had himself collected now. 'She? By "she" do you mean the entity who calls herself my daughter?'

'I mean that my daughter,' and he emphasized the word 'my', 'is still having crazy fits and she is acting just like she did last night. That new voice or new person or whatever it is inside of her...'

'The one that claims to be *my* daughter...'

'Yes. That one. She says she's homesick and she wants to go home. To your home. That you are her Pa and she doesn't know why I won't let her go live with you.' He sat down, finally but sullenly.

'Are you telling me,' Asa said slowly, 'that the entity calling itself my daughter is still inside your daughter?' Tom nodded. 'And she was there all night?' Again he nodded. 'And when Lurancy woke this morning that entity was still there?'

'If entity means ghost, yes. That same ghost is still in there and she's the one who wants to go home.'

'What do you plan to do about it?' Asa tried not to show the excitement in his voice. 'I mean, are you and Mrs Vennum willing to have the girl come to visit my home?'

'Willing? What else can we do? She says she's your daughter. She says she don't belong to us.' He got up and took a few steps toward Asa, his rough trousers pressing against the edge of the desk. 'Goddammit, what say-so do I have in this?' His voice was rising. 'Before you and that doctor came she was my daughter! I don't know what kind of magic spell you put on her but now she says she don't know me and the missus and she don't belong to us! We had a long talk after you left yesterday and she insisted that her name is not Vennum but Roff.' He turned away suddenly and stared out the window down at Walnut Street that was just coming to life. 'I don't know whether to hit you or thank you,' he said. 'Part of me wants to kill you for taking my Rancy, but another part wants me to shake your hand and hope that my Rancy is being healed.' When he turned back, Asa could see sadness in the man's eyes. 'That girl inside her told us that they had taken Rancy to some spirit place and that they was working on her. She says Rancy needs a healing in her body and in her mind and that they will take care of this over there. Damn!' He swore at the water that ran down his cheeks as he wiped it away with his gloved hand. 'I don't know where "over there" is! I don't know where they have taken my little girl's mind! I don't know if I even believe any of this is really true!'

'It is true,' Asa assured him.

'Then why in the hell didn't I ever hear of this before?' he shouted. 'Why in the hell didn't something like this happen to somebody else first? I can only know what I *know*! I can't understand things that I *don't* know.' He looked at Asa, searchingly. 'Do you understand what I'm saying? I'm trying to tell you that if I knew what was happening, then maybe it wouldn't be so frightening. My missus is frightened. She's scared out of her wits.'

'Lurancy didn't try to hurt her again, did she?' Asa was concerned.

'No. Nothing like that, thank God. It's just that this new person . . . your daughter . . . claims she doesn't know my missus. Says she ain't her mother. Says that your missus is her real mother and wants to know why she is being kept at our house like a prisoner. That's the word she used. Prisoner. It really upsets my missus.' He came back and sat down, ready now for advice, or at least ready to listen to it. 'Mr Roff, you're a lawyer and a judge and a rich man. I'm just a poor farmer. Don't have no education and never will have. I don't know what to do. But I'm not asking you as a lawyer,' he put in quickly, 'I'm asking you as a father. And it seems, if I ain't going crazy myself, that you and me may be the father of the same girl.'

After Tom left Asa tried to get some work done, but the words on the papers were so much chicken scratchings to his eyes. Even when he tried to write, the words came out crooked and misspelled.

He put on his coat, buttoned it up to the top button and tied his muffler around his throat. He put on the wool cap (he didn't care what it looked like, it kept his ears warm and that was what was important) and locked the office door behind him. Ann wouldn't be expecting him at this hour. She would probably be doing the washing or some sewing or helping Charlotte with the cooking. He was right. She was in the kitchen and breaking several eggs into a large mixing bowl.

'I'm making a sponge cake,' she said simply as he entered the warm room. It was as if she had known he would be home early. 'I'm taking it to Mary. I know that awful Hogan woman asked for it, but Mary used to like sponge cake too.

Nervie and I are going to see her this afternoon.'

'She wants to come home,' Asa said quietly. 'She's homesick.'

'I'm not surprised,' Ann replied. 'After all, Asa, it's been twelve years.'

Lurancy was also in the kitchen. Lurinda was sitting in a far corner trying to slice raw potatoes into neat slices for a baked dish at suppertime but her shaking fingers kept getting in the way of the knife. Finally Lurancy had taken the knife and the bowl from her and sliced them herself.

'This is the way my Ma always cut them,' Lurancy said in that strange voice that had appeared the night before. 'She says if you hold the potato just like this,' and she raised one to show to her mother, 'then you could slice them on a board and do it so much neater and quicker.'

Lurinda was tired of arguing with her daughter. After the visitors had left last night, Tom had called her downstairs and she timidly joined him. She expected to see Rancy all drawn up and out of her mind, but instead the girl was coherent and talkative and seemed just like the old Rancy. But then she started in on this Mary Roff business. That she wasn't really Rancy anymore, but Mary. And the unkindest part of all, that Lurinda wasn't her Ma anymore. That part hurt. Hurt a great deal.

She had found her daughter the same way this morning. Looking like the old Rancy with flushed cheeks and a ready smile but also with that strange other person inside her. She had tried to convince herself that she should be happy that Rancy was free of whatever it was that had held her and she verbally thanked God and that bearded doctor for their combined efforts, but when Rancy began speaking, all the uncertainty and confusion had come rushing back. Her daughter was her Rancy but at the same time wasn't her Rancy. She was someone named Mary Roff who had died and now was back. Lurinda thought maybe this Mary Roff person would go away in a little while and that Rancy would return to her old self. But her old self didn't appear. This Mary who was inside her wasn't like anyone she knew. And this Mary refused to call her Ma.

She had startled the girl when she had come downstairs to fix breakfast. The girl had fallen asleep on the living-room sofa. Tom hadn't put her back into the locked parlor. There she was asleep just as peacefully as you please with front door unlocked and nothing disturbed. When she had tiptoed across to look at her daughter, Rancy had opened her eyes and then pulled the blanket (Tom had thrown a coverlet on her after she had gone to sleep) over her face.

'Who are you?' she'd called out under the covers and Lurinda had pulled away the blanket so she could see it was her own mother. But the girl didn't believe her, in fact, didn't even recognize her.

'You're not my Ma!' she had said. 'My Ma is different from you.'

Lurinda was sure Rancy was still playing games and said nothing more to her. It was when she had to take her upstairs and show her where her own clothes were that she became upset all over again. There, in the dresser drawers and on the wall pegs, were the clothes that Rancy had picked out for herself from the catalogues or else had sewn before she became ill. But this morning she acted as if she had never seen any of them before. She took her pink dress (her favorite go-to-church dress) and held it up to the light as if she was seeing it for the first time. The same thing with her blouses and shawls. Finally she decided on wearing the pink one even though Lurinda protested that it was her *best* dress.

'If this is the best you have for me,' she had said, 'I see that we are going to have to go shopping this very afternoon. Where I live we would call this an ordinary workaday dress.'

'Where you live? This is where you live, young lady!'

'Oh no,' she had replied. 'I don't live here. I live with my folks, the Roffs. Don't you remember what I told you? We have that big house on the hill just above Fourth Street.' She started to get out of the crumpled pale green dress she had been in for days and asked where the hot water and soap were kept. 'You know, I can't stay too long. I can only stay a little while. I must get home tonight. Before suppertime.'

'Now, Rancy, cut that out. You *are* home and you ain't going nowhere before suppertime. You ain't been out of this

house in weeks and you sure ain't going anywhere today.'
Lurinda wished that Tom were home. He had gotten dressed and left the house before she had come downstairs. Why is it that whenever you needed a man he was never around? 'You just wait till I get you some hot water, and then when you wash you put on another dress. Not the pink one. And you are going to eat your supper right here.'

'But Loozie will have my place set for me at the table. And she gets real upset when you don't tell her you won't be there to eat.'

'Who?'

'Loozie. You know.' Then Rancy stopped and looked at her mother. 'No, I guess you wouldn't know her. She's an African woman. She works for us.'

'There ain't no black woman working for us,' Lurinda said. 'I don't know where you get these ideas! The only black woman in the entire town you know personally is Mrs Elmore and she and her husband work over at the feed store. And,' she added, 'her first name is Thelma. Not Loozie.'

'Her name is Loozie and she don't work in any feed store,' Rancy insisted. 'I ought to know. She's been with us as long as I can recall. When the war is over she's going to marry her boyfriend and they are going to live in Canada. I know this for a fact, because she told me so.'

'The war *is* over,' Lurinda said. 'But it'll start all over again, Lurancy Vennum, if you don't stop this nonsense!'

'My name is Mary Roff,' the girl insisted. 'How many times do I have to tell you? Lurancy isn't here. Lurancy is over there, on the other side. They are taking care of her.'

Lurinda started to say something else, then gave up. 'When your Pa gets back he'll have to decide what to do. I just ain't up to your shenanigans anymore. I swear to the good Lord above, I just can't take much more of this.'

And that's the way it went for most of the day. Tom returned and took his wife aside to tell her about his visit to Asa Roff's office and the fact that maybe – just maybe – there was some truth to all this stuff about ghosts and things inside Rancy's body. Lurinda had cried a great deal after that but to her surprise they weren't tears that left her sad. Somehow she felt relieved by the tears. Somehow, if she could believe that strange doctor, there was a cure for

Rancy. Maybe she would get better and not have to get locked up at the insane asylum. If only she could believe this. She tried to understand it the way her husband was trying to understand it but couldn't. Even if she didn't understand what was happening she could be glad that it was happening and pin her hopes to it. For a while anyway. Her hopes had had a very short life-span lately.

So she had gone along with the idea for the rest of the day that maybe whatever was going on would be beneficial. She hadn't argued with Rancy anymore after that but agreed with her and tried to keep up a conversation. Even when the girl used words she had never heard her use before, she didn't argue. Even when the girl called her 'Ma'am' and referred to Mrs Roff as 'Ma', she didn't object. Even when Lurancy complained about how poorly the kitchen was supplied with utensils in comparison with 'her' kitchen, she didn't protest. Lurancy seemed healthy and seemed to enjoy being out of the front parlor and helping her with the housework. They dusted the living-room and took the white things from the dirty clothes basket to soak. Lurancy had made a strange bean soup (strange to Lurinda anyway) for lunch and now was helping prepare the nighttime meal. It was the first time in weeks she had done this. Lurinda couldn't object and actually found herself thanking whatever it was for her daughter's almost miraculous recovery. And, another thing, Lurinda felt no fear. The terror of not knowing when her daughter would attack her or start doing harm to the house just wasn't there anymore. For some reason she felt safe with the child. This was a new feeling and one Lurinda cherished. If it hadn't been for the voice and the words the voice said, it would have felt like old times again. Old times when Rancy was her daughter and things were in their proper place in her tiny world.

Lurancy moved into the living-room after the potatoes were ready and Lurinda stayed in the kitchen.

'Ma'am!' Rancy called from the living-room. 'Ma'am, come quickly. Look who is coming up the walkway!'

At the girl's excited cry, Lurinda hurried into the living-room and peered out of the curtains. There were two women, bundled against the cold, in fine clothes.

'It's my Ma and my sister Nervie!' Lurancy almost

shouted. 'Oh, look at them! They've come to take me home!' She ran toward the door and pulled it open, dashing across the porch and into the snow-covered walk.

Ann caught Minerva's arm and held her back. The sight of this tall gangling girl rushing toward them, coatless in the freezing weather, was unexpected. The girl had her arms outstretched, shoved out as far as she could as if to embrace them both even before they were in range.

'Ma!' she called. 'Nervie! Oh, Ma! Oh, my dear sweet Ma!'

'Don't move,' Ann said quickly to Minerva. 'Let her come to us.'

And come she did, laughing and crying and slipping in the snow to grab both of them, hugging them, pulling them to her and trying to make her words understood even as her tears choked back the sounds. Ann and Minerva tried to pull away at first, but the grip was too strong. They let this unknown child hold them, let her stand there in the cold and let her cry.

Finally Minerva said, 'I think we'd better go into the house. You'll catch your death out here!'

'My death?' Lurancy laughed. 'I can't die.' Then she hugged them again. 'Oh Ma, we have so very much to talk about. I have so much to tell you. Both of you!'

'Rancy!' Lurinda shouted from the open front door. 'You get in here this minute.' Then in a softer tone. 'And Mrs Roff and Mrs Alter, please come in.' Then: 'Rancy Vennum, let the ladies be! Let them get inside where it's warm!'

'That woman still calls me Rancy,' the girl confided in a whisper. 'I've *tried* to tell her.'

'Well, Mary,' Ann said softly, humoring the girl and yet not finding it too difficult to pronounce the name 'Mary', 'we had better get inside, don't you think?'

'Oh, yes, Ma. Let's go in. I have some tea and there must be some bread and butter in that kitchen somewhere!' She stepped between the two women and, taking their arms, walked with them up the walk, onto the porch and into the house. Lurinda Vennum closed the door after them.

'I want to welcome you both to my home,' Lurinda said. 'If I had known you were coming I could have fixed it up a little bit, but you know things have been so hectic here lately that I really haven't had time to do anything at all.'

'Don't apologize, please,' Ann said quickly. 'Our visit was also decided upon at the last minute. We should have warned you we were coming.'

'But we had to see your daughter,' Minerva added, 'especially after what my father told us about her.'

'Oh, she's not here,' said Lurancy. 'Ma, the Vennum girl is on the other side. They're taking care of her over there. She's real sick, don't you know?'

Ann looked at Minerva and both of them looked at Lurinda, who shrugged her shoulders and twisted the hem of her apron.

'Here, Ma, let me help you with your coat. You too, Nervie. I'll take them and hang them up for you.' Lurancy quickly undid the buttons on the front of Ann's dark sealskin coat as Minerva unbuttoned her own. 'This is a new coat, isn't it, Ma? I never saw this one before.'

'Oh mercy, no,' Ann said, 'I've had this coat going on five years now.' Then she stopped. 'I'm sorry. Yes. For you, I suppose it is new. We didn't have it when you were still here . . . Mary.'

'And you look so good!' the girl spoke quickly as she hung up their coats. 'I mean, I didn't know what to expect. It has been so long! Oh, Ma, it's been so long!' She came back and embraced Ann, crying again, and not caring how her body shook with the sobs.

Ann reached up and stroked the girl's hair. 'There, there. It's all right now, child. Don't take on so. It's all right. Everything will be all right. You'll see.' As she held the body close she knew it wasn't the same body she had hugged so many times in the past. It wasn't the same body but the voice was the same. The same tones, the same inflections, the same tenderness that she had forced herself to forget. It had been better to forget. 'It's all right . . . Mary . . . it's all right. Ma's here. Your Ma's here.'

Lurinda stood watching, unable to say anything. Not knowing what was happening and not even trying to figure out where it might all be leading. 'I could put on some water for tea,' she finally said. 'I'm afraid I don't have much in the way of sweets to go with it, unexpected and all as it were.'

'We brought a sponge cake,' Minerva said. 'Mary always liked sponge cake.'

'Oh, I did, didn't I?' Lurancy laughed. 'I had almost forgotten. It's been so long since I've eaten.'

'Well, I'll get the water boiling,' Lurinda said, going into the kitchen. Lurancy watched her go and then motioned Ann and Minerva to sit on the sofa. She sat between them, holding their hands and smiling from one face to another.

'Have you come to take me home?' she asked. 'Oh, Ma, I'm so homesick for you and the boys and for Loozie. Oh, Ma, I think I'm going to start crying all over again.'

'Now we don't need any more tears,' Ann said, pulling a handkerchief out of her purse just in case. 'If you spend all our time crying your eyes out, we won't get any chance to visit now, will we?'

Lurancy shook her head. 'I'll try to be good,' she promised. 'But it is so wonderful to see both of you again!' She kissed Ann on the cheek and then kissed Minerva. 'Nervie, you smell so good! You always did buy the nicest perfumes! That old lady in the kitchen smells of onions and laundry soap. But don't tell her,' she whispered. 'She gets very upset and cries real easy.'

'I hope you haven't done anything to upset her,' Ann admonished. 'You know she is going through a difficult time right now.'

'Oh, I try to keep her calm, but she don't listen very well. I told her that her daughter wasn't here. That they have taken her away but she won't believe me. She thinks *I'm* her daughter. Ain't that crazy?'

'She probably loves her daughter,' Minerva said. 'And now that she's gone she misses her.'

'But she'll be back,' said Lurancy. 'She'll be back when she is all better again.'

'When will that be?' Ann asked hesitatingly. 'Soon?' She really didn't want to know the answer.

'I can't tell,' Lurancy replied. 'They told me that she would be gone as long as it took to cure her. She has some awful troubles in the mind and in the nerves. Something is wrong in her spinal cord and in one of the sections that pumps blood up to her brain. Somehow her brain doesn't get enough blood. Anyway, that's what they told me. And that's why I'm here! Ain't that lucky? For all of us?' She quickly kissed Ann again. 'I mean, if that girl had been in good health, I wouldn't be here now.'

'Why are you here?' Minerva asked. 'I don't quite understand how you can help her.'

'Oh, it's simple, really. That girl, Lurancy Vennum, was dying and it wasn't her time to go. So they asked me if I would come down and watch over her body until they could fix it all better.'

'Wasn't her time to go?' Ann asked in surprise.

'No. For some reason she is supposed to have a long life, but things weren't going that way and her physical self wasn't working right. Neither was her mental self. I mean, look at the way those others were able to use her. That ain't right, Ma. It ain't right that those others were able to do those things to her.'

'Others?'

'Those other people that came in and took her over. They just moved right into her and started working with her body and using her and making her do all sorts of terrible things. She even tried to kill her Ma once when one of them took her over.' The girl shook her head. 'That sort of thing shouldn't be allowed over there, but there don't seem to be any way to stop it.'

'Do you remember when you tried to kill yourself?' Ann asked, trying to test this new personality.

Lurancy stared at her. 'Me? Ma, I would never try to kill anybody!'

'When you had one of your spells, Mary,' Minerva said, 'you took a knife and hid in the woods and tried to kill yourself. Don't you remember?'

Lurancy looked from one to the other, a frown of doubt crossed her features. 'I took a knife . . . ' She shook her head, then closed her eyes. 'Are you sure?' she asked Minerva. 'Are you sure it was me?'

'Very sure.'

'I took a knife and . . . ' She was puzzled. Then her frown went to a look of recognition. 'Yes. Yes, now I recall it. But it wasn't *me* that tried to do it, it was one of them people that bothers the Vennum girl all the time. Now I remember!' She jumped up and started to roll up her sleeve. 'The scar is right here, on this arm. I took that knife and...' She stopped, puzzled. 'But the scar isn't here! Ma, the scar isn't here anymore. What happened to it?'

Minerva glanced at Ann. 'Because that's not your arm,' she said.

She stared at her skin, rubbing the exact spot where Mary Roff had stabbed her own arm almost thirteen years previously. Then she laughed. 'Of course. I forgot. That arm ain't here anymore. That arm's in the ground. They buried it when they buried the rest of me.'

Lurinda came out of the kitchen, with a brown glaze teapot on a wooden serving tray. The pitcher and creamer didn't match the pot and the plate the sponge cake was on was of a third pattern. 'I don't have a lot of nice tea things like you must have, Mrs Roff,' she apologized, 'but we seldom get visitors, and when they do come they have to take what's available.'

'Don't you worry,' Ann assured her. 'It doesn't matter what's on the outside of the pot. It's the contents inside that's important.'

Lurinda smiled and set the tray on the dining-table. She poured four cups, and after asking the two women if they took milk or sugar added it and served them. Then she cut the sponge cake and gave each of them a large slice. When it came time to hand Lurancy her cup, the girl declined.

'No thank you, Ma'am. I'm not eating.'

'Oh, just a little sponge cake, Rancy,' Lurinda coaxed. 'Mrs Roff brought it over here for you special.'

The girl shook her head. 'No, thank you. I won't eat anything at all. This body needs a rest.'

'Nothing at all, child?' Ann asked. 'Not even tea?'

'Nope. Nothing. Maybe when the body gets on even keel I can have something. But not until then. I'll know when.'

'How will you know?' Minerva asked.

'They will tell me.'

'They?' Lurinda looked at her daughter. 'They who?'

'They, Ma'am.' She smiled. 'That's all I can tell you. They don't really have names. None that you would know anyhow. But I do thank you, Ma, for bringing me that cake. Maybe later I can have some. It was real sweet of you to remember,' and she gave Mrs Roff another kiss.

Minerva was about to ask the girl how she knew her nickname was 'Nervie', when there was the sound of heavy footsteps on the front porch. All heads turned as the door opened and Tom Vennum came in with Dr Stevens. The two men stopped short in the doorway, neither of them expecting to see the Roff women.

Lurinda quickly tried to explain. 'Mrs Roff, this here is my husband, Mr Vennum.' He nodded in her direction, unsmiling. 'And this is her daughter, Mrs Alter.' Minerva smiled and bowed slightly. Neither of the women extended their hands. Ladies didn't shake hands without their gloves.

'This is Dr Stevens,' Tom Vennum introduced the tall, bearded man at his side. 'He's the one that worked on Rancy last night.'

The doctor bowed. 'Mrs Roff. Mrs Alter. Pleased to make your acquaintance.'

'Oh, no,' said Lurancy suddenly. 'This is my sister Minerva. Her name isn't Alter. At least not yet. Her name is Roff. Just like mine.'

'Why, that's no such thing,' Lurinda said. 'Her name is Alter. She's married to the assistant cashier at the bank.'

'That's right, Mary,' said Nervie. 'Henry and I got married.'

'When?'

'When the war was over Henry came back to Watseka and we was married. It's been about eleven years now.' She smiled. 'Of course you couldn't know. You went away before it happened. I thought about you a lot on the day of the wedding. You was to be my bridesmaid. Remember?'

Lurancy bowed her head. 'I remember, Nervie. And we was going to make me a long dress, peach colored, just like the one in that magazine. With all the ruffles on the front and the ribbons hanging behind.' She reached out and squeezed Minerva's hand. 'I'm sorry I went away when I did. I'm sorry if I caused you grief at your wedding.'

Minerva patted her arm.

'Don't pay it no mind.'

Dr Stevens had taken off his coat and hung it on the wall. 'Mrs Roff, I assume you have spoken with your husband over the incidents that occurred here last evening?' Ann nodded. 'What occurred has been most unusual. I have spent several years in this field and can truthfully state that I've never seen a case of possession last as long as this one already has. It's almost twenty-four hours and the entity has not departed.'

'I am well aware of who you are and what you do,' Ann said. 'I have read of your work and of your successes in some of the spiritual magazines. I want to thank you for what you have done here. You have undoubtedly saved this little girl's life.'

'I did nothing, madam,' he replied, again with a slight bow. 'All I did was clear the way for the spirit of your daughter to come in and do what she has been sent to do. It is,' he lowered his voice, 'your daughter. Isn't it?'

Ann reached out and put her arm around Lurancy's shoulders. 'Yes. I can say this quite definitely. This is my daughter. This is my Mary.'

'You are certain of it?'

'Quite certain. We have had time to talk and she has told us things that the Vennum girl couldn't possibly have known. The body is, of course, that of another, but the voice is Mary's. I've no doubt of that.'

'I'm confused,' said Tom. 'Last night she was Rancy in Rancy's body. Then she became Mary Roff in Rancy's body. She used to be my daughter and now she's not. You are her Ma and yet my missus ain't.' His voice started to rise. 'And everybody here acts as if this was the most natural thing in the world. Well, it ain't! I don't know what's happening and I don't like it!'

Lurinda stretched out her hand toward her husband. 'Don't take on so,' she said. 'These fine folks say it's all for Rancy's good. Maybe whatever is happening to her will keep her free. Will keep her out of the loony bin. God, Mr Vennum, we can't hope for anything better than that, can we?'

He sank into a chair. 'I suppose not,' he agreed. 'But I wish I understood it better. That's all.'

'But it's so easy, Mr Vennum.' Lurancy spoke up. 'Your daughter was ill. In fact, she was dying. But it wasn't her time to go. When those people started coming through her and making her sound so crazy and everything, people on the other side got worried and ...'

'The other side of *what?*' he demanded.

'The other side. You know. Where you go when you die.' She looked at him but as he didn't say anything else, she continued. 'There was much concern about her, and finally when it was decided that someone ought to come and take care of her, I volunteered. They said I could come back. It ain't usually done,' she added smiling at Mrs Roff, 'but I told them I had a great deal to make up for all the confusion and sadness I had caused my Ma and Pa when I was here before and this would be a good way to do it. I could help the Vennum girl and help my folks at the same time. They said it would be all right and here I am.'

'And you expect me to believe that?' Tom asked glaring at his daughter but already starting to treat her as if she were someone else.

'Believe it?' Lurancy was surprised for a moment. 'You mean you don't believe it? Well, sir, it's the truth. And you just have to believe the truth. Don't you, Ma? Don't you have to believe the truth?'

'It's not,' Dr Stevens said, 'that Mr Vennum doesn't believe you. It's just that it is all so strange for him. After all, this is not an everyday occurrence. To someone like the Vennums,' and he gave a deferential nod toward them, 'this is so far from anything that has ever happened to them, or indeed to anyone they have known, that it is quite difficult to understand.'

'You're damned right, it ain't easy to understand,' Tom said. 'All of a sudden my own daughter ain't who she has been all her life and instead she's the daughter of people who are perfect strangers. I can't bide that. Not just yet, anyhow.'

Lurinda decided to put her two cents in. 'And what *I* can't understand is how you, Mrs Roff, can take this so calmly. Is it because it ain't happening to *your* daughter?'

'Mrs Vennum,' Ann explained, 'twelve years ago my daughter Mary was about to be committed to the insane asylum in Springfield.'

'No! Your daughter?' Lurinda put her hand up to her face. 'I didn't know.'

'And she suffered just like your daughter has been suffering. The entire town was against us. The pressures were terrible. Then when we couldn't get help from anyone, not even our minister, we decided the best thing to do was to lock her up. The night before she was to leave she died.'

'Of what?' Tom asked.

'We don't know. Nobody knows. We heard a scream and she was dead. Just like that.'

'Oh, you poor thing,' said Lurinda. 'And that's where my Rancy was headed?'

'Obviously,' Dr Stevens replied. 'Rancy was having the same sort of attacks, only much worse. It would only have been a matter of time until she too would have died. As it is now, thanks to the spirit of Mary Roff, your daughter has been given another opportunity.'

'And you really believe this?' Tom still needed to be convinced.

'I do indeed. I've seen too much not to believe.'

'You're all talking about me as if I wasn't here,' Lurancy said. 'But I am here and I want to go now.' She got up from the sofa. 'Come on, Ma. Get your things, Nervie. Let me get my coat and we can go home now.'

'I don't think so,' Tom said.

'What?' Lurancy turned toward him. 'What do you mean? I want to go home with my Ma and my sister.'

'This is your home and you ain't going nowhere until you get a helluva lot better than you are now.' He stood up to face her. 'And that's final.'

'I want to go home!' she said in a loud but even voice.

'You are home!' he shouted. 'And you're going to stay home!'

Lurancy turned toward Mrs Roff. 'Ma! Tell this man I can go home with you. Please!'

'Well . . . ' Ann didn't want to get involved in a family fight. 'If Mr Vennum thinks . . . '

'That's right, Rancy,' Lurinda said. 'When you get better, then maybe you can go and visit with the Roffs some afternoon.'

'Some afternoon!' the girl was shouting now. 'Some afternoon.'

'Rancy . . . ' Tom warned.

'My name is not Rancy! Can't any of you see that? Can't you understand?'

'Now Rancy,' Lurinda began, but the girl spun around at her and the suddenness of it almost knocked her down.

'I was sent here to do a job,' the girl shouted. 'I was sent here and I intend to do that job! Ma. Nervie. You explain it to them. For some reason they are trying to hold me back from what I came to do. From what I *must* do.'

'Mary, dear,' Ann tried to soothe the chid. 'Maybe we could wait a few days until we see exactly how things are going to turn out. After all –'

'A few days! I don't have a few days to waste! Dr Stevens, you tell them.'

'He ain't telling us nothing,' Tom shouted. 'You live here and you're going to stay here. And one more sass out of your mouth and you're going right back into that room in there and I'll lock the door! You hear me?'

'And do you hear me?' Lurancy shouted. 'Watch closely! Watch what you are doing!'

She clutched at her throat and screamed. The others in the room backed away. Even Dr Stevens wasn't sure what was happening. Her face turned red, then began to go into a soft purple. The veins in her neck stood out. Her eyes bulged, then the pupils turned slowly upward until nothing but the whites could be seen. Her mouth opened in a cry that never was released. She sank to the floor, her face deepening in color, white flecks of froth starting to form at each corner of her lips. Her arms and legs jerked violently, quivered for a few seconds and then became stiff and rigid. She gave one loud gasp for air and her breathing almost stopped. Lurinda began to cry. Ann and Minerva stood together, watching in horror as the girl changed from a healthy teenager into an almost lifeless corpse. Tom could do nothing but stand and stare.

Dr Stevens glared at the Vennums and knelt down on the floor. Once again he began making those swooping hand movements over the girl's body. Again they hovered over her face, came down to her chest and then were raised and shaken. The hands moved and fluttered and shook until the color started to return into Lurancy's face. He passed his hands around her. Now her arms and legs became less rigid. Again the hands made their passes. The pupils of her eyes slid down into place and she closed her eyelids. Finally she sighed and took a deep breath, rolled over onto her side and pulled her legs up into a fetal position. She began to take deep regular breaths. She was sleeping.

'You know what she's done, don't you?' Dr Stevens said as he got up from the floor. 'She's shown you what Lurancy would look like if she were not inside controlling her body. You must not hinder this girl's work here on earth. To do so would mean death. Death to Lurancy and untold anguish to Mary.'

'I don't want my daughter telling me what to do,' Tom said stubbornly.

'And I, doctor,' Ann said, 'am uncertain if I want the responsibility of taking the girl into my home. Not under the present conditions.'

Dr Stevens looked at them, one at a time. 'I don't think,' he said slowly, 'that either of you has much choice in the matter. There are no roads open to agreements. You have both been given your orders. I, if you wish, will stay on in Watseka just a little longer to supervise her. I would not want the living girl's death or the dead girl's wrath on my conscience. It would be too much to bear. Much too much.'

That night after Ann told Asa everything she had seen at the Vennum home he bundled himself up in an old sweater and coat and went for a walk in the fields behind the house. It was his favorite place in the world. A place where he was always alone with his thoughts, and as the snow crunched under his boots in the darkness, he thought.

Mary was back. Mary wanted to come home. Mary, who had been dead for twelve years had suddenly appeared out of nowhere and returned to their lives. His life and Ann's life. Was this a good thing? Was it something to celebrate or to be avoided? What if he took the Vennum girl into his home and she started having those awful attacks of hers again? And if, during one of these fits, she attacked his Ann? Or did something to hurt one of the boys or the maid? Or maybe did something to hurt him? After all, when Mary had her fits all those years ago she had the power of ten men. There was no way of telling when one was going to come upon her and no way to rid her of them except letting them go away by themselves. That had been a difficult time in their lives and Ann had suffered mightily during it. Was it worth taking chances all over again? He and Ann were older now. They were no longer as young or as strong as they had been when Mary was alive. Alive for the *first* time, he added to himself. He would be sixty next year and Ann, at fifty-two, was showing her age. Did two old people dare to take on this awesome new responsibility that 'the other side' had thrust onto them? Could they handle it alone?

And what would happen to this girl, this gangling, rather plain schoolgirl, if the Roffs didn't take her in? Would she regain her health anyway? Was Dr Stevens correct in his reason for her sudden relapse tonight? Would Mary continue in her body even if she had to remain in the Vennum house? Would he, by his refusal, create further complications for a child that society had already doomed to an animal existence inside an asylum? Could he live with himself if he refused her now that she had asked him for aid and by his refusal would she worsen and die? Could he have this on his conscience for the rest of his life? Was it his decision? Did Asa B. Roff *really* have a decision in the matter?

'I thought you'd gone to bed,' he said to Ann, who was sitting in the parlor darning one of the boys' socks.

'I was waiting for you.' She looked at him and then back to her needle and thread. 'Did you decide?'

'Yes.'

'Will we bring the girl here?'

'Yes.'

'When?'

'The day after tomorrow. Give her mother time to fix her things.'

'Good.'

'I hope so,' he said and went upstairs.

February 11, 1878. A Monday. Mary Roff came home again.

Minerva had gone with Asa to help the Vennum girl pack her few things. Lurancy was Mary when they arrived. She had become Mary again shortly before she'd gone to bed the night before. She kissed Asa, calling him 'Pa', and hugged Minerva, calling her 'sister' and 'Nervie'. Tom Vennum helped carry the one old suitcase out to the buggy. His son Henry, staying home from work that morning, was formally introduced to the Roffs and gave Lurancy a close squeeze when she finally left the house. The girl had pulled away from him, embarrassed. He had tears in his eyes when his sister rejected him in this last minute. Lurinda never made an appearance. Her husband said she was upstairs with a sleeping potion and couldn't be disturbed. When Asa slapped the reins and the horse started trotting up Sixth Street, Lurancy didn't bother to look back.

From an upstairs window in the Vennum house, Lurinda pulled aside a curtain and watched them go. She wished she could cry but for some reason she was empty. All her emotions seemed to be used up.

'Ma! Oh, Ma! I'm home!' Lurancy ran up the steps onto the wide front porch and pushed in through the large double doors that led into the front hall. 'Ma! Hey, Ma!' She hurried into the first parlor and met Ann coming from the rear second parlor. They embraced, both women falling into each other's arms. Minerva stood beside them, watching the Vennum girl and her mother. Her father glanced into the room on his way upstairs with the suitcase. He almost stumbled on the first step because of the tears in his eyes.

Lurancy released her hold on Ann and stared around her. Her eyes were wide and the smile on her face was broad. 'Oh, it feels so good to be back!' she exclaimed. 'You have no idea!' She spun around a couple of times like a child playing on a front lawn. 'It feels so good!'

'Welcome home, Mary,' Ann said. 'It's been a long time. Too long.'

'Nothing seems to have changed much,' the girl said. 'That picture over there. How I used to love it. Remember? And over there you still have that funny statue!' She ran over to the table and picked up the porcelain figure of George Washington. 'Remember when that man had me do those things with this statue? Going out of the room and guessing what he did with it?' Before Ann could reply, or to get over her surprise that the incident should even have been remembered, Lurancy said, 'Oh! But somebody broke it. Look, one of the horse's feet is missing! Who did that?'

'It was Charlie,' Minerva said. 'He knocked it with his coat sleeve one day and it fell to the floor.' Then she added. 'You know. Charlie. Your brother.'

'Of course I know my brother!' Lurancy laughed. 'My baby brother! How is he? Where is he? Oh, Ma, I'm so anxious to see the boys again.'

'Well, Joe and Fen aren't here anymore,' Minerva said. 'Joe married a girl from New Jersey and he's living out there now. They have two little boys of their own. And Fen, he got married too. There was a girl at his school in Ohio and he married her and is living near Cincinnati. They have one baby, a boy.'

'Little Fen? Fenton is married? Oh, Nervie, don't joke with me. Fen ain't no more than nine or ten years old! Why I'm much older than he is and I'm only nineteen.' She laughed. 'Come on, Nervie. Tell me where Joe and Fen are.'

'They are married men now, Mary,' Ann said. 'They grew up and they went away to school and they got married.'

'But how could they, Ma?' She had a puzzled expression on her face. 'Little Fen and even Joe?'

'Time has moved on, Mary,' her mother took the girl's hands. 'Time moved on when your time stopped. You are only nineteen still. When you were here with us you were nineteen. But where you were, there is no time. Joe and Fen got older.' She laughed, 'Indeed, we all got older. You've been lucky. You've stayed the same.'

'I suppose so,' she said vaguely. 'I suppose so. But it's all so strange. I mean, to come home and not be changed at all and yet everyone around me is changed.' She sat down on the velvet sofa. 'And Frank and Charlie? Have they also gotten married since I was gone?'

'I hope not!' Ann laughed. 'Frank is but eighteen and Charlie won't be sixteen till July. No, don't make your brothers any older than they are. As it is, they think they're important men of the world.'

'They play music,' said Minerva. 'They have their own dance band and they play for parties and weddings and things. They're real good too. Frank plays trumpet and Charlie plays the piano and the violin.'

'I used to play the piano,' Lurancy said. 'Ma, do you recall how Nervie and I would play the piano and Nervie would sing?'

'You remember that?' Ann asked.

'Course I do. I used to play "We Are Coming, Sister Mary". It was my favorite hymn. Remember?'

'Heavens,' Minerva said. 'I haven't thought about that song in years.'

'I'd play it and you'd sing it and we would have such a good time!' She jumped up and looked into the front room. 'Ma, the piano ain't here anymore. What did you do with the piano?' She went over to the far wall. 'It used to set right here. What happened to it?'

'It's in Charlie's room now,' Ann replied. 'We thought it best to move it there when he started practicing so much. Anyway, he's been playing all those new waltz tunes, and they upset your father, because the boys hold the girls when they dance.'

'Is Pa becoming an old fuddy-duddy?' she laughed.

'You know,' she said, and a wistful look came over her face, 'where I have been there is the most beautiful music! It don't sound as if it's being played on anything you ever heard before. But it's there. In fact, it's all around and you don't get tired of it neither.'

'Harps?' Asa suggested.

She laughed at him. 'Oh, Pa, harps! You people on this side have some of the silliest notions! Harps!' She laughed again. 'And they don't fly around with wings, either.' Again the laugh.

'What is it like over there?' Ann asked. 'You know, child, we are all so curious. Really.'

'I wish I could explain it, Ma. I wish I could describe it the way you could understand it, but I don't think I can. It's so . . . so *different*.'

'In what way?' Asa sat in his favorite chair, ready to have heaven explained to him.

'Asa,' Ann said quickly, 'don't overtire the girl. She just got here and I'm sure we're going to have lots of time.'

'No we're not, Ma,' Lurancy said. 'We don't have lots of time.'

'What do you mean?'

'I mean that I won't be here with you forever.'

206

'But...'

'When this body is well and when the Vennum girl's mind is well, I'll be leaving you again. After all, I only came here for as long as it was necessary to help her. As soon as they tell me she's healthy again, I'll have to go back over there.'

'Oh Mary!' Ann hadn't expected this. Not so soon, anyway. 'But you will be with us for a bit? I mean, you aren't going to leave this very day or anything?'

'No, Ma,' she put her arm around the woman. 'I'll be here for a while longer. Don't ask me how long, but it will be more than just a few days. Anyway,' she said, laughing and squeezing Ann's shoulders, 'let's be happy that I came back at all! Let's not spoil it by worrying about the future. The present is the most important thing right now. The important thing is that I've been permitted to come back again. There aren't many people who've been given that special privilege. Really, it doesn't happen all the time.'

'I know,' Ann said, her voice getting husky with emotion, 'but it would be so nice if you could stay forever.'

'Ma, nothing is forever. If I've learned one thing over there it's that nothing lasts over here forever. It's always changing and you have to change with it. Those who don't change, don't grow. They say that change is as much of living as breathing is. They told me that people are not supposed to fight changes.'

'What kind of changes?' Minerva asked.

'Changes of any kind. Of loved ones, of money and even,' she smiled and kissed Ann's gray hair, 'of getting old. It's all part of their plan.'

'Whoever "they" are,' said Asa.

'Yes, Pa. Whoever "they" are. I really can't tell you who "they" are because I'm not sure myself. But I do know one thing. "They" have everything very carefully worked out in advance. We have to follow "their" plans.'

'And if we don't?' Asa asked.

'Disaster, Pa. Personal disaster.'

'Are you telling me we don't have any control over our own lives?' Asa questioned further.

'We have control in the beginning,' she said simply.

'In the beginning?'

'In the *very* beginning, before we even come into this

world.' She smiled. 'I wish you could be over there for some of the lessons.'

'I wish I could be too,' he said, 'but I'd like to return to my own home each time school was dismissed for the day!'

'Oh, Pa,' she shook her head at him, and laughed. 'Over there they say that before we decided to come back into this life we already knew what we had to do and how we had to do it.'

'Now you're preaching reincarnation,' Asa said. 'We never taught you that.'

'There was lots you didn't teach me, but I've had time to learn where I've been.'

'We choose what we want to do?' Minerva was uncertain what that meant.

'Yes. Before we return to earth in a new body we decide who our parents are to be so they can give us the proper start on the path we have to follow.'

'You mean I chose Ma and Pa before I was born?' Minerva asked.

'Yes, you did.'

'Like you chose the Vennums?' It was out before Minerva had a chance to think what she was saying.

'I didn't choose the Vennums,' Lurancy said quickly. 'That girl chose them. I chose Ma and Pa just like you did. I would *never* have chosen those people for my folks! But the Vennum girl did. Obviously there was a reason she had to live with them but something went wrong.' She sighed. 'That's the part I don't understand. I can't explain how things can go wrong when it has all been so perfectly set up in the beginning. I mean, *why?*'

'Well,' Asa volunteered, 'maybe the "why" of it is that if that girl hadn't taken sick, you wouldn't have been able to return to us. Perhaps your job wasn't quite finished when you left so suddenly. If there is a master plan to it all, your returning must be part of it.'

'Mrs Roff.' A voice called from the kitchen. Lurancy's expression changed instantly.

'Loozie! I forgot all about Loozie!' She ran through the parlor doors into the hall and directly into the kitchen. She stopped. Instead of the African woman she had expected to embrace, she saw a tall, thin, blonde woman. 'Loozie?' she called more quietly. 'Hello. Where's Loozie?'

Ann was right behind her. 'Loozie isn't with us anymore, Mary. She left here to go with her husband. Right after the war.'

'Oh, but I so wanted to see Loozie!' Lurancy's chin began to tremble. 'I had so much to tell her.'

'She went away right after you did,' Ann said softly. 'Her man came for her and they were married. Then she moved to Canada. We still hear from her every now and then. She has three little babies of her own now.'

'Three little Loozies,' Lurancy smiled. 'I'd love to see her again. And see the babies. Do you think we could go there one day before I leave and see her? Do you think we could do that, Ma? Oh, I'd really love it. There are so many things I have to tell her.'

'We'll see,' Ann replied. 'Maybe your Pa could make some arrangements. We'll see. But now I want you to meet Charlotte.' The blonde woman extended her hand. 'Charlotte, this is my daughter Mary. You know,' she said looking the woman squarely in the face, *'the daughter I told you about?* The one who has been *away* for so long?'

'Pleased to meet you, Miss Mary,' the woman said in her thick accent. 'Your Ma has told me a lot about you. I hope we can be friends.'

'Oh, I'm sure we can,' the girl replied. 'It's just that I was expecting to see my Loozie. I'm sorry if it sounds as if I'm disappointed at seeing you here instead. It's nothing personal, really.'

'I know,' the woman assured her. 'Your Ma told me all about you and all about Loozie too. I hope you are happy to be back here.' She looked at the girl and then at her employer. This was the Vennum girl. The girl that all the other maids and cooks in town had been talking about. Crazy Rancy Vennum who was dangerous and was about to be locked up. Mrs Roff had explained everything in detail to Charlotte, and the German woman supposed she could go along with it as long as it lasted. But she had warned Ann that at the first sign of any craziness on that girl's part, she was leaving. She liked the Roffs, the pay was good and the work wasn't too bad, but she didn't want to get killed. Not by some crazy. As long as the Roffs took care to see that this girl didn't get too close to her it would be all right. She had seen crazies in Germany. She didn't want any part of them here.

'Your Ma tells me you like stuffed chicken and dumplings,' she said trying to smile for the benefit of her employer, 'and I made them special for you tonight.'

'Thank you,' the girl said, 'but please don't worry about me and food. I won't eat anything for a while.'

'Not eat?' the cook's voice rose. 'I made the dumplings just for you!'

'No, thank you. I mean, *thank* you, but I'm not eating any food at all.'

'But you'll get sick and starve,' the woman protested.

'I'll be all right. I go to heaven for my tea.'

'And what is that supposed to mean?' the woman asked.

'That I get my nourishment in heaven.' She smiled. 'You'll see, so please don't fuss about any special food for me. I mean it.'

'Nothing?' The cook looked at this crazy girl and then back at Ann. 'I'm to fix *nothing* for her? Nothing at all?'

'In the beginning,' Ann said, 'let's just see what happens. You can set her plate at the table and if she eats, fine. If she doesn't that will be her affair.'

'All right, missus. You just let me know when I should start adding enough for one more person.' The crazy Vennum girl could starve for all she cared. 'Just let me know. That's all I ask.'

'I shall,' Ann replied. 'You don't worry about it.'

'I won't,' Charlotte said. And she meant it.

Frank and Charlie had been briefed – and warned – the night before about Lurancy's visit and they had discussed it between themselves that morning and then on their way home from school. Neither of them remembered their sister Mary. Frank had been almost five and Charlie not quite three when she died. They had heard about her, of course, heard about her all their lives. Mary was a strange skeleton in their family closet but that closet door had remained closed to everyone but their parents' most intimate friends. Suddenly the door was opened again and a live girl – not a ghost – came walking out.

'Lurancy Vennum, of all people,' Frank had said to Charlie when they were alone. 'Crazy Rancy.'

'She's a stick to look at,' Charlie agreed. He was almost sixteen and an expert on feminine beauty. 'I heard about what she did at school. Pushed old Miss Blades on the floor and pulled her hair. Kids said Miss Blades was screamin' and hollerin' like she was about to be butchered.' He sighed. 'Wish I had been there.' Miss Blades had never been one of his favorite teachers.

'I don't understand why Pa has to bring her into the house.' Frank was concerned. 'I mean, when her own father boarded up their windows and everything. Do we want a crazy living with us?'

'Ma says she's changed. That it's only Lurancy's body. Mary is inside. You remember how she told it. Like Mary had come back and moved into an empty house.'

'Empty head, you mean!' said Frank and they both laughed.

On their way home they agreed to be nice to the girl for their folks' sake. They both loved their Ma and Pa and both parents were so excited about Mary's return. If it would make the old folks feel better, they'd go along with it. Anyway, how long could it last? A day or two at the most. They had sat in on seances, seen spirits come in, say a few words and then go out again. They both thought there was 'something' out there all right, but exactly what they didn't know. One good thing about their folks being Spiritualists, it got them out of having to go to a Watseka church every Sunday.

Lurancy was sitting in the parlor with Nervie and the Roffs. The boys put their books on the hallway table, brushed back their hair with spittle on their palms, and entered the room.

Lurancy looked up, startled by the intruders. She rose halfway, was about to say something and then turned to Ann. 'Ma? Is this Frank and Charlie?' Ann nodded. 'Grown so big and tall! I *never* would have known you!' She rushed toward them and threw her arms around Frank and then around the younger boy. She kissed them on the cheeks and forehead. 'Oh, Frank and Charlie! Just think! How wonderful it is to see you again.'

The boys pulled away, embarrassed at being hugged and

kissed by Crazy Rancy. And in front of their parents, too. Minerva came to their rescue.

'Haven't they grown, Mary? I didn't think you'd recognize them.'

'They shot up like weeds in a bean patch!' Lurancy exclaimed. 'And so handsome too!' She put herself between them, linking arms. 'And I have so much to tell you both. Some of the things I've seen and the places I've been. Just think,' and she pulled away to gaze at them again, 'it's been twelve years since I last saw you. Twelve years!'

Both Charlie and Frank wanted to say it hadn't been but about two months since they had last seen *her*, but Ann's wagging finger kept them from mentioning it.

'It's good to see you too, Mary,' Frank said looking at his mother for a sign of approval. Which he got.

'Yes . . . Mary,' added Charlie. 'It's nice to have you home again. Been an awful long time.'

'Too long,' the girl said. 'Much too long. But we'll make all that up, won't we?' She kissed them again. 'We'll have lots of time before I go away again. Frank, dear, dear Frank, do you still like to watch the ants and the bees?'

'Huh?'

'I was just recalling with the folks how you used to spend so much time at the riverbank watching the ants and trying to catch honeybees so they didn't sting you.' She laughed. 'And you Charlie, oh, you were such a little tyke then! None of the other boys wanted you to go fishing with them because you would throw stones and twigs into the river and scare away the fish. Do you recall that?'

Frank was amazed. 'Yes,' he said quickly, 'I do remember looking at ants and insects while Joe and Fen were fishing! That's great! Ma, that's really great that she would know a thing like that!'

'She doesn't know it,' Ann said, 'she is remembering it. There's a difference.' She felt she had to give her two youngest further instructions. 'This is your *sister*. Your sister Mary who has been *away* for twelve years. You were both little shavers when she went *away*. I'm not surprised you don't remember her, but don't be surprised that she remembers *you*.'

'Is that clear?' their father asked.

'Yes, sir. That's clear,' they replied almost in unison.

'But Mary, if you've been away so long, then you must have a great deal to tell us.' Frank was warming up to the idea of having someone who had been to heaven tell him all about it. 'Is it everything they say it is? Over there?'

'Everything and more,' she replied, 'but you folks have a lot of funny ideas about it that will have to be cleared up.'

'Will you tell us about it?' he asked. 'I mean really tell us? I'm dying to know.'

'That's pretty good,' put in Charlie. 'He's dying to know and most people have to *die* to know.' He laughed. 'Do you get it, Ma? Frank said he was dying to know!'

'I got it,' Ann said sternly, 'but I didn't appreciate it.' She rose from the sofa. 'I'm sure supper is on the table by now. Let's all wash our hands and then sit down to eat. We can talk later. She took Lurancy's arm and went into the diningroom. 'Here, Mary dear, you sit beside me.' She pointed to a place setting and Lurancy pulled out the chair and sat down. In a few minutes the others were at the table, hands washed and heads bowed.

'Oh Father,' Asa prayed. 'We thank Thee for this food tonight and we especially thank Thee for bringing our daughter and sister Mary back to us. Even if it's only for a little while. We missed her and we love her and we welcome her back at our home and at our table. I'll admit that we don't understand what has happened or even why it's happened, but we thank Thee for it. We thank Thee and ask Thee to let our happiness continue as long as possible. And Lord,' he added, 'look after Lurancy Vennum.' The boys opened their eyes to catch the girl's reaction. 'Take care of her body. Cleanse her mind.' Lurancy had her head bowed. 'Make her well and whole and deliver her safely to her parents again. Thank you. Amen.' He opened his eyes and raised his head.' Now we can all eat.'

'That was a very nice prayer, Pa,' Lurancy said. 'I'm sure it will do Lurancy a great deal of good. Wherever she is.'

It took the family, all of them, two or three days to adjust to the fact that Mary was back again, even though she was in another girl's body. At first the boys would slip up and call her Rancy, at which she always corrected them. Minerva dropped in daily and had long talks with Lurancy, as the girl recalled people and events and even minor happenings from Mary's past. The most difficult part for Lurancy was accepting the fact that Nervie had married. Her husband, Henry Alter, came to visit once and she recognized him and they chatted, but it was about war things and the fears they all had that maybe Henry wouldn't come home after it was over. He had to admit that the Vennum girl knew an awful lot about the Roff family, especially the part dealing with their past. Why, she even knew things that he didn't know and he had been in the family for some twelve years. He had returned to Watseka in August of 1865, one month after they buried Mary at Old Town cemetery. She still referred to the place as Middleport. Nowadays everyone in Watseka called that part of town 'Old Town'.

Henry Alter had several long discussions with Nervie about the Vennum girl moving into his in-laws' place. It wasn't the smartest thing her father ever did, he told her. Already people in town were talking about it, wondering why Mayor Peters had countermanded his order to have the girl committed to the Springfield asylum. Lots of people thought the mayor was wrong. Almost all of them thought Asa was wrong. Instead of ridding the town of that crazy girl, Asa had brought her out into the open. Granted, the girl had changed a great deal. She was calm now and helped Ann with the housework and was giving her poor mother a rest, but the Roffs didn't keep their doors locked at night. Nobody in Watseka did. Just imagine what would happen if she had another of her fits and escaped? No, it wasn't the best thing Asa could have done for the community.

'They say she doesn't eat a bite of food all day!' Lavinia Durst was still trying to get over the shocking news she had just heard. 'Imagine having that terrible child in their own home! I can't understand what got into Asa and Ann.'

'It's all that doctor's doings. You know, the one with the full beard that's staying at the Williams House?' Sarah Thayer should have been home by now, but another minute of street-corner gossip couldn't hurt anything. 'Somehow that doctor got the mayor to agree to hold off sending Crazy Rancy away. I'm really surprised at Matt Peters doing such a thing. I doubt seriously if I will vote for him if he decides to run again.'

'And I as well! It's a disgrace that a man who is *supposed* to represent the good of the community would so *defy* us by allowing that girl to go free!'

'Just as we were all ready to breathe a sigh of relief over sending that girl away!' She adjusted her grocery parcels. 'The one I feel sorry for is poor Lurinda Vennum. When she thought her trials and tribulations were over she finds out they have only just begun. Of course her husband is worthless. Absolutely worthless. No man who was anything would permit his daughter to go and live with another family and,' she lowered her voice for emphasis, 'a family that has two young boys. If you get what I mean.'

Sarah looked at her for a second and then a smile came across her lips as she got Lavinia's meaning. For propriety's sake, she quickly turned that smile into a frown. 'Oh, I never thought of *that*. Frank and Charlie in the same house with that crazy girl. Well, anything could happen.' She cheered up at that prospect. 'What are you going to do?' she asked.

'I don't know just yet,' was the reply. 'First of all I'm going to have a talk with Martha Baker; she and the Reverend will have to take the initiative. The Vennums are members of his church.'

'Or were until Tom took a shotgun to the minister,' Sarah reminded her. That had been a great bit of news when it happened.

'And the Roffs used to be Methodists until they joined that crazy Spiritualism thing. No,' said Lavinia, 'the Reverend Baker will have to handle this.'

'And if he doesn't?'

'Then, I suppose, I will have to see to it.' Lavinia sighed at her own importance in the community.

Sarah put a comforting hand on Lavinia's shoulder. 'You are a Christian martyr, Lavinia. A Christian martyr.'

Dr Stevens opened the door to Asa's office. 'How is Mary?' he asked as he walked over to the large desk and shook the lawyer's hand.

'Fine.' Asa was glad to see him. 'Just fine. There hasn't been a bit of trouble since she came home.' He stopped and then smiled. 'You know, I do that naturally now.'

'What?'

'Call her Mary and think that she's come "home".' He shook his head. 'And it's a good feeling too.'

'And Mrs Roff, is she still of the same opinion? That the Vennum girl should stay?'

'Indeed! She's all for it. You know, Doctor, my wife has perked up and seems to be livelier since Mary came back. It's been a tonic for her.'

'And the boys? Any trouble with them?' he asked.

'None at all. Oh, every now and then they called her Lurancy, but that's over now. They think of her as their sister. It's really quite heartwarming to see.'

'How about your maid? What's her name? Charlotte?'

'Oh, no problems with Charlotte either. Just that Mary won't eat her cooking. Says she takes her tea in heaven. You know, Doctor, I'm concerned about that point. The girl hasn't eaten one bite of food since she came to live with us. It's a week today. Only a few sips of water. Is that normal?'

'Mr Roff,' the doctor had a smile under his beard, 'in this business can anything be called "normal"?'

'I suppose not,' Asa laughed, 'but I do worry about her health.'

'You are not to worry,' the doctor reminded him. 'Mary says that Lurancy's health is being taken care of on the other side. When the time comes that they wish her to eat and drink in normal quantities, I'm sure she will do it. Mary is in charge of the body now and seems to be doing a good job of it, from what I hear.'

'When are you going to come and visit her again?' Asa asked. 'It's been three days since you last saw her.'

'I don't think she needs me. Not right now. Mary is in complete control and there is nothing more I can do. I have been seriously considering going home to Wisconsin for a while. To see my wife and daughters.'

'And leaving Watseka?' Asa began to panic. 'But what if something goes wrong? What if Lurancy has another of her fits? I don't think my wife or I could handle it without you, sir.'

'I'm sure you could,' was the reply. 'Just think back to when your own daughter had her fits. You let them run their course and then you put the child to bed. Correct?' Asa nodded. 'All you have to do is the same thing this time. But, and I have been giving this case a great deal of thought, I don't think that will be necessary. The spirit of your daughter is a strong one and she is in complete charge of the girl's body. She told me herself that she expects to be around for at least three more months.'

'Three *months?*' This was news to Asa. 'When did she tell you that?'

'When I examined her the last time. She says she was told that Lurancy is making very good progress and should be ready to return to claim her own body by mid-May.'

'So she'll be with us during March and April and most of May,' he said.

'Mid-May is what I was informed. Yes. If Lurancy is indeed improving the way Mary says she is, then there is really no need for me to stay here. I will leave on the afternoon train for Chicago and then catch another train for Janesville.'

'But you'll leave your address so we can contact you?'

'Of course. I have it written here. A telegraphic message will reach me in half a day from Watseka. I can be back here in two days at the very most. However, I don't think that'll be necessary.'

'Wouldn't you like to see Mary again before you leave?'

'No, but I will return to Watseka to see her before *she* leaves. She has promised to have a long discussion with me about life over on the other side and I'll use my time in Janesville to draw up a list of suitable questions.'

'I shall tell Mary you said good-bye,' Asa said. 'She'll be sorry not to have seen you again.'

'I don't want to upset her. That's why I'm not saying good-bye personally. Let her remain in your household and let things continue on an even keel. My leaving would bother her. Just tell her I was called home but I shall return in a month or so. Tell her calmly, don't stir up any undue emotions. She needs peace and calmness around her at all times. Any major disturbance could disturb her as well and could be dangerous. For her and for those near her.'

'I understand,' Asa said.

'Thank God you do, Mr Roff. Thank God you do.'

The next evening the Vennums came to call. It had been arranged in advance. Tom had come by Asa's office that morning saying his wife was feeling much better thank you and was awful lonely without Rancy. Would it be possible to visit her? If only for a few minutes?

And so they got ready to visit the big brick house on the hill. Lurinda spent the entire day fussing over her clothes. It was the first time she had ever been in such a fancy residence and she didn't want to look out of place. She wore a green, rusty almost-taffeta dress with a full skirt and balloon sleeves. She wished she had a better visiting shawl than the white thing she had knitted herself, but it was better than nothing at all, she supposed. She combed her hair tightly back and stuck a tortoise-shell comb in the bun. With her hair back like that she could wear the gold earrings her mother had left her. She almost never wore them. Tom didn't like to see her 'all geegawed up like a fair horse'. She put on her bonnet (it *almost* matched her dress if you used your imagination) and then her heavy old winter coat over it all. She'd take her coat off just inside the door. That way only a few people would see her in it.

Tom washed and shaved and even put on a tie for the occasion. There was some minor cussing when he couldn't find his collar button. He only had one of them and it was forever falling under the dresser or into one of the cracks in the bedroom floor. He wore his church pants and a dark coat. She wished he had better shoes, but you never could tell that man nothing.

Young Henry had nice clothes. He earned them with his own money. He put on his square suit (Lurinda called it that because it had large plaids in it) and wore a pink dress shirt with a red string tie. Red ties were all the rage in Chicago, they told him when he picked it out at Wade's Clothing Store. His father wasn't so sure about a red tie for a man. He thought it was a 'sissy color' but Henry didn't care. He and Lurancy had looked at the ties together when Wade's had them in their window and she had admired the red ones. He was really wearing it for her, not his grumpy old man.

Minerva opened the door for them, shaking their hands and helping them with their coats. Lurinda was the first one out of hers and glad to leave it hanging on the hallway peg.

Minerva complimented her on her earrings and Tom just stared.

Minerva led them through the front parlor into the rear parlor, the room the entire family preferred because of its view down the fields and into the riverlands below. Lurinda kept looking to the right and left as if she were being taken on a swift tour of a museum.

'Everything is just so beautiful!' she gushed as Ann rose to meet them. 'I never saw such a beautiful house in all my born days! And look, Tom, there's a fireplace! With tiles around it. Oh, I always said I wanted to have a fireplace with tiles. Just like that one. Didn't I always say that, Tom?'

Tom grunted and shook hands with Asa. Then he introduced Henry to Mrs Roff. Minerva's husband was not there and the boys had been sent to their rooms while the visit took place. Asa didn't want any more confusion than was necessary.

'Lurancy is still upstairs in her room,' Ann explained. 'We've been working on a new dress and she's going to wear it tonight. She shouldn't be too long. Please, take a seat. Mrs Vennum, why don't you sit here on the sofa with me, and Mr Vennum, you can take that chair next to Mr Roff. Master Vennum, you can pull that chair up next to your father's. Men always have things to talk about, don't they, Mrs Vennum?' She smiled.

'They talk more than us women,' Lurinda agreed. 'But you'd never get them to admit it. And they say *we* gossip!' She leaned back on the sofa, getting the feel of the softness of the horsehair under the red velvet. She liked anything that smacked of elegance. 'You sure have a nice place, Mrs Roff. You sure do.'

'Thank you,' Ann said. Then, 'I know you are worried about your daughter, but you needn't be. She is fine. Perfectly fine.'

'You mean she is Rancy again?' Tom asked harshly. 'Or does she still think she's your girl?'

'No. She is still under the control of my daughter,' Asa put in quickly. 'It's not that she *thinks* she's my daughter, Mr Vennum, she *is* my daughter. At least in her mind. The body still is your daughter, but the mind that powers that body belongs to mine.'

'I've tried to explain things to Mr Vennum,' Lurinda said, 'but somehow it just won't stick. I had a long talk with that nice Dr Stevens. He came by the house before we left and explained what was happening in great detail. Mr Vennum, unfortunately, wasn't to home that day. I wish he had been. Maybe he could understand things better.'

'I understand things,' Tom answered, 'but I don't know *why* they are happening to our Rancy.' He waved a hand at Lurinda before she could continue. 'I know that Rancy is sick in the head and sick in the body and that your daughter came from spirit land and took her over. And will be with her till she's cured and can be her old self. I know all that. What I don't know is *why*.'

'Why? Why what, Mr Vennum?' Ann asked.

'Why it had to happen to *our* girl. Why with all the girls all over the world who get sick, did this thing, of your daughter coming in, have to happen to *her*? Why was Rancy chosen? What is so special about Rancy that this should be happening to her? Is she becoming some kind of Catholic saint, or something?'

'I don't think any of us can answer that, Mr Vennum,' Asa said. 'We don't any of us understand the workings of the spirit world. It's something we just have to accept.'

'I can only accept what I understand,' Tom was adamant.

'If it ain't before Pa's eyes where he can touch it, he won't buy it,' Henry said. 'But I know what Pa means. He means that –'

'When I need you to explain myself, Master Henry, I'll ask you.' Tom was getting embarrassed. 'Don't need no kid of mine telling the world what I think just after I've gotten through saying it.'

'Sorry, Pa.'

Ann got up from the sofa. 'I'll go and see what's taking Lurancy so long. I can understand you perfectly, Mr Vennum. It is very difficult even for Mr Roff and myself to understand the whys of spirits and the things they do. Even more difficult for us to understand why they waste time on us imperfect mortals. But they do. I believe that they do. Dr Stevens has seen much more than I have and he is convinced that spirits are operating in the human realm all the time.

And Dr Stevens is a learned man. Of that, you'll surely agree.'

'Yes,' said Tom. 'I do. He is a good man and he saved our Rancy's life. I'll always be grateful to him for that. If it hadn't been for him she'd be locked up over in Springfield this very minute.'

There were footsteps on the stairs. 'Oh, I think your daughter is coming down now,' Minerva said. Then she called: 'Mary? Is that you?'

'Yes, Nervie.'

'We're in here. In the back parlor.'

Lurancy came in through the double doors to the parlor. 'Oh Ma,' she said looking at Ann. 'Just see how nice the dress fits! It really is – ' Then she stopped. 'I'm sorry, I didn't know we was having company.'

'We ain't company, child!' Lurinda laughed. 'We're family.'

'Yeah,' Henry added. 'How you doin', Rancy?'

Lurancy looked at them. 'I'm sorry,' she said using Mary's voice. 'But I don't think we have been introduced. Pa, are these folks new neighbors?'

'These are the Vennums,' Asa said. 'Mr and Mrs Vennum and this here is young Henry Vennum.'

'Aw come on, Rancy,' Henry said. 'Say hello to Ma. She's been looking forward so to seeing you.'

Lurancy passed a hand over her forehead. 'My name is *not* Rancy, or whatever you called it. My name is Mary Roff. I hate to be insistent but I wish people wouldn't keep getting us mixed up.' She walked behind Ann's chair, standing there with one hand on her shoulder. 'This keeps happening all the time,' she said, 'and it's wearying.'

Lurinda started searching her bag; she was about to have the sniffles and wanted her handkerchief near. 'Rancy, honey,' she said, 'don't you recognize your own Ma?'

'Of course I do,' the girl replied. 'This is my Ma. This lady right here.'

'And I suppose he's your Pa?' Tom asked pointing at Asa.

'Of course he is. My Pa is Mr Roff, the lawyer.'

'And me? Who am I?' Henry asked.

'You? What kind of a funny game is this? You were just presented to me as named Henry. So I suppose you are

Henry.' She laughed but there was sarcasm there. 'And to make the circle complete, that lady is Mrs Vennum and he is Mr Vennum and that lady over there is my sister Nervie Alter. And I am Mary Roff.' She added that last with a note of finality to her voice, hoping that this name business would be finished.

'She is still bewitched,' Henry said.

'There is nothing of witchcraft here, young man!' Asa spoke up quickly and loudly. 'I don't want that kind of talk used in this house! Your sister Lurancy has gone away from her body and my daughter Mary has taken it over for a few weeks. It has nothing to do with witchcraft!' Then he lowered his voice. 'I'm sorry, but people must understand the difference. Especially you people, especially Lurancy's family. You people must understand! If you don't it will just make matters worse and take Lurancy that much longer to get better.'

'*If* she gets better,' Tom remarked.

'She will,' Ann assured him.

'How do we know?' The end of Lurinda's nose had turned pink. 'How do we know she'll get better? It looks like she is getting worse instead of better.'

'Worse?' Minerva said. 'How can you say that?'

'Well,' Lurinda sniffled, 'before she was out of her mind but she was still Rancy. Now she is out of her mind *and* her body and she's somebody else. Don't you call that getting worse?'

'No I don't!' Lurancy's voice was startlingly loud. 'Can't you people understand that Lurancy is being helped? Can't you get it through your heads that she is being cared for? Is your ignorance about the working of spirit that dense that you cannot fathom what is taking place?'

'Don't you call your Ma ignorant!' Tom shouted.

'And don't you shout at me, either! Your wife is not the only ignorant one in your household! If you had tried to understand your daughter and given her love she might not be in this situation right now!' Lurancy's voice was loud. 'But you locked her in a room and even kept her tied to the wall like some animal. When she needed compassion you gave her chains!'

'Please, Mary,' Ann reached up to comfort the girl. 'You

mustn't speak to the Vennums in that tone of voice. They didn't know what they were doing. They're sorry.'

'Now they're sorry,' she said. 'They arc only sorry that their daughter didn't die. They can understand physical death but they can't fathom the kind of spirit rest Lurancy is having. If they could have locked her up or buried her in the ground, then they would have understood. But they are lacking in many human qualities and one of them is compassion.'

'Maybe it would have been better if you had died,' Tom yelled. 'Then it would all have been over. You would have been six feet under and your Ma would have suffered but she'd have gotten over it. Alive and crazy like you are now is even worse than being dead!'

'Really, Mr Vennum,' Asa stood up. 'I cannot permit you to talk that way in my home. We have taken your daughter in to give her protection while she is being healed. Can't you understand that?'

'And who asked you to take her in?' Tom turned on him.

'You did, sir. You came to my office and asked me to take her to my home.'

'Only after that Mary thing inside her kept insisting on it,' Tom was still shouting. 'She kept up that yammering until we had to agree.'

'That yammering, as you call it,' Lurancy's tone now matched his, 'was the only way I could take the body out of that negative environment.'

'And I should have taken a switch and beat the piss out of your negative environment, young lady!' In a flash Tom was over beside her. 'This is all play-acting, and I won't have no more of it. You're coming back home with me!' He reached out and grabbed her arm. 'You're coming back to your own house where you belong!'

Lurancy stared at his finger. 'Take your hand off me, mister,' she said in a low voice.

'You get your things and let's get out of here. You don't belong here.'

'Take your hand off me.'

Lurinda talked through the tears that were falling faster now. 'Rancy, do as your Pa says. Don't get him riled up. Please!'

'And don't get me riled up!' the girl answered, and reaching across she grabbed Tom Vennum's stout fingers with her own. They came down on him like steel claws, pulling his hand away and flinging it aside. He looked at his hand, stunned by the unexpected strength and the pain.

'Goddamn you girl,' he shouted. 'You'll do as I say or else!' He swung at her, but before his hand could reach her face her arm was up, protecting. His wrist smashed into her forearm. Asa heard the crunch across the room. Tom howled and fell to the floor, clutching his wrist and cursing. Lurinda was frightened and, not knowing what to do, she began to cry louder.

Lurancy walked to the parlor doors, then turned and without even glancing at her father, said: 'I'm going up to my room now. I'm sorry this had to happen but nothing must stand in the way of this body's treatment. Nothing or nobody.' She looked at Asa and Ann, her eyelids not moving. 'I had one reason for coming back and I fully expect you two to make certain this type of interruption shall never happen again. I don't want to see these people until Lurancy is ready for them. I trust they will not be allowed back here until I have given you permission. Good-night, everyone.'

As they heard her footsteps ascending the stairs Lurinda began sobbing. 'My baby! My own baby girl! She doesn't want me anymore. Oh my God, Tom, Rancy doesn't love us anymore!'

In the days that followed some of the townspeople who had known Mary came to call. It was more curiosity than friendship. They all wanted to see this strange bird that looked like Rancy Vennum yet talked like Mary Roff.

None of them was disappointed.

There was old Doc Fowler, who came asking if he could be of some assistance even though he had been retired three years. He had never had the Vennums for patients, yet Lurancy knew him immediately.

'Did you bring those things in the bottle?' she asked.

'In the bottle?' How much had the Roffs told the girl? 'What things?'

'Those slimy things like small snakes that you used to put on my neck. You know, they drank my blood and made me feel better.'

'You remember the leeches?'

'Of course I do! I also recall that I wanted you to leave some here so I could have them as pets and you wouldn't do it. You said they cost too much money and had to come through the Rebel lines up the Mississippi.'

'Good heavens,' he exclaimed, 'that's right. I'd forgotten that. In order to get them during the war I had to have a friend send them from New Orleans by riverboat. Extraordinary,' he said to Ann, who was sitting next to the Vennum girl. 'Extraordinary!'

'That's what they've all been saying,' Lurancy replied. 'Everyone seems to think it so strange that I have a memory at all! You know I bet I recall things that other people have already forgotten. My memory always was good, wasn't it, Ma?'

Ann nodded. 'Mary never forgot a face or a birthday or a street number. I never bothered to write things down that I wanted to recall, I'd just tell them to Mary and she'd have the information whenever I needed it.'

'Well,' the doctor hesitated, 'as I hear it the Vennum girl wasn't the smartest thing at school. Didn't have no great shakes at recall. At least that's what the teachers are saying anyways.'

'That's true,' Lurancy agreed. 'That girl wasn't the brightest when it came to her books. But she was young and didn't have no real training at home. Like I did. My Ma taught me to read when I was hardly five years old. Didn't you, Ma? Remember how we looked at the pictures and the words in that little book and you taught me to read it before I started to school?'

'Good heavens,' Ann laughed, 'now it's my turn to say "extraordinary". I'd clean forgotten that you knew how to read before the first grade started.'

'You see?' the Vennum girl smiled. 'I got my Pa's brains. The Roff brains are the best brains in town!'

'Do you remember Tessie?' Dr Fowler would always remember Tessie.

'The cat? Old Tessie, the cat? Yes, of course I do!'

'Do you recall how she died?' He watched her, clinically now.

'How she died?' She shook her head. 'I suppose she got run over with a wagon or something, didn't she?'

'No,' he said. 'Go back in your mind ... Mary ... and see if you can recall how Tessie died.'

Lurancy shut her eyes and concentrated. The smile she wore turned into a frown and then into a shudder as she opened her eyes and stared at Mrs Roff. 'Ma! Now I recall how Tessie died! Oh, Ma, I'm so sorry! I didn't mean to kill Tessie! I loved that cat as much as anyone did!'

'I know, daughter. I know.' Ann was right there to soothe the girl. 'It's all right. It happened a long time ago, it's all right.'

'I cut off her head, didn't I?' Ann nodded. 'And then I drank the blood from her neck. Didn't I? I mean that's what I recall people telling me.'

'Yes, you did ... Mary,' the doctor said. 'But you were out of your mind when it happened. You didn't know what you were doing.' He shook his head. 'Extraordinary. Absolutely extraordinary.'

'This meeting has been called,' the Reverend Baker announced, 'because as concerned citizens of Watseka we have a problem that must be dealt with. That problem as you all well know is Lurancy Vennum.'

He looked, from the raised stage and from behind the pulpit, at the fifteen or so members of his congregation who had asked him to chair the committee that would get the Vennum girl placed in the insane asylum where she belonged. Lavinia Durst was there, he nodded to her. So was her close friend Sarah Thayer. His wife was there, in the back row, always so modest about exalting her position where he was concerned. Noticeably missing were Mayor Peters and Asa B. Roff. Colonel Peters had been invited but he had declined, saying he couldn't spare the time from his bookshop, and Mr Roff was missing because, frankly, he hadn't been invited. The Roffs hadn't been inside the Methodist Church since that fracas with the Reverend Dille some twelve years before.

'The background of the case is well known,' he said in his rich preaching tones, 'and rather than go into the past at this time I think we should decide what has to be done now, in the present. We cannot have our children and our womenfolk endangered by this wild girl who is permitted to run loose in the streets. There is a place for everyone in our community. Everyone who is normal and productive,' he added. 'When a member of society falls behind in their mental abilities and becomes a menace to the productive Christian members, then we must examine our Christian consciences and resolve to do what is best for that individual. We must search our hearts and decide not how *we* would benefit but rather what would be the best thing for the unfortunate individual who is unable to care for himself. Or herself, as in this case.' He paused, waiting for the discussion to begin, the image of Tom Vennum waving a loaded shotgun at him ever present in his mind.

'Would someone like to start?'

Sarah Thayer stood up in the pew. 'I think it's a disgrace.' She sat down. There was mild applause.

'A disgrace? How so?'

'Well,' she got up again, 'it has been proven that Lurancy Vennum is crazy. I mean, our own doctors said she was. And even the mayor agreed that she was. Then all of a sudden, because of some quack doing hand gestures in the air, she is permitted to come out of her room and roam the streets. That's what I call a disgrace.' She sat down again.

The Reverend Baker passed his hand lightly over his prematurely balding head. The short beard under his chin was to compensate for the lack of hair on his scalp. 'What Mrs Thayer says is perfectly true. The best medical minds in the country agreed that the girl was insane. Incurably insane. Then this Spiritualist *minister*' – he chuckled at the word 'minister' – 'came into town and suddenly she has been cured.'

'What does he know that our own medical doctors don't know?' someone called out.

'And then he goes off again, pretty as you please, and leaves us with her. I know, because I saw him go.' This was Miss Alice Williams's contribution. She ran the hotel where the strange doctor had been allowed to spend a week. Well, he wouldn't get back in *her* place again. She ran a respectable house for respectable people. 'He called himself a doctor, but I didn't see any medicine.'

'He heals with the wave of his hand,' the Reverend replied. 'Just a few passes in the air and everybody is fine and dandy again.'

'Too bad he wasn't here to work on old man Palachek's horse,' a man in the second row said. 'Might have saved the beast.' There was general laughter after that.

'I have a sow that won't breed,' another man spoke up. 'Do you suppose the doc would cure her?' Much more laughter.

'I'm glad to see we are all in such a good mood,' the Reverend said. 'Decisions like we have to make are never best made under stress or anger.'

'Well, I'm angry.' Lavinia Durst stood up. 'I'm very angry that we cannot be safe in our own homes at night. I hear tell that the Vennum girl is no longer Lurancy Vennum but instead has become Mary Roff and is all sweetness and light. Well, she can hoodwink such old fools as Doc Fowler and Emaline Parker, but she can't hoodwink me. I remember what Mary Roff was!' She turned so that everyone could see how well she remembered. 'And if Crazy Rancy Vennum is now Crazy Mary Roff, then we have two crazies to contend with, not just one! Either the authorities do something or else we will do it! There can't be any shilly-shallying this time!'

'I spoke with Lurinda Vennum,' a woman said, 'and she claims that ever since this Mary thing took over her daughter's body she's been much better. In the head.'

'Of course, she'd say that!' Lavinia was still standing. 'She's trying to protect her own daughter. I'm not surprised at that. I'd probably do the same thing in her place. You can't go by what either the Vennums or the Roffs say. You have to go by the facts.' She took a deep breath. 'And the facts are that we have a *certified* crazy girl in our midst and none of us are safe!' She sat down, folded her hands in her lap and felt the full power of her own worthiness.

'Maybe Lurinda Vennum thinks it's better that her daughter go live with the Roffs than in the mental institution', a woman spoke up.

'Well,' the Reverend's wife was heard from, 'I would

rather have a child of mine locked up in a crazy house than become a *Spiritualist*!'

'Oh yes.' 'We agree.' 'Tsk tsk.' 'Absolutely.' 'Did you ever?' Murmurings from all over the room.

'As I see it,' Lavinia spoke up, 'there is only one thing to do. We must go to Mayor Peters and get him to sign another paper to commit that girl. We must get him to see that Asa Roff and his crazy spirit religion have made a fool out of him and in front of all the folks in Watseka. The mayor must know that he is in that job to do his duty to *us*, the citizens who voted for him.'

'If you wish,' the Reverend folded his hands across the paunchy stomach protruding from his thin frame. 'If you wish, I shall take it upon myself to call on the mayor ... in his capacity as mayor and not as a seller of books and periodicals ... and demand he do something about getting the Vennum girl committed to Springfield.'

'Or anyplace,' a woman called out.

'Yes. Just get her out of Watseka.'

'Fine,' the Reverend said. 'I shall go but I need another member of this group with me, so that Colonel Peters will see that I have the concerned citizenry behind me.'

'It should be Lavinia,' the second row man said. 'Everyone respects Lavinia.'

Sarah Thayer spoke up. 'You are definitely the one we all want.' Then to the others, 'Isn't that so?'

Much yessing. Much applause as Lavinia stood up, smiled, took a humble but well-rehearsed bow, smiled at the minister and said: 'If you really want me, I'll try and do my best.' Then she sat down. Triumphant. She had waited and the opportunity had come. Twelve years was a long time to wait but now she was ready. Ready to get back at the Roffs for all those wrongs of more than a decade ago. 'I'll do my best,' she said again. 'You can be sure of that.'

It frightened everyone the first time it happened.

Lurancy was in the kitchen with Ann and Charlotte, sitting on a high stool in the corner watching them make mince pies. Frank had gone hunting the day before and shot a deer. After he dressed it and cut up several hunks for his friends, Charlotte and Ann ground the rest of it and canned it for mincemeat. The pies being made today were from the batch that didn't get canned and tucked away in the fruit cellars in the cold corner of the basement.

'I sure wish you would eat some of these pies.' Charlotte never called the Vennum girl 'Mary'. Ann pretended not to notice. 'You've been here goin' on a month and not one bite of food have you taken into your stomach. Nobody can survive on that, not even a spirit like you!' Charlotte had almost gotten used to the strange child in the household. Almost, but not quite. She slept with her door bolted and a butcher knife on the chair next to her bed. She also hung a length of sleigh bells around the door knob before she went to sleep. If anyone tried to force the door open, the bells would ring and she'd be out of bed, knife in hand, in seconds. Neither Ann nor Asa suspected their housekeeper's fears.

Charlotte kept a close watch on the food that was served in the house. She put the leftovers in the icebox every night and carefully inspected them in the morning. If something had been eaten she questioned the boys about it. Almost always they had been the ones who had taken the food. (One embarrassing night shortly after the Vennum girl arrived, Charlotte heard the icebox door open. Because of the handle's snap lock, there was always a noise when the door closed. Sure she had caught the Vennum girl in the act, she jumped out of bed and into the kitchen, wearing only her nightgown and carrying her butcher knife. Instead of Lurancy she caught Asa stealing a chicken drumstick.) After that she waited until the family was at the breakfast table to make her investigations. No, Lurancy or Mary or whoever she was hadn't eaten a thing as far as she could tell. And it had been over a month. It just didn't make sense.

Yet, everyone agreed, Lurancy looked fine. She hadn't lost any weight. In fact, it seemed as if she had gained a couple of pounds. Her face was flushed her eyes sparkled and her hair was becoming thick and lustrous. The boys admitted that she looked a lot better now than she did when she first arrived.

'I was telling Nervie,' Ann was saying, 'that when the weather gets a little better, maybe we will all go to Chicago for shopping and maybe go to the theater. Would you like that, Mary?'

'Oh yes, Ma. I can't recall when I was last in Chicago. The boys have a picture book of it and it looks mighty big. Scary almost,' she replied.

'I was in Chicago when I first came west,' Charlotte said. 'I didn't like it much. There was too much people and too much noise. Friends of my father live there. They have a hat store. I stayed with them for a few weeks before coming down here.'

'The food is good in Chicago,' Ann commented. 'They have marvelous French and Italian restaurants. The one I recall best sits on a pier over the river and the fresh breezes blow right in on your table.'

'That must be in summertime,' the cook laughed, 'for if it was in the wintertime the breezes would blow you clean into the river! God! I never saw such winds as in Chicago!'

'Mary, do you recall the windstorm that blew down the trees along the river? You were just a tyke then, but it howled and we all thought it was a tornado.' Ann kept searching for items out of their pasts to test the girl. So far everything had checked perfectly. She was getting used to having her daughter home again. 'Mary? Do you recall that windstorm?'

Lurancy didn't answer.

'Mary? Don't you recall that? The sky got black all of a sudden and Loozie and I had clothes on the line and they began to blow in all which way directions?' Ann looked up from her pie dough at the girl. 'Mary?'

Lurancy was sitting there, eyes wide and staring around her. She was working her mouth, trying to speak. 'Wha – ' was the only sound that came out. Tears welled up and as they ran down her cheeks, they unloosened her voice. 'Where am I? Where's my Ma?'

'I'm right here, dear,' Ann said, wiping the flour from her hands and going over to the girl. 'What's the matter?'

'Where's my Ma?' she said again. 'I want my Ma!'

'Mary, what's the matter?' Ann's voice rose in concern.

'Where am I?' She stared at Ann and then at Charlotte. 'Where am I? Who are you people?'

'I'm your Ma!' Ann said loudly, 'and this is Charlotte.'

'No!' The girl jumped off the stool and looked wildly around her. 'I want my Ma! I want to go home!'

'Oh my God!' Ann's breath caught in her throat. 'Lurancy is back!'

Charlotte took several steps backward, toward her bedroom with the protection of the closed door and the butcher knife.

'I want my Ma! Please,' she looked at Ann. 'Tell my Ma to come get me.'

Quickly Ann untied her apron and tossed it on a chair. 'Charlotte, go fetch Mr Roff at the office. Tell him Lurancy is back and she wants to go home.' Charlotte just stood there staring. 'Go ahead!' Ann commanded. 'Have him come as fast as he can!'

Lurancy moved out of the kitchen and into the hallway. She kept looking at the walls and the floor, seeing them for the first time. 'Where am I?' she kept saying. 'Where's my Ma?' She looked in through the front parlor doors and called: 'Ma? Ma, are you in here?' Then she turned and saw Ann right behind her. 'Where's my Ma?' She began to cry.

'Your Ma left you here for a few hours, Lurancy,' said Ann. 'She'll be after you in a little while. Now why don't you just go upstairs to your room and calm down till she gets here.'

The girl shook her head. 'I want to go home. Now!'

Ann reached for her, but missed by inches as Lurancy ran down the length of the hallway and yanked open the front door. She dashed out into the cold March air.

'Rancy!' Ann screamed. 'Come back in here. You'll catch your death out there!'

The girl turned around, took one more look at Ann and jumped off the porch into a snowbank that had drifted against the house. It was over six feet from the porch to the ground and she fell heavily into the ice-encrusted pile. Ann hurried down the steps, ran beside the porch as best she could in her full skirts and high-heel boots and caught the girl just as she tried to right herself.

Lurancy pushed her away and, lifting her dress, started plunging through knee-deep snow straight across the lawn toward the street. Ann kept right after her, following in the path she was clearing.

'Lurancy, please!' Ann pleaded. 'Come back into the house! Nothing is going to happen to you! Come in and wait for your folks!'

'I don't know who you are!' the girl screamed. 'Please let me be! Let me get back to my Ma!'

'Lurancy, please!' Ann was getting short of breath and the cold air she gasped into her lungs burned her insides. 'Please, Lurancy. Listen to me! Listen to reason!'

The girl continued her knee-deep plunges into the heavy snow until she came to the edge of the lawn. From there the property sloped downhill, down to the street where piles of snow had been banked in layers to let people and horses move freely. Lurancy took one last look at Ann, then stumbled into the snow, rolled down and thudded against the deeply packed mounds of ice, dirt, straw and manure.

'Lurancy!' Ann screamed and slipped, tumbling down the embankment after her. She rolled next to the girl. Lurancy didn't move.

Ann forced herself to her feet and, with hands that were already numb with cold, tried to lift Lurancy, but she was too heavy. No matter how she struggled or pulled, the girl didn't budge. Ann began to cry, in anger now more than anything else, and kept pulling at the girl's clothing. 'Please, Lurancy!' she gasped. 'Please get up! Please!'

'Ann? Ann are you all right?' She heard his voice and looked up. Asa and Charlotte were coming up the street in the buggy. 'Are you all right?' he shouted again.

'Yes!' she managed to call. 'But hurry! It's Lurancy. She's out here and she seems unconscious!'

Asa beat the horse until it was beside the two figures in the snow. He jumped out and Charlotte was right behind him. They picked up the girl, Ann at her feet, and stumbling and slipping managed to get her into the buggy. Asa threw his lap robe over Lurancy and then helped Ann inside. He put another robe around her shivering frame.

'Are you all right?' he questioned.

'Yes,' she said through chattering teeth. 'I'm okay. Just get the girl into the house!'

Asa slapped the reins and the horse took off, heading

down the street and turning into the driveway and up to the rear entrance of the house and the warm kitchen.

And across the street someone in a horse and buggy sat watching. She had followed right behind Asa's buggy, meeting it as he passed her corner. Wearing a warm coat and covered by a lap robe, the woman quickly jotted down notes of everything she had seen and heard. These notes would come in handy. She slapped the reins and her horse turned back toward the center of town. After she finished her shopping, she'd stop by the church and tell the Reverend Baker what she'd seen. He would be impressed with her detective work. But then, he was always pleased with any information Lavinia Durst gave him.

Lurancy slept all afternoon and into the early evening, Asa and Ann by her bed. They hadn't notified the Vennums. It wouldn't have done anything except cause more confusion. Besides, Mary had ordered the Vennums not be allowed back into the Roff home until she said it was all right to return. Now, as they sat watching the sleeping girl, they wondered who would return when she awoke. Would it be Lurancy or Mary?

It was Mary. She rolled over onto her side, opened her eyes and looked at the Roffs. She breathed deeply, more like a sigh, and smiled at them. 'I'm sorry,' she said. 'They wanted to test the body. I tried to tell them I didn't think it was ready yet, but they insisted. So I stepped out and she came back.' She reached out a hand and put it over Ann's. 'I'm sorry, Ma. I really am. But I tried to tell them.'

'That's all right,' Ann replied softly. 'Your father and I are happy just to have you back.'

'You gave your Ma a fright,' Asa said, 'but we're glad you came back to us. We would have missed you if you hadn't.'

'They may do that from time to time,' said the girl. 'This testing, I mean. I really don't have no control over it, so don't be surprised if it happens again.'

'What do we do?' Asa didn't like the idea of today's scene being repeated. 'I mean, we can't keep you locked in your room like the Vennums did. And I can't endanger my family.'

'It won't be so bad the next time,' the girl answered.

'They've already explained to Lurancy what happened and where she was when she came back.'

'How do you know?' Asa asked.

'I was there when they told her,' came the matter-of-fact reply. 'The body was here, asleep, but Rancy and I were over there together. It was strange. It's the first time we've had a chance to talk.'

'Well... I don't understand,' Ann said. 'If you weren't in the body and neither was Lurancy, who was taking care of it? I mean, they didn't just let it lie here, did they?'

'Oh no. There was somebody in it. One of the other people over there who does these things.'

'And what if that person had woken up and not known where he was? Wouldn't that have been worse?'

'Oh, no, Pa. He couldn't have woken up the body. His job is to keep all the parts functioning, but he can't wake it up and make it move and talk or anything like that. No, don't worry about that. Lurancy and me are the only ones that can use this body. Unless, of course...' her voice faltered.

'Unless?' Asa asked.

'Unless one of those other people, like that awful Hogan woman, catches it at a weak moment. But that ain't likely to happen.' She laughed and sat up, putting her feet over the side of the bed. 'Anyway, I'm hungry. Let's see what Charlotte has in the kitchen.'

'Hungry?' Ann was delighted. 'You mean you're going to eat something?'

'Ma,' she said, running a brush through her hair, 'I'm going to eat *everything*! I'm starved!'

The entire family stood around the table watching Lurancy eat as if they were watching a traveling minstrel show. Ann insisted on doing the cooking herself, starting out with scrambled eggs and a thick ham slice and ending up with two glasses of milk and a large piece of freshly baked mince pie.

That night, when everyone was in bed, Charlotte pushed her chest of drawers up against her door. It would be one more safeguard when the crazy started attacking again.

Lavinia stayed after the service the next Sunday to remind the minister of the scene in the snow on Friday.

'I tell you it was a disgrace! That poor Ann Roff, aged and infirm as she is, out there bare-headed and bare-shouldered and trying to get that girl up onto her feet! My heart went out to her. It really did.'

'I believe you,' he said. 'It was a scene that would have melted many a Christian heart.'

'And so unnecessary! I mean if they hadn't interfered the way they did, poor Ann wouldn't be in this situation right now! But no, Asa and his crazy imported preacher had to have their own way! I tell you, Reverend Baker, that girl is doing more damage over there than she ever did in her own home!'

'Didn't you volunteer to help poor Mrs Roff?' he asked.

'Just as I was about to do so, Asa came down the street lickety-split in his buggy and with that German woman who works for them. You know that nice Charlotte Wiedener who comes to church sometimes.' He nodded. 'Well, when I saw Asa and the cook had everything under control, I didn't get out of the buggy. But I was about to. I was about to.'

'I'm sure you were.' He was in no mood for chatter right now. His sermon on how evil can come up like a March wind had not been well received. Nobody had to tell him, he could sense it by the way the congregation squirmed and the way men honked their noses into their handkerchiefs. A really good sermon rarely got a honk at all. This one sounded as if a gaggle of geese had come marching down the center aisle. 'I suppose,' he said, 'the only thing to do is to see Mayor Peters and get that new writ ordered.' He looked at his watch. 'How about if we call on him together on Wednesday?'

Lavinia shook her head. 'How about if we do it tomorrow?'

He sighed. Better get it over with. 'Tomorrow it is. Here at the church at 11 a.m.?' She smiled her agreement. 'Then we'll go straight to his store and get this matter taken care of once and for all.' Old mother Spangler came out of the church, past the minister and, instead of shaking his hand, loudly blew her nose. The Reverend Baker turned abruptly from Lavinia and disappeared through a side door.

There was always an unusual amount of mail and boxes to open after a weekend and Colonel Peters didn't cotton to people disturbing his Mondays with business that had nothing to do with his bookshop. He could be found every Wednesday at the City Hall and the preacher and the old gossip knew it. Yet they stood there yammering at him about something that was none of their concern.

Lavinia had quickly worked herself into her normal level of righteous indignation. 'We, the voters of this town, expected more of you than broken promises! I know that I speak for all the concerned citizens of Watseka when I ask – nay, sir, *demand* – that you do something about this Vennum girl!'

He stopped yanking at a sealed carton and glared at her. 'Mrs Durst,' he said slowly, 'the last person who *demanded* that I do something was a Rebel officer who surprised me while I was on a mission to Stone River, Tennessee. He came from behind and demanded that I surrender.'

'What did you do?' The preacher had also been with the Union forces.

'I shot him, sir. Right between the eyes!'

Lavinia gasped and thought she would faint but looking around she saw there wasn't a comfortable place to fall, so decided against it. 'You weren't getting paid by voters then, young man,' she said. 'You were in the army and had to defend yourself. Now that you are the mayor you have an obligation to listen to the very people who put you into that office.'

'And who can also take me out? Isn't that right, Mrs Durst?'

'Yes,' she said emphatically, 'who can also take you out.'

'So,' he put down the books he had taken from the carton and stared at both of them. 'What you are basically telling me is that if I don't recommit this innocent girl you will have my job.'

'We don't mean it to sound so crass, sir,' the minister said, 'but that is the general feeling of the town.'

'My answer, Mrs Durst, is no. An imperturbable, unbending and unmitigated no.'

'But you can't!' she protested.

'Oh, but I can. I'm still the mayor here, Mrs Durst. Not you. My word is law, not yours. And while I have the power the people have invested in me, I shall do nothing to harm that child.'

'But she's a menace!'

'To whom? Have you seen the change that's come over her in the past month? Did you see what an animal-like creature she was before? Did you bother to try and talk to her, to reach her at that place wherever her mind had gone? Did you, Preacher Baker? Did you even bother to *try* and *help* her when her own father had her tied to the wall and beat her when he couldn't control her? Did you try to help that child?'

'I went over there a couple of times,' the minister said, 'but her father chased me away with a gun.'

'I heard about that,' Colonel Peters tried not to smile. 'But did you try again after that?' The Reverend Baker shook his head. 'Why not? You were in the army, sir. You have faced guns before. You were even wounded in the line of duty. So why did one little gun affect you so badly? How come you ran from one lone man with one lone shotgun?'

'Colonel Peters, sir,' the minister pulled himself up to his full five feet ten inches, 'I did not come here to be insulted. I served my country in the last great conflict and I served it honorably and bravely. I will not stand here and allow you to impugn my patriotism.'

'I'm not saying anything about your patriotism, sir. What I was questioning was your bravery. But let it pass. The damage has been done. After Tom Vennum grabbed his gun you went along with all the others in condemning the girl on hearsay.'

'All that is water under the bridge,' Lavinia said angrily. 'The problem is now. Today. What are you going to do about that Vennum girl *today*?'

'Not a thing, Mrs Durst. Not a thing. She is living in the Roff household and is on the road to recovery. I have seen her and I have talked with her and she is vastly improved in every way to what she was a month ago. To interfere now would set her back to her old pattern and eventually lead to her death.'

'But she is crazy!' Lavinia insisted. 'She thinks she is someone else! She thinks she's that awful Mary Roff who died long ago! Is that normal to you, sir? Is that what you call improving in every way?'

'That is what I call improving in *her* way,' he said. 'And that is the way I must respect.'

'But the Roffs are Spiritualists!' the Reverend Baker blurted out. 'Certainly that household is no fit place for a mentally disturbed child! They are Spiritualists!'

Colonel Peters clutched his fingers tightly around a newly arrived novel. It was all the rage in London and it gave him the strength he needed not to put his fingers around the preacher's neck. 'I don't see anything wrong with being a Spiritualist, sir.' His face was getting redder. 'I believe they are also Christians and as Christians the Roffs have opened the doors of their home to this sick child. Show me the *Christian* member of your congregation who was willing to do the same.'

Colonel Peters bent back to his pile of books. 'If you both will excuse me, I have work to do.'

'So you refuse to help?' Lavinia asked.

'I do. I also refuse to discuss the matter any further.'

'Does that mean we have to take matters into our own hands?' she looked him squarely in the eye. 'We can do it, you know. We don't need you.'

'And I don't need you,' he said, the red coming back into his face. 'Please get out of here or I shall forget that I am a gentleman and that you are masquerading around town as a lady. The door is that way. Good morning and good-bye!'

Watseka, Illinois
March 20, 1878

Dear Dr Stevens:

I sincerely hope you are well and that your wife and daughters are likewise. It has been over a month now since you left and I am writing to tell you how things are going here and how I am faring. It was kind of you to send me the lovely letter and the small picture of you that I requested. I keep it beside my bed and say a special prayer to it each night before I blow out the candle.

My Mother and my Father are also very fine and so are brothers Frank and Charles. It is so wonderful to be with them all again. Of course Nervie is busy with her husband and her family duties but she does come to see me almost every day.

The weather here has been cool but now it seems to be warming up. Pa says that spring is almost here and I am glad. Yesterday I went to shop with Ma and we put on just a light jacket and shawl. There are some flowers coming up back in the woods and many of the trees and bushes have the tiniest little buds on them already. I do hope spring hurries and gets here before I have to leave again.

I've told my folks that I'll be leaving one of these days. They don't like it and Ma gets real sad. I get sad too but there is nothing any of us can do. I just give thanks to the Lord (and to you!!) that I was able to return for a visit that has lasted this long. I didn't expect it to be more than a few days and look how time has flown!

I have had some news from the other side and they tell me that the Vennum girl is doing real nicely. Her nerves are much better and that problem with her spinal cord is much improved. Her heart is also getting stronger and she is learning many things over there. She will be a changed girl when she gets back here. It is my prayer that her family will treat her differently when she does come back. She has not had a very happy life, poor thing.

They also gave me some information that I was to pass along to you. They said that one day soon you will get a letter from heaven. It has something to do with one of your patients. That's all they told me, but you are not to become discouraged with some problem with a patient because they will send you a letter from heaven that will explain everything.

I must close now, dear, dear friend, because Pa is going back to the office after he has his lunch and I will ask him to post this letter for me. Please come back and see me real soon. We must have that little talk we spoke about and time is drawing nigh to the day I shall have to depart forever.

              May God bless you in all your endeavors,

Your obedient servant and friend,
Mary Roff.

P.S.
There is trouble brewing in the air. They told me that when they told me about your letter. They also told me I had to be strong. With God's guidance and your prayers, I shall be.

Mary.

She handed the letter to Asa when he was about to leave the house. 'Pa, will you please post this to Dr Stevens for me?'

He took the envelope and felt a lump form in his throat. For years he had carried, in his wallet, a little poem Mary had written for him when she was a patient in Peoria. How many times over the years had he taken it out and reread it? He knew it by heart. He also knew the handwriting by heart. This envelope was addressed in that very same handwriting.

The next Sunday was almost summerlike in its warmth and soft breezes. The following day was just the same, a rural peace and tranquility hung over the town as men worked their fields in their shirtsleeves and women brought out their rugs and furniture for airing. A kind of calm lay over everything in Watseka, with two exceptions: the Reverend Baker and Mrs Lavinia Durst, who had got out of a buggy across the street and were coming up the walk of the Roff home.

Ann and Charlotte were in the backyard, beating at two floor rugs they had hung over a heavy clothesline. The boys were in school and Minerva was at home doing her own chores. Lurancy was alone in the house and went down to open the door when the pull bell jangled for the third time in a row.

'Yes?' she said.

Neither Mr Baker nor Lavinia had expected the Vennum girl to be the one to greet them. They both took a step backward.

'Yes?' Lurancy said again. 'Do you wish to speak with my Ma? She's out in back, but I can fetch her in a minute.'

Lavinia glanced at the minister. 'Well,' she said, 'we do wish to speak to Mrs Roff but we've also come to speak to you. Maybe it's better this way,' she said to the minister. He nodded in agreement. 'Why don't we just sit out here on the front porch?' the woman suggested.

'Oh, but the chairs are all dirty,' Lurancy protested. 'We haven't gotten around to cleaning off the winter soot yet.' She didn't think it would be polite for two finely dressed people to sit on dirty chairs. 'Please come into the house. I'll go and fetch Ma.'

'Well, we will come in, but just for a little while,' the man said. 'We have other business to attend to this morning. At least *I* do.' He wanted Lavinia to understand he had no intention of taking all morning with this Lurancy Vennum matter.

'Please,' the girl held the door open and they entered the house. It was the first time either of them had been inside the Roff home and Lavinia looked around eagerly.

'I'll go and get my Ma.' Lurancy had started for the back door when Lavinia called her.

'No. Let her tend to her duties for a few minutes. It's you we really wish to talk with.'

'Me?'

'Yes, child,' the woman said. 'We have heard a great deal about you and we have come to see you for ourselves.'

'See what?' Lurancy pulled back a bit.

'Well, they are saying in town that you are Mary Roff.'

'That's right, I am.'

'Returned from the grave.'

'From the grave?' she repeated.

'Yes,' the Reverend Baker added, 'returned to life after more than a decade of being dead.'

'That's true,' Lurancy said. 'I have returned to life but not from the grave. If I had come from the grave I wouldn't have this body now. I'd have another. My own.'

The minister changed his tactics. Obviously the child was lying. 'Who told you to say those things?'

'Told me? Told me what?'

'To say that you were Mary Roff and not Lurancy Vennum. Lying is a sin in the eyes of God. Do you know that?'

'I'm not lying,' she replied with a tremor in her voice. 'What I'm telling you is the truth! I am Mary Roff.'

'You are Lurancy Vennum,' said Lavinia quickly. 'And we know all about your shenanigans.'

'Shenanigans?' Lurancy took another step backward. She didn't like these people, whoever they were. 'I don't understand.'

'You'll understand soon enough when you get to Springfield!' Lavinia raised her voice.

'Now, Mrs Durst,' the minister said. 'Please. Let me handle her.'

'Can't you see she's lying?' Lavinia got up and went toward Lurancy. 'One look at her will tell you who she is. She is Lurancy Vennum body and soul! I've seen the girl with Tom and Lurinda a million times and so have you!'

'I am Mary Roff!' she protested. 'Let me get my Ma.'

'Just you stay put, young lady,' the minister said. 'We aren't finished.'

'I don't know who you are,' said the girl.

'You certainly do!' Lavinia corrected her. 'You've gone to his church many times. He is the Reverend Baker, minister at the Methodist Church where you are a member.' She smiled at this child who thought she could hoodwink her by lying so badly. 'Now suppose we get to the bottom of this. If it's play-acting you're doing, forget it. We didn't come here to see a show.'

'Who are you?' Lurancy asked. 'What right have you to come into my house and torment me in this manner?'

'Lurancy Vennum, you know perfectly well who I am,' Lavinia almost shouted. 'And this ain't your house. This house belongs to Asa Roff. Your house is on Sixth Street and belongs to Tom Vennum.'

'I am not Lurancy Vennum,' the girl insisted. 'I am Mary Roff.'

'Well,' and Lavinia snorted, 'if you are Mary Roff, then you *certainly* know who I am! Mary and I had quite a set-to when she was alive.'

The girl looked closely at the lined face under the white hair and the hat with the black egret feather. 'You do look like someone I used to know,' she admitted.

'Used to know. You know me very well, if you really are Mary Roff!' She came closer. 'Look at me. Doesn't my face tell you my name?'

'Really,' the minister said, 'I think you are going at this in the wrong manner.'

Lavinia ignored him. She'd waited too long for this moment. 'Look at me. Look well and then tell me you don't know who I am!'

The girl tried to pull away but Lavinia had her almost up against the parlor wall. That old face was just inches away from hers and she could smell the cologne that Lavinia used on her tongue to mask the odor of rotting teeth. 'Who am I?'

Lurancy's eyes grew wide. 'Mrs Durst!' she exclaimed. 'You are Lavinia Durst!'

'That's correct, but it doesn't prove you are Mary Roff. The Vennums know me. All Watseka knows me. That ain't such a marvelous feat. Tell me something that Crazy Rancy don't know. Tell me something that only Mary Roff knows.' She turned back to the minister. 'That'll be the day. When this girl comes up with something that only Mary could know.'

'I do know you now,' Lurancy said. Her voice and manner were calmer. She had gotten herself under control. 'Yes, I recall you quite well as a matter of fact. You were the old busybody who tried to have me committed to Springfield.'

Lavinia didn't know whether to slap the child or sit down. She decided on neither. 'Don't call me names, you crazy girl! I didn't come here to be insulted.'

'Why did you come here?' It was a new voice entering the room. Ann made them all turn and look in her direction. 'Why did you come here, Lavinia Durst? You were certainly *not* invited.'

'I am a member of the concerned citizens committee,' Lavinia said, 'I don't have to be invited. The committee has powers.'

'Not in this house, it doesn't.'

'We should have notified you beforehand,' the Reverend spoke up. 'Maybe we could have planned the visit better.'

'No amount of planning would have induced me to permit either one of you to come into my house.'

'You watch your tongue, Ann Roff,' Lavinia warned, 'you are talking with a man of God.'

'I am talking with a man,' Ann replied, 'who happens to also be a minister. There is a big difference in that and a man of God.'

'Now see here, Mrs Roff,' the Reverend Baker protested. 'I have my credentials –'

'And I have my feelings. My feelings are, at this moment, that the two of you have barged uninvited into my home and I shall have to ask you to leave.'

'You can't throw us out!' Lavinia shouted. 'We are the citizens committee.'

'You are troublemakers!' Ann was surprised at her own display of strength and she would tell Asa later that it must have come from that protective instinct a mother has for her children. 'Please leave,' she said and began walking toward the door. 'It's this way.'

'You can't do this to us, Ann Roff.' Lavinia was beside herself with these insults from her old adversary. 'We have the power and we will make sure this crazy girl gets her due! We are going to have her locked up and the key is going to get thrown away! Don't think you can stop us! We represent the people!'

'You represent shit!' The voice was loud and masculine and it came from Lurancy who was standing against the wall with her arms crossed and a smile on her face. 'You old bitch,' said the male voice. 'All you've ever done is cause trouble. All the business you ever mind is somebody else's. Get the shit out of here and don't come back or I'll bust your old ass into a thousand fragments!'

Lavinia screamed and ducked behind the Reverend as the girl walked toward her. 'Don't touch me,' she cried. 'Reverend Baker, don't let her touch me! She's crazy!'

'Mary!' Ann shouted. 'Stop that kind of talk this instant!'

Lurancy laughed. 'Mary ain't here! She's gone. This old bitch frightened her away. Don't worry, lady,' the voice said to Ann, 'I ain't gonna hurt you. I just wanna get my hands around that scrawny chicken neck and squeeze.'

'She's mad!' Lavinia was screaming. 'She's mad and she's going to kill me!'

'How right you are!' Lurancy pushed at the minister.

'Get out of my way, you turn-collar old fraud, and let me get my hands on that troublemaker! Mealy-mouthed old fart!'

'Oh my God!' Ann had her hands up to her face. 'Look what you've done now! Just see what the two of you have done!'

'Get out of my way!' Lurancy pushed at the minister but he held his ground, bracing his legs on the carpeted floor. The girl took a swing and with one blow to the side of his body knocked him halfway across the room. He fell against a small table, knocking the pictures and ornaments to the floor. Lurancy grabbed Lavinia and dragged her across the rug to the sofa. 'That ass will be in a thousand pieces,' the man inside the girl laughed. 'Lots of folks are going to be mighty pleased at my handiwork.'

'Oh my God!' Ann screamed. 'No. Mary, please don't! Please!'

The girl ignored her, tossed Lavinia onto the sofa and raising her arm, brought her open palm down on Lavinia's rear end with a sound that could have been mistaken for a pistol shot.

Lavinia felt the pain and fainted.

Up again went the hand, accompanied by the mannish laugh, but the palm didn't descend. 'She's out cold,' the voice said. 'Damn! That takes all the fun out of it.'

Ann grabbed Lurancy but instead of the struggle she expected, felt her crumple in her arms. As Lurancy slid to the floor Ann fell with her.

The Reverend Baker, seeing his opponent on the ground, rushed over to Lavinia and started slapping her hands and face to revive her. 'Mrs Durst! Mrs Durst. Please! Let's get out of here!'

Lavinia moaned, her eyelids fluttered and she stretched out her arms for the minister to take. He helped her to her feet, her hat over one eye, her egret feather broken in two places.

'Mrs Roff,' the Reverend said, 'you can be sure we will be back again! We cannot permit this kind of conduct from anyone in our community. We shall be back. And we shall have a warrant for that girl's arrest.'

'Can't you see what you've done already?' Ann shouted

at him. 'Are you so blind not to see the damage you've caused?'

'I am not blind, Mrs Roff, not at all. I have excellent eyesight and it has shown me the *true* side of this disgraceful story! The girl is infested with demons. I will not permit her to stay in this house or this city!'

'You can do nothing about it!' Ann shouted. 'You are not God!'

'No. But that girl is the Devil! She cannot go unpunished.' He and Lavinia were almost to the front door. 'And neither you nor your husband will go unpunished. You can be sure of that! Spiritualism is the curse of the Devil! The Devil is in this house but he shall not stay long!'

Asa sent the telegram to Dr Stevens:

> COME AT ONCE. TERRIBLE UPSETTING EXPERIENCE HAS REMOVED BOTH MARY AND LURANCY FROM BODY. WE NEED YOU. ASA ROFF.

Three days later the doctor arrived on the 2.34 from Chicago. Asa was at the station with his horse and buggy to meet him.

'She's been unconscious ever since the incident,' Asa told him as they drove toward the house. 'She seems to be having nightmares and rolls and tosses but won't awaken. Of course both Mrs Roff and myself are terribly upset over it. We fear the worst, obviously. I just hope there is something you can do.'

'And the girl's parents. Have you told them about her?' the doctor asked.

'No, I haven't.'

'Strange,' was the comment. 'Why not?'

'Well, they came to visit her once, about a week after she moved in, and so upset the girl that Mary asked us not to have them back until she gave the approval. I didn't want to call them now, especially when Lurancy is so physically ill. They could just up and cart her off to their house again. You know,' and he looked at the doctor, 'we don't have any legal papers saying we can keep Rancy. They can take her away anytime they choose.'

'I know. I've thought about that. Why do you think they haven't come for her before this?'

'It's Mrs Vennum. She's not well. Nervous disorders and crying fits and the like. Probably she doesn't want Lurancy back because she knows she can't handle her.'

'How is *your* wife taking all this?'

'Not very well, I'm afraid. She's been sleeping in the same room with the girl ever since the incident. Hasn't gotten much sleep, actually. She wakes up every few hours to see if she needs another cover or if she can get some water down her or anything. You know, doctor, it's almost worse than the first time. With our own daughter. Ann is older and she feels maybe she didn't do the job she should have with Mary. That if she had given Mary more attention perhaps things would have turned out differently. I don't know. Maybe she's right. I was so busy building a business I was lax in my attention to her too.'

'Come now, sir, you can't blame yourself for something that was predestined! Of the people in this town you above all know that. Mary had to die when she did. You will have to die when you do. We all will have to die when our time comes. No sooner and no later. Surely you know that, believe that?'

'I suppose I do. I mean I know it. I don't know if I *believe* it. It is all so difficult, Doctor. Just when you feel you have the answers, along comes a whole bushel basket of new questions. Mary's reappearance has unleashed a waterfall of questions and doubt.' He looked at the bearded man beside him. 'Yes, doubt. Doubt that I know anything or that any of us knows anything about that world out there. Or "over there" as Mary calls it.'

'But it hasn't shaken your faith, has it? I mean in Spiritualism?'

'It has only shaken my preconceived notions. My faith is still strong. My basic faith. The one I had even before I ever heard about Spiritualism. And that faith is that there is a God and He is wondrous and works strange things of which we mortals can only stand in awe.'

They pulled up the driveway, clear now of snow. The

long thaw had melted all the winter's leavings that were on the ground. A few barn roofs had vestiges of the white flakes and some front porch tops were still hidden by the stuff, but mostly it looked as if winter had never been there at all.

Ann met them at the front door and hurried the doctor upstairs. He found Lurancy in bed, asleep but with a frown on her face and perspiring heavily.

'She started that sweating last night,' Ann told him. 'Along with the groans. I try to talk to her but she won't listen.'

The doctor examined the girl's eyelids and then held her wrist as he counted her pulsebeats against his round gold watch. Then he took off his jacket and asked Asa to help him turn Lurancy onto her back. When this was done he covered her with a thin blanket and flexed his fingers. 'I'll try the passes on her,' he said to no one in particular.

His hands were just a few inches from her face as he started moving them slowly down to her chin, her neck and her chest. Then he swooped them into the air and shook them, fingers spread apart, trying to remove some invisible substance that had stuck to them. Back the hands went to the top of her head, then down her face, her throat, her chest and then were shaken. Again they fluttered in front of her, passed, swooped and were shaken. The girl didn't budge.

'Help me sit her up,' he ordered Asa, and as they raised Lurancy into position, Ann pushed several feather pillows between the girl's back and the headboard. Still she didn't open her eyes.

The doctor shook his fingers, said a silent prayer and started the hand movements again. Over the head, down the face, the neck, the chest and then the swooping and the shaking. Once again. And then again. No response from Lurancy.

Dr Stevens rubbed his hands together and placed one of them on the girl's forehead and the other on the back of her head. He began to press his hands and shake his body. His arms shook as if they were being tossed in a strong wind. Drops of sweat ran down his forehead and into his thick black beard. He took away his hands, shook them and placed them again in the same spot, making a sandwich of Lurancy's head. He prayed silently and then he prayed aloud. There was no reaction. Lurancy sat there, propped up by the pillows, like an overlarge rag doll.

'I'm sorry,' he said after about an hour of this, 'but I can't seem to get through to her. I don't know what it is. There is nothing more I can do at the moment. I have already been told that I've done enough for now. They have told me,' he said. 'They always do. All we can do now is pray that the energies will work and will have a reaction.' He gave each of them a faint smile. 'I'll try again later. Maybe it is the exhaustion of my trip. Perhaps that's what it is.' He seemed relieved by this explanation. 'When I've had a chance to recoup my own energies, I'll try sending them to her again.'

Asa and the doctor left the room after pulling Lurancy back down into a lying position. Ann covered her with a blanket and placed a pillow under her head. She stood there after the two men had gone, staring down at the sleeping face of this girl who was her daughter and yet who was no relation at all. 'Please get well, Mary . . . or Lurancy,' she said as she kissed the girl on the forehead and settled herself in a chair next to the bed.

The doctor was shown to his room. Asa insisted he stay in the house and wouldn't hear of him checking into a hotel.

Frank and Charlie had taken a great deal of ribbing at school when word got around that Crazy Rancy was staying with them. Their friends joked about soon having to lock up the entire family because madness was a disease that might be catching. Their teachers questioned them outright on what was going on and wondered aloud if their father really knew what he was doing. One day there was a crayon drawing in the boys' toilet on the second floor. It showed two stick boys having sex with a stick girl who was tied to a bed. The names Frank, Charlie and Crazy Rancy pointed with arrows to the figures. Mr Haley, the principal, heard about the drawing and after inspecting it ordered it washed away. He also ordered that the subject of Miss Vennum's illness was not a fit one for frivolity and threatened any student caught making light of her predicament with a severe caning and six weeks of detention. The jokes about Lurancy and the Roff boys stopped after that. They would have anyway because most of the students liked Frank and Charlie and were already bored with the Crazy Rancy story.

Twice a day for the next few days Dr Stevens gave his treatment to Lurancy. There was no response. Each morning and afternoon he would leave the bedroom more discouraged than ever. Once he even suggested sending for a friend who 'maybe was better than I am' in St Louis, but it was only an idea. Asa knew Dr Stevens could cure her and knew that Mary's spirit – if it was still around – trusted this man over any other doctor.

Those were silent days in the Roff home. Ann hardly ever left the girl's side and Charlotte was tired of doing all the housework and the cooking by herself. She grumbled that she had to take a tray up to Ann three times a day and grumbled when Ann didn't eat half the things she put on it. If she wasn't careful, Charlotte told her, she would get sick herself. She had to eat. Ann promised but only picked at the food. Nervie tried to help with some of the work but found it difficult doing things with Charlotte.

'You know, Mrs Alter,' the German woman said one afternoon when they were ironing clothes, 'maybe it would be better for everybody if that girl went back home. She is killing your mother.'

Nervie was furious. 'Charlotte! You know what those Vennum people would do to her! She'd be dead in a week.'

'And that would be such a bad thing? I mean, between what she is now and dead, that's so bad?'

Minerva threw down the shirt she was ironing. 'Mrs Wiedener. Please remember your place!' She stomped out of the kitchen and would have slammed the door except it was on swinging hinges.

'I'll remember my place, okay,' Charlotte said aloud. 'And my place is to look after me and not get killed by some crazy girl.' She went on with her ironing, deliberately pressing a wrinkle into one of Lurancy's muslin blouses.

By April 8 Dr Stevens was still trying. The results were still negative. He had no idea what was going wrong. The girl had been like this since March 25, a full fifteen days. She hadn't eaten or taken a drop of liquid. She hadn't performed any of her 'necessities', hadn't soiled the bed once. The only good sign was that she didn't seem to be losing weight; neither Asa nor Ann thought she had changed physically. There was no unpleasant odor to her body, the sweating came at infrequent intervals and never lasted more than a few minutes. She made no noises now, even though Asa had told him about the 'nightmares' that caused her to move in bed. Since the doctor's arrival she hadn't even done that. She just lay there like an illustration of a sleeping princess in a children's book of fairy tales. Maybe that's what she needed, Charlie had said at dinner one night last week, a prince charming to come along and kiss her. No one at the table thought it was the least bit funny and Charlie was excused before the dessert was served.

On the night of the eighth, Dr Stevens retired early to his room. He wanted to read, to meditate, just to get away from everyone and try to decipher what was going wrong. Maybe it was he himself? Possibly the powers were leaving him. It had happened to others. One day 'they' had taken the powers away. 'They' gave them and 'they' took them back again. Perhaps 'they' had done it to him, yet he couldn't quite understand the logic of it. Why permit his powers to bring in the Roff girl and then deny him the powers to revive her?

'It's not fair!' he heard himself say aloud and he jumped a bit at the sound of his own voice. 'I've tried everything I know how! I have prayed and I have worked and still nothing has been worth the effort! It is not fair!' He got up from his chair and began to pace the room. 'It's not fair. It isn't fair to me and it certainly isn't fair to the Vennum girl. And especially not to Mary!' He said that last sentence a little louder than the others. 'It isn't fair to Mary. First you bring her back from her heavenly rest and ask her to assume the responsibility for this new body and then you abandon her! Yes, I said abandon! After all she has gone through for you, you abandon her!' His voice was getting louder. He didn't care. He was getting angry and his voice always rose when he was angry. 'I try to do my best. I try to follow all the orders you give me. Even the stupid ones. Yes, don't be shocked. Sometimes your orders don't make a particle of sense but I do them! I carry them out to the

252

letter. Don't I?' He didn't wait for an answer. 'I put my life and my reputation on the line and what do you do? You ignore me when I need you most! And what's worse, you ignore Mary! Do you realize you are ignoring her?' His voice bounced back at him from the flowers on the wallpaper. He heard it and lowered it somewhat. 'I want you to know something,' he said looking up, not at the ceiling, just up. 'I want you to know that this is the last time I'll work on one of these cases for you! That's right. The *last* time! Mark it down in your calendars! I am fed up with you! With all of you!' His voice was rising again. 'You ask me to give up my life, my family and my friends and when I do it all for you, yes for *you*, you refuse me your support! Well, I am getting out! Out. Do you hear me? Out!' He passed the front of the dresser mirror and saw how he looked shaking his fist and staring at nothing up above him. 'And you are a fool,' he said to his image. 'A fool to keep on following orders from whoever *they* are! A fool, and a fool deserves everything he gets!' He stopped, staring at the man in the mirror with the red face above his thick black beard, wearing shirtsleeves, no collar and no tie. 'Ah!' he said, dismissing him with a wave of his hand. 'Go to bed. Fools need sleep too.'

Mechanically he undressed, hung his trousers in the wardrobe along with his jacket and threw his shirt onto a chair. He had already taken off his shoes, so only the stockings needed to be removed. He pulled each one off and tossed it angrily onto the wrinkled shirt. Then, wearing only his long woolen underwear, which he never took off until the first day of summer, he scratched inside at the armpits and at his groin and got into bed.

He was about to blow out the oil lamp when he saw it. His arm, reaching for the lamp, froze in space. There, drifting from the ceiling, slowly, slowly turning in a breeze of its own making was an envelope. An ordinary short white envelope. It fell lazily downward and onto the carpet. He stared at it for a full three minutes before he had the courage to get out of bed and pick it up. Trembling, he opened it.

'There are three points on the Vennum girl's body that are in need of physical therapy.' It was written in script, with a kind of European slant to the letters that seemed to have come from an aged and infirm hand. 'You are to heat some camphor and rub it briskly into her wrists and her ankles. Then rub some more camphor into the veins that are on both sides of her neck. When this has been accomplished, place a flannel cloth that has been soaked in warm castor oil at the base of her spine. Secure this flannel with a strip of cloth, tying it tightly so the oil will fully penetrate the nerves and muscles of that area. Do this three times in three days but for periods lasting not more than one hour each. On the third time, proceed as usual with your magnetic passes.'

Dr Stevens read the paragraph over again, unable to believe yet knowing it was happening to him. There was one line at the bottom of the page, all by itself. He drew nearer to the lamp to read the tiny script. All it said was: 'God is with you.'

'Thank you,' he said, pulling the paper close to his heart, feeling very humble and very much ashamed. 'Thank you.'

In the morning he showed Asa and Ann the letter. Surprisingly, he had slept very well that night, once the excitement of getting the letter had worn off. It was an assured sleep, the assurance coming from the fact that the girl would definitely be healed and that he, most definitely, had not lost his powers.

'Mary told me I would get a letter from heaven,' he said to them. 'She wrote and told me I'd get it. She said it would save someone's life.' He smiled. 'Little did she know that it would be her own.'

As soon as Oren's drugstore was open, Asa was there buying the camphor and the castor oil. Ann heated the oils herself, not wanting to let Charlotte have anything to do with them after Nervie reported her conversation with the woman. She cut one of Asa's old flannel nightshirts into large squares and tore an old sheet into strips.

'It must be the shock of that other person, whoever he was, that came through her was too much,' the doctor said as he applied the warm camphor to Lurancy's ankles and wrists. 'The shock must have upset things on a more physical level than even the other side could handle. That's the way I see it, anyway. They must have hoped the magnetic passes would be enough but obviously they needed to be accompanied by this outside stimulus. I've never heard of hot castor oil, though. That's a new one on me.'

'I have,' Asa said. 'When I was a boy my aunt used to put a castor-oil pack over her liver. It took the pain away in no time flat. Where she learned it, I have no idea. But it worked.'

They turned the girl over, and while the men looked away, Ann pulled Lurancy's nightgown up around her shoulders and then brought up the blanket so it covered her buttocks. The men turned around when they were given permission and the doctor placed the castor-oil pack at the base of her spine. Ann tied it securely and tightly.

After about forty-five minutes there was a low moan from the girl. But it was a sound. The three adults were jubilant. Later that afternoon Lurancy moved by herself, turning onto her side and pulling her legs up against her stomach. Ann cried a little when she reported it to her husband and the doctor. That night Ann slept in her own bed. Exhausted but relieved.

The next day the treatment was repeated. This time, not more than ten minutes after the castor oil pack had been in place, Lurancy fluttered her eyelids and tried to form a word. Ann patted her head and murmured tenderly to her. Later that afternoon she was able to give the girl a sip or two of warm milk.

On the third day Dr Stevens began his passes over her once the camphor and the castor oil had been applied. After the first swooping movements, Lurancy opened her eyes and tried to lift her head.

'Ma?' she called. 'Ma?'

'Right here, darling. Your Ma is right here.' Ann lightly brushed the girl's hair back from her eyes.

'Ma?' Lurancy smiled. 'It's gonna be all right. The body's going to be all right.'

Ann hesitated before she touched the girl again. 'Is that you, Mary?' she asked timidly. 'Is that Mary?'

'Yes, Ma. It's me. Mary.' She smiled and reached out an arm to catch hold of Ann's full skirt. 'The body's gonna be all right. Everything's going to be all right.' She fell asleep still clutching Ann's skirt.

Sunday, April 14, 1878, saw the Methodist Church decked out in daffodils, and even a few potted lilies, which struggled mightily to be seen above the silks, satins, nets, gauzes, velvets, brocades and feathers of the ladies of the congregation.

The Reverend Baker had a smile on his face as he stood there looking at the flock. 'It is a blessed day,' he intoned, 'a blessed day to give thanks.'

The pianist played a spirited rendition of 'Christ Our Lord Is Risen Today' and everyone sang the 'hallelujah' chorus with much gusto and feeling. Just before the collection was taken (and it was always a good one on Easter, with backsliders putting in enough to ease their consciences for another year), the minister had 'a few announcements'.

'As you are all aware, we have formed a citizens committee to help an unfortunate girl in our community. This child, who shall go nameless from the pulpit, is a member of this church, of this congregation. Recently she was to have gone to Springfield to begin needed medical treatments, but outside influences halted that treatment and the poor child has been forced to remain here in Watseka, where she is lacking entirely the moral and medical care she was prescribed. The child has been taken from her parents' home and is now living in a deluded state of mind in the home of citizens in Watseka who shall also not be named from this pulpit. This gentleman and his family were at one time members of this congregation but they withdrew and are not members of any certified or reputable Christian congregation.' He paused to let his eyes wander over the gathered devout. He didn't need to name names; from the way they were looking at each other and from the few whispers he managed to hear up where he was standing, they knew who he was talking about.

'A petition has been written up, a petition that will be presented to those in authority in this city, demanding that this child be taken care of in the proper manner. I fervently ask you to sign your name to this petition as you leave the worship service this morning. Mrs Lavinia Durst will be at a table in the vestibule with this paper and with pen and ink available. Examine your hearts and ask yourself why you too cannot come to the aid of this poor child who has been abandoned by her parents and left to suffer alone in the midst of non-Christian strangers. Now,' he said changing his tone and smiling, 'while the collection baskets are passed will you open your hymnals to page one hundred twenty-seven and sing the first two verses of "Let Me Walk in Thy Footsteps, Oh My Lord".'

Two days later, on April 1, Lurinda Vennum made a batch of vanilla-frosted chocolate cupcakes. Chocolate cupcakes were Rancy's favorite. Lurinda put them all in the cake safe except one. This one she placed in the center of a blue plate and then stuck one small pink candle into the top of the cake. She lit the candle and began to sing softly: 'Happy birthday to you, Happy birthday to you. Happy birthday, dear Rancy. Happy birth . . . ' Her voice broke, she sat on a kitchen chair and cried.

The next two weeks, as the petition circulated around town, Ann and Minerva spent as much time as they could with Lurancy. They heard the rumblings and knew what was being said about all of them. Not to be liked in a small town was one thing but to be denounced from a pulpit was something much worse. It was the equivalent of being excommunicated for a Catholic or having a picture in the post office for a criminal. The Roffs had been branded and were expected to knuckle under to the demands of the townspeople. No one was beyond town justice. Especially not the Roffs who, in spite of their money and position, were already outside the church.

Because of this, the Roff women insisted to Lurancy that she should get acquainted with the Vennum family.

'But I don't like them,' she said. 'We don't have anything to talk about to each other.'

'Mary,' Ann pleaded, 'one of these days you are going to go away and Lurancy will come back and Lurancy will have to return home. To the Vennum home.'

'That's her and not me. When I go the next time, I'll just keep right on going.'

'We know that,' Minerva said, 'but think of poor Mrs Vennum. You can see how happy we are to have you here; imagine how she must feel not to have her daughter there.'

Lurancy sighed. She supposed they were right. 'Oh, well,' she said. 'I'll go and visit the lady. It can't hurt anything.

Her daughter is much stronger now and so am I. I won't let them get to me, that's all. I promise.'

So, on Monday, May 6, Asa Roff was surprised in his office when Lurancy suddenly came in, put her arms around his shoulders and said: 'Pa, I'm going with Mrs Vennum to visit today.'

Asa looked up. There in the doorway stood Lurinda Vennum. She looked paler than he had remembered and there seemed to be more lines in her face, yet she was smiling.

Lurancy was at home, at the Roff home, by four. She seemed exhausted after her visit and Ann told her to lie down. 'Did anything happen?' she asked, almost afraid of what the reply would be.

'No,' the girl said. 'Nothing. We had a pleasant afternoon. She showed me some of Lurancy's clothes and things and a scrapbook that her daughter made from the ladies' magazines. Mostly she just sat there and stared at me. We had tea and fresh-baked cupcakes and I ate one just for her. You know, Ma, I don't like cupcakes at all, but I ate one just to please her.' She put an apron over her dress, ready to help with the evening meal. 'I feel sorry for that woman. She is so alone. I suppose it'll be good for her when Rancy comes back.'

'Yes,' Ann replied sadly. 'I suppose it will be good for *her*.'

The next morning, after breakfast the men had gone to work or school. Charlotte was washing the dishes. Lurancy took Mrs Roff by the hand.

'Ma, can I talk with you? Private?'

Ann nodded and the girl led her into the back parlor and closed the doors. She motioned the woman to sit on the sofa and she sat down beside her. Again she reached for her hand.

'Ma, I've got some sad news for you. I don't know how to tell it.'

'Sad? I'm used to sadness, Mary. Don't be afraid.' She clenched the girl's hand in hers. 'You can tell me.'

'Yesterday at the Vennums, Lurancy came back.'

'Came back? What do you mean?'

'Just that. I was sitting and talking with Mrs Vennum when Lurancy came back and took over her body. She was so happy to see her Ma and they hugged each other and cried and then Lurancy went away again. That's why I was so sad yesterday when I got back here.' She got up and went to look out of the window and to delay her tears. 'Ma, I don't know what this all means. I don't know when that girl will be back for good! Do you hear what I'm saying, Ma? I don't know how much longer we will be together! Oh Ma,' and she rushed into Ann's arms. 'I don't want to leave you again. Not again! Please, Ma! Don't let them take me!'

Ann wanted to cry herself, but held back. 'Mary, child, *my* child. It'll be all right. It has to be all right. Don't take on so!'

'But I want to stay here with you and Pa. Forever!'

'Nothing is forever. You told me that yourself when you came back here. We love you. Your Pa and I haven't been so happy in years as we have these past weeks. We love you and don't want to see you leave us, but you know you *have* to. You *know* that!'

'I suppose,' she said, 'I suppose I do. But that doesn't make it any easier.'

'You should be glad you were able to come back at all. Look at what a wonderful opportunity you've given us. And what great solace and strength you've given Dr Stevens.' She sat the girl on the sofa again. 'Don't worry, we'll be together again. Your Pa and I will soon be over there where you are and then we'll be together for an awful long time.' She stroked Lurancy's hair. 'This has all been expected. We've been knowing it was coming. It ain't so terrible.'

The girl leaned back onto the sofa and wiped her eyes with the edge of her apron. She bit her lower lip and closed her eyelids. Then she sighed deeply. She folded her hands in her lap and sighed again. Ann watched her for several minutes and then quietly stood up and walked toward the closed doors.

She heard the cry coming even before it was out of the girl's throat.

'Who are you? I want my Ma!'

'Lurancy?'

'Yes. Where's my Ma?'

Ann took a deep breath. 'Your Ma isn't here right now.'

'Where is she?'

'Over to her place.'

'Why'd she leave me here?' the girl's lips began to tremble.

'She didn't leave you here. My daughter Mary Roff brought you here.' She paused watching how this information reflected on the girl's face. 'You were sick in the body and my daughter brought you here to get well.'

The girl started to get off the sofa. 'Please let me go home,' she said. 'I don't want to stay here.'

'Do you want me to get your coat?'

'Yes, Ma'am. Please. I want to go home.'

'You just sit right here. I'll fetch your things.' The girl remained on the sofa as Ann went into the front hallway where Lurancy's winter coat was hanging. 'It had to come sometime,' she said aloud to her reflection in the hall mirror. 'I just wish Asa had been here, that's all.'

She brought the coat into the parlor. 'Here, put this on and I'll walk to your place with you.'

The girl was still on the sofa, her hands over her eyes. When she took them away, she smiled at Ann.

'Oh Ma! Did you see? Did you see how she comes and goes now? But she let me come back again, Ma! She let me come back again!' The two embraced. 'Don't know for how long Ma, but I'm going to appreciate every minute of it.'

On Monday, May 13, Asa had two visitors in his office. One was the Reverend Baker and the other was Mrs Lavinia Durst. They didn't beat around the bush.

'We have something for you,' the minister said, reaching into his briefcase. 'This paper.' He put it on Asa's desk, right under his nose.

Asa didn't touch it. 'What is it?'

'A petition. A petition that you surrender Lurancy Vennum to the proper authorities and permit her to start her treatment in Springfield.'

'It's been signed by four hundred and twenty-eight persons,' Lavinia said. 'All of them citizens of Watseka and all of them anxious to see justice carried out!'

'You call this justice?' Asa asked, still not touching the document. 'Take an innocent girl away from her family and friends and lock her up for the rest of her life? Is that justice in your terms?'

'Don't try your theatrics on us, Asa Roff.' Lavinia wasn't about to take anything from him now. Not now. 'You know what we mean. That girl is dangerous and I am the one that has the emotional scars to prove it.'

'And the bruised ass,' Asa said sarcastically, 'if what my wife tells me is true.'

'Really! Reverend Baker, do you see how he mocks us?'

'I don't mock you and I don't like you. I only can tell you one thing. I have no intention of giving up the Vennum girl to you or anyone else. I know my rights as a citizen and I know her rights. I'm a lawyer and a judge, don't forget. I can drag things out for a mighty long time. And I will drag this out until the Vennum girl is cured and able to return to her real home.' He got up and walked toward the door. 'Until that time comes, I respectfully ask both of you not to bother me or Lurancy again. There are laws against harassment and invasion of privacy, you know.'

The minister didn't move. 'Mr Roff, you have always been known as a reasonable man.'

'Why don't you have the mayor with you?' Asa asked. 'After all, he's the one who must sign her commitment papers.'

Asa laughed. 'But he told me he threw you out of his store and now I'm going to throw you out of my office. The two of you are certainly getting special treatment in town, aren't you?' Asa opened the door, and pointed into the hallway. 'If you don't mind. I have work to do.'

'Then we won't disturb you, Pa. Dr Stevens and I can come back later.' Lurancy was standing there, her hand still raised as she was about to knock on the closed door.

'Lurancy!' Asa was not happy to see her. 'What are you doing here?'

'We were out for a stroll and thought it would be nice to

drop in for a visit,' Dr Stevens replied. 'I'm sorry if the moment was inopportune.'

'No. Come in, sir,' the Reverend Baker said. 'As a matter of fact, I've been anxious to meet you.'

Asa shrugged and took the girl by the hand. 'You might as well hear this, Doctor,' he said. 'This is the Methodist minister I was telling you about and this is Lavinia Durst.'

The doctor's eyes widened. 'Indeed? Well, this is a surprise. I've been looking forward to meeting both of you.'

'They brought me a piece of paper,' Asa said. 'A petition that I send Lurancy away to Springfield.' He motioned to the folded sheets on his desk. 'I haven't touched it yet, so legally I haven't received it.'

'You've received it,' said Lavinia, 'because we've given it to you. Don't think you're so smart, Asa Roff. I knew you when you were just a shoe salesman and don't forget it.'

Lurancy was hanging onto Asa's hand, staring at Lavinia Durst. Lavinia pointed a finger at her. 'Don't look at me like that, young lady! I'm wise to you. I'm aware of your tricks. You've played your last one on me!'

'Pa?' and she drew closer to Asa. 'Who is this woman?'

'Nobody important,' he said.

That cut Lavinia quickly and deeply. 'Nobody important! You'll see how important I am! You don't own Watseka, Asa Roff, and you don't own me either. You think you're so powerful with your fancy house and your judge titles; well, you are a nothing and a nobody and you ain't got a friend in this entire town!' She grabbed the petition and waved it in his face. 'There are four hundred and twenty-eight names on this paper and they are all your enemies! I got them onto my side now.' She threw the petition back on the desk. 'And you say I'm not important in this town.'

'Don't you talk to my Pa like that!' Lurancy said. 'It ain't fair.'

'Your Pa?' Lavinia laughed. 'Look who this crazy girl is calling her Pa. Why, just look, Reverend Baker, she's still as loony as a hoot owl!'

'I ain't loony!' the girl protested.

'Loony as a hoot owl, that's what you are, and as dangerous as a coiled rattlesnake. Never know when you're gonna strike.' She nudged the minister. 'I guess we don't have to see any more, do we? I guess we have enough to tell the others, if necessary.'

'What others?' Dr Stevens asked.

'In the governor's office.' Lavinia was playing her last trump card. 'I have influence in the state capital. If this loony girl doesn't get committed soon, I'm going straight to the governor.' She cupped Lurancy's chin in her hand. 'How do you like that, Crazy Rancy?'

'Don't touch me!' The girl pulled away. She was about to say something else when she stopped and put her hand over her eyes.

'Now what?' Asa asked quickly.

'Nothing, Pa,' Lurancy replied. 'I'm listening.'

'Listening?' Lavinia snorted. 'Listening to what?'

'If you'd be quiet, I could hear,' she said softly. 'They are talking to me.'

'They?' the minister asked.

'They are those on the other – ' Dr Stevens broke off his remark. 'But why bother? You're a Methodist minister. You'd never understand.'

'Work of the Devil, that's what it is.' Lavinia edged toward the open door. 'I don't have no mind to get caught up in it again.'

Lurancy took her hand away from her eyes and looked at Dr Stevens. 'They said there was nothing to worry about. They had everything under control.'

'Control my foot!' Lavinia was in the doorway. 'It'll take more than your demons to keep you here in Watseka, young lady!'

'They said you were to take this as a warning and not to bother me again.'

'And so have you been warned. By four hundred and twenty-eight signatures.' She went down the hallway, the Reverend Baker following right behind.

'She's been warned, Pa,' the girl looked at Asa. 'I tried to tell her but she won't listen. She's been warned.'

That Friday evening the front doorbell rang and when Charlotte opened it, there was Henry Vennum.

He had his hat in his hand. 'Please, Ma'am,' he said. 'I wondered if I could see my sister? Lurancy Vennum? She's a guest here.'

'I know who she is,' the German woman replied. 'But I don't know if she's allowed visitors. You wait here.' She closed the door and went into the back parlor where Asa and Lurancy were quietly talking.

'Excuse me, sir, but there is a young man outside who has come calling on Lurancy Vennum. Says he's her brother.'

'Her brother?' Asa got up from his chair. 'What does he want?'

'He wants to talk to Lurancy,' replied Charlotte.

'But Rancy isn't here,' the girl said. 'She's still away on the other side.'

'I don't know about that,' said the woman, 'but he's out on the porch. What'll I tell him?'

'Tell him to come in, of course,' Asa said. 'Have him come in here.'

When the woman left, Lurancy looked at Asa. 'Wonder what *he* wants? Do you think there's been some sickness at the Vennum place?'

'I don't know,' Asa replied. 'We'll find out soon enough.'

'He's about the only decent one of that whole lot,' Lurancy said. 'Still, he's a bore. Only talks about his old job at the feedstore. That's all he knows.' She stopped speaking and smoothed her dress as the young man came into the room.

'Mr Roff? Excuse me, sir, but I wondered if I could talk to Rancy?' He stood just inside the doorway talking to Asa but looking at his sister.

'She isn't here right now,' Asa said. 'If you know what I mean.'

The young man nodded. 'Yes, sir, I do, but her Ma is not too well and I was kind of hoping that maybe Lurancy would make her feel better if she talked with her.'

'Is something wrong with your mother?' Lurancy asked.

'It's her nerves. She's been doing a lot of crying and ain't sleeping much. Mostly because of the petition.'

'The petition? What petition?' the girl asked.

'You know what I'm talking about, don't you, sir?'

Asa nodded. 'I do indeed. I haven't told Mary much about it though.'

'Good. No use having her upset too.' Asa motioned him to a chair and he sat on the edge of it. 'You don't think there's a chance, then.'

'Of your sister going to see your mother?'

'Right.'

'I don't know. I doubt it. Lurancy isn't here right now. I'm sorry but there's not much I can do about it. You understand?'

'Yes, sir. I do.' He rose to his feet. 'Well, I thought I'd try. Ma being so nervous and all.'

'I'm sorry,' Asa put his hand on the young man's shoulder. 'I can understand what your mother is going through. But it won't be for much longer. Lurancy is getting better every day. Frankly, I wouldn't be surprised if your sister would be home before the month is out.' This was May and Mary had told Dr Stevens 'they' expected Lurancy to be well by the middle of it. Today was the seventeenth. It could happen at any moment.

'What are we going to do about the petition?' Henry asked him. 'I mean, what good is all this if they end up putting her away?'

'I don't think they'll put her away. Your sister has some new and powerful friends she didn't have before. Not only on this side but on the other side as well.'

'I sure hope so. It would just kill Ma if anything more happened to Rancy.'

'Henry! Oh, Henry!'

The two men turned. Lurancy was sitting on the sofa, her eyes wide and her arms outstretched. 'What a wonderful surprise!' She jumped up and embraced him. 'It's so good to see you! Mr Roff, ain't it a surprise to see Henry again?' She had tears in her eyes. So did Henry. So did Asa.

'I'll let the two of you alone,' the older man said. 'I'm sure you have a million things to say. I'll be in the next room if you need me, Henry.'

After he had gone, Lurancy held her brother out at arm's length. 'Just look at you! So handsome and so tall! Come, let's sit on the sofa. Tell me all about everything. I want to hear everything!' They sat and she held his hands. 'How *are* you? Tell me what you've been doing since I left.'

'I'm fine, Rancy. Real fine. The job at the feedstore's going good. I can't complain none.' He reached up and touched her lightly on the cheek. 'We miss you at the house, Rancy. I miss you real bad.'

'Oh, and I miss you!' she said. 'But it won't be for long. I won't be away much longer. I'm getting much much better and they tell me that I'll soon be ready to come home for good. Won't that be wonderful?' She squeezed his hands. 'How's Ma?'

'Not too good,' he said sadly. 'She misses you terrible and gets those crying fits and sometimes can't seem to stop. Rancy, do you suppose you could go over and see her?'

'Now?'

'Yeah. Now. I've got the buggy outside. It wouldn't take but a few minutes to bring you there. And she'd like it so! She really would.'

The girl pulled back a little. 'No,' she said shaking her head. 'I can't leave here. Not just yet. They asked me not to.' She reached up and put her fingers to his lips. 'Why don't you bring Ma over here? That would be fine, I'm sure!'

'Well, I don't know. You recall the last time she was here and Pa and Mr Roff got into a fracas and there was bad blood all around.'

'Things are different now, Henry. Pa understands things a whole lot better than he did then. The Roffs understand better too. Henry, the Roffs have been so marvelous to me. You have no idea.' She got up and opened the door.

'We are much obliged to them, I know,' he said.

'For as long as I live, I'll be obliged to them. Let me see if it's all right for Ma to come here. Mr Roff,' she called, 'could you come here for a minute?'

Asa hurried into the parlor. He hadn't told Ann about this. She was over at Nervie's and he didn't want to upset her by calling her home.

'Mr Roff,' Lurancy said, 'Henry says that Ma is feeling awfully sad that I ain't back to the house yet. He wants me to go over there, but they have told me to stay here. Would it be all right if he brought Ma over here?' She touched the sleeves of his coat. 'Please?'

'Of course, it would be all right,' he answered, 'but will you stay here while Henry is gone? I mean,' he said, 'will Lurancy remain in the body all that time?'

'No,' she answered matter-of-factly. 'I won't. I'll go away now and Mary will come in. Then I'll come back when my Ma gets here. Don't worry,' she said and put her arm through his. 'Henry, didn't I tell you? These folks have been so good to me!'

'I'll go and get Ma,' the young man said excitedly. 'Shouldn't be more than ten minutes.' He started for the door. 'Rancy,' he said, stopping and looking at her, 'please be here when Ma gets here. Please?'

'I gave you my word, Henry. You just fetch Ma. I can't wait to see her.'

The young man ran out of the house and jumped into his buggy.

When the door closed Lurancy said: 'You know, Pa, he isn't such a bad fellow, and it did Rancy a great deal of good to see him. She really misses her folks. I just hope her Ma doesn't take on too much while she's here.' She kissed Asa on the cheek. 'I'll go and freshen up and put on that new dress Ma made for me. Mrs Vennum will like seeing her daughter looking pretty.'

In less than ten minutes the front doorbell rang again. Asa answered it himself.

'Mr Roff,' Lurinda almost hugged him. 'I do so want to thank you for letting me come and see my Rancy! You are a true gentleman!'

'Not at all, Mrs Vennum. Please do come in. Rancy's gone upstairs to pretty herself up for you. Let's wait for her in the back parlor.' Henry took his mother's arm and led the way. Asa followed after them. 'I'll tell her you're here,' he said. 'Excuse me a moment.'

'How does she look?' the woman asked. 'Am I gonna get a shock? I can't take many more shocks, Henry.'

'Just you wait and see. She sure looks a mighty sight better than when she was at our house,' he said. 'She's got life to her now and her eyes shine and she takes care of herself. Combs her hair and washes her face and all those things she never did before.'

'I always combed my hair and washed my face, Henry

Vennum!' Lurancy came running into the room. 'Ma! My own dear sweet Ma!' Lurinda gave one mighty sob and clutched her daughter to her. They didn't speak. Everything they had to say was said in that embrace.

Asa closed the double doors and went out onto the front porch. The night was warm and there was a large moon. He sat on the steps, took out a cigarette, lit it and inhaled deeply. A cricket whirred somewhere a few feet away and far in the distance a flock of starlings, startled by something, rose to be silhouetted against the moon. He didn't think of anything, didn't want to think of anything. All he wanted was peace and quiet inside as well as outside himself. The last few pieces were being put into place. Soon the puzzle would be complete and he would see what the entire picture looked like. There was one piece that didn't fit in as yet. It had Lavinia Durst's face on it. That piece bothered him. That piece could destroy the entire puzzle.

The next morning the Roff family was having breakfast together. It was a Saturday and the boys didn't have school and Asa had decided not to go to his office. Lurancy sat with them, eating a large bowl of oatmeal, scooping it up with a piece of homemade bread liberally covered with peanut butter.

It was when Charlie passed her some more milk that she realized the other boy was missing. 'Where's Frank?' she asked. 'Ain't he going to eat?'

'He's already had his breakfast,' Ann said.

'So soon?'

'He had to go to the train station,' Charlie said. 'To fetch somebody.'

'Fetch somebody? Who?'

Charlie was about to tell but Ann put her fingers to her lips. 'Now Charles, it's to be a surprise.'

'Not for long,' Charlie shouted. 'The buggy just drove up the driveway.' He jumped from the table and ran down the hallway toward the front porch.

There was a long silence in the dining-room. Lurancy could hear Charlie's voice rising excitedly and then much laughter. She glanced at Asa but he shook his head. 'You just wait right here.'

The girl shut her eyes, almost not breathing as she waited

for the doors to open. There was rustling in the doorway of the dining-room and she knew Ann and Asa had gotten up to greet whoever – or whatever – it was. There was some whispering and then Ann's voice said: 'All right, Mary. You can look now.'

Lurancy opened her eyes and stared at the figure in the doorway. It was a large figure wearing several petticoats and a neat little bonnet. The hands and face were dusky black.

Lurancy gasped, then rose halfway from her chair. 'Loozie! Oh my heavens, it's Loozie!'

The rest of that day (and if Lurancy had had her way, most of the night) was spent talking with Loozie, reminiscing with Loozie and just being close to Loozie. The entire family had a million questions for her and she, in turn, had a thousand for them. She talked about her babies and gave a daguerreotype photo in a folding brass frame as a gift to the family. The photo was of her family. Her oldest, Asa, now almost eleven, stood solemnly beside his sisters Grace Mary, who was eight, and Elizabeth Minerva, who was six. Loozie and her husband posed behind the children, wearing their finest clothes and trying to look serious instead of proud.

Ann had written her about Lurancy and so the woman knew how to react to this stranger with Mary's voice and mind. She had been studying the spirits all her life. What was happening at the Roff home intrigued but didn't frighten or confuse her. She believed in the powers on the other side. She had come from a long line of believers and considered it an honor to be a witness to what Mary had been sent back to accomplish.

The next day was Sunday and after breakfast Loozie and Lurancy took a walk. Loozie hadn't been in Watseka for twelve years and kept oohing and aahing over each new building, each new residence and each new improvement.

'It looks like the same old place,' she told the girl, 'and then we turn a corner and there's something I never seen before!' She laughed. 'Still ain't much of a town, though. Not like Chicago or Toronto or some of the cities I've seen.'

They walked hand in hand, Loozie paying no attention to the stares they were getting. She had been in Canada long enough to forget about prejudice. When she was the only African in Watseka there had been no racial discrimination, just curiosity. People wanted to know her because she was one of a kind, and she loved it. But now, since the war, stories started coming from other places about how Africans would kill a white man just as soon look at him or how they would steal anything that wasn't nailed down or how they had this terrible smell in their armpits. Therefore the stares and the mutterings as she walked hand in hand with Crazy Rancy Vennum.

They passed the courthouse, all red brick and white wood trim with a tower supported by six white Grecian pillars. 'My,' exclaimed Loozie, 'will you look at that! Wasn't half finished when I was here. Nothing but a hole in the ground and a lot of bricks in a pile. And look what they done to it! Ain't it a pretty place, though?'

When they came to the next corner, Loozie stopped. 'And look what they've done to the Methodist Church! I declare there must be more money in this town than I thought.' She pulled at Lurancy's hand. 'Come on, let's peek inside. I want to see what it looks like when there's a service going on.'

'I'd rather not, Loozie. I don't like that church.'

'Oh, come on, child. That's your church. That's the one your folks go to! Come on. Listen you can hear them singing. Come on. Just for a peek.'

Reluctantly Lurancy followed the African woman up the front steps of the frame building. There was no one in the outer hall and the doors to the auditorium were closed. The singing got louder as Loozie pushed one of the doors open and peered inside. 'My, my! They went and put a carpet in the aisle and fancy paper on the walls that looks just like marble!'

'Can we go now?' the girl insisted.

'Sure, honey. Let's.' They started for the outside door when a side door opened. Lavinia Durst stopped stock still. The pen and inkwell in her hand fell to the floor.

'That girl! You brought that girl here to torment us!' Lavinia was shouting, her face white with fear.

'We was only looking,' Lurancy said in a low voice. She tugged at Loozie. 'Come on!'

'In my church!' Lavinia yelled. 'On a Sunday! Oh my God!'

There was a noise from inside the auditorium. The doors opened and several people came out.

'What's the matter?' a man's voice asked.

'Look!' Lavinia was leaning against the wall. 'It's that crazy Vennum girl. She's come to destroy us!'

'Look, missus,' Loozie started to say. 'All we did was look inside. It was my idea.'

'Lurancy Vennum?'

'Here? That crazy girl?'

'Outside in the vestibule! For the love of Pete!'

'What does she want? She's got a nigger woman with her!'

'That girl's here for no good. Mark my words, no good!'

'We didn't do anything!' Loozie had to shout to make herself heard. 'We just wanted to look inside!'

'What are they doing here? Crazy Rancy loose?'

'In the vestibule? Don't let her in here! Does she have a knife?'

'Oh Edgar, I think I'm going to faint! Who let her in?'

'I thought Asa Roff was taking care of her! Keep her away from me!'

The Reverend Baker hurried off his platform and elbowed his way up the aisle and into the vestibule. 'Lurancy Vennum!' he said. 'What are you doing here? And who,' he said to Loozie, 'are you?'

'Let's get out of here, Loozie,' Lurancy said. 'Come on!'

Loozie tried to push her way toward the door, but there were too many people in her path. Children from the Sunday School classes had come pouring in the front door when they heard the racket.

'Hey look! It's that crazy girl! The one who hit Miss Blades.'

'You know, Crazy Rancy! What's she doing?'

'Lift me up, I can't see.'

'Hey, Freddie, come here.'

'They got Crazy Rancy cornered in here!'

Loozie was getting frightened but didn't dare show it. Not to these people. 'Just let us pass,' she commanded. 'You folks just let us pass!'

'Loozie, please!' Lurancy began to whimper and try to hide herself in the folds of the large woman's clothing.

'Let us pass!' Loozie demanded. 'This child here ain't well. She needs fresh air.' She pushed and managed to get a few feet closer to the door. 'Let us pass!' she demanded.

'That child is crazy!' Lavinia screamed. 'She's crazy and should be locked up. That nigger woman should be locked up too!'

'Let us out of here!' Loozie pushed a few feet closer to the door. Lurancy was crying openly now as unknown hands pulled her hair, yanked at her clothes or slapped her face.

The African woman shoved harder; the crowd gave in a little. People were yelling, some women were screaming, the children who had been pushed to the floor were crying. She managed to get almost to the door when Lavinia screamed:

'We have her here now! Don't let her get away!' She bent down quickly and snatched up the fallen inkwell. With one well-aimed throw she sent it sailing through the air. It struck Lurancy squarely in the side of the head. She crumpled into Loozie's arms.

'Blood,' someone said. 'Look at the blood!'

The voices stopped. Everyone pulled back, silently. Loozie picked the unconscious girl up and cradled her in her arms. This time she didn't have to ask. The members of the congregation parted silently, and Loozie carried Lurancy outside and down the sidewalk. When she reached the street she turned and looked back at the faces in the doorway. It was a long, full, careful look as if she was engraving each and every countenance on her memory for a long time to come. 'Mrs Durst?' she called. 'Mrs Durst!'

Hands propelled Lavinia to the door.

'As I understand it,' Loozie said to her, 'you have been warned. Now take this as another warning.' Loozie smeared her finger in the blood that was slowly covering Lurancy's face. Then she knelt and traced a cross on the sidewalk. 'That is another warning,' she said. 'You have been doubly warned.'

Then she turned and started carrying Lurancy in the direction of Minerva's house, three blocks away. She didn't know how long they stood watching her for she never turned to look at them again.

*

Lurancy acted, that evening, as if nothing had happened and, indeed, she seemed quite content. She told the Roffs, as well as Loozie and Minerva, that everything was going to be all right and insisted they not worry. She had regained consciousness in Minerva's house, had walked home rather than ride in the buggy and what most surprised the family about the entire incident: by sundown the wound on her temple had healed. There was no blood, no bruise, no scar. Nothing. 'They have taken care of it,' she said. 'The way they are going to take care of everything else.'

In the morning she asked Asa to have the entire family gathered at home after dinner.

'Everyone?' he asked. 'Why?'

'There is going to be a manifestation. Just for the family. And for Dr Stevens and Mayor Peters. And for Loozie and Charlotte too, of course. They told me last night. They want the back parlor room cleared of all furniture, and chairs enough for everyone placed in a circle.'

'Are we going to have a seance?' he asked.

'I don't know, Pa. Something like that. They want everyone to be there. Even the boys. I gather it's going to be rather special. Will you make the arrangements? Call the folks together?'

'Of course I will,' he said. 'You can't tell me any more?'

'I don't know any more,' she said.

'How about the Vennums? Tom and Lurinda and young Henry?'

'No,' she said emphatically. 'They are not ready for it. Not ready at all.'

Because there would be so many people to dinner, Charlotte, with Loozie's help, prepared a buffet-style meal. The weather was warm enough to put everything out on the front porch and on the lawn. There was cold roast beef and fried chicken. Baked beans and creamed stringbeans. Potato salad and macaroni salad. Fresh radishes and fresh baby onions. Chocolate cake and strawberry pie. Rice pudding and Knox Gelatin and large pitchers of lemonade. There was a picnic atmosphere about it all and everyone ate more than they should have. Except for Lurancy. She didn't eat a bite. No matter how they coaxed her or pressed a forkful of this or a spoonful of that just to taste, she shook her head.

The women brought all the dishes into the kitchen and while they were washing and stacking them Frank and Charlie pushed aside the parlor furniture and placed eleven chairs in a circle.

Lurancy came in to inspect their work. 'Add one more,' she said.

'Why?' Charlie asked. 'There's only eleven of us, counting you.'

'Add one more,' she repeated. 'There are to be twelve chairs and one of them is to remain empty.'

The boys shrugged, found another chair and enlarged the circle.

When the sun had gone down all the way, Lurancy told Asa she was ready. 'Will you call them, Pa? I'll be in the parlor.'

One by one they came in and Mary told them where she wanted them to sit. 'It's as if we have a big clock,' she explained, 'and we should have a man sitting next to a woman and then another man as much as possible.' She drew a pencil diagram from her dress pocket.

'I'll sit here, at twelve o'clock,' she said, 'and Pa, you sit at one o'clock, and Dr Stevens, would you please sit at my right at eleven o'clock. Now, Loozie, you will be at two o'clock and Colonel Peters next to her at three.' She waited until they took their places. 'Now, Nervie, you sit at four and Charlie at five. The six o'clock chair, the one right opposite me, is to remain vacant. Is that understood?' She looked sharply around the room. 'Nobody is to sit there. Ever.'

Charlie sat in his five o'clock position and edged slightly away from the six o'clock forbidden chair. 'Is there someone sitting there now?' he asked with a nervous laugh.

'Not yet,' was the reply. 'But there will be.'

'Can't I change seats? I mean, can't you put Frank or somebody here?' He was serious.

'I don't want to sit there,' Frank laughed. 'You can have it.'

'Good,' Lurancy replied, 'because I want you to sit at the seven o'clock chair. Just on the *other* side of the empty one.'

'Oh cripes!' Frank said.

'Frank!' Ann spoke up. 'Watch your language, please.'

'Ha!' Charlie felt better. 'You got the other side! Good!'

If it had been any other time or place Frank would have taken a poke at his younger brother. Instead, he sat resignedly in the seven o'clock seat.

'Now, Charlotte, will you sit beside Frank at eight o'clock?'

'I wasn't planning on sitting anywhere at all.' The woman was in the doorway still wearing her apron, not at all happy about what was taking place.

'Please, Charlotte,' Lurancy said. 'It's very important that you do.'

The woman looked at Ann. 'Do I have to, missus? I would prefer if not.'

'Can't she be excused, Mary?' Ann looked at her daughter.

'No, Ma. She can't.' The voice was determined.

'Then please, Charlotte,' Ann said. 'Come in and sit beside Frank.'

The woman muttered something in German, something none of them understood, and slowly took her place. She scowled, making sure they all saw she didn't like it at all.

'Henry Alter, will you please sit at nine, beside Charlotte, and Ma, will you sit between Henry and Dr Stevens.'

Minerva's husband took his place beside the cook and glanced unhappily down at four o'clock where his wife, Minerva, was sitting. 'I've never been to one of these things before,' he said. 'I don't think I know what to do.'

'The best thing to do when you don't know what to do,' Dr Stevens said, 'is to do nothing. Just sit there and await the happenings. If you are supposed to do something or say something you will know it at the right time.'

'Correct,' Lurancy said. 'Absolutely correct. There is one more thing before we begin.' The girl was very businesslike. 'Charlotte, I need a small basin of water. Would you fetch one, please. A small one, about as big as a dinner plate.'

'But filled with water?' the woman asked. Lurancy nodded and the cook, glad to get out of the room, if only for a minute, went immediately to do as she was asked.

'And Loozie,' the girl said, 'dear, dear Loozie. I want you to go upstairs to my bedroom. There is a loose edging on the dresser. Will you remove it and take out the small carving?

Remember when we put it there so many years ago?'

Loozie stood up, swaying slightly with the shock of this child recalling something that she had almost forgotten, and that had happened to another child, a child who had been dead going on thirteen years. 'You remember that thing?' she said in amazement. 'I had clean let it go out of my mind.'

'What thing?' Asa asked.

'Something I gave Mary when she was about to go to that awful place in Peoria. And this child remembered it.' She laughed and shook her head.

'It's just where we put it, Loozie,' Lurancy said. 'Just where we put it.'

Charlotte came back with the basin of water. 'Where do you want it?' she asked.

'In the center of the circle. Yes. That's about right. Right there.'

'There are only two of us here who have never attended one of these things,' Henry Alter said. 'You and me, Charlotte. Good thing they put us next to each other.'

'Well,' she answered, 'I'm sure the colonel there has never been to one of these seance things.'

'Don't be so sure, Mrs Wiedener,' he laughed. 'I've attended many of these in my lifetime.'

She demanded, 'What's going to happen?'

'I can't tell you,' the mayor answered, 'for I don't know myself. But if it's a good one – and I'm sure it will be – it could change your entire life.'

'Nothing could change my life,' she scoffed. 'I am too old to change. My life is in a pattern. And it's a good pattern.'

'Then you don't want to change,' he suggested.

She grunted, crossed her arms and said nothing.

Loozie came back into the room. 'Here it is,' she beamed, 'just like Mary and I left it.' She had uncovered the small dark wood carving from the piece of red cloth and held it in the palm of her hand. The single blue bead in the featureless face caught the glint of the oil lamps for an instant.

'Can I see?' Charlie rose up and reached out his hand.

'No!' Lurancy's voice was loud. 'Nobody is to touch it. Loozie, you may show them if you wish, but nobody is to touch it. I don't want any outside energies on it.'

Charlie sat back down, slightly miffed at Lurancy, and waited his turn as the black woman moved from chair to chair holding the ugly little wooden man with one hand over his heart and the other on his buttocks. 'A woman gave this to my own Ma years ago,' she explained. 'That was when she was a slave. The woman who gave it to her came directly from Africa. I never did know that woman. She was dead before I was born.'

'What's it for?' Colonel Peters asked.

'It's to keep away evil. Things like ghosts and demons and the evil eye. I gave it to my Mary.'

Ann looked, wide-eyed, at Asa, but neither said a word.

'It's ugly!' Charlotte turned her face away.

'Evil always is,' Lurancy said softly.

Loozie took her chair, holding the figure in her hand. Minerva had gotten up and turned down all the oil lamps. There were three of them and they glowed faintly in the far corners. The room was dark, but there was still enough light to see the faces of those sitting in the circle.

Lurancy took a deep breath. 'I want you all to join hands,' she said. 'Take the hand of the person who is sitting next to you.'

'What about me and Charlie?' Frank asked. 'We've got this empty chair between us.'

'Reach out and take each other's hand,' the girl said.

'You know what this brings to mind?' Ann broke the silence. 'The time Reverend Dille did this with Mary. Right here in this parlor. It didn't have the best outcome.'

'This time things will go better,' the girl replied. 'Many things have changed, Ma. I know much more than I did back then. Trust me.'

'I do, dear. I trust you completely.'

'Good. I must have the trust of everyone in this room and I must have it at all times.' She closed her eyes. 'I am going to sit here for a few minutes. Please do not disturb me by talking or making any movement whatsoever. Dr Stevens' – she didn't look at him – 'please keep sending me as much of your energy as you can.'

'Of course,' he said softly.

She took a deep breath. Then another. All eyes were on her face, except for Henry Alter, who kept glancing at his wife's face to see how she was accepting it all. The breathing got deeper, the sounds of air being taken into her lungs grew farther and farther apart. Loozie, the amulet now resting in her lap, watched the girl's face intently. Colonel Peters never took his gaze from her. Charlotte let her eyes wander from Lurancy's face to Ann's. When this Crazy Rancy business was all over, she told herself, she would get another job somewhere. She couldn't stay on in a house like this much longer.

Lurancy took another deep breath. Then she shuddered. They could feel the ripples of her shudder through their circle of hands. Henry glanced again at Minerva. He would have to have a long talk with her when this was all over.

'Henry Alter!'

He turned back in astonishment at having Lurancy call his name.

'Yes?' he said, then wondered if he should have broken the silence.

'You look fine, you old son of a gun!'

'What?'

'I said you look fine! Little more around the middle than you used to have, but that's what comes with prosperity.' The voice was coming out of Lurancy's body, but it wasn't Lurancy's voice. It was a man's voice, a voice he thought he recognized.

'Ask him his name,' Ann whispered.

'Me?'

'Yes. He's obviously here for you. Ask him his name.'

'What – ' he felt very foolish ' – what is your name?'

'How about if I give you a hint?'

Henry didn't say anything. 'Speak to him!' Ann whispered again. 'You have to keep talking to them.'

'Okay. Sure,' he said, 'give me a hint.'

'Let's put the booze in the poison bottles! There! Now do you know who I am?'

'Let's put the booze . . .' Henry repeated. 'I can't think of what that could mean. No,' he shook his head, 'that doesn't mean anything to me at all.'

'Fifty-second Kentucky Infantry. November, 1864. Georgia. We got that shipment of booze and all the officers wanted some. We took empty poison bottles from the infirmary and filled them full of booze. Didn't have no trouble with our booze after that.' The laugh came again. 'Now do you remember, Brother Booze-hound?'

'Shorty Stewart!' Henry was stunned. 'Shorty Stewart! Nervie, that's the fellow I told you about. The one who worked in the hospital camp with me.' Minerva nodded. 'How incredible!' Then he stopped. 'But you ain't dead, Shorty! We got a Christmas card from you and your wife last year. No!' He shook his head. 'I'm sorry. I don't believe you. Shorty ain't dead.'

'Shorty?' Minerva spoke at Lurancy, 'Henry's right. We did get a Christmas card from you and your wife. It can't be you. Not unless you passed over since then.'

'You must be Brother Booze-hound's wife,' the voice said. 'Pleased to meet you. No, it's me all right. If you save your cards, find the one my wife sent you and look at it again. It only has *her* name on it. I kicked the bucket in May. Hell,' Lurancy smiled, 'that's a year ago this month! Don't seem possible.'

'We were planning on coming to Kentucky and visiting with you one day,' Henry said. 'I'm sorry to hear you're gone. How did it happen?'

'Don't know. Didn't know then and still don't know. I was sitting in the shit house . . . ' The voice stopped and gave a polite laugh. 'Excuse me, ladies. I was sitting in the *out*-house as nice as you please and I just fell over on my face. When I came to I was gone.' He laughed again. 'Gone for good. I guess I really took a healthy one, eh, Brother Booze-hound? Gone from both ends at the same time!'

Charlie and Frank laughed and the colonel tried not to. Minerva and Charlotte tried not to be shocked. Ann didn't try. She was shocked.

'Really, Mr Shorty! I do think you could watch your language. There are ladies present. This is not an army camp. This is a private home.'

'Umm uh! What you went and married into, Boozie old boy! Well, I'd better get out of here before they start quoting the Bible at me too.'

'Do they do that over there?' Dr Stevens asked. 'Read from the Bible?'

'I was just joking,' the voice said. 'They don't mention it over here.'

Dr Stevens was very disappointed. They could see it on his face. 'Well, maybe,' he suggested, 'you are in a special place where the Good Book isn't read. But they do read it in other places. I'm sure of that. Quite sure.'

'You ever been here?' the voice questioned.

'No,' the doctor replied, 'but I've communicated with many spirits from the other side who have assured me –'

'Then don't try to tell me what they do and don't do.' The voice was irritated. 'I'm over here and you ain't. Okay, Hen, I'd better get back. Couldn't resist this opportunity to come in and talk to you, though.'

'Shorty,' there was emotion in Henry's voice, 'are you happy over there?'

'Hell, Boozie, did you ever know me when I *wasn't* happy?' The laugh came again. 'Good-bye. Was real nice talking to you.' The laugh came again and then there was silence.

'Why "poor"?' Dr Stevens asked. 'Obviously he is in no pain and enjoying himself wherever he is.'

Henry laughed. 'Shorty would enjoy himself no matter where he was, even in the firepits of hell.'

'Well, from the way he was speaking,' Ann said, 'that just may be the spot he's in!'

'Aw Ma!' Charlie objected, 'the man was a soldier so he talks like a soldier.'

'A man is first of all a gentleman no matter what he later chooses as a profession, young man, and don't you forget it.'

'Aw Ma!'

Lurancy had been sitting there with her head bowed ever since Shorty Stewart had left her. Now she moaned and all attention was fixed on her again. 'Dr Stevens?' she said. 'Dr Stevens?'

'Yes, I'm here, child.'

'Dr Stevens?' She moaned again. 'Daddy? Daddy, can you hear me?'

Asa looked at the doctor but didn't say anything.

'Do you mean *me*?' the doctor asked. 'Is it *me* you are calling Daddy?'

'Daddy,' the voice inside Lurancy was light and feminine. 'This is Emma. How are you, Daddy?'

'Fine, Emma! Just fine!' He beamed at Lurancy. 'Nice to talk with you again.'

'It's always a pleasure for me too, Daddy. I use every chance I can to come through to you.'

'I should explain,' the doctor said to the others, 'that my daughter Emma has come through at many gatherings like this one. She passed over in forty-nine, that's almost thirty years ago, isn't it? My how time flies.'

'Daddy, I've been watching what's happening with the body here.'

'You mean the Vennum girl's body?'

'Yes and it's coming along very nicely. I wonder if I could take it for a while. I'd love to go home and visit Mother in it. Do you think I could?' Lurancy's face was turned toward the man. 'Do you think Mr and Mrs Roff would permit me?'

'Well, I don't know.' He was flustered by the idea. 'After all, it's up to those on the other side, really. Not my say-so at all. You should know that.'

'I do, but I thought if you and the Roffs gave me permission they might let me have it. Only for a few days.'

Both Ann and Asa were looking at him, questioningly. He shook his head at them. 'No,' he said, 'I don't think it's a good idea. The Vennum girl will be needing that body very soon. It shouldn't stray from here now.' He shook his head again at the Roffs. 'Besides, your mother would be extremely perturbed by such an action. She loves you, of course,' he added quickly, 'but such a visit wouldn't be wise. She is not a young woman, you know.'

'Yes, she is. Daddy, she's only twenty-eight. That ain't old!'

'You're forgetting, my dear, that you have been gone almost thirty years. Your mother is *fifty*-eight now. You people on the other side lose all track of time. We've discussed this before.'

'Yes, I know we did.' The voice sighed. 'Well, it was just an idea, anyway. Please give my love to Mother when you see her and to my sisters.'

'I will, Emma dear. I will. Thank you for coming.'

'Thank you, Father, and thank this instrument for me when she awakens.'

'I will.'

'Good-bye.' She was gone and Lurancy's head fell forward onto her chest.

'Dr Stevens,' Colonel Peters said. 'You amaze me. I mean when your daughter came in, you did it all so . . . so,' he searched for the words ' . . . so matter-of-factly. As if it is an everyday occurrence.'

'Well, not precisely *everyday*, but I've been in this field for many years now. Emma has come through mediums all over the country. She's a very powerful entity and my judgement of a good seance is whether she makes an appearance or not. I would have been most disappointed had she not come through today. But I couldn't let her see her mother right now.'

'I'm glad,' Ann said. 'I would have hated to see Lurancy leave now.'

'She won't be here for much longer, Mrs Roff,' the doctor warned. 'You had all better make up your minds to that fact. The Vennum girl is almost completely healed. She will want to take control of her own body very, very soon.'

Lurancy groaned again. 'Charlotte!' a voice from inside her called. 'Charlotte *mein Liebchen*!'

The housekeeper's eyes opened wide. '*Ja?*' she responded automatically to the German words.

'*Wie geht es Dir, mein Kind?*'

'*Gut.*' Charlotte's eyes bore into Lurancy's face, trying to see the face of another. '*Wer bist du?*'

'*Deine Grossmutter Stoner. Wie geht es Dir?*'

'*Grossmutter!*' Then in English to those in the circle: 'It's my grandmother. She says it's my Grandmother Stoner!' Ann smiled at how excited the woman had become. '*Grossmutter? Bist Du es wirklich?*'

'*Charlotte, ich bin van Weitem hergekonnen um Dich zu sehen.*'

'*Grossmutter, Kann ich Dir glaüben?*'

'In English!' commanded Dr Stevens. 'Speak to one another in English! In English so we can all understand,' his voice was loud and firm.

'I ... will ... try ...' the old woman inside the girl said slowly, 'but it is not ... my ... language.'

'We understand that,' the doctor said, 'but if you really are from spirit you can speak to us in any language you choose. We are all Americans here. Here we speak English.'

'Here we speak ... English,' the voice repeated. 'All right. So I too will speak ... English.'

Charlotte had tears streaming down her face. *'Es ist unmöglich, mein Gott!'*

'Mrs Wiedener,' the doctor was insistent. 'I must ask that you speak only in English.'

'I said it is impossible. That my Grandmother Stoner should be here! Should be in America! My grandmother was my very favorite person when I was in Germany. When I was growing up.'

'And now look at you,' the old woman's voice said. 'All big and a woman and here in America. It has been such a long time!'

'Yes, Grandmother, such a long time.'

Lurancy looked at Dr Stevens, her eyes still closed. 'I do not like this,' the old voice said. 'I do not like this apartness that I feel. I will do something. *Ja?*'

'Anything you choose,' he said.

'Good.'

There was a whirring sound and a rush of warm air down the center of the circle. Ann screamed and Loozie half rose in her seat. Lurancy's chair was empty.

An old woman sat in the six o'clock chair. Sat there firmly, holding hands with Frank and Charlie. 'Enough,' she said. 'Take apart the hands.' Gladly the boys released her old hands, unable to understand how they were holding them in the first place.

The old woman rose from the chair and walked over to Charlotte. 'I want to embrace my granddaughter,' she said. 'It has been much too long since the last time.' Charlotte started to rise. 'Undo the hands,' the old woman ordered Frank and Henry. 'Let her get up.'

Charlotte rose unsteadily, reached out and embraced the woman, her hands feeling a strong body and her fingers touching the coarse dark shawl her grandmother always wore. Even the lace cap on her gray head was exactly as Charlotte remembered it.

'Grandmother,' she began to cry. 'How good it is to hold you again! I missed you terrible when I went away.'

'We missed you too. Very much.' There were no tears in the older woman's eyes. 'Your mother was unhappy for months after. But she got used. She got used to the idea that you were never coming back.'

'And mother,' Charlotte cried, 'how is mother? Is she with you?'

'She is over here but she cannot talk with you. She needs more time. She is pig-headed like you. She needs to see more things before she makes up her mind.'

The link of hands broken, Ann touched Dr Stevens on his arm. 'Where is Lurancy?' she whispered. 'What happened to her?'

He shook his head. 'I don't know. This is most strange.'

Charlotte's body was still shaking with the joy-grief she felt at holding her grandmother again. 'Are you all right? Over there?'

'Of course!' came the reply, 'and so is little Helmut.'

'Helmut? My *brother* Helmut? He's dead?' Charlotte began crying louder. 'Helmut is dead?'

'Years ago,' came the reply, 'from a stupid battle in a stupid war. It was quick, though. He didn't suffer. He helped bring your mother across. It was easier for her with him there.'

Dr Stevens spoke to the apparition. 'What have you done with Lurancy?'

'With who?' She looked at him.

'With Lurancy. The channel you used to come through. Where is she?'

The woman shrugged. 'How do I know? Somewhere, I suppose.'

'I think she should come back now,' he said. 'She is not in the best health.'

'I am not finished with my granddaughter. For too many years we have not seen each other.'

'I think you should go and allow the girl to return,' he insisted. 'What you are doing is not good for her.'

'What I am doing? I am doing nothing!'

'Please go,' Ann said. 'Let the girl come back.'

'Yes,' Colonel Peters added. 'It would be the best for everyone.'

'Everyone but me and Charlotte. Yes?' She gave her granddaughter one more embrace. 'A kiss for you,' and then in German : 'We'll see you on the other side.'

'Good-bye, Grandma,' Charlotte searched her pockets for a handkerchief as the old woman sat down in the six o'clock chair.

The same rush of air was heard and Lurancy appeared back in her seat.

'Everyone!' the doctor commanded. 'Join hands quickly!' They reached out for each other in the semidarkness. Dr Stevens grabbed the girl's right hand as Asa grabbed her left.

She sighed. 'I'm all right.' She opened her eyes and smiled at the group. 'Really. Everything is fine.'

'Are you sure?' Ann asked.

'Yes, Ma. I told you. This won't be like the last time. I know what I'm doing but there is one more thing that must be done. Loozie, are you ready?'

'Ready for what, child?'

'Ready to follow instructions when they are given to you? They may come awfully fast.'

'I'm ready. Count on me,' the African woman replied.

'What is about to happen,' she explained, 'is something *they* want to happen. I have known about this for several days now. It was confirmed yesterday. Do not blame me for it afterward. Please! I have no control in the matter and do not blame Lurancy when she returns. It is *their* plans and *their* doings. They tried to have things happen differently but it didn't work out that way. This is the only way left to them. Please, Ma,' she looked at Ann, 'don't blame me and don't blame Lurancy. Don't you either, Mayor Peters. We, Lurancy and I, are only being used as instruments.'

'What's this all about?' the mayor asked. 'Blame you for what?'

'You'll see. That's all I can tell you now, but when it's over, you'll see. And I hope you'll understand.'

Lurancy sighed. Her body began to shake. She closed her eyes. 'All right,' she said. 'They're ready to begin.'

Henry Alter thought he felt something move against his

trouser leg, but when he looked there was nothing there.

Ann sensed a movement behind her, she wanted to turn around but didn't dare.

Lurancy moaned and one of the oil lamps went out. Heads turned to stare at it, but there was nothing to be seen.

Charlie felt something blow past the back of his neck. Just the idea of it gave him goosebumps. He looked quickly past the empty six o'clock chair toward Frank, but his brother must not have felt anything, for he was staring at Lurancy.

The second oil lamp flickered and plunged that side of the room in darkness.

'Oh, my,' Minerva said.

'Amen!' Charlie added.

Again Lurancy moaned, but this time it was deeper, almost an imprisoned sob. Ann looked anxiously at the girl. It was difficult to see her face, with the two lamps out. 'Is she all right?' she whispered to Dr Stevens.

'I think so,' he answered.

That was when the third lamp went out. Charlotte screamed at finding herself in the dark and Colonel Peters asked: 'Is this really necessary?'

A harsh strangled cry came from the twelve o'clock chair, from Lurancy's chair. 'They have come,' she cried out. 'They are here!'

There was a brilliant flash of light, like lightning across an August sky. Everyone instinctively shut their eyes at the unexpected glare and pulled back.

'Keep your hands joined!' the doctor commanded. 'Don't break the circle!'

The flash came again, throwing the farthest corners of the room into sharp relief. Again Charlotte screamed as Charlie and Frank gasped.

They gasped because there was someone sitting on the number six chair. It was a man and he was wearing almost nothing, just a piece of cloth around his waist. He was barefoot and barechested. His skin was dark, but not as dark as Loozie's.

'Good evening,' he said. Now everyone saw him. Saw him solid and heard his breathing. Frank and Henry Alter had to hold on tightly to Charlotte's hands as she tried to get away, out of the circle completely.

'Good evening,' the strange-looking man repeated. 'Do not be alarmed. I am not here to harm you. I am here to carry out a mission.'

'A mission?' Dr Stevens was the first to regain his composure. 'Can you tell us what it is?'

'I cannot. You will discover for yourselves.'

Asa looked at Lurancy's seat. She was not there. 'Where is the girl?' he asked.

'Gone.'

'Gone? Gone where?'

'Just gone. She will be back. Please,' and he unclasped his hands from Frank and Charlie's, 'do not ask so many questions. I have work to do and not too much time nor energy to do it in.' He stood up and they could all see him clearly now, even with the lights out. His skin glowed with an inner radiance of his own. He looked to be over six feet tall, with dark heavy hair that came just below his ears. There was no hair on his muscular body. His nose and lips were almost classical in their straightness and fullness. He stood in front of Loozie, who was looking at him with eyes as big as teacups.

'Give it to me,' he said, holding out his hand.

'What?' she asked.

'The figure. The carved figure we have been saving for so long.'

Loozie undid her hands from Asa's and Mayor Peters's and handed him the amulet that had been resting in her lap.

He held it up and stared at it for a few seconds. The single blue eye gleamed in the reflection of his skin. Then he raised the figure far over his head, holding it aloft for a minute or more, before he shouted and threw it with all his force into the basin of water that was in the center of the circle.

Immediately there was a gigantic puff of flame and smoke. It roared up out of the basin and the heat pressed harshly against the faces of everyone in the circle.

Ann screamed and jumped up, getting away from the flames. Minerva and Charlotte did the same. The men pushed back their chairs, Charlie fell over backward and scrambled to get out of the way.

'My God!' Asa shouted. 'What are you doing?'

'He's going to burn down the house!' Henry yelled.

'I want out of here!' Charlotte rushed toward the door. 'They're locked,' she screamed. 'I can't get out.'

'Desist!' the stranger shouted. 'There is no danger. Stay where you are!'

The command of his voice brought a stillness into the room. They stood there staring at the flames that rose straight up out of the basin. The flames were high and hot, yet they didn't expand. It was like a flaming ornamental fountain rising up smoothly and forcibly and with directed purpose. No one in the room had ever seen anything like it before, but no one approached to investigate it closer.

On Hickory Street, Lavinia Durst put down the novel she was reading. She sat for a moment wondering if she had heard something or whether it was her imagination. No, there was somebody in the front hall, inside the front door.

'Who's there?' she called. Nobody answered. 'Sarah, is that you?'

Every now and again Sarah Thayer would drop in either to borrow something or return something. When there was no answer, Lavinia got up from her easy chair and walked to the hallway. 'Sarah?'

Two people stood inside the door. Two girls. One was Lurancy Vennum. The other was Mary Roff.

Lavinia screamed, a high shattering scream that shook her entire body. She clutched at the wall, trying to steady herself. Her breath came in short burning gasps.

The girls stood there, together, not saying anything.

Somehow Lavinia regained enough strength to move back into the front room. The girls followed, silently.

Lavinia put her hand over her heart. She was sure it was going to burst. She wanted to scream again, but no sounds would appear.

The two girls advanced closer to her.

She collapsed into a chair. Her hands were trembling so badly she couldn't control them to come up and cover her eyes.

'You were warned,' Mary said.

'More than once,' Lurancy said.

Lavinia took a deep breath. 'Get out of here!' she managed to say. 'Both of you!'

'We warned you,' Mary said.

'You wouldn't listen.'

'You're crazy,' the woman gasped. 'Both of you are crazy! Leave me alone.'

'You didn't leave us alone,' Mary said.

'I – ' Lavinia gasped. 'As soon as I get my breath I'm fetching the police!'

'Why did you do those things?' Lurancy asked.

'Why didn't you leave us alone?' Mary asked.

'I'll get the law on you,' Lavinia choked, 'you'll see. I'll get the law.'

That's when she smelled the smoke. It started as a wispy curling around the feet of the two girls and slowly came up their skirts and down their arms.

'You're on fire!' she screamed struggling to get out of the chair. 'Fire!'

The flames followed the smoke, bursting the girls' skirts into brilliant blasts of red and yellow. They stood looking at her, not smiling, just looking.

Lavinia couldn't rise from the chair. Her legs were weak and her arms shook. 'Please,' she began to whimper. 'Please.'

Then the flames spread. From the girls' skirts to the Persian rug on the floor. Then from the rug to the legs of the sofa, then up the side of the sofa to the pillows and the draperies behind the sofa.

Lavinia couldn't move. She clutched at her heart.

'Why did you do those things?' Lurancy asked again.

'You were warned,' Mary said.

The fire then came up the legs of the chair where Lavinia sat. It jumped into her lap, sizzling the fabric of her dress and turning the white ruffles of her blouse into black slivers. The woman gave one last cry before the flames roared into her body with full force. Then all at once the entire house burst into flames. Glass shattered in the upper windows, the roof screamed with the force of the flames and the sudden wind that had appeared from nowhere. Floor timbers gnawed by fire shriveled and collapsed. Finally, just minutes after the flames had reached it, the roof caved into the scorching shell of Lavinia Durst's house.

At that moment the shooting pillar of flame in the Roff

parlor went out. The oil lamps came back up. The stranger vanished. Lurancy was sitting in her twelve o'clock chair.

She opened her eyes. 'It's over,' she said. 'It's all over. The seance, everything. It's over.'

The guests began to talk at once. 'What was that all about?'

'What happened? Who was that man?'

'How did he make water burn like that? Mary, where did you go?'

Lurancy stood up and put up her hands, asking for silence. 'Ma, I'm very tired. I want to go to bed.'

'Of course, dear,' Ann said. 'I'll come up with you.'

'Hey!' Charlie shouted. 'Listen. The fire department is going somewhere.' They could hear the clanging of the bells. 'Wonder where it is. Come on, Frank, let's go.'

'Can we, Ma?' Frank asked.

She nodded. 'I suppose so. The seance is over.'

'You won't see much,' Lurancy said. 'It's all over. There's nothing left.'

The boys ran out of the room, followed by Henry Alter and the mayor. Henry was a member of the volunteer fire department and wanted to get there as soon as possible. The mayor was the man in charge of all city departments. He should be there too.

Dr Stevens put his arm around the girl. 'Are you all right, Mary?'

'Yes,' she said. 'Now I am. Everything is going to be fine from now on.'

'That was a most impressive demonstration,' he said. 'That seance was quite unusual. I'm glad I was here to see it.'

'I'm glad you were too,' she said. 'You have been a great help to me and the work I had to do.' She kissed him on the cheek, above the beard.

'Let's get to bed, young lady,' Loozie said. 'You've had a long day.'

'I will, Loozie, but first there is something I have to say. A kind of announcement. Ma. Pa. Dear Nervie and Dr Stevens. What I have to say is sad but it is also happy for some people.'

'What is it, dear?' Ann asked.

'Tomorrow I am going away.' She paused. 'For good.'

'Tomorrow!' Ann felt the tears welling up in her eyes. 'So soon?'

'Tomorrow. My work here is finished. Lurancy is well and normal. Tomorrow at eleven o'clock in the morning, the Vennum girl will come back to claim this body.'

Ann reached out and hugged the girl to her.

'Oh, Ma!' she said, starting to cry. 'I don't want to go! Really I don't. I want to stay here with you and Pa and the boys! But I can't, Ma. I can't!'

Ann wiped away Lurancy's tears. 'You've got to be brave,' she said. 'We've all got to be brave about this. We've known it was coming and we thank God that He let us have you for as much time as He did.'

'Nervie, will you come for the Vennum girl tomorrow at ten thirty?' Lurancy asked. 'Will you take her back to her folks?'

'Of course I will.' She also had tears in her eyes.

'And, Pa, will you have the Vennums at your office tomorrow at eleven? That's where she wants to meet them.'

'Don't worry,' he said. 'They'll be there.'

The girl gave Loozie a kiss and a lingering hug, then embraced Dr Stevens again. 'I'm very tired. I want to go to bed now, Ma. I really do.'

By the time the boys returned to tell their Pa that Lavinia Durst's home had been completely destroyed, Lurancy was asleep. Asa was on the front porch, in the rocking chair, in the dark.

'And the place just went up like a tinderbox!' Charlie reported. 'Nothing could be saved.'

'By the time the fire engine got there the roof had caved in. You should see it, Pa,' Frank said, 'it's all burnt down into tiny ashes.'

'Yeah,' added Charlie, 'as if there had never been a house there at all.'

'Or a woman,' Frank said. 'They are sure old lady Durst died in the fire.'

'Aren't you gonna go see it?' they asked.

'No,' he said, never stopping his rocking, 'I'm not. Their work is always effective and complete.'

'What?'

'Nothing,' Asa answered. 'Nothing at all. Just thinking. Why don't you get to bed? Tomorrow'll be another exhausting day around here.'

'Why?' Frank asked.

'Your sister is leaving tomorrow. For good. Lurancy Vennum is going to take over and go home.'

'Really?' The boys looked at each other. 'Can we stay home from school?'

'You'll see her at breakfast. It's best not to have too many people around. Now go on upstairs and get to bed.'

'You coming too, Pa?'

'No. I'm going to sit out here a while longer. There's some things I want to sort out in my mind.' The boys went in and closed the door. Asa kept rocking in the chair, staring off into the blackness of the Watseka night. Somewhere out there were a million unanswered questions waiting to be asked. A million concepts and ideas waiting to be accepted. A million ways of looking at things and reacting to them. Standards broken, theories upset. Ignorance banished. Superstition destroyed. Jules Verne had written a popular book about going to the moon and people wondered if they'd ever get there.

'That's as far as man aims,' Asa said aloud into the night, 'only to the moon. That's not where the answers will be. That's not where they'll be at all.'

Tuesday, May 21, 1878, dawned chilly in Watseka. A fog had settled in the lowlands and the river seemed to be steaming with mist. Loozie and Ann helped Lurancy pack her belongings into a suitcase. All the clothes and gifts that she had acquired during her stay at the Roffs were going home with her. They belonged to Lurancy even though they had been given to Mary. Ann didn't want them around. There would be enough memories without coming across a cameo brooch or a piece of tatting to remind her of her daughter's second death. And that's what it felt like, she told Asa as he was getting dressed that morning, a second death. Mary was dying all over again.

The girl didn't eat hardly any breakfast. She had been

crying during the night and her eyes were red. She didn't want to leave her family again, but there was nothing else she could do. It had been part of the bargain. The only consolation, and yet she didn't like to think of it, was that Asa and Ann were not getting any younger. Asa would be sixty soon. A few more years and he would be on the other side with her. Ann would follow shortly. She could wait those few years. She could wait because afterward there would be all eternity.

Frank and Charlie hugged Lurancy and kissed her several times. 'You come back and see us,' they said.

'Lurancy will come back,' the girl corrected them. 'I won't be able to. Not any more.'

'Well, anyway it was real fine having you home with us, Mary. We'll miss you.' Frank hugged the Vennum girl once more. 'Look,' he said surprised at the emotion that he felt welling up in his chest, 'we gotta get to school.' Damn! He didn't want them to see any tears! 'You take care of yourself, Mary. You hear?'

'I hear,' she said smiling at him. 'And you take care too. I don't want to see you where I'm going for a long time yet.'

'Not if we can help it,' laughed Charlie. 'I got lots to do yet and lots of places to see.'

'Then do them,' the girl said, 'and remember me.'

'I will, Sis. I will.' He kissed her. 'Gotta go,' he added as he too felt the pressure behind his eyes.

After they had gone, Asa rose from the table. 'I'll get over to the office and I'll take your things with me. I mean, I'll take Lurancy's things with me and give them to her parents.' He checked his pocket watch. 'You'll be there at eleven?'

'Yes, Pa.'

He started toward the rear door, where the horse and buggy waited.

'Pa?' the girl called.

He stopped, 'Yes?'

'I love you, Pa. I really do.'

'I know,' he said, 'and I love you.' As he reached the buggy he stopped and wiped his eyes with his coat sleeve.

Ann and Loozie busied themselves with housework and

Charlotte spent more time than usual at the market. Dr Stevens sat in his room, writing.

'The girl seems much saddened by her departure this morning. There is a feeling of grief over the house, as when one dies. Of course the Vennums must be happy and I'm sure that is the only consolation in this case. I suppose Mrs Roff will take the departure the hardest of anyone. She has borne up under the strain of the events remarkably well, but I detect a few cracks in her façade already and I shall stay on in the house for a few days in case she needs my services.

'I will confess that I shall also miss the girl. As Mary she was bright and independent and industrious. We had many long talks and some of the things she told me about the other side are so overwhelming that I fear to put them on paper (even to you my dear) for fear of derision and ridicule.

'There is a whole world over there, and yet it isn't really a world at all. It is a state of mind, or energies if you will, where the wrongs of the earthly plane are corrected and where learning is a full-time occupation. The learning process never stops, she told me, because each soul must advance and prepare for his next lifetime. Apparently (and this I have never considered) a soul doesn't necessarily return to this planet for each lifetime but goes to other planets where there is life as well. I almost said "populated planets" but Mary tells me there can be intelligence without there being form. (You see what I mean about the prospect of ridicule?)

'Apparently our beliefs about reincarnation have to be revised. A soul is never *forced* to return to earth if he doesn't choose to. And the limits of fate do not necessarily stop at personal relationships but cross all barriers of both time and space. And (oh yes, this!) there is no time. Not really! Now don't ask me to explain this any better than those simple four words. That's what she told me and no amount of explanation made the slightest dent upon my mind. It is something to do with everything happening at the same time and yet there is no time! There is no yesterday or tomorrow. There is only right now. I hope I shall be able to fathom that out before I make my own transition.

'There was a terrible fire in Watseka last night. It happened while we were holding a most remarkable seance in the Roff parlor. I haven't questioned the child about it yet (and I never shall!) but my suspicions are that somehow "they" had something to do with it. A woman was killed in the fire. As you know, I am the last person on earth to condone destruction but "they" seemed to have a reason for it. I cannot argue with "them". The few times I've tried, I've always come out second best. I cannot argue with "them" nor can I fully understand their motives for everything they do. Can an ant understand the phases of the moon? Or indeed, is the ant even aware that the moon exists?

'I pray for enlightenment and for knowledge of God's mysteries. I also pray that I shall be back with you very soon.

'All my love,

'Winchester.

'P.S. Emma came through the girl at the seance last night with some preposterous plan to take over her body and come visit you in Wisconsin. Really, that Emma is a caution! Will she *never* grow up?'

When Minerva arrived at 10.30, Ann called Dr Stevens downstairs. 'She will be going soon,' she said. 'I know you wanted to say good-bye.'

The girl was in the parlor, sitting on the velvet sofa with Loozie. Tears glistened on the African woman's face.

'You take care of yourself now, child, you hear?'

'I will,' she promised. 'Loozie, I shall try and come to you. When you need me, please call me and I'll try and come.'

'In a body?' the woman asked.

'No, I'll just *be* there. You'll feel my presence, but you won't be able to see me.'

'I'll see you, child,' the woman assured her. 'I'll see you in my heart! You'll always be there. Always!'

'Mary,' Ann said. 'It's getting close to time. Dr Stevens would like to have a prayer.'

Ann sat on the sofa beside the girl and Loozie. Minerva and Charlotte stood behind the sofa. Dr Stevens stood in front of them.

'Oh Lord. If it can be that an angel is in our midst, and

about to leave us and join her own spirit-life, will God in all His goodness look after her and protect her and thank her greatly for the happiness and the solace she gave those of us who must remain behind. We ask You to bless her forever and keep her memory alive as an inspiration to others who walk in darkness and doubt. Amen.'

'Amen,' the girl said.

Charlotte came around the sofa and Lurancy got up. 'I want to hug you,' the woman said, 'and tell you good-bye. In the beginning I didn't think you were really who you were. I didn't know what to think. But I know now.' She reached out her arms and the girl came into them. 'You come back and see us. When you are Rancy, I mean. Remember that there will always be cakes and cookies and things just for you. Oh,' she tried to laugh, 'look at me. Frogs in my throat!'

The girl returned the embrace. 'Thank you, Charlotte. Thank you for everything.'

Dr Stevens stood beside her. 'Mary, I shall miss you but I shall always treasure your memory.'

'Pray for me, sir,' she asked. 'You have been a wonderful, wonderful friend. Without you none of this would have been possible.'

'Nonsense. I didn't do anything.'

'You opened the doors. I stood on the other side knocking, but you opened the doors. There must always be two. One on this side and one on the other.'

'Mary,' Nervie said. 'It's almost time.'

The girl stood in front of Ann and then dropped to her knees, her head in the woman's lap. 'Oh Ma! I really am sorry that I have to go away. How I wish I could stay and be with you always, but it can't be done. Pray for me, Ma, and don't forget me. Ever.'

Ann caressed the girl's hair. She wanted to say so many things, things she had saved for this moment, but all the words that would come out were, 'I love you, daughter. Now you'd better go. The Vennums are waiting.'

The girl lifted her face and Ann kissed her on the lips.

Nervie touched her shoulder. 'Mary, we must be going.'

Lurancy arose and gave a brave smile to everyone in the room. 'I feel sad at parting with you all, for you have treated me so kindly. Your sympathy and love has helped me to cure this body.' Then to Minerva: 'Please. Let's go.'

The sound of the closing front door echoed forever in Watseka's memory.

Epilogue

By the time they got to Asa's office Mary was gone and Lurancy had returned for good. She called Asa 'Mr Roff' and embraced Tom and Lurinda Vennum.

She willingly went home with them and was completely restored to health. No more fits, fainting spells or seizures by other personalities. She was enrolled back in school that September and graduated with the rest of her class.

When Lurancy was eighteen she married a local boy named George Binning and two years later they moved from Watseka to Rawlins County, Kansas. They bought a farm and she had eleven children. While visiting one of her daughters in northern California in the late 1940s, she died.

Asa and Ann Roff were besieged with hundreds of letters from skeptics and believers when the story appeared on the front page of the *Watseka Times* and was later published in several national Spiritualist magazines. After one year the pressure of prejudice in Watseka forced them to sell their home and move to Emporia, Kansas. Seven years later, when the incident had time to cool down, they returned to live with Minerva and Henry Alter and to die of old age. They are buried in Watseka.

Charlie Roff was the first of the children to join Mary. He died in 1885, at twenty years of age, of consumption. The other boys have faded into history.

Tom and Lurinda Vennum stayed on in Watseka for many years. Finally, he died; she sold the house and moved in with Lurancy and her children. There is no record of what happened to Henry.

Dr E. W. Stevens lectured on 'The Watseka Wonder' for eight years before dropping dead at a friend's home in Chicago a few days before Christmas, 1886.

Colonel Peters did not get re-elected mayor of Watseka but influential friends brought him into state politics. In 1879 he was elected to the Illinois legislature by the National party. In 1884 he ran for state senator as a Democratic candidate. He lost, returned to Watseka and remained one of its most illustrious citizens.

Charlotte Wiedener went to Chicago when the Roffs were forced to move to Kansas.

Loozie has any number of great-great-grandchildren scattered about Canada.

Over the years some streets were renamed in Watseka and a great number of the older homes were torn down. Surprisingly, both the houses in this story are still standing. The Roff home, located at 300 East Sheridan Street, is owned by attorney Ivan Looker. Henry and Golda Sobkoviak own the Vennum home, the address of which is now 135 Belmont Street.

Mary Roff never returned again.

THE EXORCIST
by William Peter Blatty

The Exorcist is a terrifying mixture of fact and fancy.

Well researched, written in a literate style, it comes to grips with the forces of evil incarnate, and there are not many readers who will be unmoved.

'THE EXORCIST is as superior to most books of its kind as an Einstein equation is to an accountant's column of figures.'
                                    THE NEW YORK TIMES BOOK REVIEW

0 552 09156 1   £2.50

WHAT ABOUT THE BABY
by Clare McNally

EVIL HAS COME FOR HER BABY

1824 A young mother returns home to find her infant son brutally murdered in his cradle. Her tortured grief led to a consuming desire for vengeance . . .

NOW For beautiful Gabrielle Hansen, 17, orphaned and pregnant, her lonely world becomes a place of unimagined terror. Bizarre chants invade her mind . . . Death plagues her dreams . . . Blood desecrates her room . . .

For she has been adopted by an undying evil from the past, an evil that has come for only one precious thing – her baby.

WHAT ABOUT THE BABY?

0 552 12691 8   £1.75

PSYCHO
by Robert Bloch

THE STORY THAT ALFRED HITCHCOCK MADE INTO HIS MOST SPINE-CHILLING FILM.

She stepped into the shower stall. She let the warm water gush over her. That's why she didn't hear the door open. At first, when the shower curtains parted, steam obscured the face. Then she saw it . . .

A face peering through the curtains. A headscarf concealed the hair, and glassy eyes stared inhumanly. The skin was powdered dead white and two spots of rouge were centred on the cheekbones.

She started to scream. Then the curtains parted further and a hand appeared, holding a butcher's knife. . . .

0 552 08272 4   £1.50

PSYCHO II
by Robert Bloch

THE LONG-AWAITED SEQUEL TO THE CLASSIC THRILLER THAT STARTED IT ALL!

For the last 20 years, Norman Bates has been in a state hospital for the criminally insane. With the help of his psychiatrist, Norman appears to have been cured of his mother fixation, and now decides that he wants OUT. His opportunity arises when he is visited by a nun. He kills her, uses her habit as a disguise – and escapes.

The psycho murders are about to start again . . .

EVEN MORE TERRIFYING THAN PSYCHO!

0 552 12186 X   £1.75

GHOST HOUSE
by Clare McNally

You won't be able to stop reading until the nightmare is over . . .

A dream house that traps a family in horror.

The beautiful old mansion on Long Island's South Shore seemed the perfect home for the Van Burens and their three young children. What happened to them inside that house is an experience you'll pray couldn't happen to you.

At first the Van Burens believed there had to be some natural explanation. Before it was over, they were fighting for their children's lives against an obscene manifestation of evil that engulfed them all in a desperate nightmare.

Not even *Flowers in the Attic* prepares you for

                GHOST HOUSE

0 552 11652 1   £1.95

GHOST HOUSE REVENGE
by Clare McNally

The Ghost House horror lives on . . . for revenge.

Only nightmares and broken limbs remained to remind the Van Burens and their three children of past terror. And when the physical therapist and his shy daughter arrived, the family dared hope for a return to normal life . . .

But somewhere within the ancient Long Island mansion, something was laughing, mocking, plotting . . .

They prayed it wasn't the same as before. It was not – it was much, much worse. Soon they were fighting for their lives against a shape-shifting horror of insatiable evil. A malevolence that lusted with hideous pleasure, and killed with raging delight . . .

0 552 11825 7   £1.95

A SELECTED LIST OF HORROR TITLES AVAILABLE FROM CORGI BOOKS

THE PRICES SHOWN BELOW WERE CORRECT AT THE TIME OF GOING TO PRESS. HOWEVER TRANSWORLD PUBLISHERS RESERVE THE RIGHT TO SHOW NEW RETAIL PRICES ON COVERS WHICH MAY DIFFER FROM THOSE PREVIOUSLY ADVERTISED IN THE TEXT OR ELSEWHERE.

☐ 13000 1	**THE INTRUDER**	*Thomas Altman*	£2.50
☐ 09156 1	**THE EXORCIST**	*William Peter Blatty*	£2.50
☐ 12186 X	**PSYCHO 2**	*Robert Bloch*	£1.75
☐ 08272 4	**PSYCHO**	*Robert Bloch*	£1.50
☐ 13135 0	**POLTERGEIST II**	*James Kahn*	£1.95
☐ 12691 8	**WHAT ABOUT THE BABY?**	*Clare McNally*	£1.75
☐ 12400 1	**GHOSTLIGHT**	*Clare McNally*	£1.95
☐ 11652 1	**GHOST HOUSE**	*Clare McNally*	£1.95
☐ 11825 7	**GHOST HOUSE REVENGE**	*Clare McNally*	£1.95
☐ 12587 3	**MINE TO KILL**	*David St. Clair*	£2.50
☐ 11132 5	**CHILD POSSESSED**	*David St. Clair*	£2.50
☐ 10471 X	**FULL CIRCLE**	*Peter Straub*	£2.50

All these books are available at your book shop or newsagent, or can be ordered direct from the publisher. Just tick the titles you want and fill in the form below.

ORDER FORM

TRANSWORLD READER'S SERVICE, 61–63 Uxbridge Road, Ealing, London, W5 5SA.

Please send cheque or postal order, not cash. All cheques and postal orders must be in £ sterling and made payable to Transworld Publishers Ltd.

Please allow cost of book(s) plus the following for postage and packing:

U.K./Republic of Ireland Customers:
Orders in excess of £5: no charge
Orders under £5: add 50p

Overseas Customers:
All orders: add £1.50

NAME (Block Letters)..

ADDRESS ....

....